THE BEAUTY OF THE END

THE BEAUTY OF THE END

A NOVEL

LAUREN STIENSTRA

Little a

This is a work of fiction. Names, characters, organizations, places, events, and incidents are either products of the author's imagination or are used fictitiously. Otherwise, any resemblance to actual persons, living or dead, is purely coincidental.

Text copyright © 2025 by Lauren Stienstra
All rights reserved.

No part of this book may be reproduced, or stored in a retrieval system, or transmitted in any form or by any means, electronic, mechanical, photocopying, recording, or otherwise, without express written permission of the publisher.

Published by Little A, New York

www.apub.com

Amazon, the Amazon logo, and Little A are trademarks of Amazon.com, Inc., or its affiliates.

ISBN-13: 9781662525650 (hardcover)
ISBN-13: 9781662525667 (paperback)
ISBN-13: 9781662525643 (digital)

Cover design by Kimberly Glyder
Cover image: © THEPALMER / Getty

Printed in the United States of America

First edition

To my mother, Maggie Stienstra, who showed me how to love literature, motherhood, and most importantly, myself

CHAPTER 1

By the time I was five years old, I knew I didn't want children.

And while I didn't use those words exactly, I telegraphed the sentiment as clearly as a freshly minted kindergartener could:

"But Maggie . . ."

By stretching out that last syllable for a full three seconds, I could only hope that my sister might understand—and respect—that I didn't want to play house. Not on the first day of school, at least, not when we didn't know anyone. But in our short lifetime together, my sister had already developed an indifference to my complaints. She dismissed my protest with a roll of her gingerbread eyes and marched me over to the jungle gym to assimilate into her fictitious household.

"There," she said, stuffing my hand into the clammy grasp of a scrawny redheaded boy we'd just met. "You'll be the mommy, and Nolan will be the daddy."

The boy's eyes bulged at the contact. I wasn't sure which shocked him more: the fact that Maggie and I were carbon copies of each other—not a lot of kids in town had ever actually seen identical twins—or the fact that he was touching a girl.

Annoyed by the arranged marriage, I dropped the carrottop's hand.

Nolan looked confused by my rejection and tried to steer us back toward the game. "So, uh, don't we need a baby?"

My heart stuttered. I hadn't wanted to play house, but if Maggie was going to bully me into it, I wasn't going to tolerate a baby. I'd seen enough of them in our church's nursery—their cries set my teeth on edge, they always seemed sticky, and there was only so much diaper stink that powder could cover up. But these nuisances paled in comparison to the source of my true discomfort.

Having a baby meant that *I* would be a *mommy*.

Maggie eyed a sniveling bespectacled boy across the yard. "What about Christopher? He cries a lot."

I stamped my brand-new Mary Janes into the wood chips. "No. Babies."

Maggie recoiled with a look just as baffled as Nolan's. "How can you be the mommy if you don't have a baby?"

If anyone could've understood why I didn't want to play mommy, it should've been my sister. Maggie had gone through the same childhood I had: surrendered by our immigrant parents, adopted by someone new—and all before the tender age of two so we wouldn't resent it.

Despite this intention, I did from time to time. Deep down, I wasn't sure what I'd done to deserve abandonment, and I wasn't sure why I'd been chosen either. This left me incredibly confused about my purpose in my family, and the easiest way to avoid any heartache was to refuse to think about it at all. The fact that Maggie had forced it upon me on the first day of school felt like the ultimate betrayal.

I retreated to our classroom before losing the battle against my tears.

On the bus that afternoon, I chose a lonely-looking seat in the front row. Window seats weren't generally available to the smaller kids, so if I wanted to lean my head against something, I needed to subject myself to the proximity of the driver. Sensing my displeasure, my sister turned up her nose and chose instead to sit next to Angela, a bubblegum dealer with a generous reputation. In an act of sisterly defiance, I committed to embracing my solitary trip—but just as the folding doors closed, the reedy boy from the playground scooched in.

"Do you want to hear some jokes?"

Jokes were a poor substitute for the apology I wanted, but Nolan didn't wait for permission.

"What has four wheels and flies?"

My unflinching gaze fixed on something outside the window. "I don't know."

"A garbage truck."

I wasn't sure which irritated me more: the dumb punch line or the fact he hadn't taken my hint. I shot the rascal a dirty look. "That's a riddle, not a joke."

Immune to my irritation, Nolan's eyebrows danced with his next setup. "Then what do snowmen eat for breakfast?"

"Frosted flakes," I snipped. "That one's on the back of the cereal box."

Nolan's eyes twinkled. "So, what's brown and sticky?"

I had no excuse for not anticipating the potty humor. I was just as five as he was.

"A stick!" Nolan cried, an enormous grin splitting his freckled face. "You thought I was going to say poop!"

His zeal drew a giggle from me. "How do you know so many jokes?"

"My mom taught them to me. Moms are the best, you know."

As the bus lurched to a stop, Nolan twisted sideways so I could exit. Out the window, I spotted my mother and her much younger sister, both waving eagerly. In terms of parental responsibilities, Aunt Frankie filled in for my father from time to time, and the substitution didn't bother Maggie or me one bit. Though my mother seemed disappointed she *still* hadn't finished community college, Aunt Frankie got to stay up late and watch all the newly released movies, modeled the hippest sunglasses under freshly crimped bangs, and even ate leftover birthday cake for breakfast every once in a while.

Maggie and I couldn't wait to grow up to be her.

Lithe and tawny, Aunt Frankie offered me a fishnet-gloved hand as I stepped down from the bus. "So how'd everything go today, Charliebear?"

An innocent question, but a match in my powder keg.

I buried my face in her denim jacket and let loose my tears. "Maggie tried to make me the mommy," I wailed.

Incautious and overconfident, my sister refused my mother's assistance and jumped down the bus steps herself. "I was just trying to help her make friends!"

Aunt Frankie sighed as she rubbed circles into my back. "Oh, Charlie," she said. "I did tell her to watch out for you."

My mother, however, had broken up enough sisterly spats to know this wasn't the first time I'd rejected faux motherhood.

"Darling, why didn't you just tell your sister that you didn't want to play house?"

My eyes dropped to the ground as I toed the gravel. "I don't know."

The first of many bald-faced lies. I *did* know. I just didn't have the courage to tell her. As much as Maggie antagonized me, my sister was my security blanket—the only thing I'd held on to since birth. More often than not, Maggie *was* exactly what I needed: when I felt shy, she drew off attention; when I felt fear, she stood up for us both; when I needed comfort, she was there. Usually. Being with my sister was so much easier than being alone that I couldn't risk losing her—even if her recklessness pained me.

Eager to move beyond the tiff, Aunt Frankie posed a new question as she pushed open the front door. "Well, did you two make any friends?"

Maggie swaggered through our wood-paneled entryway and dropped her book bag on the sofa. "One nice boy, named Nolan. He's got a lot of freckles. Also Jessica, who's really good at playing four square, and Gloria—she can tie her own shoes! At lunch, I sat next to Candace . . ."

She went on to name half the class. I went up to our room.

The Beauty of the End

My pity party was interrupted ten minutes later, when the buttery aroma of popcorn wafted into the room. When Maggie plopped the bowl on my bed, I rolled away to face the wall.

"I'm sorry, Charlie," she said, in the monotone of obligation.

My mother must have compelled the apology. Instead of accepting, I clutched my favorite stuffed animal and continued to brood.

Miffed by my silence, my sister spoke up.

"Why are you so scared?" she asked, her tone not at all sympathetic.

I sat up to object, irked by having to lie again. "I'm not scared," I said. "I just don't want to be a mommy."

That last part was true. It must have sounded as much, too, because Maggie softened for her next six words.

"I was just trying to help."

That sounded true too.

The truth, however, would become increasingly scarce.

The change began just a few years later, when my father began hiding the newspaper. Not *hiding*, exactly, but stowing the paper on top of the fridge after he'd finished reading it—and he often finished reading it long before Maggie and I came down for breakfast. We still wanted to read the comics, but that section, along with all the others, was stashed well out of reach.

One morning, I stumbled into the kitchen in my unicorn pajamas, still rubbing the sleep from my second-grade eyes. "Daddy, can you please get *Garfield* down for me?"

My father stood next to my mother at the sink, where they'd been talking in hushed tones. He shook his pasty hands dry and moved to retrieve the requested funny pages.

"Of course, sweetheart," he boomed.

"Why don't you just leave them on the table like you used to?"

He winked. "You wouldn't want me to spill my coffee all over *Calvin and Hobbes*, would you?"

Though I was tempted to believe such a quick and jolly explanation, there was a sadness in his sunken eyes that suggested something far more insidious might be afoot.

My mother's behavior corroborated this initial suspicion. She liked to watch the morning talk shows while cleaning up after breakfast but would flip off the television the moment Maggie or I ever entered the room. Somehow, she'd kept her record perfect until the spring of that year, when I managed to tiptoe into the kitchen and catch a glimpse of whatever she was trying to hide.

A rambunctious litter of golden retrievers chasing a bucket of tennis balls, apparently. The accompanying banner read:

Nationwide puppy shortage? Canis familiaris registers at 99*

Big words for a seven-year-old. While I'd sung the national anthem often enough to figure out "nation," and "puppy" had been one of the first words I'd learned to spell, "shortage" took me a moment—just enough time for my mother to notice.

She ushered me out of the room in a huff. "Let's go, Charlie. There's nothing here you need to see."

That, of course, told me that there was. I took my inquiry to the school lunch table.

"Oh yeah, I heard about that," Allison said. "My dog just had puppies, and my dad thinks we can get a thousand dollars for each of them now."

"No way," countered Brendan, one of our more belligerent classmates. "No one is going to pay a thousand bucks for one of your stupid mutts. Anyone who wants a dog will just go to the pound."

Nolan pulled his sandwich from a paper bag. "They can't."

"What do you mean 'they can't'?" Brendan slammed his juice box on the table. "Anyone can get a dog for free at the pound."

Nolan took a bite of his peanut butter and jelly. "Doesn't matter how much money you have. The pound is empty."

Everyone at the table stopped chewing. The pound was never empty. In fact, the kennels were always too full. Our school had just hosted a turkey trot at Thanksgiving to raise money for the animals at risk of being put down. As the top fundraiser, Maggie had taken first prize.

Nolan pulled the crusts from his bread. "My mom took me last week, and they only had cats. She said the news is making everyone crazy—something about dogs dying out. She used the word 'hoarding,' but I don't really know what that means."

Maggie took a bite of her turkey and cheese. "As long as I can still get a poodle," she said. "They're the smartest, you know. And can learn the most tricks. Aunt Frankie told me she's seen one ride a skateboard." My sister looked over at me. "Plus, we could get one with dark, curly hair, just like us."

"I don't care what kind it is as long as it sleeps in *my* bed," I replied. "But there's no way our parents get us a dog. Not if they cost so much."

We looked to Nolan for his canine fantasy.

"I don't want a dog," he said, slumping into the cafeteria bench. "I want a brother."

Maggie and I faltered.

"Are you sure?" she asked, her eyebrows reaching for the ceiling.

"You don't have to share your snacks with a dog," I reminded him.

"Or the TV," Maggie added.

Nolan sighed. "That's why my mom took me to the pound. She thought a dog would keep me company until a brother comes along."

Maggie's face dropped as if whatever she was about to say was either illegal or ill advised. "Is your mom . . ." She looked both ways to check if anyone else was listening. "Pregnant?"

Crestfallen, Nolan kept his eyes on his unfinished crusts. "I don't think so. My dad just got a new job at the baby food factory in Scranton, so he's been away a lot."

"So no dog *and* no brother?" I confirmed.

He shook his head. "Not for a while."

Inspired by the lunchtime conversation, Maggie spent the rest of the day plotting how to ask our parents for a puppy. Her plans, of course, included me as an accomplice.

"I'm not doing it," I said. "Mom and Dad already told us the Super Nintendo was too expensive, and apparently a dog is way, way more."

"Oh, come on, Charlie," Maggie nagged. "If you don't *ask*, you don't *get*. That's what Juliana's always saying, and she always gets what she wants."

Juliana was the teacher's pet—and her advice sounded terrible. But Maggie could hardly contain herself as we got off the bus.

"Mom! Mom! Mom!" she chattered. "Allison's dog just had puppies. Can we get one? Pretty, pretty please? Our birthday's next month!"

Our mother let go a forlorn breath. "Oh, girls. I don't know what you've heard at school, but the situation with dogs has gotten a lot more . . ." She looked nervously between us. "Complicated."

"But we really, really, *really* want a dog," Maggie continued. "Allison says the puppies will be ready for new homes when school gets out. It'll be summer, which means Charlie and I can take care of it every day. You and Dad won't have to lift a finger."

My mother bit her lip as she herded us into the house. "Girls, your father's already been working extra shifts to make your birthday extra special this year. The gifts are on layaway, but he'll be able to pick them up in just a few weeks. I think they're really going to make your summer."

Undeterred, Maggie got on her knees to beg. "But Mom, a puppy would make our summer the bestest, most special, most unforgettable summer *ever*."

"Maggie," my mother snapped. "I'm telling you *no*. And it's time you drop the subject—before I think you're ungrateful."

The reprimand sent Maggie storming upstairs. I followed her, unwilling to risk my mother's temper. But as we departed, I heard my mother whisper something I'm sure I wasn't supposed to hear:

"I don't think you have to worry about this summer being forgettable."

CHAPTER 2

April 26 started off routinely enough: after combing our hair and brushing our teeth, Maggie and I stood obediently in front of the fireplace so our mother could snap our annual birthday Polaroid.

"Oh, you make it look like such a chore!" she chirped, shaking out the picture as it developed. "Now let me see what I can do to make you *actually* smile."

Little did we know that our mother had quite a bit of fun tucked up her sleeve. At breakfast, she poured chocolate milk over our cereal and let us watch cartoons at the kitchen table. When the bus arrived, she handed us a grocery bag of party favors and treats to hand out, instantly improving our popularity. Finally, at lunch, she delivered surprise cupcakes for our entire class. As my mother cleared away pastry crumbs and frosting smears from the lunch table, she couldn't help but giggle.

"Your father has quite the surprise for you when you get home."

Maggie's eyes widened as visions of poodles danced through her head. I, on the other hand, tried to keep my expectations in check. One of our neighbors had advertised his trampoline for sale a few weeks prior, and that seemed like a strong possibility.

Playful though it was, our mother's tease tortured us the rest of the afternoon. Maggie, distracted from school for perhaps the first time in her entire life, didn't answer every single question asked in class. Similarly preoccupied, I doodled pogo sticks and inflatable swimming pools on the back of my social studies handout. Both behaviors drew ire from our teacher, who modestly admonished us for the inattention. School, I was sure, would last forever until that last bell rang.

Maggie and I raced to the bus.

"Do you think it's a puppy?" she asked, heaving herself into the front row.

"No," I rebuked, slightly shocked she was still considering it. "But you'd better be happy with whatever they've gotten us."

"I will, I will," she conceded. "But you don't always have to burst my bubble, you know."

Before I could answer, the bus pulled up to our stop. Maggie bolted to the door and I followed, not far behind. Our blessed mother stood by to greet us, but we outran her to get to the house.

"Happy birthday!" my father cried as we barged through the front door and into his open arms.

Maggie stopped short, as if she were waiting for a furball to run up and greet her. When it didn't, my eyes roamed the room looking for a pile of wrapped boxes, a "Happy Birthday" banner, pennants, garland—anything that might indicate something festive was afoot. But the house seemed entirely devoid of anything canine or celebratory. I looked to my father, who seemed delighted by our confusion.

"But where's . . ."

"Your presents?" He turned his bottom lip outward and waved away our expectations with all the camp of a circus clown. "Nope, no presents this year. Lost all my money playing poker with the squad."

"Daaaad," Maggie groaned, sensing the gag.

An impish smile crossed his grizzled face. "You girls might as well go mope up in your room."

We took the time to shed our backpacks only to be faster up the stairs.

At the threshold to our room, Maggie and I found the doorway crisscrossed with a barrier of rainbow streamers. Together, we crashed through the crepe-paper blockade to find a veritable kaleidoscope of technicolor balloons kissing the entirety of our ceiling. The strings of these prismatic dirigibles floated lazily over two brand-new banana-seat bicycles—complete with purple wicker baskets and shiny sterling bells.

Exactly what we'd asked for before we'd heard about Allison's puppies.

After disposing of our momentary disappointment, Maggie and I rode those bikes as often as our parents would let us—which was every day, more or less. Both our mother and father seemed to want us out of the house as much as possible. Fresh air, my father said, was good for growing girls. My mother appreciated that it gave her and my father more time to talk, which they seemed to be doing a lot.

Friday nights were our favorite, of course. Our parents would order the local pizza deal and let us ride around the cul-de-sac until sundown. As the hazy evening light drained from the mulberry sky, Maggie and I alternated between slices of pepperoni and daring each other to attempt every stunt we could think of. She could think of, really. Dropping off the Maxwells' uneven curb, riding as far as we could one-handed, skid-stopping without catching Dad's reproach—Maggie never missed a chance to push herself toward grade-school glory or serious injury.

The two were too close for comfort for me, and I frequently stepped back from the ledge.

Maggie needled me. "Come on, Charlie. Don't be a fraidy-cat!"

My parents supervised these escalating antics from our front porch swing. While Maggie and I often called for their attention with a gleeful "Look at me!," they could rarely be torn from their private conversations. A dismissive wave or a distracted "aha!" was often all we got. And while they didn't seem to have much to say to us, they certainly had a lot to say to each other. The creases in my father's brow deepened every week, and my mother seemed to blanch another shade of pale. Nonetheless, they both always managed to smile when Maggie and I hauled our trusty steeds back to their corral.

Unfortunately, the last Friday in May broke the pattern of that weekly ritual. After getting off the bus, my sister and I only managed two steps into the house before our mother handed us two plates of pizza and a warning.

"You two will need to be in bed early tonight," she said before returning her attention to the pizza box she was struggling to stuff in the trash.

Maggie's mouth was half-full of cheese. "But what about our bikes?" she protested.

My mother defeated the recalcitrant cardboard with a final shove. "I'm sorry, girls. It's going to have to wait. You two can watch a movie, but then it'll be time to get upstairs."

She promptly inserted *The Little Mermaid* into the VCR. Usually, Maggie and I would've belted out Ariel's heartfelt ballads while dancing along to Sebastian's punchy calypso, but instead we sat placidly and nibbled. My mother, on the other hand, had returned to the kitchen to click on the radio. Whenever she was cooking or cleaning, she generally preferred the accompaniment of smooth jazz, but that night she did neither. Instead, she focused her attention on a radio news broadcast that not even my father could pull her away from. When he happened to nag her about picking up the mail or taking out the trash, she sniped at him with the same refrain she'd delivered earlier: "It's going to have to wait."

Just as the undersea credits rolled, my mother gathered up the paper plates and escorted us to our room.

"Are you sure we don't have time to ride?" Maggie pleaded. "You *always* let us ride late on Fridays."

My mother was already pulling a nightgown down over my head. "Next week," she said, sounding just as harried as she looked. "Time to go brush your teeth."

With an exaggerated sigh, Maggie shuffled off to the bathroom. I couldn't blame her for capitulating—compared to me, she'd already put up a valiant fight for our weekly tradition. Watching her retreat, I decided that I couldn't surrender so easily—not unless I wanted

Maggie harping on my cowardice again. If you don't ask, you don't get, I reminded myself.

Looking up at my mother, I made my best doe eyes as I climbed into bed. "Since we didn't get to ride, can we at least make ice cream sundaes?"

My mother pulled a blanket up under my chin. "Sorry, Charlie," she said. "The president's giving an important speech in just a few minutes, and I need to listen. You girls best be asleep."

Per our normal routine, my mother reached across the bedside table to flick on the night-light. Unnecessary, she noticed, because at six o'clock, sunlight still poured through our back bedroom window.

She stood up to draw the curtains instead. I used the delay to pick at what little detail my mother had revealed.

"What kind of speech?" I asked.

"A long one," she answered.

Again, I told myself. Try again. That's what Maggie would do.

"About what?"

She snapped the drapes together. "Some news."

The tone she used signaled that she knew what I was up to and that I was about to lose my television privileges for the week.

"Well, that sounds boring," I conceded, content with my attempt at resistance.

My mother crossed the room to kiss my forehead. "We can only hope."

Having gone to bed early, my sister and I woke to ravenous pangs of hunger just as the sun came up. Given that my mother despised being roused predawn, Maggie and I stalked down to the kitchen to scrounge up some breakfast—only to find our glassy-eyed parents nursing what had to be their third carafe of coffee. When we appeared at the bottom of the stairs, they rushed over to pull us close and stroke our hair. Their overblown affection disoriented me.

Maggie and I had come down for milk and cereal, not hugs and kisses.

My father moved to distract. "You're in luck, girls. French toast is on the menu!"

He turned to the pantry to collect the ingredients while Maggie grabbed the step stool. French toast was our favorite—my sister and I had spent many Saturday mornings developing our "secret" family recipe: thick slices of stale toast dredged through a generous lacquer of eggs swirled with milk, then gussied up and fried with aromatic flourishes of cinnamon, orange zest, and vanilla. While the scent of bright citrus and seductive spice perfumed the kitchen, my sister armed herself with a spatula and challenged my father to duel. While he parried her advances with his own plastic saber, I snapped a picture with the Polaroid camera my mother had left on the counter.

That photo would later be held sacred on our fridge as the last moment we'd known of the "before times."

The diversion worked until I replaced the camera to the shelf. There, I noticed the light on my mother's sink-side radio was conspicuously dull. Last night she'd been glued to it, but this morning the kitchen was quiet—and remarkably so. It reminded me of my mother's concern.

I turned toward my parents, who were plating the toast. "Mommy, what did the president say last night?"

Drip.

Drip.

Drip.

The syrup my mother had been pouring started running off the countertop. She gawked at me as if I'd taken the luck I'd pushed last night and just shoved it into a nearby ravine.

My chest tightened. How could such an innocent question have gotten me so quickly in trouble?

My parents exchanged an uneasy look before my father took a seat at the kitchen table. It was the same seat he usually took when I was about to get a talking-to, and my stomach dropped instinctively. But on that suspicious spring morning, the blood drained from my father's fleshy cheeks instead of flushing them. His eyes were wet with sadness, not frustration. The hand that usually curled into an angry fist moved gently to my knee.

"Well, sweetheart," he began, glancing back over his shoulder to make sure Maggie was listening too. "President Canfield gave us some big news last night. News that's going to change a lot of things for a lot of people. But I want you to know that you, Maggie, your mom, and I are all going to be okay."

My eyes followed his to my mother, who looked far less certain.

"So what is it, Daddy?"

He hesitated, looking again to my mother, who shook her head. But my father may as well have been allergic to lies, so he took my hands into his and tried to tell the truth.

"Well, girls, eventually—but not right now, and probably not for a long, long time . . ."

Whatever words he was trying to summon seemed stuck to the roof of his mouth. After a flurry of stammers and false starts, he finally surrendered to candor.

"There won't be any more babies."

I took a sip of orange juice and smacked my lips. "That's okay. I don't really want any more babies."

The words flabbergasted my father but animated my previously stoic mother.

"Leave it, Jim." With both her eyes and her words, she begged him to ignore my innocent retort.

Impervious to her assertion, my father continued. "The problem is, darling, if there aren't any more babies, then there won't be any more grown-ups . . ."

My mother crossed the room to intervene. "Jim, you don't have to go there," she petitioned. "Not right now. It. Can. Wait." Her pleas fizzled to a whimper. "They're only eight."

Impervious to her desperate appeal, my father tumbled headlong into his conclusion with one final gulp. "And if there aren't any more grown-ups, there won't be any more people. Ever."

My mother buried her face in her apron and left the room. Comparatively unfazed, Maggie and I dug into our plates.

Some might have assumed that children our age couldn't fully register the meaning of my father's reveal. In all honesty, we might not have if our house hadn't been fumigated for termites earlier that year. When we were allowed back inside, Maggie peppered my parents with all sorts of uncomfortable questions as they swept the dead insects out the back door. How did they die? What killed them? Did they stop breathing? Why didn't they run?

I, on the other hand, didn't know what else to do but watch the horror unfold.

Even though the extinction my father described didn't involve anything half as sensational as our recent termite annihilation, he spent the rest of breakfast reassuring Maggie and me that no harm would come to our family. No one we knew was going to die tomorrow, and beyond that, the effects of the announcement didn't really concern second graders. It didn't occur to me or Maggie to mourn the future we were about to lose, as my mother already was. Nor did we realize that such grief would begin a lot sooner than my father suggested.

Because what President Canfield had told the nation was not "a long, long time." What he'd told the nation was "four."

The average American family would last just four more generations.

CHAPTER 3

Everyone thought the world was ending—at least for the first few weeks.

My parents kept my sister and me home for the rest of the school year. They, along with everyone else, weren't quite sure how other people would react to the suggestion that humanity was about to extinguish. By the summer, though, most of the population had figured out that not much had changed. No one was dying—at least not any faster than they had been before—and these very lively people still needed groceries and haircuts and bank accounts. Soon, everyone went back to work. Everything went back to normal.

At least in the eyes of us children.

Two years passed before any adults officially explained the crisis. When Maggie and I were in the fourth grade, the school handed everyone in our class a government-issued booklet and a VHS tape—both featuring a giant orange-eyed cicada on the front. From the brief orientation we received in class, the disappearance of these horrendous-looking insects had led to the discovery of humanity's expiration date. We were to review both the booklet and the video with our parents and return them before the end of the year.

Brendan saw me thumbing through the material on the bus ride home.

"Psh," he scoffed. "Cicadas aren't even real."

I looked at him and then back down at the magazine. "There's a photo of one right here."

His ratty lip pulled into a sneer. "But have you ever seen one?"

"No," I said. "That's what happens when things go extinct."

Brendan snatched the video from my lap and passed it to one of his cronies. "My dad says the whole thing's a hoax."

I grabbed for the cassette, but the boys were already playing keep-away: Timmy tossed it to Travis, who lobbed it to Keith two rows back. I'd get detention if I didn't return the tape in good condition, and at this rate it looked like I might be spending Friday afternoon with Principal Allende.

"Your dad works at the gas station down the street," Maggie interjected, seizing the video from Keith's unsuspecting hands.

"Shut up, hula girl. We dropped nukes on your island for a reason."

It was no great secret that Maggie and I were adopted. Our skin was eight shades darker than our lily-white parents', and we'd spent a lot of show-and-tell time explaining why. Much to our teacher's surprise, talking about our adoption didn't bother us much anymore—the transaction had occurred when we were toddlers, and the full emotional embrace of our second family had all but tranquilized our sorrow. What was most awkward, actually, was that most kids thought that hailing from the South Pacific meant we'd been born knowing how to surf. Maggie and I didn't disabuse them of the notion but didn't reveal that we'd been born to immigrants in Arkansas either. Much to my relief, I avoided having to confess that I'd never actually seen the ocean.

The insults, though. Those were new. The existential stress of the past two years had left many families raw, ours included. Maggie looked ready to spit in Brendan's face when Nolan stepped in front of her.

"Get lost, Brendan," he said. "You can't even point to the Marshall Islands on a map."

"Isn't that cute! The ginger's standing up for the orphans."

Brendan took a swing at Nolan's face, but our friend ducked the punch just before the bus jerked to a halt. The hefty bus driver threw the gearbox into park and lurched down the aisle to grab Brendan by the ear.

"You'd think with the end of the world round the corner, y'all could at least be decent to each other," she said.

Clutching the VHS tape tight to my chest, I disembarked the bus as quickly as I possibly could. Brendan, relegated to a seat on the front bench, scowled at me. As she followed me out, Maggie parried his grimace by sticking out her tongue. Nolan also got off at our stop, intent on walking us home.

"You both were really brave back there." I sighed. "Thanks."

Nolan's freckles faded into a field of red as he pulled at the straps on his backpack. "Somebody had to do something. I'm glad it made a difference."

Maggie seemed far more annoyed than flattered. "You can't be afraid to stick up for yourself, Charlie. It's the only thing bullies understand."

After seeing us to our driveway, Nolan made for his own house up the road. As he turned away, I found myself wishing I'd hugged him. But the moment was gone. Instead, I trudged up the gravel with my sister, who was making the case that we should avoid telling our parents about what had happened. I agreed. With all that was going on, they didn't need another reason to worry, and Maggie jumped right into explaining our homework instead.

"First, they want us to read the brochure and ask you questions. Then, they want us to watch the video." She eyed my father, who looked less than enthused. "*Together*. As a *family*."

"Sounds like we got our work cut out for us," he mused, his gray eyes puffy from two weeks of graveyard shifts with the police department. "Let's take care of this before I have to head in."

I settled into the pamphlet while my mother fixed us a snack. Eight pages, two columns, and plenty of pictures of long-dead bugs. How such a thing could explain the end of our species, I didn't know.

It was the cicadas that gave it away.

Apparently, billions of these insects, a batch known as Brood X, should've made an enormous emergence in 1987. They'd just spent seventeen years underground metamorphosizing from larvae into adults. Seventeen years. A biological miracle, really, that so many bugs took so long to mature. Even more impressive was their simultaneous resurrection. Every seventeen years, in the same few weeks, every single member of Brood X climbed out of the soil, shook off the dirt, and proclaimed its existence to the world with a fantastic and earsplitting shriek. So dazzled were the scientists they'd dubbed these heinous, noisy creatures *Magicicada*.

The public was far less enchanted.

My father recalled the weathermen describing the incoming plague like a late-season blizzard: *flurries* of insects were scheduled to *drift* into the region just as soon as ground temperatures warmed past sixty-four degrees. The bugs would *accumulate* in the trees at *unprecedented levels* and call to their mates with a deafening "song." Not long after, the cicadas would copulate, lay their eggs, and die, leaving behind a *blanket* of carcasses to clog up the sidewalks and gutters. Measurements would be made in *inches*; the inconvenience would last *weeks*.

"The forecasts had everyone so worked up that pretty much every hardware store sold out of push brooms." My father chuckled. "The best I could do was take the snow shovel out of storage and buy your mother a pair of new galoshes."

But the cicadas never showed up.

That whole summer, not a single one was seen, heard, or stepped on. Suddenly, gratefully, curiously—they were gone.

Perhaps more accurately, the missing cicadas never actually *were*.

Maggie piped up when she reached the third page. "What's an en-to-mo-lo-gist?"

My parents flicked uncertain looks at each other. Both had a high school education, but neither would've called science their strong suit.

"A person who studies bugs," I answered. Having paid attention to the nature shows on public television, I knew more about biology than most.

Not being a particularly well-funded branch of science, it took months for the entomologists to investigate the cicadas' disappearance. What they found disturbed them: seventeen years prior, the previous batch of Brood X had produced plenty of excruciating noise but not a single viable egg.

No viable eggs meant no subterranean larvae. No 1970 larvae meant no 1987 emergence. No 1987 emergence meant no more Brood X cicadas.

The bugs were extinct.

I put down my booklet.

"We didn't think it was such a big deal at first," my mother explained, plopping our baby book in the middle of the table. She flipped to one of the early pages and pointed to a note she'd written under the heading titled "Current Events":

In 1987, God had to exterminate the cicadas to make room for other pests: these two!

"It's hard to believe we ever made that joke." She let go a regretful sigh.

My father swallowed. "Isn't it time for the video?"

Our family then migrated from the kitchen table to the living room.

"Do you think we should invite Aunt Frankie?" Maggie asked, popping the tape into the VCR. "They did tell us to review the video with our *entire* family."

My father shook his head and scoffed. "Aunt Frankie is a little . . ."

"Preoccupied," my mother finished, in a tone that did not invite questions.

Whatever Aunt Frankie was up to, she'd been up to it for months. In the wake of the president's announcement, Maggie and I had seen less and less of our favorite aunt. She'd looked pretty ghoulish that last time I'd seen her. Drawn and dirty, with yellowing skin and loosening teeth—pitiful, in a word. My mother had lured her over on the promise of Sunday dinner but kept an eye on her pocketbook throughout the meal. Afterward, my father warned Maggie and me never to let Aunt Frankie in the house unless another adult was present.

After the VCR finished calibrating, the TV screen filled with dramatic clips of concerned scientists examining half-filled test tubes.

Toxins. Radiation. Global warming. Scientists around the world considered all possible explanations for the missing cicadas before ruling each and every one out. Frustrated by the lack of answers, an enterprising young researcher employed an experimental technique to analyze the cicadas' inner mechanics. While genetic sequencing hadn't been utilized much beyond bacteria, Dr. David J. Carmichael took it upon himself to reach out to the people who collected old, dead bugs to request samples from the various batches of Brood X insects: 1970, 1953, 1936, 1919, and so forth. It took him nearly two years to decode all that DNA, but his results approximated something between astounding and horrific.

Eventual, irreversible infertility had been written into the cicadas' genetic code.

A monumental discovery: significant enough to merit several first-rate journal articles, sensational enough to draw a prime-time news spot.

Our video cut to footage from that first interview: Dr. Carmichael must have been running late, because he'd been shoved onstage in his still-wet trench coat.

"Well, when we looked at the DNA from the 1970 cicadas, we didn't find anything of interest, to be honest," he started. He pulled his sleeve across his face to catch the rain that dripped from the end of his nose. "It all looked the same. It all looked normal. But we found something important when we compared it to the samples from 1953 insects. The 1970 sample was shorter."

The news anchor's head cocked against her bulky shoulder pads. "And what does that mean, exactly?"

"The older cicadas had a particular sequence that the younger cicadas did not," Dr. Carmichael continued. "We call that sequence the 'LMT' gene, an abbreviation of the protein it codes for. And when we looked at insects from the 1936 batch? They had two copies. The 1919 group had three. One collector brought us a uniquely well-preserved specimen from 1868, and just as expected, that bug's DNA contained six copies of LMT."

Maggie jumped off the couch and pointed at the television. "That's why they call it the Limit!"

"Shhhh!" I hissed, waving her out of my view.

A keen eye could spot the anchor counting on her fingertips. "Sounds like some kind of . . . biological countdown."

"An apt comparison—except this time bomb detonates with extinction instead of explosion. Brood X, it seems, had a fixed number of generations, with every reproductive cycle ticking one away. By 1970, no LMT genes remained, and, well—it ended the species."

The anchor shifted in her seat. His tone thick with reassurance, Dr. Carmichael preempted her next question.

"No other species has ever demonstrated similar reproductive decay," he soothed. "This condition may be as unique to the cicada as its seventeen-year life cycle."

"When will you know?"

"Soon," he answered. "As soon as we can examine some samples from other extinctions."

A savvy move, the narrator explained. Dr. Carmichael had been trying for months to secure the cooperation of coy private collectors and haughty museum directors. Even the questionable taxidermists hadn't taken his calls. But within a week of that interview, they all came forward to offer hair, nails, and feathers from their most privileged specimens: dodo birds, Tasmanian tigers, woolly mammoths.

Geneticists located the cursed gene in every single one. Much to the misfortune of life on our planet, these creatures hadn't fallen victim to overhunting or habitat loss or climate change, as previously hypothesized.

They'd simply expired according to a preordained genetic schedule.

I looked over at my parents. Their hang-dog faces fixated on the screen, but I could tell their minds were elsewhere. My sister, too, seemed entranced—but her eyes sparkled. And not in a way that made me feel safe.

CHAPTER 4

The television cut to static when the credits ran out. Maggie stood up and switched it off.

"So," she said, addressing the room, "how many generations do *we* have left?"

"Four," my father said, dodging her eye contact.

"*Maybe* four," my mother countered. "Four is the average. Since humans don't reproduce all at once like the cicadas, there's some difference between people. Some have two, some have six . . ."

"Some people already have none," my father scoffed.

My mother ignored his flippant contribution. "They're working on a test right now so everyone can figure out what they have."

Maggie's unsatisfied look chilled the room. "So what are we going to do?"

She gestured toward the now blank screen. "*We* should be doing something. Like that doctor in the video. There's got to be something we can do. To save the species. To save . . ." She waved indiscriminately around the room. "Us."

"The scientists *are* doing things," my mother answered. "Along with the test, they're also working on a cure."

Maggie paced in front of the fireplace. "But what about *us*? There has to be something our family can do to help."

"This isn't like the fundraising for the pound, darling," my father replied. "There's not a lot you or me or any regular person can do right now, so you might as well relax. The scientists will get this sorted out. I'm sure by the time you're our age, they'll have some kind of pill or a shot you can take to get yourselves fixed up."

Maggie stopped in the middle of the living room. "Waiting around doesn't seem like enough."

"Well, what do you want *me* to do about it? I'm just a cop."

The dismissive remark brought angry tears to Maggie's eyes, and my mother moved to defuse the impending detonation. "Sweetheart, I'm sure if you just wait patiently, everything will be fine."

The salve was anything but, and Maggie stiffened into a wooden doll. "I don't believe you," she muttered.

I couldn't tell whether her fists were clenching from fear or frustration.

That night, exhausted by her outburst, Maggie fell asleep as soon as her head hit the pillow. This left me with plenty of time to think about all I'd seen on that tape. And while my sister was eager to figure out what we could all do, I was struck by how much had already happened.

And how none of it was good.

After Dr. Carmichael's discovery, every laboratory in the country pivoted to studying the world's newfound genetic hazard. Unfortunately, it still took months to properly analyze even the simplest organisms. It wasn't until 1991 that a team at Johns Hopkins determined that the common fruit fly still embodied one hundred thousand generations. A number so high, in fact, that the principal investigator assumed his equipment had malfunctioned. He marked the result with a "*" to indicate his doubt and asked independent laboratories all over the world to rerun his experiment.

Over the course of the next month, these labs not only confirmed his result but adopted his notation.

100,000*. While most people sighed with relief, the scientific community seized with anxiety. A generation of fruit flies lasted all of 28 days, meaning the entirety of *Drosophila melanogaster* would last no more than 8,500 years. The blink of an eye on the geologic time scale, but inconceivably distant for most humans. Public concern abated, at least until the restaurants started running out of calamari.

And the hydrangeas didn't bloom.

And no one could remember when they last saw a porcupine.

As more and more creatures vanished, so did the world's indifference.

Beset by urgency, corporations, universities, and governments all surged their resources into anything that might clarify these dreadful timelines. Genetic technologies, centralized studies, and cooperative agreements—all were put to work assessing longevity of the world's creatures. The work began with the simplest invertebrates, with barnacles clocking in at 80,000* and sea urchins at 50,000*. Fish followed, with all but the most sophisticated varieties containing at least 12,000* or better. Birds and reptiles would endure for centuries as well, with most species averaging 1,000* and 3,000*, respectively. And while each of these experiments generated journal-worthy results, it was the sum of their parts that truly caught headlines:

The more complex the creature, the nearer its reproductive end.

This did not bode well for mammals. Lab rats were the first to have their sunset calculated: as a species, *Rattus norvegicus* averaged just 400*, which meant most would expire within two hundred years. Most. The rats in the study, however, demonstrated significant individual variation. The rats bred for genetic experiments—those that reproduced early and often for science—registered at 100*. The rats bred as pets or for long-term study exceeded 550*. And while these bloodlines would long outlast those of their "more productive" brethren, no rat could escape the ultimate end.

Extinction could be delayed, but not defeated.

For a while, each new study intensified the collective dread. But somewhere between the domesticated cat (*Felis catus*, 72*) and chimpanzee (*Pan troglodytes*, 18*), the public deadened to new results. The only finding that mattered was for humans, and that work was expressly prohibited by international law on the grounds that it might cause panic. But by Christmas of 1993, the world had already worked itself into hysterics, thanks to the quacks and the charlatans and the death cult leaders who'd been exploiting the speculation for years. The United Nations Special Commission on Natural Extinction had no choice but to embark upon a definitive study, the results of which were finalized on Friday, the thirteenth of May.

The date was, of course, a coincidence.

At least that's what they told us.

By the time Maggie and I reached the middle of fifth grade, the Limit had already begun to curb the population—at least according to the statisticians. The rest of us couldn't tell. There were still plenty of buyers and sellers, producers and consumers, doctors and lawyers and engineers. What the world was losing was babies. Every year saw fewer and fewer, and eventually, we'd all run out.

On the first day back at school after spring break, Maggie and I found Nolan sitting against the playground's rear fence, picking at the errant weeds.

"My dad lost his job," he said, ripping an unassuming dandelion from its roots.

I took a seat next to him. When Nolan's father had come in for career day, he'd brought tiny jars of mushy peas and pureed carrots. He worked for Gerber, at the baby-food plant, and while the slop made everyone gag, his presentation had won over the entire class.

"They're shutting down the factory," Nolan continued.

The news flushed away Maggie's usual perk. "What's going to happen to your family?" she asked. "Will you have to move?"

"I hope not," he said. "My mom's working on a plan."

29

"Moms make the best plans," I assured him. But it was Maggie who gave him a hug.

My sister and I spent the rest of the day trying to cheer Nolan up. I gave him my at-bats during kickball while Maggie let him cut the lunch line. I shared my chips while Maggie offered to do his math homework. Nothing really worked, however, and our job wasn't made easier when Mrs. Aoki handed us official-looking forms to take home.

Maggie turned it over a few times. "What is this?"

I scanned the first few lines. "A permission slip. They want to take some blood."

It was here. Genetic persistence screening had finally become both available to and mandatory for ten-year-olds across the country, and now the entire fifth grade was about to find out just how long their families had left. Until that moment, the Limit hadn't changed all that much about our daily lives: the lights had stayed on, the pantry remained stocked, and school, somehow, continued—much to our chagrin. This test was, quite literally, the first pinprick of change.

My mother reviewed the forms as soon as we shoved them into her hands. "Sounds like they want you two to submit for a finger stick sometime next month," she announced.

"I'm sure it won't be anything more than a few drops," my father assured. "It's the results that could be far more painful."

My mother twinged. "You girls will be brave enough to do that, right?"

"Of course," Maggie replied. Too busy trying to subdue the growing squall of alarm inside me, I let my sister's response stand for my own.

I spent the next few weeks trying not to think too much about the upcoming test. Instead, Maggie and I focused on Nolan: she drew elaborate pictures of us all playing together; I made him a bracelet from the beading kit we had received for Christmas. Though Maggie had already used most of the brighter gems to make matching necklaces for herself and Aunt Frankie, plenty of browns and greens and "boy" colors still lingered in the box.

I gave Nolan the totem when we lined up outside the school's gym for screening. My heartbeat quickened as I tied the drably beaded cord around his narrow wrist.

"Here," I said nervously. "Friends forever. No matter what."

Unlike our initial kindergarten contact, Nolan didn't seem to mind my touch. And for the first time since he'd told us about his father, I saw my best friend smile, setting both my heart and my eyelashes into a flutter. A nurse rescued me before Maggie noticed.

"Mr. Kincade?" she called. "You're next."

※

Two weeks later, the nurse called my sister and me into her office for our results. Given that we were twins and our results would be identical, Nurse Pierce didn't see any harm in scheduling our appointments together. When we met our parents at the school's front door, my flustered mother fussed with her hair and clutched at her handbag. My father, however, reached for Maggie with his right hand and me with his left and led all of us down the hallway.

Together. As a family.

Nurse Pierce fumbled through an off-kilter stack of files as she called us in.

"How I miss the days of Band-Aids and bloody noses," she tutted. "Please, take a seat."

We couldn't, at least not immediately. My father had to upright the chairs that encircled her desk while my mother cleared a handful of tissues from the floor.

Whoever had gone before us hadn't gotten good news.

Nurse Pierce pushed a wisp of white hair away from her face. "Ah, yes, thank you for that. Let's see . . . Taglieri . . . Takana . . . ah, Tannehill. Here we are."

Her pudgy fingers split open the marigold folders as she peeked inside.

"Lord have mercy," she said, crossing herself. "You both screened 5*."

My mother loudly expelled the breath she'd been holding. For once, I found myself grateful for such theatrics—my mother's outsize relief distracted from my own discomfort. Uncertain what to make of the news, I could only sit on my hands and swallow. Based on her own enduring silence, the news rendered my sister equally perplexed. It was my father who finally interjected.

"That, uh, sounds like a good thing?"

"It is and it isn't," Nurse Pierce replied. "A lot of responsibility comes with these results. Charlie, Maggie, you'll be able to have children—but there will be increasing pressure to do so too. Your genes might be the ones that break the Limit, you know."

The cheeky wink she delivered turned my stomach.

"Just to be clear, any children you have will be 4*, their children 3*, and so forth. You're all quite fortunate that you'll never see the end of your family line—at least not with your own eyes." She paused for a moment. "That's not something I get to tell everybody."

I'd spotted Brendan's mother weeping on a bench during recess. No wonder he hadn't returned to class.

Nurse Pierce returned our files to the stack and forced a smile. "Girls, why don't you head out to the playground. I need to discuss some of the specifics with your parents."

While the dismissal was gentle, her tone was far graver than before. I eased out of my chair obediently, happy to ignore the ugly details as long as possible. Maggie, however, didn't budge.

"I'm not going," she said.

"Unfortunately, dear, this is a conversation for grown-ups." Nurse Pierce's nervous eyes darted to my parents for reinforcement.

"You heard Nurse Pierce, Mags," my father added. "Don't you worry your precious little head about what's going on in here. Remember what your mother always says: if you wait patiently and quietly, everything will turn out fine."

While the condescension was enough to raise my hackles, Maggie's were on the ceiling. At a loss for words, but not emotion, she slammed the door so hard that Nurse Pierce's nameplate dropped to the floor. My sister found her voice a few minutes later.

"I don't believe you," she spat at no one in particular.

Those were words I'd never forget.

※

When we got to the playground, Maggie threw herself belly-first onto the swings.

"I don't understand why they don't just tell us the truth."

I settled into the swing beside her and rocked. "Maybe they don't know what to say."

Maggie spun around, winding up the chain as she went. "The adults aren't doing enough. This test doesn't really *do* anything. It doesn't help find a cure at all; it just makes people nervous."

"Well, maybe when you grow up, *you* can do more. You seem to really care about this, Maggie. Maybe you can find the cure."

When her swing couldn't take any more, Maggie let go and unwound in a great tornado of chain links and curls. When she finally came to rest, she looked up at me.

"I do *really care*. Everyone should *really care*. But right now, the only thing I *really care* about is Nolan having to move."

Grateful for the change in subject, I nodded. "Me too."

"What if we raised some money?" she asked, finally sitting up.

I looked over to find Maggie's eyes glinting. Despite her best efforts to keep a straight face, the corners of her mischievous mouth had turned upward.

"If we help Nolan's family make their bills, they won't have to move," she asserted, her voice purring with excitement.

"But how much would we need?"

Maggie kicked off the ground and started swinging. "I don't know, maybe two hundred? I've still got twelve bucks from last month's allowance."

"That seems like a lot of money. The two hundred, that is."

Maggie pumped her legs with increasing speed, reaching heights far higher than I'd ever dared.

"I know," she said as she passed through the trough. "But if we don't do anything, Nolan will *definitely* have to move. We have to try something."

I kicked at the groove that previous children had worn into the ground. "I guess we could mow lawns."

Maggie was now moving so fast she almost had to shout. "What about a lemonade stand?"

With that, my sister leaped from the apex of her now astronomic arc and sailed through the air like a squirrel. She landed deftly on all fours, then stood up to dust off her hands on her pants.

"It'll make us feel better to do something, Charlie. Anything."

§

My parents collected us from the playground a few moments later, looking visibly lighter than before but still not quite relieved. The empty gaze my mother carried suggested she still might be wrestling with whatever she'd been told.

Maggie tried to pull her out of it as she opened the door. "Being a 5* is a good thing, right? Our family should have nothing to worry about."

"You're right," my mother agreed. "At least not yet."

"Not yet?" snapped Maggie. "What do you mean by '*not yet*'?"

My father cut in with just a twinge of aggravation. "She means that we'll tell you when you're older, sweetheart. You two should just focus on your childhood. Ride your bikes, build forts, go swimming, catch fireflies. Open a lemonade stand, for crying out loud. But for heaven's sake, let the grown-ups take care of the worrying."

His upper lip stiffened as he braced for Maggie's retort.

Instead, my sister raised an eyebrow.

"Can you help us with the lemonade stand?"

The next Saturday, my father made good on his promise and hauled a cooler of ice to the curb. He then helped us dissolve the stubborn lemonade powder into our mother's Tupperware pitchers and even turned on the lights of his cruiser to advertise. But just after lunch, our financier and chief operations officer was forced to relinquish his budding juice boutique to his "more than capable" understudies. Unfortunately, he was due back at the station for overtime.

The elderly Maxwells stopped by first. They were just strolling through on their daily walk, so they didn't have quarters on them, but both seemed glad to see Maggie and me out and about. Not a lot of kids were outside doing kid-like things anymore, they said. Desperate for marketing, my sister and I gave the doddering old couple two cups of lemonade after they swore to spread the good word. But an hour later, when the midday sun grew hot, we still had nothing to show but the pocket change my father had left us with.

Maggie wiped her sweaty face with the front of her favorite shirt. "This isn't working," she said. "Why don't you stay here—I'll go drum up some business."

That's when she took off on her bike to solicit donations instead. A few of our neighbors took pity on our struggling business and kicked in a dollar or two. Mrs. Dunkley from down the street found Maggie's pitch so adorable she offered up a twenty. My sister continued her campaign until thirst overpowered her. She plopped her sweaty wad of bills on top of the cooler and gulped down three of my prefilled cups.

"It's amazing what people will give if you just ask."

"$52.75," I counted. "A good start, I guess."

Maggie swigged another cup and then tapped the icebox. "We can try again next week. The closer we get to summer, the more people will need cool drinks."

She then shoved the money back into her pocket and mounted her bicycle once more.

"I'm going to bring this to Nolan," she said, snapping closed the clasp of her helmet. "You should come too."

I wasn't ready to see Nolan, not when I looked so sunburned and frazzled. "Don't you think we should wait until we have two hundred?"

"It's almost the end of the month. That's when money runs tight at our house. Maybe this can cover the cable bill or something."

With that, we were off.

Nolan lived in a proper Dutch colonial half a mile up the main road. After a few minutes of vigorous pedaling, Maggie and I ditched our bikes in his yard so she could race up the porch and pound on his crimson front door. Halfway out of breath, I scrambled up behind her just as Mrs. Kincade appeared. Hair like rosewood and skin like ivory, her apple hadn't fallen very far from its tree.

"Hi, Mrs. Kincade," Maggie started. "Is Nolan home?"

"I'm sorry, girls. He's out fishing with his dad. I'll let him know you dropped by."

Mrs. Kincade lingered in the doorway, waiting for us to turn back to our bikes. Maggie just fidgeted her hand in her pocket.

"We, uh, heard that Mr. Kincade lost his job," she blurted. "We wanted to give you this."

My sister produced her wad of cash and thrust it in Mrs. Kincade's direction.

Nolan's mother eyed the money but made no motion to receive it.

"You girls are just too sweet," she said. "But right now, our family's doing just fine. I can't take this."

"But you have to," Maggie replied, her tone a bit more forceful. "We don't want Nolan to move."

"All right, all right," she conceded. "But let me walk you home."

※

On the way back, Mrs. Kincade made lovely small talk. She complimented our bikes as well as our curls, then asked how school was going. When Maggie proudly announced that we'd screened as 5*s, Mrs. Kincade told us there weren't too many people like us out there. Because of that, she said, we might take a little more care in being out on the street alone.

Our mother, apparently, shared the same opinion.

She burst through the front door as soon as we turned into the driveway. *"Magnolia Bea and Charlotte Mae,"* she called. *"You get your butts in the house right now!"*

I realized then that we'd forgotten to tell her where we were going.

"Jesus." She cursed, not quite under her breath. "I thought somebody kidnapped you."

Maggie and I knew better than to cross her in a mood like this and swept up to our room without another word. Once upstairs, I cracked a window to eavesdrop on the proceedings. Perhaps my mother's furor would recede once she realized how charitable Maggie and I were trying to be.

"Thanks for bringing them home, Janet," she said.

"No trouble," Mrs. Kincade replied. "I also needed to give you this."

She passed my mother Maggie's roll of bills.

My mother shook her head. "I'm so sorry. When the girls told me they wanted to sell lemonade, they didn't say what for."

"It's really very sweet that they want to help."

My mother then invited Mrs. Kincade to take a seat on the porch swing. Then, because she could never let good sugar go to waste, she poured Nolan's mother a tiny cup of lemonade.

"So how's Sean doing?"

Mrs. Kincade took a polite sip. "The formula line got hit first. The company thought more mothers were just switching back to breastfeeding, but now it seems like the demand will never return." She knocked back the rest of the juice with one swallow. "They're reducing their workforce in accordance with the population decline."

My mother refilled the tiny paper cup. "So what are you going to do?"

"Well, the school nurse told me the government is going to start offering stipends for women to reproduce. I guess we have to consider it."

Money? For babies? I could hardly believe what I was hearing. Maybe Nolan did have a chance to stay.

"The girls have mentioned Nolan wanting a brother. Are you sure you're ready to go back to the newborn phase?"

"I'm no spring chicken, that's for sure," Mrs. Kincade laughed. "But the payment increases as you get older—something about lengthening generations. Anyhow, with my fortieth on the horizon, Sean and I might be able to really cash in."

"Happy birthday to *you*," my mother cooed. If Dixie cups could clink, I'm sure I would have heard them. Instead, I heard the flick of a lighter.

"Would you like one?" my mother asked, no doubt offering Mrs. Kincade one of the clandestine cigarettes she'd promised she'd quit. My mother only smoked at her wit's end, and it seemed that Maggie and I had driven her there.

"I haven't had one of those in years," Mrs. Kincade replied. "So that's a yes."

My nose then filled with acrid wafts of tobacco smoke as their fumes drifted up to the second floor.

"Is having a baby something you and Jim would ever consider?" Mrs. Kincade's voice was smoother now, more supple and even. "I'm happy to pass along the brochure."

My mother's had similarly mellowed. "I really wish we could. But Jim and I struggled to get pregnant. Turns out it wasn't his sperm count or my 'hostile uterus.' We'd run out of generations—just like the cicadas."

Mrs. Kincade didn't quite know how to respond, but my mother had manners enough to move the conversation along.

"So how do you get the money?" she asked.

Mrs. Kincade took a long drag from her cigarette and blew out one flawless ring. "Starts with a visit with someone called a Mendel."

CHAPTER 5

The Mendelia was never humanity's first choice. The Mendelia was, in fact, humanity's last option, born of failing science and frazzled nerves. That's what Dr. Rubino explained at our sixth-grade assembly. She'd been sent by the organization to proselytize, and our school welcomed their envoy.

Dressed in a long white lab coat, she tapped the microphone a few times to get our attention.

"Good morning," Dr. Rubino started. "The Mendelia sent me here today to talk with you about our work—and how you might help."

Dr. Venita Rubino was a lot younger than I imagined she'd be. Young, svelte, and brimming with confidence, Dr. Rubino could run both literal and intellectual circles around Nurse Pierce. After a janitor finished assembling her projector, screen, and slide carousel, the woman in white pointed her remote at the ancient machine and clicked.

An image of goggle-clad scientists toiling over a lab bench flashed onto the screen.

"Ever since President Canfield announced the Limit, more than a million different scientists have tried to defeat it. Bioengineers have tried replicating the gene and inserting more copies of it into the sequence. Data scientists have combed through thousands of genomes in search of chance mutations. Nutritionists, physiologists, microbiologists—they've all had their own approach. But none have produced a solution."

She paused to let the information sink in. Whatever my parents had said about "patiently waiting" suddenly seemed impossibly naive.

Dr. Rubino clicked again, and the on-screen scientists were replaced by a thick herd of fluffy sheep.

"In the absence of a quick fix, humanity must revert to old habits. Habits with a demonstrable record of success. Husbandry—the practice of careful breeding—can lengthen the span of generations and buy our species a few more decades for research."

Another click, another slide. This one with some basic computations.

"Most individuals in our species only have four generations left," she said, holding up a handful of manicured fingers to emphasize the point. "Since humans, on average, reproduce every twenty years, scientists have only eighty years to make a discovery."

My breath hitched. Eighty years was just one lifetime.

My lifetime.

"But if we extend that term to twenty-five, we delay our extinction by one hundred years. At fifty, we double that."

Mrs. Kincade suddenly looked like a hero.

"Purposeful reproduction can also accelerate adaptation." Dr. Rubino brought up an image of uniformly yellow sweet corn alongside its far more prismatic Indian brother. "Instead of breeding *out* spurious mutations, as has been done in agriculture, we now have renewed interest in breeding such variations *in*. The smallest change might break the Limit. And while the world's scientists might endeavor on hundreds of new laboratory experiments every year, 364,000 babies are born every single day."

Dr. Rubino produced a ravishing smile.

"Each is an opportunity."

After another Hollywood-quality pause, Dr. Rubino flipped through a rapid sequence of very different images: colossal mansions, flashy super cars, well-groomed horses, piles of cash. Any normal twelve-year-old would've salivated, but my innards calcified into something both heavy and nauseating. Maggie's heel bounced furiously against the floor.

"Now," Dr. Rubino continued. "Let's talk about the benefits."

"If you can resist the temptation of children until age forty, you'll be rewarded with a grand lump sum—one that grows larger with every year you age. If you can't wait, prolific breeding is also an option. Women who roll the biological dice as often as possible are rewarded with modest monthly payments for each child they spawn.

"In either case, one thing is certain. The higher you screen, the more children you should have. The species depends on it."

My breakfast curdled in my stomach, and I felt certain I was about to vomit. My status as a 5* suddenly seemed more curse than blessing.

Dr. Rubino turned off her slide projector. "Questions?"

Stunned into silence, the room couldn't even manage a whisper until Allison's hand shot up.

"Are we allowed to wait until we're thirty? And maybe just have two children? That's what my mom and dad did."

Dr. Rubino clasped her hands together with all the rehearsed refinement of a choir girl. "Of course, of course," she tutted. "At this time, the Mendelia have no interest in curtailing normal reproductive behavior. The government just won't pay for it."

Greed, it seemed, might possibly save humanity.

Maggie, Nolan, and I trudged through the remainder of sixth grade. The Mendelia's assembly worked exactly as intended, and our classmates spent the better part of the year plotting the best ways to satisfy their financial and familial goals. We'd barely had sex ed, but now most kids were planning enormous broods or geriatric pregnancies to fund their million-dollar dreams.

While I found the exercise excruciating, it devastated Nolan. After Memorial Day, we found him sitting alone at his desk before class. Not smiling, not sleeping, just sitting. Quivering.

Maggie and I rushed over.

"My dad's moving to New Jersey," he whimpered.

Maggie flared with excitement. "He found a job?"

"No," Nolan replied. "He found another woman."

"What?" For once, Maggie and I responded in unison.

"My mom hasn't been able to get pregnant, so the Mendelia's money hasn't come through. Instead, my dad's going to try and make a fortune by having a bunch of kids with this lady he met at church." Nolan's head dropped to the table. "He promised to send us some."

My whole body deflated. Mr. Kincade couldn't just abandon his family. There had to be rules about that, right?

"My mom kicked him out." Nolan pulled a snot-stained sleeve across his teary cheeks. "She said that if he's going to go off and have his own family, she's going to go off and have hers. We're moving in with my aunt in Minnesota next week."

༄

Imploding families. Impending desertions. Chaos. These had not been on Dr. Rubino's menu of perks. When Nolan quit school to help his mom pack, I felt like my life was collapsing. I failed tests I should have aced, ignored all my homework, and didn't even keep up with my regularly scheduled after-school television programming. For the whole week, I just wanted to get in my bed and cry.

If I was in shambles, I couldn't imagine how Nolan could keep going.

My mother let Maggie and me stay home the Friday the moving truck came. She knew we needed to say goodbye and told Mrs. Kincade to call before they left.

My father was coming off a night shift, so Maggie and I had to play quietly in our room so that he could get enough rest. Just after lunch, my mother caught Mrs. Kincade's call on the first ring and then poked her head in our room.

"Girls," she whispered. "It's time."

She then roused my father, and the whole family piled into our four-door sedan. Together, we'd made Janet and Nolan a little care package for their drive: an assortment of chips and drinks that Maggie and I handpicked at the gas station, a few well-loved comic books and word-search puzzles, a bottle of wine for the hotel later that night. The centerpiece, however, was the plate of homemade chocolate chip cookies. Maggie and I had baked them the night before, and our mother had shown us how to sprinkle a little bit of sea salt on top to make them even more delicious. I got to carry the tray.

Down the front steps, over the gravel, and into the car—I gimbaled the cookies deftly enough until we pulled in front of Nolan's house. That's when panic seized me—the moving van was pulling away. But before I could even cry out, I noticed Nolan and his mother in the driveway, loading the last of their luggage into their old station wagon.

We weren't too late after all.

With a meek smile, Mrs. Kincade placed the chips and wine in the passenger seat. "As usual, you're really too sweet."

Nolan leaned against his mother. Thin as a beanpole, he looked as if he might snap under the weight of what was about to happen. The poor boy kept his eyes on Maggie and me as we gathered around the trunk—I could only imagine he was trying to drink in the last images of his closest friends, because I was doing the same. But as we approached the end of our gentle farewells, I felt his gaze lock onto me.

I handed him the cookies and gave a little wave. "I'm going to miss you."

"I'm *really* going to miss you," Maggie added as she ran up and threw her arms around him. Nolan bobbled the plate and just barely managed to hand it off to his mother before my sister consumed him.

Nolan held that embrace for as long as he could—his rosemary eyes clamping down tightly, his knobby fingers digging into Maggie's shoulders. I'd never seen anyone hold on to something so desperately, and I found myself wishing it were me.

We left before anyone could break down in tears.

No one spoke on the car ride home—not until my father felt compelled to state the obvious.

"Now that," he said, pointing back toward Nolan's house, "is a tragedy."

"It just seems so unnecessary," my mother continued. "Janet was busting her butt waiting tables, but she was making ends meet."

My father scoffed. "Sean's just using the Limit to justify his affair."

"A lot of people are using the Limit to justify a lot of things," my mother mused. "Some of it's real, though. Some people have lost everything."

"Frankie?" he asked.

My mother smacked her lips together with the slightest hint of disdain. "Yep."

As my mother told it, Aunt Frankie had been a lot like Maggie before the Limit was announced. Both had been forces of nature. Strong-willed, sharp-witted, smooth-talking women who long ago decided that they themselves could conquer the world. For instance, by the end of elementary school, my sister had already earned the approval of both teachers and administrators alike with her perfect attendance, ingenious artwork, and 99th-percentile test scores. All this earned her a spot on the school's academic achievement plaque—only three names below Aunt Frankie's.

Despite her superlative scholastic performance, Aunt Frankie found herself unable to attend a real university due to the financial damage that the savings-and-loan crisis wreaked on her bank account. Instead, she focused on real estate, answering phones and filing paperwork at the local agency so that she could pay for all the right classes. Everything started coming together when she turned twenty-six—she'd lined up an internship and even scraped enough cash together to print her own business cards. But a month before she was supposed to sit for her licensing exams, the president made his announcement.

A declining population meant there'd always be more homes than people. Property values bottomed out, and real estate was cast aside as frivolity along with Aunt Frankie's dreams.

Like so many of her peers, Aunt Frankie grieved the loss of her future with alcohol and drugs. After bankrupting my grandparents with multiple stints in rehab, she found herself more at home in a crack house than an apartment. Grandpop and Gam Gam died on the assumption their youngest daughter wouldn't be far behind.

By the time Maggie and I turned thirteen, we'd seen enough public-service announcements to know that Aunt Frankie had a drug problem. Cigarettes, liquor, ecstasy, cocaine—my parents tried to keep her worst episodes out of sight, but there were times she'd show up at our house completely strung out, stoned, or wasted, and sometimes all at once. And while Maggie and I loved how friendly Aunt Frankie was when she was intoxicated, we knew it wasn't real. She was coping with the Limit the only way she knew how.

My parents, however, couldn't stand it. They fought every time she visited—with her, with each other, and sometimes even us. When my father saw Maggie showing Aunt Frankie too much affection, he'd lash out, convinced that his dean's list daughter might fall into the same habits as his derelict sister-in-law.

There were times, though, when I felt like Maggie and I might be rubbing off on Aunt Frankie more than she was on us. If we invited her over to braid hair and paint nails, she found a way to maintain sobriety for at least half a day. We could stretch out those four hours even longer by adding lunch and dinner on either end. Ice cream sundaes? Another hour without using. While we might not ever cure her, Maggie and I could at least postpone the inevitable.

Simple delights might just be enough to keep her demons at bay.

Back in the car, my father placed his hand on my mother's knee. "Frankie'll make it back to the straight and narrow," he said. It was kind of him to reassure her, even though I knew he didn't quite believe it. "But speaking of tragedies, did I tell you about Mrs. Novak?"

My mother searched her memory. "The chief's secretary?"

"Yep. Had her first child last week."

"Wow," my mother replied. "Isn't she . . ."

"A woman of a certain age? She sure is. Well, her check from the Mendelia arrived three days ago. The first thing the old bird did was take herself down to the dealership and the department store—bought a brand-new convertible and a fox fur stole."

My mother smirked. "After carrying a pregnancy at her age, I'm sure she deserved it."

"Maybe," my father replied. "But what if I told you she drove off into the sunset without ever looking back?"

Bile stung the back of my throat. Maggie's systems would be revolting, too, I knew—she and I had spent many dark hours talking about this particular paranoia. Despite our love of our adopted parents, fears of abandonment lurked in the darkest corners of our minds. And as gentle and generous as my father often was, he seemed completely aloof to our sensitivity. We knew he didn't mean to be uncaring or unkind—he'd just never been adopted.

My mother answered in a tone that made me think she knew Maggie and I were suffering. "You're kidding."

My father didn't take the hint. "Left her newborn in the arms of her unsuspecting husband. No joke."

Tension poisoned the rest of the drive. Desperate to escape the cruelty of my father's benign neglect, Maggie and I flung open our doors and heaved ourselves out of the vehicle just as soon as it rolled to a stop. The last thing I heard before retreating to our room was our mother:

"The Limit's tearing all sorts of families apart."

She never suspected that ours would be next.

CHAPTER 6

In the beginning, my family's formation story had been relatively straightforward. Though the term had yet to be coined, my parents' naught condition left them unable to conceive, no matter how much money or medicine they threw at it. After trying but failing to have children for more than five years, Jim and Sherry Tannehill threw in the towel and decided to adopt.

The transaction occurred in Springdale, Arkansas, where my father had taken the only policing job he could find. The economy was down and money was tight, but my mother was desperate for children—and my father was in no position to deny her. He'd been the one to drag her away from her family in the Poconos to a lonesome existence in the Ozarks, after all. And she wasn't keen to let him forget it.

Luckily, a contact from work put my father in touch with a one-woman adoption "agency," and in just three months' time, the deal was done. Perhaps too quickly and too cheaply, but Jim and Sherry weren't especially eager to count the teeth of this particular gift horse—they were too head-over-heels for their new toddler girls. Daughters of Marshallese immigrants, they were told, from a couple who couldn't afford the expense of twins. Rather than choosing to keep one or the other, they'd given us both up in hopes we could stay together—and thanks to Jim and Sherry, we could.

What we couldn't do, however, was stay in Springdale. The chaos of "two under two" overwhelmed my mother, and it wasn't long before our new family retreated back to Pennsylvania for support. My mother's much younger sister—Francis—had volunteered to babysit, and two years of work experience was enough to get my father hired on with a new department much closer to home.

They should've known that things had gone too smoothly. Few adoption stories are free from drama or disturbance, and ours began on the first day of seventh grade. Maggie and I were puttering through our algebra homework when the phone rang, and my mother was still on the line long after we'd finished our worksheets. My appetite was starting to nag, so I decided to inquire about dinner. She refused my advances, but not with her typical brush-off. Instead, she cowered against the wall, pressing her free hand over her ear.

"I don't understand," she said, her voice eerily low. "It's been years."

Her posture frightened me. From what little I could see of her withering expression, she was trying hard to focus on, or consider, something far more serious than what to put on the table. Ten minutes later, she closed the call.

"Thank you. Please let me know."

What my mother wanted to know was this: Did she and my father have legitimate parental rights to my sister and me? It hadn't been in question until that call. But during that conversation, an Arkansas state attorney explained that Ms. Fabiola Lang had been charged with adoption fraud. In a class-action suit, a number of families from Springdale, Arkansas, had accused her of exploiting their local immigrant community. In the Marshall Islands it wasn't uncommon for families to place small children outside the home during difficult years, but these arrangements were understood to be temporary. What the profiteer hadn't told my biological parents—and so many like them—was that in the US, such adoptions were permanent.

Instead of the Good Samaritans they believed themselves to be, my adoptive parents had suddenly been cast as kidnappers.

The next year was hell. As the Arkansas attorney general investigated and prosecuted the case, his team made weekly requests for documentation. I spent many late nights helping my mother photocopy and mail birth certificates, adoption contracts, any correspondence with Fabiola she could find. One fine summer evening, my father was summoned to give a deposition. That sent my sister and me into a tailspin.

"Why are they doing this?" Maggie wailed, her face ruddy from a potent blend of rage and tears.

My father had only just gotten home. The sun had long ago set, but the day's thick, warm air still hadn't cooled. A thin film of sweat glistened over his forehead.

"The Limit," he said, and loosened his tie. "Children, and people's rights to them, have become all the more complicated."

I tried to meet his gaze. "But do we get to stay with you?"

My father kept his eyes on the glass he'd pushed under the tap. "We don't know yet," he said, watching it fill.

"What do you mean?"

He gulped down most of the water before answering. "Obviously, your mother and I are doing everything we can to keep you. But the attorneys think it might be more appropriate to reunite you with your biological parents."

My father swirled the last swallow of liquid around in the glass as if it were vodka. "That being said, the social workers haven't been able to find them, so you could be in foster care for a while."

Maggie and I stood stock still.

Neither of us wanted this. Neither of us had asked for this.

"I won't go," Maggie asserted. "I won't go to Arkansas, and you can't make me."

My aggravated mother snapped a dishtowel over the sink. "Look, Jim, now you've got them all upset."

My father slammed his glass on the table. "It's not my fault that damned woman put us in this terrible bind!"

I couldn't bear to hear my parents argue and blitzed out of the kitchen into the backyard. While I didn't know where I wanted to be, I couldn't be in that house for one moment longer.

Down toward the back of our property, our yard sloped into an old creek bed where the mid-June fireflies lolled about in the tall grass. Their fairy lights caught my attention, and for a moment I wondered whether these insects—any other creature, really—could truly understand how the Limit had changed their fate.

Ignorance really did look like bliss.

Maggie caught up to me and took a seat on a nearby log.

"I didn't mean to make them fight, I promise. I was just trying to help."

It was the excuse my sister always used to pardon her behavior. While always well intentioned, Maggie had a penchant for obstinate, objectionable, and otherwise uncooperative conduct, which often precipitated unfavorable results. Now I had to worry about the stability of my parents' relationship on top of whether we'd be shipped off to Springdale.

"Too much is changing," I said, trying to subdue my sobs. Hot, angry tears still stung at my cheeks. "We can't be two places at once. We have to love one more than the other. They're making us choose." I paused to catch a breath. "And I resent it."

"Let's make a pact," Maggie said, taking her feet. "Our biological parents gave us away because they wanted us to stay together, right? So even if we don't go back to them—even if we stay with Mom and Dad—we still can honor their wishes."

Maggie held out her pinkie. "We'll stay together for as long as we can."

Such a small gesture—a door prize compared to our actual return. But it was more than nothing. And although I'd never met my biological parents, I knew they deserved something more than that.

My sister waggled her little finger. "Agreed?"

I used mine to grab it, and we shook.

No one in our household got a proper night's rest that evening. Not the one after either. Not until the prosecutor reached a plea deal, really. Fabiola would spend ten years in a minimum-security prison, two if she cooperated with locating the birth parents. Vaitea and Fiva Riklon, however, couldn't be found. Too many years, too many address changes, no current phone number. The social worker we spoke with wasn't even sure if they lived in the US anymore.

"I'm sorry," she said. "Your best chance is going out there, and that's not something we can fund."

After that, the unwelcome phone calls from Arkansas grew further and further apart. One month stretched into two, and later, into twelve. By the end of middle school, our family had given ourselves permission to start counting in years—but not before my mother lost twenty pounds and my father's hair washed out to gray. While nothing about the structure of our family had fundamentally changed, my attitude about it had. Strangers had victimized both sets of my parents: Vaitea and Fiva, swindled; Jim and Sherry, wrongly accused. Both the criminal and the state had treated Maggie and me like commodities—no different from a sack of flour or an ounce of gold. But all of our parents loved us. It had taken all of Vaitea and Fiva's love to let us go and all of Jim and Sherry's to keep us.

Parenthood, as far as I could tell, was nothing but strife.

CHAPTER 7

"Open wide."

The dentist pulled his stool up to a recumbent Aunt Frankie, who lay in his exam chair. An intermittent affair with methamphetamines had taken much of her hair and some of her teeth—damage no amount of teetotaling could completely repair. And while her mouth still resembled the end of a battered bowling alley, two years of sobriety had done great work restoring the light in Aunt Frankie's eyes. It had not, however, cleaned up her mind.

A smirk crimped my aunt's skinny lips. "My mouth or my legs?"

The joke left the dentist aghast but sent Maggie and me into cackles. My unamused mother, however, remained silent. She needed only her pigeon-blue eyes to convey the strongest of reprimands.

Aunt Frankie turned back to the dentist. "Sorry. You've gotta have a sense of humor in my line of work."

The misfired apology intensified our laughter, which had the same effect on our mother's glare. She swatted us with a magazine while Aunt Frankie made her correction.

"My, uh, *former* line of work."

Not knowing what else to do, the befuddled dentist began his exam.

Given the duration of Aunt Frankie's sobriety, my mother felt it was time for her sister to start looking the part. A department store makeover went a long way, but there was something a few well-styled outfits and a fresh haircut couldn't fix, and that was Aunt Frankie's teeth. My mother spent every last penny of her inheritance sponsoring her sister's dental rehabilitation.

"Anything to help make the temperance stick," she added.

So on the third Thursday of every month, my mother dragged Aunt Frankie to the local dentist's office for a regimen of cleaning, filling, and denture fitting. While she'd been relatively careful about keeping Aunt Frankie's addiction out of sight when we were young, my mother had no problem grandstanding her sister's recovery now that we were teenagers and often brought Maggie and me along.

"Twelve steps is a lot for a person who couldn't get themselves out of bed two Christmases ago," she said. "And that deserves celebrating."

And celebrate we did. In addition to observing and rewarding every chip, milestone, and anniversary, my mother started involving Aunt Frankie more with our family. Once she pinched enough pennies to afford a heavily used car, Aunt Frankie was awarded the distinguished responsibility of driving my sister and me to and from our after-school activities. Maggie swam anchor for our high school's medley relay team and always needed a ride to the gym; I preferred shelving books at the community library on the other side of town. While my mother was happy for the help, my sister and I not so secretly preferred it. Aunt Frankie let us play rap music, always brought Slurpees, and once again became our favorite adult.

One brisk spring evening during our freshman year, Aunt Frankie took us out for a late-night snack at a local hamburger stand. We stood at the counter and tried to order, but the staff seemed indisposed, huddled around a tiny black-and-white television at the back of the kitchen. This still happened whenever Limit-related developments hit the news—the whole world stopped.

Unable to discern exactly what the restaurant staff were seeing, we piled back into Aunt Frankie's hatchback and headed for home.

"I always get nervous when this happens," she grumbled. "You never know how people are going to react."

It didn't take a big-city detective to know she was talking about herself. Relapse was always a risk, and none of us knew what might set it off.

The ride was unusually morose as we contemplated what new twist of cruelty the Limit might impose. Animal extinctions, however sad, felt quaint compared with the political upheaval, international trade wars, and religious violence that brewed in the headlines. Nothing we saw at the restaurant gave any clue as to which may be transpiring.

I sat on my hands to quell the jitters. Knowing, not knowing—both were awful.

Maggie, however, had a preference. "So what do you think it is?"

We'd just pulled up to the house, so I helped myself out of the car and slammed the door. "I heard Disneyland is going to have to raise ticket prices," I said, with all hope that the most innocuous explanation might be correct. "They're already seeing drops in attendance."

"That's hardly news," Maggie retorted. "I bet it's New Zealand. Their population is declining so quickly that the prime minister is offering citizenship to any immigrants over 3*. Sucks being an island, I guess."

Aunt Frankie took a step up onto the porch. "That's nothing. Did you two hear about the hooker who woke up in a bathtub full of ice? Her ovaries were cut out. They're blaming it on a street gang called the Oviraptors."

Maggie pawed the inside of her purse in search of her house key. "Isn't that the name of a dinosaur?"

"Yes," I said, already slipping mine in the lock. "It's Latin for 'egg thief.'"

"Frankie." A brutish voice called out of the darkness, and I spotted my mother sipping a glass of wine in the porch rocker. "Could you not go out of your way to frighten my girls?"

"I'm not trying to frighten them," Aunt Frankie replied, her enthusiasm cooling with every word. "I'm telling them the truth."

"Your 'truth' sounds a lot like that urban legend about black-market kidneys."

"I don't disagree," Aunt Frankie replied. "But this hooker was my friend."

"You're friends with hookers?"

I regretted the question as soon as it left my lips. Of course she was. Friendship was the only safety net in that occupation, and Frankie had only retired just a few years ago.

My aunt didn't break eye contact with my mother while she answered me. "I used to be. And this one was a real gem. Smart, genuine—maybe a bit too naive. Not a whole lot different than you, come to think of it."

The venom of truth stung in a way I hadn't expected. And while Aunt Frankie had intended to wound my mother, I couldn't help but feel the victim.

"Maybe it's time you told these girls the reality of their condition, Sheryl. Before either of them gets hurt."

Aunt Frankie turned and stomped back to her car. My mother didn't come in until well after Maggie and I had gone to bed.

§

The next morning, the paper told Maggie and me everything we needed to know.

Woman found in bath; ovaries missing

"They didn't say 'stolen,'" my father pointed out.

My mother glared down her nose. "Not helpful, Jim."

He skimmed this piece over my shoulder. "No mention of a street gang, though. Probably just the mob."

When I grimaced, he raised his hands in defense. "What? It happened in New Jersey."

"The girl was a 5*," I announced. "Just like us."

Before Maggie could react, my mother snatched the paper from my hands and crumpled the page. "You should probably stop telling people that."

Maggie was first to retort. "What do you want us to do? Lie?"

"We want you," my father said smoothly, "to bluff."

Maggie and I exchanged quizzical looks while my father poured himself another cup of coffee. "It's time I taught you girls to play poker."

After explaining the rules of Five-Card Draw and issuing us a few fistfuls of leftover Easter candy, my father dealt everyone in.

"Use the candy to wager," he explained. "My chips are down at the station."

My mother reviewed her cards and knocked her fist on the table. "Call," she said.

"I raise . . . three jelly beans," Maggie said, pushing the treats toward the center of the table.

I only had a pair of tens but knew I shouldn't bow out. That was the whole point of this exercise. "I see your beans and raise you two marshmallow bunnies."

My father folded his hand. "Too rich for my blood."

My mother considered her fan and then pushed the requisite candy into the pot. It was time to discard.

My mother handed two cards back to my father and sighed. "Girls, when we first got your screening results, you might remember that Nurse Pierce wanted to talk to us privately."

Maggie blushed as she recalled the incident—and her tantrum. "Sorry," she said, and collapsed her whole hand to pass it back to our father. I kept my tens but discarded the rest.

My father collected our stacks, then dealt out what we all needed.

My mother picked up her new cards. "You screened very highly—a good thing, by all accounts. But dangerous too."

The Beauty of the End

I pulled up mine—another ten. I made a very conscious effort to still my face.

My father thumbed the deck. "She told us you need to watch out for men."

My mother nodded but kept her eyes on her cards. "The disgusting ones will want to marry you as a means to extend their family names. The dangerous ones will want to sell your fertility on the black market." She pushed two lemon drops into the kitty. "In matters of romance, you'll need to guard your genetic gifts just as closely as your hearts."

"I'm all in," Maggie said. She used both hands to shove her remaining gummy bears into the pot.

"That's not to say you might not meet the perfect guy," my father added. "But even if you do, Nurse Pierce told us that your children, and their children, and then their children, too, will bear witness to . . ." He looked to my mother. "What did she call it?"

"Progressive social collapse."

All eyes fell on me. Not for my reaction to this devastation, but to decide whether to call Maggie's bet. Like my parents' aging computer, I struggled to process two things at once, especially when the present and the future seemed so disjoint. Especially when I didn't even want children. It didn't help that my sister was trying to peek at my cards. Maggie shrank back into her seat when I batted her away with my free hand.

"I was just trying to help," she said, unable to restrain herself.

In terms of my hand, three of a kind seemed good but not great—just like being a 5*. But I couldn't play cards and hold this conversation at the same time. Just like having babies and saving the world, the pressure of having to do both at once was far, far too much.

"Fold," I said.

"Me too," my mother added.

Maggie turned over her hand. Nothing but mismatched spot cards and the queen of hearts.

My father reached over to ruffle her hair. "Grade A bluff," he said. "That's my girl."

59

He re-formed the deck and shuffled. While he flexed and broke the brick of cards, my mother went on to explain that while our greatest grandchildren might yet break the Limit, society's slow descent into dystopia could render the discovery moot. The bulk of humanity would perish over the next eighty years, and <u>those left behind would have to grapple with dwindling resources, rising crime, and pervasive depression.</u>

My father tapped his stack against the table to knock the cards back into alignment. "There might not be a world worth living in, even if your offspring can still produce life for it."

Maggie recoiled. "Then what's the point in being a 5*?"

After an uncomfortable beat, my father gestured for my mother to continue. "Come on, Sherry. You promised you'd tell them."

My mother bit her lip. "There is . . . a more *unusual* way to use your eggs," she said. "Although there are some—including myself—who consider it a bit extreme."

She paused, as if leaving an opening for my father to concur. When he didn't, the burgeoning silence compelled her to continue.

"The Mendelia need high-screening eggs for their research," she said. "Donating your ovaries guarantees you a career in the program."

My father tapped his temple. "A smart move, considering that entire professions are collapsing."

My mother swallowed hard. "While you do secure a steady paycheck and a lifetime pension, you forfeit the ability to have children."

Those last words rang like a bell inside my mind.

Finally, a way out.

My mother's chin quivered as she rushed through her final lines. "But it's not a decision that you and Maggie need to make right away. That being said, it's not one that can be indefinitely postponed either."

Human eggs, like most things biological, were most viable young and fresh.

"The Mendelia want them before your eighteenth birthday."

CHAPTER 8

The world started to fall apart a little bit more after that, and in a much more physical way. Seven years had passed since the announcement about the Limit. Seven years' worth of people had died—sixteen million, at least in the US. While this reflected a normal trend compared to prior years, the replacement rate hadn't kept up: the country saw only ten million births, down from fourteen million the year before.

For a country that had only ever known growth, contraction was especially hard. Companies consolidated. Jobs were lost. Everyone had less money to spend. Our hometown of Hawley, Pennsylvania, fell into disrepair, just like everywhere else: houses crumbled, sidewalks split, and street signs rusted over. An enormous pothole opened up in our cul-de-sac, and my father had a habit of bottoming out his cruiser in it as he rushed home from work.

His face burned hot as he shed his gun belt at the door. "When are they going to fill that doggone crater in front of the house? The department's going to garnish my wages if this keeps happening."

Maggie, my mother, and I sat at the kitchen table, paying bills and finishing our essays on seventeenth-century European politics. "You might try taking that turn at a different angle," my mother suggested. "I don't think the town's going to fix it anytime soon."

He kicked off his boots. "And why's that? In exchange for my taxes, they're supposed to keep up the roads."

"Why don't you try filling it yourself?" Maggie added. "If road workers can do it, it can't be that hard."

My father's eyes narrowed as he unbuttoned his uniform shirt.

My sister raised her hands in an indignant shrug. "What? I'm just trying to help."

As Maggie flitted upstairs, my mother rolled her eyes. "Look, the town just doesn't have as much money as it used to."

Down to his undershirt, my father waltzed over to the table to kiss my mother atop her head. "Of all the things the Limit has caused, I never would've guessed tax evasion."

"Fewer people means fewer taxpayers." My mother clucked. "The town can either raise rates or reduce services. Guess which one they're not going to do?"

My father, already digging through the pantry, pulled out a bag of pretzels. "Since when did you become a government accountant?"

"You're not the only one who reads the paper, darling," she said, and turned back to her checkbook. "Let's just hope it doesn't get worse."

It would. Because it was the future that portended, not the present. And that could be seen in the markets, which shifted and stalled unpredictably as investors reconsidered the prudence of their long-term investments. Their speculation wrung our college accounts dry, as well as our hopes for gainful employment. The few jobs left in rural Pennsylvania—cosmetologist, truck driver, landscaping, retail—were demoralizing and dead-end. After dating an upperclassman so desperate to get out of town that he'd joined the army, Maggie flirted with military service as well.

The mere suggestion made my mother faint.

※

Hawley wasn't exactly a place that most people thought you needed to escape from. Only ninety minutes outside New York City, the town had originally been pitched as a bedroom community for Manhattan.

Its developers pledged to establish a suburban paradise of organic grocers, fitness facilities, and pet hotels—an exclusive community to lure family-minded financiers and publishing giants out of their high-rise apartments.

They only needed to generate some demand.

So after building some basic tract homes as cheaply as possible, the developers sold those plots to blue-collar families in fringe towns nearby. The wine bars and outlet malls and boutique bakeries would surely follow.

At least that's what they told everyone.

Many working-class folks—my parents included—took that bait. But not the grocery store managers and gym execs and animal hoteliers. The city that never slept had no use for a place to rest its head, they knew, and Hawley's new residents were left with cheap housing and not much else.

The Limit had only intensified their distress.

To make sure we at least had something to put on a résumé, my father insisted Maggie and I get part-time jobs in our sophomore year. My sister, ever the hero, took work as a lifeguard; I opted to stock shelves at the local pharmacy. But that didn't stop his anxiety from coming to a head on the last day of our spring break. Maggie and I were munching through some toast and taking turns reading the newspaper's advice columns when my father sauntered up with a fresh cup of coffee.

"Girls, have you thought about what comes after graduation?"

I cringed at his failed attempt at nonchalance, but Maggie didn't even look up from her page.

"You must be joking," she scoffed.

I hadn't stopped perusing the horoscopes. "We know we need to have a plan."

"Well, now's a good time as ever to start making one," he said, pulling down the paper to eyeball me. "You don't want to end up like I did."

It hadn't been easy for my father to find work when he was first starting out. He'd spent a whole year unemployed, living in his parents' basement with my mother until he found that opening with the Springdale Police Department. His new salary had been enough to get them by—but just barely. My mother told us they argued constantly about money and could never really enjoy what little they had.

"It was a lousy way to live," he reminded us, "and the Limit's not making it any easier."

"We know," I said, and pointed to the pharmacy polo I'd slung over my backpack.

Maggie scraped her crusts into the garbage can. "I don't work double shifts at the pool for nothing!"

"It's just that I haven't heard you girls talk much about what you want to do with yourselves after graduation."

I drummed my fingers on my glass of orange juice. Of course he hadn't heard me talk about what I wanted to do with myself—what I wanted to do with myself flew in the face of what was expected of me. If I'd had my druthers, I would've pursued a career in ecology or zoology or some other science that didn't have to work on the Limit. But that's not what anyone wanted to hear. As a 5*, I was supposed to be refining my plan to pump out kids. Lots of them. For the sake of humanity.

There was no easy way to tell people I planned on shirking this duty. I still didn't understand how someone like me was supposed to fit into this world, especially with *progressive social collapse* just over the horizon. After all I'd been through already, and all that was yet to come, all I wanted was stability. As much as my mother scorned it, the Mendelia could offer just that.

I feigned annoyance. "We're only sixteen, Dad. Who knows what jobs will be around tomorrow—or even in thirty years? I think it's okay if we take some time to figure everything out."

His lips pursed as he looked both ways to check if my mother was around. "What about this Mendelia business?"

Maggie's dish clattered in the sink. "What *about* this Mendelia business?"

"Sounds like good money for important work. And you can't beat the benefits," he blustered. "It'll get you both out of this dump too. We all know you need that."

Maggie dampened some paper towels and began wiping down the counter. "That's all well and good," she snipped. "But are you really ready to give up your grandkids?"

"Excuse me?"

It was hard to tell whether my father was objecting to Maggie's question or her tone.

Maggie kept her eyes on the laminate and intensified her scrubbing. "They collect your ovaries when you join, remember? Not just your eggs—your whole ovary. Both of them. If Charlie and I pursue it, we won't be able to have any kids."

"I know, I know. I remember. It's just . . ."

While my father's heart was in the right place, he didn't know just how much family meant to my sister. Or how much ours meant to me. But crucifying him over it wouldn't help him learn.

"We know what's important to you, Dad," I said, trying to avert the crisis. "Good job. Steady paycheck. No worries. Got it."

But my father couldn't resist the final word. "I just don't see why it's not worth it."

Maggie gave up her scrubbing and pitched the glob of paper towels into the trash. "It's not that hard to understand, Dad. We don't want our children taken from us the same way that shady adoption agency took us from our parents."

I shuddered. Not for our parents, biological or adoptive. Not for Maggie. But for myself. If Maggie didn't want to join the Mendelia, I didn't know what I was going to do. We'd promised to stay together, so I couldn't do it without her.

The future, it seemed, was already driving a wedge between us.

After upbraiding my father, Maggie pushed me out the front door. "Why does he keep doing this?" she huffed.

"He just wants what's best for us," I said, struggling to pull on my jacket and my backpack.

Maggie marched toward the curb. "How could he possibly know what's best for us? Our lives couldn't be more different than his."

"Maggie," I sighed, irritated as much by our sudden departure as by her arrogance. "He's just trying to help."

The words cut down her vanity with extreme prejudice. She recognized them, I knew, and probably resented that I'd used them against her. Not until Aunt Frankie's clunker pulled up could she manage another word.

"Come on," she mumbled. "We're late for class."

Not that either of us was looking forward to it. Every year of high school finished with the same full day of "family life education." The material, which originally discouraged teenage pregnancy, had been completely revamped. The informational videos now showed happy teenage pregnancies carried by happy teenage parents who seemed entirely content forgoing happy teenage lives. Or normal ones, at least. How did we know what was normal? It was still in the books we read. *Jane Eyre*, *The Catcher in the Rye*, *The Outsiders*—none of the teens in those stories seemed the least bit preoccupied by rapidly forthcoming extinction.

Exhausted by the day and the emotions it surfaced, I resigned to my bedroom shortly after dinner. It wasn't long before Maggie joined me—not for sleep, but for company. There were things she needed to discuss.

"You've never really wanted babies, have you?"

Even in front of my sister, I hated admitting that I didn't. It made me sound so callous, so selfish. Maybe I was those things, but I didn't need to advertise. It took me several contemplative breaths to manage an honest reply.

"No."

"Do you know why?"

The Beauty of the End

I mulled it over for a long minute, retracing the lines of reasoning that my mind had worn into my skull.

"Not exactly," I muttered. "I know that I should—have babies, that is. But I think having kids is one of those things you should feel strongly about. Mom and Dad did. So did our biological parents. They let us go because it was best for us, right? And I don't know that I could do what they did. I don't think I can love like that. If I can't, I probably shouldn't."

Maggie didn't say anything more. Not because she didn't have anything to say but because she was waiting to be asked.

"What about you?" I obliged.

"I do." The words fell crisply from her lips. "But I can't tell whether making a few babies for myself is more important than making hundreds of babies for other people."

I shouldn't have been surprised. When Maggie turned ten, she started rocking babies at church—and not just because she didn't like sitting through the sermons. She felt more helpful in the nursery than in the pews. That's why she'd taken the lifeguarding job too. While I teased her about saving the world one whistle blow at a time, I knew she truly believed it. The drowning child she pulled out of the deep end of the pool? Might go on to break the Limit.

"While I'm pretty sure having kids will make me happy, I *know* helping others will," she prattled. "I think I'm pretty good at it too. Mom, Dad, our teachers, my supervisor—they've all told me. But none of them can know whether I'll be a good parent. Or if I'll even like it. That's a complete gamble."

"I get that," I said, happy to hear my sister and I shared at least something in common.

"Also, anyone can be a parent. Because anyone can have a baby. Well, not *anyone*, I guess—that's the problem. But maybe my talents are more unique than my eggs. And maybe I should put those talents to good use."

My pulse quickened. If she wanted to enlist, then I could, too—and be off the hook for saving the species with my reproductive system.

"Did . . . you just talk yourself into enlisting?"

Her voice warmed with the slightest bit of laughter. "If you try hard enough, Charlie, you can talk yourself into anything."

Out the window, the sun waxed low over the darkening pines. Though I'd gone to bed eager for the bitter day to conclude, I now felt more optimistic than ever. Maggie. The Mendelia. Maybe my future as breeding livestock wasn't quite a fait accompli.

While I didn't want to jinx it, the sudden onset of hope brought along jest.

"So when are you going to tell Dad he's been right about the Mendelia?"

"I'm not sure I'd go that far, but he's . . . not wrong," she said, sidestepping the concession she couldn't quite bring herself to make. A quiet minute passed before she piped up again. "Would you come with me?"

There was an unfamiliar humility in her request.

Maggie's next words spilled out quickly. "I know you're lukewarm about the whole thing, but it might be your best chance to do something smart. They field teams in pairs—the Mendel works directly with clients, but their technician runs the laboratory and conducts all the screenings and stuff. You'd be great at it."

She was wrong about the first part but right about the second. In most cases, I preferred pipettes to people. In middle school, I'd written fan mail to the scientists behind the Human Genome Project instead of the hottest boy bands. By high school, I was skipping pep rallies to spend more time running biology experiments.

I'd fit right in as Maggie's scientific understudy.

Maggie yawned. "Also, I'm not sure you have much choice in the matter. You know I can't leave you."

As she waved her pinkie in the air, I could almost hear her grinning.

Three birds, one stone. By joining the Mendelia, I'd get to leave Hawley. I'd get to stay with my sister. I'd surrender my ovaries and everyone would stop bothering me about kids.

It was almost too good to be true.

"There's just one last thing," I said. "What are we going to tell Mom?"

CHAPTER 9

My mother had never been keen on the Mendelia. She bristled whenever she heard the word and would leave the room whenever their advertisements aired—which was daily, at least.

She clicked off the television. "It's no wonder they have to work so hard to recruit. What did they expect, asking women to give up their ovaries?"

"Men have it so much easier," Maggie agreed. "Quarterly samples? That's hardly a sacrifice."

I shot my sister a disgruntled glare. We'd planned to tell our mother about our intent to enlist after dinner. Casually deriding the Mendelia a few hours before wasn't going to help her swallow that pill.

Maggie sighed. "I was just trying to help."

I didn't have time to be annoyed with her, because we'd agreed to meet our father by the grill and inform him of our decision first.

"I'm glad," he said, just as he flipped three sizzling burger patties. "I'm especially glad you two will be going together." He turned over a fourth—the puck of ground turkey for my mother, who'd been watching her weight. "Though I have to tell you, that won't make things any easier on you-know-who. The Mendelia might be offering you two tickets to better lives, but it'll shortchange your mother of her grandkids. She'll start missing the birthday cakes she'll never get to decorate and the school plays she won't attend. Halloween will be the worst."

He used his spatula to call our attention inside, to the mantel above the fireplace. On top stood a parade of mismatched picture frames, each containing a photo of Maggie and me dressed up in that year's particular fantasy: barnyard animals, favorite cartoon characters, astronauts—whatever we'd asked for, year over year. My mother always stood proudly behind us and rarely looked happier.

"You have to understand just how hard she had to work to build her family," he said. "She can't fathom why you'd just give yours away."

Where would our eggs go? Into the bodies of infertile women, ultimately. While the naught condition arrested a woman's ability to produce viable eggs, it didn't kill her biological drive to procreate. Most naughts still wanted children and desperately so. And while the DNA of naughts was no longer viable, their uteri still worked exactly as designed. They could carry a pregnancy to term, as long as they had a fertilized egg.

That's what the Mendelia promised to provide.

My sister and I slept in the morning after we told our mother. She took the news just about as well as our father predicted, so we cut her a wide berth by skipping breakfast and lurking upstairs. The fact that it was Saturday eased our exile: we didn't need to occupy her kitchen or washroom to pack lunches or launder PE uniforms. The only thing we really had to do was practice for our driving test. Though the exam was scheduled for the following weekend, neither Maggie nor I had perfected the dreaded three-point turn. Once our mother departed the premises to go grocery shopping, my sister and I pulled our father's rusted-out station wagon out to practice.

"Okay, first, all the way left . . ." The metal steering wheel squealed as Maggie pressed an extra rotation into it. When she couldn't turn it any farther, my sister took her foot off the brake. The car jerked forward, then continued rolling.

Maggie held on to the wheel as we very quickly approached our neighbor's yard. "Then," she narrated, "pull up to the edge of the opposing . . ."

Before she could finish her sentence, the wagon bounced dramatically off the opposite curb.

"Lane," she added.

"Too far," I said, rubbing my neck.

Maggie grinned before shifting into reverse. "No such thing. Just the fail-safe way to find where to stop."

The absurdity made my eyes roll, which means I didn't catch my sister craning her neck toward the back window.

"Then, reverse and turn the wheel toward the right . . ."

The car skittered backward until we jolted against the curb once more.

"Too far *again*," I said, my displeasure intensifying.

Maggie winked. "But it got the job done."

When she put the wagon back into drive, we glided back into the center of the lane. After about ten yards, Maggie parked the car and stepped out into the street.

She dangled the keys in my direction. "Okay, your turn."

I surveyed the street and Maggie's rusty red scuffs. "We're going to end up going in circles, aren't we?"

My sister leaned against the wagon and threw me a reproachful look. "Don't sound too excited there, Charliebear. Mom will be back in no time if she hears us having too much fun."

I dropped into a slouch against the bumper. "I just can't stop thinking about what she said last night."

"About the Mendelia? Or us?"

The hem of my T-shirt did nothing to buff out the scratch Maggie had scored across the bumper. "The Mendelia, actually," I said. My mother's emotional tirade had included several hurtful words about the organization as well as my sister and me, the latter of which I was content to forget. "You don't think they're *that* evil, do you?"

"No," Maggie answered "Well, not as much as Mom thinks, at least. But Mendels do get a chance to play God, so I can understand why she's . . ."

My sister looked up. "Suspicious."

The irreverent twinkle had returned to her eye. No doubt my sister was already contemplating the auspicious combinations she'd put together. A Sudanese egg with a Swedish sperm. A felon's egg with a Mensa sperm. An athlete's egg with an obese sperm. The genetic material of all sorts of people were stored in a bank, and soon, she'd be drawing down from it to make embryos for all sorts of worthy naughts. All in the name of the Limit.

"But who wouldn't want to toy with all those combinations?"

"Me," I replied. "But that's why I'm going as your technician. What I was trying to get at, though, is this: given that we're Marshallese 5*s, our eggs should be pretty popular. Mom will get *plenty* of grandkids. They just won't exactly be hers."

Maggie shook away an errant and disappointed snort. "If only she could see it that way."

"Can you imagine a thousand little yous and mes running around?"

Maggie pressed the key ring into my palm. "They'll keep the driving instructors in business, that's for sure."

Too wounded by our decision to enlist, my mother couldn't bring herself to accompany us to the clinic for the procedure. Instead, it was my father who roused us out of bed. He rushed around our room, pulling open the drapes and singing the same little ditty he did when we were small:

> Good morning to you,
> Good morning to you,
> You might make good Mendels . . .
> We need to leave in a few!

Those last two lines were new.

While my father laid on the cheer pretty thick, he couldn't paper over the fact that our mother hadn't emerged from their bedroom. She was hurting, I knew, but her absence felt like punishment. For what crime? I wasn't quite sure.

When Maggie and I descended upon the kitchen table, my father presented us with carefully crafted breakfast sandwiches.

I couldn't quite hide my disappointment when I asked, "No French toast?"

My father sagged. "Sorry, darling. I just didn't want to make this morning any more . . . emotional. Especially for your mother."

While I found his compassion valiant, Maggie found it misplaced.

"But what about *us*?" she asked, toggling a finger back and forth between her and me. "We're the ones getting cut open."

He checked his watch. "Speaking of, you two should dig in. You've only got ten more minutes before I'm supposed to stop you from eating or drinking. As for your mother, she'll come around."

My father continued his happy charade all the way down to Scranton, where the nearest Mendel clinic had embedded in the federal courthouse. Standing atop its grand marble staircase, most recruits probably felt like they were about to do more for humanity in one afternoon than they might otherwise accomplish in a lifetime.

I, however, blanched at the sight.

Maggie squinted up at the monumental facade. "Are you ready?"

"Probably not," I confessed, keeping my eyes on the palace before us. My mother's behavior had dampened my spirits, and I could feel my feet growing colder by the minute.

"It's not like they're gone forever, you know." Maggie interlocked my elbow with hers. "Although most of your eggs get used up in practice, you can earn a few back if you're successful. Any small discovery is worth an egg or two—even if it doesn't break the Limit. Same with persuading a woman to use separate fathers. Or convincing a fifty-year-old to have a second child. They use eggs like bonuses. Keeps Mendels motivated."

"I'm not sure that's going to work for me," I muttered.

"I'd like to earn back at least a few. With IVF, it's still possible to give Mom those grandkids, since they don't take your uterus." One of Maggie's hands drifted to her belly. "Wait, don't tell her I said that. Let's not get her hopes up."

After one last reflective moment, Maggie took a step forward and dragged me toward the oaken doors. "For what it's worth, I've heard the paperwork is the most painful part."

Those rumors bore out. Over the course of the next hour, half a dozen aluminum clipboards bounced between Maggie, myself, my father, and the Mendel. We'd just about closed the deal when one of the staff summoned the doctor into the hallway to chide her about recruiting identical twins—genetic duplicates—into the program.

"We're supposed to be diversifying the inventory!" the woman hissed, apparently unaware that she hadn't quite stepped out of earshot.

The Mendel could barely suppress her frustration. "Inventory? What inventory? We won't have any inventory if we can't get people to enlist. We've got recruiting targets to hit, Maeve, and Headquarters won't be thrilled if we miss our quota again."

"But there's little to no variation between them. If we're hunting for biological anomalies, this doesn't buy us anything."

An unrepentant scoff escaped the Mendel. "If that was HQ's primary concern, they'd institute a draft. Until then, the program's still voluntary. At least these girls are 5*s."

The clinicians proceeded to squabble, but in the end, the Mendel pulled rank. She returned to the room and gave Maggie the honor of inking the final signature.

My sister showed no hesitation.

Compared to the paperwork, the procedure was an absolute cakewalk. Though performed under anesthesia, the keyhole surgery left me only mildly disoriented and a tad bit sore. Maggie and I held hands throughout recovery, breaking our grasp only so that the nurse could pull out our IVs.

"Congratulations," she announced, shaking our hands. "With that step complete, you're no longer my patients. You're my colleagues."

Maggie leaned over the railing of her hospital bed. "So, coworker, is this a promotion or demotion from sister?"

I pulled the adhesive from my forearms with a grin. "As long as you don't call me coconspirator, we'll call it a lateral transfer."

After we pulled on our sweatpants and oversize shirts, the nurse handed us our discharge papers. "You'll have a follow-up appointment with the Mendel next week. Then you'll be off to training! I loved it, but I have to tell you, half my class failed out because they couldn't hack the counseling. Brush up on your people skills just as much as your physiology and you'll do fine."

A few minutes later, I walked out of the clinic free from my ovaries but imprisoned by a whole new set of concerns.

The Mendelia operated four convents to train their recruits. Scattered between the urban East, the dirty South, the Great Plains, and the mountainous West, each campus proudly proclaimed a unique and attractive lifestyle. Alongside images of inquisitive scientists and industrious students, the informational brochures teased manicured plantations, roughneck cowboys, sunset skylines, and snowcapped highlands. My father had perused them thoroughly while waiting for us in recovery and handed us the glossy double-sided handouts when we got to the car.

"Don't think it'll matter all that much," he said. "I hear it's much more West Point than Wellesley. You two will be lucky if you get to keep those long locks."

Maggie pulled a few ringlets between her fingers. "Is it really that much like boot camp?"

"I don't think so," he conceded. "But I wouldn't get too excited about delights and diversions. My lieutenant says his son is in class from dawn 'til dusk and *still* has to attend mandatory study hall after dinner. Poor guy barely gets time to take a piss, let alone a shower."

I suddenly became very aware of the plaque on my teeth. "Well, that sounds inhumane."

"Maybe. But it's the only way the government knows how to make a doctor in two years flat."

The Mendelia had opened their first convent in Baltimore, Maryland, at Johns Hopkins University, the national nexus for all Limit-related research. After that, they placed another campus in Ponce de Leon, Florida, to serve the South. Considering that breaking the Limit pretty much amounted to a species-wide search for the biological fountain of youth, that location seemed especially apropos. The flyover states were covered by a convent in Manhattan, Kansas, which was about as close as you could get to the geographic center of the country without having to stand in a cornfield. Lastly, a facility in Tehachapi, California, served the West. It wasn't a town most people had heard of, but it was one of the few places left in that state with cheap land and labor.

Much like the military, Mendelic recruits didn't get a say in where they were assigned, so Maggie and I didn't waste too much breath on it. But when a girl from our school confused her Manhattans, we couldn't help but gossip.

"How did she *not* know it was Kansas?" Maggie handed me a basket of laundry. "The pictures were all over the recruitment materials. Not Broadway or Times Square or Central Park. Silos. Silos and cornfields."

I started folding the dryer-warm clothes while she continued her rant.

"The swamps were for Florida. The harbor and shipping containers, Baltimore. The mountains must have been California. I don't know much about Kansas, but I know there's no mountains." She dropped a handful of socks onto the couch in conclusion.

"Flatter than a pancake," I said, matching the pairs. "I took a history class with that girl, though. She wasn't exactly what you would call 'Hopkins material.'"

Maggie looked over at me. "I'm sure you're hoping we get California?"

A fair assumption. I'd spent the past few evenings trying to gin up my enthusiasm for the work by dreaming about endless sunshine, surfing lessons, funky art museums, hip cafés—all the things people gushed about in television shows and magazines. Boardwalks, ski slopes, movie stars, and eventually, wine country. Those were the types of things that got everyone else excited. I could only hope they'd work for me too.

"If only . . ." I sighed, feigning a lust I did not feel. "But I doubt we'll get that lucky. You want Hopkins, don't you?"

As the Mendelia's flagship facility, Hopkins doubled as the program's Headquarters and got prestige and talent to match. They only admitted the best, and my sister could probably count herself among them—she'd aced all her classes and blown the curve on the tests. But Hopkins was a pressure cooker. The same program that could polish Maggie into a diamond would grind me down to dust.

Maggie smirked. "What makes you think that?"

"Your grades, your drive, your insatiable thirst for recognition," I taunted. "All the top scientists go there—don't tell me you don't want to be close to them."

She tossed me two of my work polos. "Look, Mom and Dad would freak. Baltimore's the murder capital of the country."

"I can't believe you'd lower your standards."

"I'm not," she tutted, firing a rolled-up ball of socks at my head. "I just have other motives."

I ducked the projectile. "So, Ponce de Leon? To swim with the manatees?"

"More like alligators, so no."

I knew there was only one reasonable option left. "Are you telling me you're hoping for California too?"

She put the basket on her hip and began to make her way upstairs. "I wouldn't mind the smaller pond. Easier to be the biggest fish." She turned and waggled her pinkie finger in my direction. "And I think we made a promise."

I couldn't tell which of her answers constituted more of the truth. Maggie enjoyed being the first, the best, the only—and it would be easier to be all those things in Tehachapi. I still couldn't accept that she'd really reject Hopkins, but in her decision, she was making room for me. And no matter her reasoning, and no matter where we ended up, the outcome would be the same.

I'd be with her. That's what mattered.

CHAPTER 10

On April 26, 2005, we returned to the Scranton clinic for our final inspection. The date was significant for another reason, too—our eighteenth birthday. After taking a quick look at our healing wounds, the technician shuttled us into a formal office, where the Mendel paged through our charts. We took the seats in front of her desk just as she looked up.

"Good afternoon, ladies," she said, her whole face beaming. "It's not often that I get clients coming in on days they should be celebrating! Did you mean to book this appointment on such an important occasion?"

"No, ma'am," replied Maggie, a bit too quickly for me to believe. She had that roguish glint in her eye again. What exactly she was up to, I had no idea.

"How serendipitous," the Mendel clucked. "And that's the art of Mendelia, really. There's science to it, absolutely, but there's also a lot of luck. Speaking of, have you girls thought about which convent you'd like to attend?"

I glanced over at Maggie, who never looked back at me.

"Tehachapi," she said.

The Mendel clapped her hands. "Well, considering it's a very special day for two very special people, let me see if I can pull a few strings."

Maggie smiled. At that point, I knew she'd planned this coincidence. And while I wanted to ask how she'd conceived of such a brazen plot, there was no opening. The Mendel plowed on to other news.

"I have two more things for you ladies, both of them good. First, now that the Mendelia have your eggs, you'll receive further details about your new careers. Most of my recruits get their orders before graduation. Second, your incisions look great, so the scarring should be minimal. You're both cleared to attend prom—if your school is having one."

An unfortunate reminder that most weren't. Two weeks prior, the class president of a private academy in Georgia had turned his cotillion into a homicide by spiking the punch with cyanide. He didn't want anyone to have to live in a world with no future—at least that's what he put in his note. Now schools across the country were canceling their formal events to prevent copycats.

Wisely or not, our principal doubled down on the event on the grounds that the young adults in his school deserved at least one morsel of normalcy. Shortly after the gala was announced, my father hauled us down to the local off-price retailer and handed us two hundred-dollar bills.

"I'll pick you girls up in an hour," he said.

While I marveled at the single largest bill I'd ever seen, Maggie pocketed hers.

"And what will *you* be up to?" she asked, a narrowed eye on our father.

"Stocking up on Kleenex. Your mother nearly blew the house down when you enlisted, and seeing you two dressed up like princesses will no doubt bring about a second squall."

After nodding in agreement, my sister and I pushed past the fur-trimmed boots and velour sweatsuits to the formal section, where we found two overstuffed racks of last season's unwanted frocks. Maggie snatched the first one that caught her eye.

"Lavender spaghetti straps would look great on you!" she squealed. When she pulled the dress against her own body to check the length, the curling corners of a carpet square caught the skirt. "You'd probably need to get it hemmed."

I felt my intestines twist. Spending such an exorbitant sum on something I'd only wear once already seemed like a sin—there was no way I could justify adding alterations to such an expense.

"Pastels aren't really my thing," I replied.

Maggie returned to the rack to weed through the options when a nearby slip dress caught her attention. The momentary distraction allowed me to probe my far more serious interest.

"So how did you know?"

Maggie ran a swath of silky teal between her fingers. "Know what?"

"How to get the Mendel to pick a convent for us."

My sister pulled the gown and held it aside, never once inviting my opinion. "A rumor. Mandy from stats said something similar happened to her, so I just went for it."

"Bold, don't you think?"

Her bottom lip protruded into a bulbous pout. "Not really. Just a little bit of scheming around the calendar."

"But what if she found out?"

Maggie's face dropped from general ambivalence to extreme annoyance. "Nothing would've happened, Charlie. Nothing at all."

I felt my eyes narrow. "Don't you ever worry about taking things just a little too far?"

Maggie forced the sequined halter she was examining back into its flock. "No, I don't, actually. Sometimes, a little gall gets you a long way. Like into the Mendelia, for instance. God, Charlie, why do you always have to be so nervous?"

She held out another dress in my direction.

"Hmmm. Let's see . . . this seems like you. Pepto pink with a sweetheart neckline."

"And what do you mean by that?"

"That you're sweet. And slightly medicinal."

Disgust pulled at the corners of my mouth. "Maggie . . ."

My sister flicked up a second svelte number. "What about black, and backless, with a thigh-high slit? You could totally pull this off! Matches your hair, your eyes, and your totally rebellious attitude."

"Well, that's aspirational."

"It should be," she sneered. "This dress would show off your backbone just as well as your boobs if you'd only consider growing one."

I threw up my hands. "Wow. I didn't realize that going dress shopping with you would turn into such a character assassination."

Maggie's hands wrenched around the plastic hanger. "It's not my fault—you started it."

"How?"

"You called me careless!"

I couldn't help but screech. "And you called me a coward!"

Our escalating voices drew a glare from an older woman browsing the lingerie. Maggie's voice dropped low.

"You needed to hear it."

Of all the knives she'd thrown at me, those words twisted the one in my heart. My sister had gall, that was true—gall enough to berate me in public. Hurt spilled from my eyes before tears could come. When she noticed, I saw Maggie's fill with regret.

I turned to storm off, but my sister caught my elbow. "Look, I know I got out of hand, but I was just trying to help."

"Stop. Saying. That," I spat. "You've got to stop saying that. You *always* use those six words to cover up your mistakes. You took a risk, you said something awful, and now you can't walk it back. When will you ever just take responsibility?"

I lurched forward when she released my arm. "Whatever, Charlie. What you're not changing, you're choosing."

Things were frosty between Maggie and me after that. But because we still shared a room, the kitchen table, and most of our classes, we had to remain civil. It wasn't that we didn't love each other—I had no doubt we still did—we just couldn't stand each other.

"Sisters," my mother said knowingly.

Despite our animosity, Maggie and I still managed to go to prom together. Neither of us had dates—not many boys were interested in girls who'd just torn up their tickets for free government cash. But we owed it to our mother. After all the heartbreak we'd already caused her, we could at least don our discount dresses and smile so the poor woman could get her costumed Polaroid.

After putting her camera away, she handed each of us a bottle of water. "Stay safe, you hear. And don't drink the punch."

Maggie and I then piled into a rickety school bus to spend a "magical" evening in a "grand" hotel ballroom dancing away the last cherished moments of our youth. After milling about and making chitchat with a handful of kids I'd probably never see again, I caught up with Maggie in the bathroom.

"I can't believe they actually went through with this. Security guards around the food, individually packaged drinks—Principal Gorman confiscated Nicole's breath mints at the door. If they really think this is really that dangerous, we shouldn't even be here."

Maggie reapplied her lip gloss with a smack. "The things we do to make the adults feel like everything's all right."

A rustle from the handicap stall interrupted our banter. Ashley Killion pushed through the door moments later, flaunting a heavily pregnant belly under thick layers of tulle. We paused as she waddled back to the dance floor.

I moved to the sink to wash my hands. "Half the girls here look like they have soccer balls stuffed under their gowns."

"The Macy's in Stroudsburg opened up a whole section for maternity gowns," Maggie said. "Apparently they couldn't keep them in stock."

"Their local Mendel must push breeding pretty hard."

Maggie hoisted herself onto the counter. "I guess you haven't heard about our very own basketball team," she said. "When none of the girls got scouted for college ball, all nine went down to Stroudsburg and got the Mendel to convince their parents to let them get an early start. *For the benefits.*"

"Is that even legal?"

Maggie handed me a paper towel and shrugged. "Their parents consented. Once the babies are born, the girls will be pulling down a couple hundred bucks a month. Chump change right now, but Natalie Grundmeier told me it's only going to take one more kid for her to afford her own trailer. Steffi Yao has even bigger plans. She thinks that by kid eight, she'll be able to afford a beach house on the Jersey Shore."

"Wow," I said, shaking my head. "Their wildest dreams don't even take them that far."

"Come on," Maggie replied. "I called Aunt Frankie to come pick us up."

Maggie and I pushed through the crowded ballroom to get back to the lobby. Electronic music throbbed behind us, and the whole place smelled like sweat. I was grateful Aunt Frankie was just pulling up. Maggie slipped into the front seat while I took the back.

Aunt Frankie plopped a six-pack of wine coolers into Maggie's lap. "Here," she said. "It's prom. Maybe it'll help you two be friends again."

Maggie passed two fluorescent pink drinks back to me. I almost didn't want to touch them and immediately racked the bottles into the hatchback's cup holders.

"Aunt Frankie," I said. "You know we're not supposed to . . ."

Aunt Frankie put her car into drive. "Have a little underage fun? What's the point of being the 'cool aunt' if I don't get to do things like this? Come on, Charlie, don't be such a drag."

"She's not a drag," Maggie said, cracking the lid off her drink. "She's responsible. Someone's got to be." She threw Aunt Frankie a knowing look. "You know how it is."

I couldn't tell if Maggie was defending or demeaning me, but the effect was the same.

As much as I wanted to believe that we were some kind of threesome, Aunt Frankie was always closer with Maggie. They shared a moxie that I did not; both felt comfortable breaking rules and flaunting authority, while I preferred a far less risky existence. But in the end, I was grateful for the difference. Aunt Frankie always turned to Maggie before me, and in many cases that was a blessing. I was reminded of it when Maggie cornered me at my locker later that week.

"Has Aunt Frankie ever talked to you about our enlistment in the Mendelia?"

I searched for my physics homework. "No, not really. But she didn't exactly seem thrilled when we told her."

That was an understatement. Aunt Frankie had pitched an enormous fit when we'd broken the news at Sunday dinner. Unlike my mother, she wasn't upset that we didn't want children. Aunt Frankie's outrage stemmed from our moving away.

"Yeah." Maggie sighed. "I think she's jealous that we get to move on with our lives."

"Can't say I blame her."

Maggie slumped against the metal cabinets. "Well, she asked me something awkward before I left for work the other day."

Uncomfortable questions weren't unusual for Aunt Frankie, but Maggie bringing them up was. I raised an eyebrow. "And what's that?"

"If I could make a baby for her."

I flinched. Like our mother, Aunt Frankie was a naught, and when the Mendelia first launched their embryo placement program, she applied. But the Mendelia were careful with their embryos. While they were always in need of a womb, they weren't eager to place a child with a recently reformed drug addict with no reliable employment. They couldn't afford to tarnish their reputation. And that's what Aunt Frankie was in their eyes: a blemish. She visited three different Mendels and was denied each time.

"That seems . . . like it probably violates a code of ethics or something," I said.

"It does. I went to the library to read the policy. The Mendelia's rules are just like medicine's—you're not supposed to treat your own family."

"So what did you tell her?"

Maggie's eyes shifted out the window. "That I wasn't going to make any promises."

I slammed my locker door. "You're not actually thinking about giving Aunt Frankie a baby, right? You're not even a Mendel yet—you probably shouldn't be breaking their rules."

The bell rang. Maggie had a few more moments to explain herself.

"No. Absolutely not. Aunt Frankie's a train wreck; everyone knows that. But I can't help but think a child might be good for her. When Mom let her into our lives, she got sober. Maybe a kid would help her, I don't know, grow up. Move to the city or something. If she does, maybe Mom and Dad can finally leave this shithole too."

Everything she'd said was true. Maggie's motivations weren't misplaced.

"Sounds like a pretty high limb to go out on," I said.

"I know," she replied, her gaze shifting to the distance. "I'm just worried about her."

Content that she'd heeded the warning, I snapped closed my lock and spun the dial. "Leave the worrying to me. It's what I do best, honestly."

Whatever Maggie told Aunt Frankie, it wasn't enough to spoil their relationship. I was working my shift at the pharmacy the following Saturday when I noticed Maggie browsing the wound-care aisle. She was wearing her work uniform—red nylon shorts, a fresh YMCA T-shirt, and a blue fanny pack slung low around her waist—but that wasn't what caught my eye. Surgical tape ran round her forearm. Inky splotches percolated through the gauzy dressing. I stalked her to the front counter, where she paid in cash. After ducking back into Aunt Frankie's hatchback, they sped off toward the pool like Thelma and Louise.

A few days later, my mother noticed Maggie's sudden preference for long-sleeved shirts, and it didn't take long for her to correctly conclude that her rapscallion daughter had gotten a tattoo.

She hoisted Maggie's wrist into the air to examine the evidence. "Is this your aunt Frankie's doing?"

My sister snatched back her arm. "No," she said. "It was my idea. There was this artist who owed her a favor, and he's moving out of state next week."

My mother turned to the sink to take out her frustration on the dishes. "A favor? I hate to think what for. But you! You let Aunt Frankie's 'friend' permanently brand you?"

"Oh, come on, Mom. I'm eighteen. And it's not like I got skulls or hearts or flames or anything." Maggie pushed up her sleeve and pulled off the dressing. "It's just a basic outline of some sweet pea blossoms."

My father peered over his reading glasses. "Seems pretty tasteful to me."

"But what's it mean?" My mother's face looked just as accusing as her tone.

My sister didn't appreciate the continued inquisition. "Excuse me?"

My mother returned to scrubbing. "Don't tell me you picked a tattoo that doesn't hold any meaning."

Maggie pulled her sleeve back down. "Fine," she said. "It's our birth-month flower."

My sister's eyes skipped over to me, and my mother's glare followed. "Is that true?"

I wanted no part of the argument and gave the least committal answer I could think of. "Maybe?"

My mother turned back to Maggie. "And Aunt Frankie got one to match?"

"No, actually," Maggie snapped. "Aunt Frankie got a bow and arrow. To symbolize that by being drawn back, she's ready to launch forward."

"Well, that's far more inspirational than I've ever known my own sister to be. I'm assuming you came up with it?"

Maggie's chin lifted in pride. "I did."

My mother sneered and returned to her suds. "I just wish you both weren't so . . . impulsive."

What was done was done, my mother finally concluded. But there was something more concerning about Maggie's new ink that my parents didn't realize and that I didn't mention. Pea plants were the experimental subject of Gregor Mendel, the namesake of our recently chosen profession. My sister took no interest in the astrological assignments of random plants. She'd imprinted herself with a patron symbol of her future career. And while Maggie had always been impulsive, she usually channeled her urges into far more grounded activities: charity car washes, holiday food drives, emergency blood donations—not some self-indulgent devotion to something she didn't really know.

While we'd always had our differences, the tattoo marked the first time I felt truly distinct from her.

Perhaps my mother's concerns weren't misplaced.

Little more than a weatherproof shack, Hawley's post office became my favorite destination at the end of the school year. Our training assignments were due to arrive, and I couldn't help but visit almost every day. My veins surged with emotion each time I keyed the box: anxiety, excitement, but most often, disappointment. Twenty-nine times I opened that door and found nothing. Not nothing, exactly—there were always flyers and junk mailers. But not what I was looking for. Wiser women and statisticians would have given up, but on the thirtieth try, I found it: a pink postal slip referring me to the front desk for a certified delivery.

Even though the line was short, I could barely stand having to wait and fidgeted for the entire five minutes. When I finally handed the slip to the clerk, the pudgy old woman smiled.

"I've seen you come in every day this past month," she said. "And I think whatever you've been waiting for has finally arrived."

My nerves forced a joke. "I hope so, ma'am. If I have to make any more trips, I'm going to owe my dad an oil change."

After a hearty chortle, she pulled two large manila envelopes from a nearby shelf. I scribbled for the delivery and offered a million uninterrupted thank-yous before snatching the packets and heading back to the car. But as I crossed that parking lot, my excitement subsided into reverence.

Our new lives were described within those envelopes, and they deserved respect.

Or at least an audience.

I needed to find my sister.

I dropped the mailers on the passenger seat and reversed out of the parking lot. Like Maggie and me, the packets were identical but for our names—both of which had been hand-printed. An oddly personal detail for such bureaucratic mail. Both envelopes carried the Mendelian seal in lieu of a return address, and both had been postmarked from Baltimore. A clue? Perhaps. But more likely an artifact that they'd all been sent from Headquarters.

Frenzy surged through me as I pulled into our driveway. Maggie could be anywhere in the house, and I burst through the front door fully prepared to conduct a search. But there she was, just across the room, loading the dishwasher. I slung her envelope across the counter.

"Do we wait for Mom and Dad?" Her question was earnest, but her patience, short-lived. "Never mind, I can't."

When Maggie tore open her envelope, half a ream of multicolored forms spilled onto the floor. Having opened mine more carefully, I got a head start skimming the cover letter. My eyes flitted down the page: a boilerplate greeting, several inches of generic congratulations, a paragraph or two of programmatic overview. Finally, on the back of the page, I found it.

REPORTING LOCATION: TEHACHAPI, CALIFORNIA.

Maggie beat me to the exclamation. "California!" she yelped. "We got in!"

"*You* got us in!" I answered. "I can't believe it worked!"

We flapped the papers in exaltation and came together. It had been weeks since I'd felt my sister's touch, and the contact of her body warmed my soul. Everything we'd argued about fell away as our future came into focus. Our embrace was heartfelt, relieving, and brief—we both wanted to get back to the details.

Registration forms. Supply lists. Dental insurance. Retirement investments. There was so much to do before our scheduled onboarding on Labor Day. But with every passing minute of quiet reading, more wrinkles creased my brow.

Maggie's rumpled too. "They want us to prepare for altitude sickness."

I looked up from a pamphlet. "And bring heavy winter coats."

"Charlie, do you know where Tehachapi actually is?"

We moved to the study, where Maggie sat down at the computer and pulled up a map of California. Tehachapi wasn't anywhere near San Francisco, but to say it was close to Los Angeles was an overstatement. Far from everything we'd ever heard of, Tehachapi was nestled in a mountain range that bordered the eastern part of the state.

As curious as we might have been about our new home, we lacked the patience for more research and suspended our confusion in favor of celebration.

It was California. It was what we wanted. We were finally getting out, moving on, growing up.

We should have been fine. But we had no idea what was really in store. And that, frankly, wasn't exactly our fault.

CHAPTER 11

My father sold the station wagon to pay for the flight. Both he and my mother knew that Maggie and I would never move home again, and my parents needed the money more than we needed the vehicle. Neither of them, however, could talk about those things with us—in the last few weeks of August, the car was gone and airline tickets had materialized under a fridge magnet.

The sun-bleached photo of the spatula fight had finally been replaced.

The night before the flight was a quiet one. My mother splurged on a feast of baby back ribs, which my father grilled along with some fresh farm-stand corn—our favorite summertime meal. While she still hadn't warmed to the future Maggie and I had chosen, my mother wasn't going to let us leave her house on an empty stomach.

I met her by the garbage can to scrape in the leftover cobs. "Does this mean you've come around to the idea?"

"Not entirely." She sighed. "But I'll get there. 'Have to accept what I cannot change' and all that."

Maggie swooped by to empty the bone bowl. "Don't let the Limit hear you!"

After waving my sister away, I smiled and kissed my mother on the temple. "I wish you could come with us."

She dabbed away the slightest of tears and then threw her arms around me. "Unfortunately, among all the things I must come to grips with, your father's name is already on the ticket."

While most families would've loafed through the remainder of the idyllic summer evening under the stars or next to a campfire, there was only one way the Tannehills knew how to spend their last night together. And that was playing cards.

After we'd learned to play poker, my father started instigating card games at the end of every supper. Before that, we'd closed our meals by dutifully reading a chapter of the Bible aloud, an homage to my parents' childhood traditions. But as the Limit radicalized more religions and churches became hostile, my parents found table games a safer forum for fellowship and congregation. And while each night had been independently delightful, their cumulative effect was profound. As Maggie and I mastered everything from spades to gin rummy to bridge, she and I felt mature, impressive, and most of all, connected—hard feelings to come by for teenagers of any generation, but even more so in the wake of the Limit.

The night of our departure, we agreed to play hearts. After a few contentious hands, Maggie won by shooting the moon.

"And with that, I think I'll call it a night," she said, slapping her knees. "Best to go out on top."

"Wait," my father protested, already reshuffling the deck. "One more hand. You can't leave me a loser in my own home!"

She pushed back from the table. "Sorry, Pops. We've got an early flight to catch, and now I've got a reputation to maintain."

I stood up to join my sister. "I have to agree. About the flight part, at least. It's almost midnight—if we go to bed right now, we can still manage five hours of sleep."

"Maybe four," my mother countered. "There's no way you'll fall asleep right away, considering how uptight you've been."

"That's why I suggested we go to bed three hours ago!"

Having already made it upstairs, Maggie crossed her arms over the top railing. "Sorry, Charlie. While you might be the responsible one, you're not all that convincing."

By the time I nabbed a cushion to sling at her, my sister—and everyone else, for that matter—had disappeared into their beds.

⚇

Having never flown before, I'd spent several days fretting over things that wouldn't matter: traffic, the security screening, air sickness. My father had told me not to worry—as our chaperone, he wouldn't let anything happen. These platitudes did little to shrink my anxieties, and the frenzy within my mind didn't quiet until we finally made it aloft.

While I'd always known the United States to be a large country, soaring above it humbled me. Diminished me. Feeling so small left me breathless. And though the sojourn left me fighting for emotional air, the wind wasn't truly knocked out of me until we made a rock-hard landing in Los Angeles: a jaw-clattering lurch, unsuspecting gasps from nearby passengers, ear-splitting whines from both the tires and the engines. While the whole episode ended before I understood exactly what was going on, the abrupt touchdown heralded all the friction that lay ahead. A near-tragic mix-up at baggage claim delayed us in securing a rental car, and this was just enough time for an unfortunate amount of traffic to congest the city's central knot of freeways.

Time passed more slowly than the miles, but as the city relaxed into suburbs, finally, so did I.

Despite three hours of driving, Tehachapi was still a hundred miles off. According to my father's map, somehow that amounted to only one county, and not even California's largest. But as we transitioned between Los Angeles and Kern, scrubby plains of chalky soil replaced the well-manicured lawns. The once-cloudy sky opened up into a great yawn of cerulean; cracking riverbeds contoured the now-barren landscape.

For all we'd heard about sophisticated Los Angeles, and for all we'd read about the mountainous convent, none of us expected a desert to lie in between.

Yet another new experience. Too many, perhaps, for one day, but my choice in the matter had long ago been rendered moot. Half-exhausted, half-awestruck, I marveled at the desolation for almost an hour before Maggie broke the reverie.

"Dad, can we find a gas station?" Outside the window, her hand surfed eddies of hot air.

My father checked the dashboard. "Tank's still a quarter full."

"But I need water," Maggie said. "And ChapStick."

He was already testy—the high price of gasoline had intimidated him into renting a midsize sedan instead of something more festive. "The heat's dehydrating you. You should close the window."

Maggie obliged and then laid her carob curls against it. "Still thirsty and dry, Dad."

"Can't it wait?"

My sister's sunglasses weren't dark enough to hide the fact that her eyes were rolling out of her head. "If you want me to turn into beef jerky, sure."

I felt the urge to come to her defense. "I'm kind of wilting, too, Dad."

"That's because of the elevation," he said. "Passed a sign a few miles ago that said we're already over two thousand feet. That's twice what it is back home, and we're not even in the mountains yet."

"We're not due at the convent until tomorrow morning," I reminded him. "Are you sure we need to drive straight through?"

My father drummed his fingers on the wheel. "Charlie, weren't you the one who insisted we leave the house at four a.m. so we wouldn't miss the flight?"

"You're right, I'm sorry. But we're here now, so I think it's okay to slow down."

He hit the blinker. "You girls are lucky my patience hasn't drained as fast as this gas tank. I can't believe we already need a second fill."

"Should've gotten the damn convertible," Maggie muttered.

We refueled at a dusty pump station just off the highway. The farther we drove, the more the metropolis decomposed—mansions diminished into houses that devolved into shacks. Radio stations dwindled from too many to too few. Multilane freeways collapsed into lonely highways and finally poorly paved streets. At some points, it seemed unwise to even stop the car.

People who lived this far from society did not want to be bothered by it.

For mountain-dwelling people like us, the sight of dark hills developing along the horizon brought relief. Our eerie desert transit was nearly complete. These hills, however, were not like those we knew from Pennsylvania. No granite, no pines, no river-cut chasms or grass-lined meadows. Windmills colonized every available slope—each a mindless drone spinning within the greater hive.

No one spoke as we coursed through the interlocking peaks and valleys; our eyes fixed instead on the mechanical infestation.

Daylight slipped away as we crested the ridge and a small nucleus of lights appeared in the bowels of the valley below. After a quick truckstop dinner, we checked into a homely roadside motel. Maggie tried to convince us to spend the rest of the evening exploring our new home, but neither my father nor I had the appetite. I, for one, was too tired to even don my pajamas and tucked into our shabby queen bed still in my traveling clothes. After describing himself as "bushwhacked," my father did the same. My sister must have been, too, because she accepted our refusal without complaint but snuck in a final whisper between my father's snores.

"I can't believe we finally made it," she said. "Thank you for coming."

The Mendelia's use of the term "convent" was especially apt in Tehachapi. The epitome of austere, the campus comprised a small collection of concrete buildings nestled between the scabrous mountains we'd passed through the previous night. It had also, most recently, been a prison. We discovered this the next morning at the diner where we stopped for breakfast.

"Good morning, y'all."

A gaudy waitress poured my father a preemptive cup of coffee. We mumbled our greetings as we dropped into the booth. The waitress pointed the carafe in Maggie's direction. "You know the fastest way to the convent, dontcha?"

Maggie pushed her mug forward. "You oughta tell him," she said, nodding toward our father. "He's the driver."

"Well, this town's so broke they haven't changed the signage yet. But if we keep telling the new arrivals to follow the signs to the old penitentiary, maybe the Mendelia will kick in for it."

"Excuse me?" my father sputtered, reaching for a napkin.

The server had one at the ready.

"Yup, the fastest way to get to the convent is to follow the signs for the California Correctional Institution. The Mendelia took it over just a couple of years ago. Welcome!"

The waitress poured my cup next, and I asked for two creamers. "How did you know where we're headed?"

She cracked her chewing gum. "Honey, this town has just one high school, and I see those kids all year long. Fresh faces like yours in early September means only one thing."

My gaze followed her sweeping gesture around the dining room. Peppered in among the truckers and transients was a handful of nervous-looking teenagers.

The waitress pulled a pencil from behind her ear. "So what'll it be?"

Both Maggie and I preferred sizing up our classmates to the menu, so we blindly ordered French toast. My father, on the other hand, indulged himself in an exorbitant platter of country-fried steak since my mother wasn't around to nag about his diet.

After we'd finished our meals, the waitress delivered the check. "I'm a 1*, you know. I have a daughter, too—so she's a naught." She handed my father his change. "No babies for her, no grandbabies for me."

The melodrama didn't register well with me. Thanks to our sacrifice, this family surely had other options. Maggie must have felt the same, because her lips puckered in disbelief. "Why not get an embryo?"

"Darling, if my daughter was interested in raising other people's children, she'd adopt. At least you know what you're getting when you sign up for that." The waitress proceeded to wave in the general direction of the convent. "Who knows what those scientists are really up to—some of those babies are nothing more than wild experiments."

The older woman must have seen Maggie bristling, because she adjusted her tone. "But I'm sure that's not y'all. You look responsible."

"Take care, now," she added.

My father left a tip, but Maggie snatched it off the table as we left. Once the front door shut behind us, she lampooned the waitress's conspiracy.

"I can't believe her," Maggie started. "If the government was up to something that immoral, everyone would know. The evidence would be too hard to hide, because babies are too hard to hide."

As much as we belittled the woman's small-mindedness, the waitress had been right about one thing—the signage. The russet-brown placards for the California Correctional Institution were easy enough to spot, and we wound our way back to a secluded paddock on the far side of town without much trouble. After the final turn, the two-lane road straightened out and ran for a mile up to the main gate.

"Makes it easy to see anyone coming or going," my father said. "And the sight lines are good if you need to take them out."

Not unlike Hawley, the Limit was also eroding California's population—as well as its tax base and crime rate. It only took a few years for the state to realize it needed income more than it needed empty prisons—and began selling off assets. The Mendelia picked up the CCI facility for a lot less than they'd planned and spent their surplus converting it. Prison cells were recast as dormitories; visitation rooms and common areas transformed into classrooms and laboratories. The cafeterias and libraries required no change.

After verifying our identities at the front gate, the armed guards directed my father to a parking lot in front of our new residence, where he pulled the parking brake at exactly 10:03 a.m. I noticed the time because I was antsy: our first assembly was scheduled for noon, by which time all new recruits needed to be moved in, and any accompanying adults needed to have moved on.

Two hours didn't seem like enough.

It was. Maggie and I barely had a duffel apiece. Aside from a few changes of clothing and a good winter coat, the Mendelia didn't require us to bring much, and it didn't take long to unpack those few things into our small shared room. We stowed our clothes in wooden bureaus and hung our jackets in the empty closet. My father stashed our bags on the highest shelf and idled.

There was only one thing left for him to be helpful with: a gracious exit.

Maggie took pity on him and initiated the departure. "Dad, I can't thank you enough. We couldn't have asked for a better chauffeur."

"I'm sorry I was cranky yesterday," he sniveled. "Try not to remember me like that."

"Would you prefer us to remember you losing at cards?" Tears had begun to well in her eyes too.

Mine, too, were dewing. "I'm going with the version of him who can't resist fried beef for breakfast when Mom's not around to bother him about his sodium intake."

He pulled us together with both arms and muffled his sob in my shoulder. "I don't know what we're going to do without you two."

After a long embrace, we thanked him again for driving and promised to visit. One of those statements was true, the other, a courtesy.

Not long after he'd departed, the housekeeping staff brought by fresh sheets and towels. I'd never had such service before and couldn't quite believe I deserved the hospitality. But a laminated sign taped just above the door handle reminded me why the convent provided laundry, meals, and housekeeping: not to make us comfortable, but to free our time for study. We weren't supposed to waste precious government time dusting or mopping or anything unrelated to our primary purpose.

We were supposed to be breaking the Limit.

I stacked my linens atop the dresser and slung the remaining sheets at my sister. Neither of us needed to ask for help—we'd tag-teamed bed-making duty for our entire lives.

"And thank *you* too," I said, billowing the flat sheet out over the mattress.

Maggie smoothed out the wrinkles. "For making you do this?"

"And not leaving me to rot in Hawley."

Maggie smirked. "Well, as long as you promise to keep making beds with me while we're here, we'll call it even."

I lifted my chin toward the door. Several wayward students were floating through the hallway in search of assistance. "At least we don't have to beg strangers for help."

Maggie tucked her last hospital corner. "Could be a good way to meet people," she said. "So never mind the bed making. Promise me you'll loosen up?"

"I'll try," I said. "But if you fail, they send you home. And I don't want to go back to Pennsylvania. Which is why we should get going."

Maggie's face drooped as she looked at the clock. "We still have half an hour, Charlie."

I shouldered my backpack. "But we don't know where the auditorium is, you have no idea how long it takes to get there, and I'm not interested in being late."

She lifted her brow. "Remember what I said about loosening up?"

CHAPTER 12

Whatever money the Mendelia had saved on their prison deal, they'd spent on their posh new auditorium. The crown jewel of campus, the theater smelled of freshly unwrapped upholstery and still-drying paint. We entered the dimly lit room from the back—the rim of a steep bowl of stadium seats complete with crushed-velvet cushions and retractable writing desks. My feet sunk into the thickly carpeted steps while Maggie led me down to the front row.

Just because she wasn't early didn't mean she wasn't eager.

Over the next few minutes, 398 other recruits filtered into the auditorium, a near-even mix of men and women. A patchwork of skin tones, body types, hair styles, and face shapes, the audience—my classmates—represented all that the Mendelia wanted in their inventory: diversity. I started to wonder if my father's concern about military-style training would hold up. That's when the superintendent, lanky and bespectacled, shed a trench coat and took center stage. Maggie elbowed my ribs.

"That's Dr. Carmichael!" she squealed, barely able to maintain a whisper.

What was the world's leading Limit scientist doing at a convent? Teaching, of course, but rumors abounded. Some said he'd washed up; others thought he must enjoy the dry mountain climate. But my sister discovered the truth, and many months after that first assembly. The truth was that Dr. Carmichael had come to enjoy an existence out of the spotlight. There were advantages to obscurity, he said: if he put enough distance between himself and Headquarters, his work would never be scrutinized.

This was the most dangerous lesson he would ever teach her.

Just as the clock struck noon, Dr. Carmichael began his presentation. His opening statements comprised a bouquet of flowery pleasantries: a welcome to the convent, introductions of himself and key staff, and finally, respect for his audience.

"You've already made an incredible contribution," he said. I felt the faintest tingle in the scars below my waistband. "But through training and practice, all of you are about to accomplish so, so much more."

Dr. Carmichael rapped his knuckles on the podium. "The way I see it, seeking life beyond the Limit is like charting a voyage to an unknown land. No one has ever been there, and no one knows the way. But just like the other great pioneers before us, we can turn to the skies for guidance. Let genetics serve as our North Star. In constellation with the other supporting sciences, we can build a celestial map to navigate this crisis."

I looked over at Maggie. Her mouth had fallen slightly agape.

"So far, the Mendelia has established an expeditionary fleet: its clinics. Each of these is a ship; every client, a passenger. And what is your role? Mendels, you shall be our captains: reading the stars, eyeing the seas, charting the way. Without you, our ships are lost."

It was the kind of work Maggie dreamed of. Her eyes glittered at the call to action.

"Technicians, you are the crew: fueling the engine, tending the ballast, keeping the watch. Without you, our ships are dead."

What he described was honest work. Humble work. With Maggie at the helm, the raging seas of our future seemed infinitely more navigable. My sister must have felt equally encouraged, because she reached across the armrest to squeeze my hand.

"And so, as partners, you will endeavor to reach the land beyond the Limit. Like Columbus and Magellan before you, seek out an end you can only dream of. Cast aside the anchors of humility and doubt, and you will give our species the best chance for a future we all deserve."

The resulting cacophony was immediate. Maggie was moved to her feet, and others quickly followed suit. The applause ceased only when the superintendent bowed out through a side door, yielding the floor to another administrator who struggled to control the room.

"Wonderful, isn't he? So romantic." As the clamor subsided, the lean, polished woman stepped away from the podium and clasped her hands tightly together just below her waist.

It was then that I recognized her.

"I'm Dr. Venita Rubino, dean of administration here at the convent. Unfortunately, I have the responsibility of explaining your next few years here in much more pragmatic terms. But before we get started, I do have some news about an exciting development in the way we do business. As you know, we divide our recruits into Mendels and technicians, and up until this point, recruits have had a choice in the matter. This year marks a change in the way we make those assignments."

Dr. Rubino strutted around the edge of the stage with an unchecked confidence. "Survey after survey has shown that our clients—our mothers—prefer to consult with another woman when making decisions about their fertility. Therefore, starting this year, all female recruits will train as primary scientists and reproductive consultants. Ladies, you will be our Mendels."

A collective gasp murmured across the audience. It was my turn to grab Maggie's hand.

Having no doubt expected the upset, Dr. Rubino ignored the fervor and continued. "But humanity cannot be saved on the backs of women alone. Gentlemen, you will serve as technicians. As Dr. Carmichael noted, our clinics cannot run without critical laboratory work. That's where you come in."

The blood that thundered in my ears drowned out anything else Dr. Rubino had to say. While I knew I should be taking an interest in the details, no amount of focus could muffle the shriek of the sudden, irreparable change that scraped the inside of my brain.

Was I really going to have to do this alone? Without Maggie?

My pulse hastened.

What was I going to do? Would they even allow me to quit?

My breath shallowed.

Is this how I would lose my sister?

Full-blown panic felt just moments away.

Dr. Rubino returned to center stage. "Let me remind you: humanity needs more Mendelia in the field as soon as possible," she said. "Thousands of people get pregnant every day, hundreds more yearn for children. They all need our guidance.

"Let us meet that demand."

The lights came up just as Dr. Rubino exited. While most other recruits stood up to leave, I stayed seated, unsure if my body could hold up the weight of my dread.

Maggie offered her hand. "We'll get you through this, Charlie."

Maggie could barely keep up as I scurried back to our dorm.

"If you really want out, you can just fail your classes," she wheezed. It would be weeks before we'd fully acclimate to the thin mountain air.

"And then what?" I spat, equally breathless. "Go back to Hawley?"

She shrugged. "Dad didn't seem like he would mind."

I shoved through the building's front doors. "They promised me a technician job. I gave them my ovaries. Isn't this a breach of contract or something?"

"Good luck suing the government," Maggie scoffed. "I'm not a lawyer, but I'm sure there's something in the fine print about 'other duties as assigned.'"

She keyed the door so that I could flop onto my freshly made bed.

"Look, there's no good option," Maggie continued. "I know you're afraid of it, but I still think becoming a Mendel sounds better than frittering away your life back in Pennsylvania."

That wasn't the half of it. Yes, I was afraid of becoming a Mendel. And, yes, the pharmacy would be a dismal place to spend the rest of my life. But worse than that, turning back to Hawley meant leaving Tehachapi.

Losing touch with my sister.

A gentle knock interrupted my dismay. In the doorway, a mop of rusty-brown hair had appeared.

A familiar mop of rusty-brown hair.

And rosemary eyes.

A small beaded bracelet ran around his right wrist.

"You ladies ready to grab some supper?"

"Nolan?" I asked, half under my breath.

"Nolan?"

Maggie screamed, then leaped up to throw her arms around our long-lost friend.

My heart danced staccato inside my chest. Nolan? After all these years? Not probable. But possible. And actual. Because there he was, standing in my doorway.

I wanted to jump up and hug him too but couldn't bring myself to produce the same zeal as my sister. Bashfulness impinged on my sentimentality, and instead, I gave an awkward wave from my bed.

"What are you doing here?" I asked.

Before he spoke, I felt Nolan's gaze snag on mine for the briefest of moments. "The same thing you are," he said. "Though I could hardly believe my eyes when I saw you in the auditorium. Aren't you both 5*s or something?"

"Yeah," Maggie confirmed. "But this was the only way to get out of Pennsylvania."

"I'm only a 4*, and Minnesota was no better," he said, nodding his affirmation. "Plus, who wouldn't want a chance to save the world?"

Me, I thought. Too much pressure. But my newfound obligation felt quite a bit lighter in Nolan's presence.

He gestured toward the cafeteria. "Come on. I've heard the kitchen staff put together a real Okie feast in honor of our arrival."

※

Maggie, Nolan, and I spent the rest of that first afternoon catching up on all that had happened since he'd left. In between updates about high school, our parents, and then enlistment, our trio worked through a veritable feast of Oklahoma favorites: crispy fried okra nuggets, tangy stalks of pickled asparagus, overcooked pinto beans spilled over tough cuts of pork. Right before dessert, Nolan mentioned his hometown girlfriend, Val, who'd also joined the Mendelia. Though I could tell my sister was trying to hide it, disappointment had punctured her revelry.

Neither Maggie nor I should've been surprised that Nolan had come to the convent attached. Given his obvious magnetism and pre-eminent charm, of course someone would've taken an interest—and she was probably just as charismatic and entertaining as he.

But why wasn't she here?

While I wanted to know why this notionally perfect couple hadn't enlisted together, Maggie ignored Nolan's reveal.

"Where did they get all of this?" she said, marveling at a heaving slice of walnut pie. "I've never had anything like it."

Whether her heart ached like mine or she just wanted to duck the discomfort, my sister's redirection worked.

"Prized family recipes of the lunch ladies," Nolan replied. "All descended from Dust Bowl refugees."

While Nolan looked relieved that the conversation was moving on, Maggie blithely licked flakes of pastry crust from her lips. "And how do you know?"

"Edith." Nolan pointed to a venerable old woman working the hot-food counter. "She takes considerable pride in this spread and went out of her way to remind me that everything we're having today is far tastier than the dandelion salads and canned tumbleweeds she had to eat."

Edith was right. The food was uncommonly delicious. So much so that, between the meal and the company, I'd all but forgotten my newly discovered fate.

The first few months at the convent had slipped away just as quickly as my belief in perennial California sunshine. Despite Nolan's steady luminescence, by November I felt as if my whole life had dimmed. As days fell off the calendar, so did minutes of sunlight, dissolving the warm, windy summer into a pungent, putrid fall and finally a great, gray winter.

And that wasn't the worst of it.

As my father predicted, my schedule was regimented to the minute with class, laboratory time, and study hall. Neither Maggie nor I had time to fuss about Nolan, especially since the object of our affection remained committed to his relationship. Instead, we focused on our schoolwork—just as the government intended.

My courses progressed as quickly as the seasons, and while I was passing my exams, I wasn't exactly excelling. Not like Maggie, at least. She was making grades and turning heads, spending extra hours in the library as well as the lab. Dr. Carmichael even asked her to assist on some of his research projects.

While Maggie radiated devotion to her craft, I seemed to reflect it. I dodged all the extracurriculars and enrichment activities and left class as early as the faculty would allow. Who was I to determine how and when couples should procreate? Why should I decide their future?

I hadn't even been able to do that for myself.

Learning to make placements was the worst. Naughts wanted babies, and I needed to make them—and I needed to make them in a way that might break the Limit. That meant learning how to select the eggs and sperm that might produce a spontaneous mutation. The tens of thousands of samples contained within the Mendelia's genetic library could be combined in billions of ways, and somehow I'd been charged with divining the particular pairing that might save the human race.

The odds were astronomical, and so was my blood pressure.

"Don't worry," Dr. Carmichael started. "As long as you make a baby, you're moving in the right direction. More humans means more procreators, and eventually, more scientists. Perhaps more Mendels if we're lucky. All of this buys our species more time and better odds."

Maggie's favorite instructor had the distinct pleasure of teaching the introductory genetic innovation course. The classroom he taught in was rumored to have previously served as the prison's solitary confinement ward. Fitting, I thought, for how lonely I felt. I hadn't even been able to call my parents during those first few months—not only could I not find the time, but I didn't want to admit how desperate I felt.

Whether out of camaraderie or pity, Maggie and Nolan sat beside me in the back row while Dr. Carmichael paged through his notes.

"It is, however, better to produce a baby with a little something new. None of our existing DNA can beat the Limit, so we need to search for something novel. Something different. Not too different, mind you. Some differences must be avoided. Down syndrome, for example. Tay-Sachs. Duchenne muscular dystrophy—these genetic disorders are entirely incompatible with a long, productive human life."

The hairs on the back of my neck stood up. In middle school, Maggie and I had known a girl with Down syndrome, and despite her "difference," she always seemed to be thriving. I saw my sister raise her hand to challenge the point, but Dr. Carmichael waved it away.

"Or at least life as we *want* it. That being said, to advance our research, you must seek out and promulgate conditions that may have gone unappreciated in the past. This might mean working with DNA from someone who is genetically deaf. Or has sickle cell anemia. Or Ehlers-Danlos."

Nolan leaned over with a whisper. "Is that the one that makes you bald?"

Maggie shook her head. "That's alopecia. Ehlers-Danlos makes your skin elastic."

Understanding released Nolan's furrowed brow. "Ah, so they want us to work with conditions that are inconvenient, but not . . ."

"Incompatible with life," I finished.

CHAPTER 13

The arrival of the winter holidays brought a brief reprieve. Despite its generally solemn atmosphere, the convent wasn't completely devoid of holiday spirit: string lights had been woven into the razor wire, and the housekeeping staff had hung a few fir wreaths on the most important of doorways. The Mendelia also suspended classes for two weeks to allow the staff a chance to visit their families, but Maggie and I stayed behind. She wanted to study, and I needed to rest; it wasn't like we could afford to fly home anyhow.

Our parents compensated with a well-timed gift.

"Let's open it!" Maggie cried, as soon as the janitor delivered the package. Though she'd just returned from a long lab session, you might've thought there was a poodle inside for how excited she sounded.

Before I could protest, my sister stripped off the packaging tape and began rooting through the parcel's interior.

I hesitated. "Don't you think we should wait until Christmas?"

"Oh, come on, Charlie. It's December 23. Isn't that close enough?"

When she made her best puppy eyes, I crumbled. Joy was a rare treat on campus, and seeing my sister so enthusiastic revived my own childish delight.

I joined Maggie in dumping a mountain of packing peanuts on my bed.

"Let's see what we have here," she said, and ripped open a small snowman-clad brick. A deck of law enforcement–themed playing cards fell into her lap.

I skimmed my mother's explanatory note. "From Dad. He says to use the sweets as chips: candy canes, $1; gingersnaps, $5."

Maggie rolled a handful of tinsel-wrapped chocolates through her fingers. "God, I miss those nights. What about these plastic boxes?"

My eyes skimmed over my mother's page. "Tupperware. Aunt Frankie's hosting parties. Apparently she got laid off from the laundromat."

Maggie turned back to the pile to finish skinning the wrapping paper from some of the more oddly shaped items.

"One big jar of maple syrup, one tiny bottle of vanilla extract, and a bundle of cinnamon sticks," she said.

I pulled a few portly fruits from underneath the tissue paper. "Not to mention a few oranges."

A spark ignited my sister's grin. "Are you thinking what I'm thinking?"

Of course I was. There was only one thing we could do with these ingredients, and neither of us could wait until morning.

Maggie shoved the foodstuffs into her book bag, and we sped across campus.

Had we not known where to look, Maggie and I would've missed what little light projected from the back pantry. Edith was staging the kitchen for supper.

My sister and I barged in, with Maggie heaving her backpack onto the countertop. "Ms. Edith, would you mind if we made our own dinner tonight?"

"We won't need much besides a few slices of bread and an egg," I added.

The crone dusted a bit of flour from her hands. "Girls, you might not know this, but yours ain't the only mouths I gotta feed round here. If you wanna cook, I'll let ya, but you've gotta make enough for all of us."

I wasn't sure how far two oranges and a tablespoon of vanilla would go, but Maggie seemed unconcerned. "And how many is that?" she asked.

"Just you, me, and Dr. Rubino," Edith answered. "And that bird don't eat much."

Half an hour later, Maggie and I plated up two servings of Tannehill French toast and sent them out the door with Edith so she could enjoy a night off. For our second batch, Maggie went a bit heavier with the extracts and filled the whole space with the festive scents of butter, sugar, and spice. To further embellish the mood, she performed a brazen acapella of "Sleigh Ride" that she danced out across the empty linoleum floor.

"So like you," I snickered.

After catching her breath, Maggie hoisted herself up on the countertop. "And what do you mean by that?"

"You're just so . . . audacious."

My sister grabbed a plate and speared three bites of syrup-laden toast with her fork. "Oh, come on! Our DNA might hold five generations, but we only get to live one."

I couldn't help but roll my eyes. "You're insatiable."

"And you're"—she chewed—"a drag."

I dropped my utensils in surrender. "Can we not fight on Christmas?"

My request silenced Maggie, but I wasn't sure for how long. Arguing with my sister was like wrestling a pig in mud, Nolan had said—after a while, you realize the pig likes it.

Maggie must have agreed to the truce, because she turned back to her plate. "At least it kind of smells like home."

"Kind of tastes like it too."

"Not as good as Dad's, though," she said. "Too much vanilla."

I looked over to catch her punctuate her retort with a wink.

"I miss them," I said.

"Me too," she added.

"Think they'll come out for graduation?"

Maggie dropped her plate into the industrial sink. "I'm sure they will. But that means you actually need to graduate, you know."

"No pressure." I sighed. "No pressure at all."

The next morning, Maggie and I decided we could spare one wintery afternoon to finally explore the town we'd already been living in for four months. Given that it was Christmas Eve, we thought we might even get a little bit of shopping in.

The shuttle from campus to downtown Tehachapi was empty except for us.

"We'll meet you here at nine thirty," Maggie told the driver. "*Please* don't forget about us."

Stepping off the bus was like stepping back into Pennsylvania. The roads were sludgy from winter weather treatment, not to mention completely devoid of sidewalks. Maggie and I had to trudge down half a mile of muddy shoulder before arriving at a half-vacant strip mall, only to find a seedy pawn shop, an empty hair salon, and an off-brand dollar store. Piles of road salt occupied most of the parking spaces.

"So what's next?" I asked, rubbing my freezing hands together.

Maggie craned her neck upward. Two lonely gliders dawdled against the steel-gray sky, circling the town like vultures. "There's got to be an airport around here. That might be something to see."

The suggestion failed to light the fire of my enthusiasm. "Let's go home. If I'm going to be bored, I want to be warm."

"Don't be such a spoilsport," Maggie said, her cloudy breath fogging the crystalline air. "Fifteen more minutes."

It was too brisk to stand too still for too long. After another miserable half mile, Maggie spotted the airstrip in the distance: it paralleled the same highway that'd brought us into town. A powdered-sugar snow dusted the mountains beyond.

"I can't make it that far," I said. My chattering teeth made it difficult to get the words out.

"You won't have to." Maggie smiled.

She pointed to a Mexican restaurant just a hundred yards ahead. I'd been so focused on the horizon I hadn't been able to see what was just off my nose.

A few freezing minutes later, Maggie threw open a heavy blue door and together we crossed over into an oasis of warmth. Rustic adobe decor, the strum of a mariachi guitar, the smells of corncobs charring over a charcoal fire—the ambiance sucked the cold right from my bones. A giant mural of tropical ferns, sparkling waterfalls, and stepped pyramids further convinced my mind that I'd somehow transcended the desolate mountains of Central California into the luscious jungles of Mexico.

The bartender waved us over. The dining room was full; the seats in front of him were the last in the house. With no concern for our age, Maggie pulled back a stool and ordered two virgin margaritas.

As we crunched our way through a boat of tortilla chips, Maggie and I talked a little about home, but mostly about school. There wasn't much to our lives besides it at that point. My sister was on track to be the top of our class, and there'd be privileges for such excellence: choice in technician, as well as in residency. These were decisions that few got to make—less superlative students like myself would be matched with technicians and clinics by algorithm. The faculty had explained it just one week before.

"Partnering," Dr. Varghese said, "is tantamount to arranged marriage."

A favorite among students, Dr. Brinda Varghese was round and warm and forgiving—all the things the convent and its curriculum were not. She had a way of delivering bad news gently and could always manage a spoonful of sugar even when the cupboards were bare.

"As faculty, we use our expertise and intuition to pair you together. While we know that many of you would prefer to make this choice for yourselves, trial and error is a process for which you do not have the time and we do not have the patience. The Mendelia need practitioners out in the field—and while we will consider your preference, it will be your personality and performance that matter most in our decision."

A handful of girls in the front row snarled in disgust. We'd just spent the past three months learning how to coach and control our clients, but now that the shoe was on the other foot, it blistered.

Dr. Varghese could sense the tension in the room and pivoted toward more alluring subjects. "And while your first year here is focused on developing individual skills, your second will be spent practicing with your partner to confirm compatibility. At graduation, viable pairs receive residency assignments, complete with travel itineraries and housing arrangements. I can tell you it all happens a lot more quickly than you expect."

If only, I thought. The finish line that Dr. Varghese teased was still eighteen months out. Given all that had happened, I just wanted to know whether I'd fail or succeed, fall back to Hawley, or move on to a clinic. Whether I'd need to accept that I'd wasted two years of my life or spend the rest of them in practice.

Hell, it seemed, was in between.

"Before Memorial Day, you will complete all of your assessments and preliminary exams," Dr. Varghese continued. "You will also submit a list of three names. Your partner *preferences*," she emphasized. "Though they may not weigh heavily on the balance of our decision, they may yet tip the scales. Please do remember the gravity of these selections. Your partner may be the most important relationship of your career—if not your life."

I had no doubts about who Maggie would choose. Much like my sister, Nolan had distinguished himself with outstanding performance and unmatched technique. It didn't hurt that he'd become obviously and increasingly enamored with her. Over the past few months, Nolan had taken to walking my sister to class, bringing her coffee, and running all sorts of other errands for her—girlfriend or not. He'd even left her a Christmas present: a beautiful watercolor painting of a climbing sweet pea vine.

The pity I felt should've been for Nolan's girlfriend, but I kept it for myself.

I might have been envious of my sister's fledging romance if anxiety hadn't completely consumed me. Because I wasn't Maggie, because I wasn't exceptional, the trajectory of my future was about to be calculated by an unfeeling, unthinking algorithm. My future would be decided by the tests I barely passed and the partner the faculty thought I should have. Disaster, it seemed, was assured—but whether it escalated into full-blown catastrophe would be determined by one remaining uncertainty: where my sister and I would end up for residency.

If we were close, I might yet survive. But the Mendelia were still trying to open clinics in every domestic zip code and still had ten thousand more to go.

We'd be lucky to land in the same time zone.

Separation was painful for me to even think about, much less talk about. Maggie and I had never spent more than a week apart—when her swim team won the state championships in Pittsburgh during our freshman year. Even that had made me nervous; whether it was logical or not, physical separation felt like the first skid down the slippery slope of total estrangement. I still needed my sister, and I wasn't ready to break our pact—even though she might be.

We were on our fourth margarita in half as many hours when I began to suspect they'd lost their virginity. The bartender confirmed my hunch by throwing a flirtatious wink in Maggie's direction. However much tequila he'd given us, it was enough to swell my courage.

I ran my finger around the rim of the shapely cocktail glass. "So in terms of residency, where are you thinking?"

My sister sipped her drink. "We'll see where they put me."

"Don't tease, Mags. You know you're going to be valedictorian. You'll get to choose. I'm the one who's going to have to roll dice with the algorithm."

"Okay, okay," she conceded. "But first, why don't you tell me what winning the residency lottery looks like for you."

No matter where I ended up, it wouldn't be with my sister. To dodge the superfluous question and spare my own feelings, I again feigned interest in the same manufactured dream I'd projected about the convent.

It was just as believable as it was false.

"Eternal sunshine. Coconut trees. Everything about California that Tehachapi isn't," I said. "Is a little bit of seaside sanctuary too much to ask?"

Maggie smiled. "I don't know, but according to the travel magazines in the clinic lobbies, lapping waves and coastal breezes sure do soothe the nerves."

We shared a snicker. The hopes and dreams that had once been quite commonplace seemed absurd in the shadow of the Limit. There could be no relaxation while humanity sat on the threshold of extinction's door.

As our cackling subsided, I reversed the question. "So what about you?"

"The same," she teased.

The drinks had weakened my dignity. "Oh, come on!" I whined. "I know you want more than sunsets and scenery!"

"You're right," she said. "But where I want to end up has the same things you want, so the statement remains true."

I groaned. "You know I don't enjoy riddles! Tell me what you're really after."

Maggie pushed back her unfinished drink. "Would you believe me if I told you 'remnants of ancient DNA'?"

I must have recoiled, because my sister felt the need to offer a more complete explanation.

"It's the work I've been doing with Dr. Carmichael. He's been studying some promising sequences, and many of them are very, very old. Archaic, really. He thinks that Neanderthals and other protohumans may have left behind some biological keys that could unlock the

Limit. But to take his work any further, I need to work with the people who actually carry some of these genes."

I pulled at the edge of my napkin. Whatever she was planning sounded very, very far away.

"And where would they be?" I asked.

Maggie wouldn't look at me, but I kept my eyes on her.

"Melanesia, ideally," she answered. "The people there have the highest concentration of prehistoric DNA."

I knew it was coming. I wasn't so foolish as to think our pact could last forever. But *we* weren't agreeing to end it, as I always thought we would. She'd already made the decision.

Alone.

I withdrew into a corner of myself that not even Maggie could reach. She might have been able to, actually, if she'd held up her pinkie finger. But as minutes went by, the promise never appeared.

My next question was as flat as my affect. "Is that even in the US?"

"No," she sighed, her voice heavy.

For a moment, I felt relief—the Mendelia wouldn't send freshly minted residents abroad. Experience was a requirement for international assignments.

"But there are parts of our country that are close enough."

I stared a hole through her. "Hawai'i?"

Maggie made more eye contact with the bottles behind the bar than with me. "Much, much farther than that."

"Then where, exactly?"

She swiveled on the barstool to meet my gaze.

"The Marshall Islands."

My sister put her hands up in defense. "I know what it looks like, and I promise you I'm not using this as an excuse to go find Mom and Dad."

"You mean Vaitea and Fiva?"

My sister didn't answer, but I didn't have any more questions.

The next fifteen minutes passed in silence. When the bartender offered to refill our drinks, we refused. When the waiter brought us a fresh basket of chips, we declined. But when the barback asked if we wanted our check, Maggie ordered a plate of sopaipillas.

She pushed the cinnamon-encrusted pastries in my direction. "Here. It's the closest thing they have to French toast."

As I picked at the peace offering, I tried desperately to understand my sister's choices. How her motivation could be so much different than mine. How she could feel so certain about something she barely understood.

I handed my empty plate to the busboy and turned to her. "How do you know that it's worth it?"

"The Marshall Islands?" she replied.

"Yes, the Marshall Islands. And everything else. All the effort you put in at school. In the lab. At the library. Everything you're doing to break the Limit. Which, I remind you, has been studied for almost fifteen years by world-renowned scientists and still seems pretty unbeatable."

She snickered before throwing back the last of her drink. "I don't know if it's worth it. All I can tell you is that it makes me happy."

We were startled back into reality as the host switched off the lights in the dining room. Maggie checked her watch: 9:20 p.m. We'd lost track of time. In a great swirl of activity, I grabbed my purse while my sister flung a handful of bills at the bartender as we both ran toward the exit. The host smirked as he opened the door.

A whole foot of snow had accumulated.

There was no way we'd be able to make the shuttle. But we seemed like the only ones who were anxious about getting home. The waiters had strewn themselves over the furniture while the cooks passed around cold beers. The reposing staff only startled into activity when three giant pickup trucks pulled into the parking lot. Everyone piled in without a backward glance, except for the dishwashers, who had to lock up. They jabbered at us in Spanish. While we couldn't understand exactly what they were saying, their meaning was clear: get in the truck or sleep on the floor.

We took the back bench of a battered cab alongside the dishwashers. The driver, one of the cooks, craned his neck. "A dónde?"

Maggie knew there was only one question he could be asking. "Mendelia. Gracias."

He nodded. The host and the bartender, both on the front bench, started exchanging jokes. It was gibberish to us but for the laughter. We hadn't heard such a ruckus since arriving at the convent, a place so dour that a stolen snicker amounted to a scarlet letter. The raucous Spanish exchanges continued until "Feliz Navidad" came on the radio, at which point the driver drummed the steering wheel while the host and the bartender clapped exuberantly. The dishwasher who sat next to Maggie started elbowing her in the ribs, goading her into singing along. She gave in. And not just with a halfhearted mumble, like me. Maggie flourished invisible maracas while she half screamed, half sang, *"I want to wish you a Merry Christmas!"* Our companions doubled over. Soon, everyone was trying to outperform one another in the most absurd singalong I had ever witnessed, all of us howling a cross-cultural Christmas carol in the middle of an unexpected blizzard.

As we made our way down the long road toward campus, our pilot performed a flurry of gestures that we deciphered as a request for further directions. I tried to explain that we were happy to walk the rest of the way, but when Maggie reached for the latch, our hosts replied with an unmistakable chorus of nos. After several broken exchanges, we determined that they wanted to drop us near our room so that we wouldn't have to slog through the now knee-deep snow. After seeing us to the walkway of our dormitory, they waved jovially, reversed quickly, and were never seen again.

The still-falling snow snuffed out any remaining sound from the departing truck. The sky had completely darkened by that time, and the storm's fat flakes fell gently, but constantly. The cold air and dark skies seemed to pressurize the silence. Neither Maggie nor I spoke, nor made immediately for the door. We drank deeply of the stillness. The sanctity. The moment stretched into seconds, the seconds into minutes.

While it wasn't the California dream I'd envisioned, it stunned me nonetheless.

CHAPTER 14

A week later, coursework kicked in with a vengeance. The convent added clinical rounds to our academic schedule so we could start observing client consultations and embryo implantations. As if I needed more stress. But not having disrupted our study habits with too many festivities, my sister and I found ourselves more prepared than most.

While others struggled to rejoin the rhythms of the convent, Maggie found more time to take walks with Nolan. Unsurprisingly, he'd broken up with his girlfriend over the break, and while he claimed to be taking a bit of time for himself, it was hard to deny that he could always be found with my sister. Even I had to concede they were an item. On February 14, the two headed into town for a meal at the same Mexican restaurant where Maggie and I had drowned Christmas. It wasn't until after they'd left that I realized it was Valentine's Day.

There was no sense in waiting up for them, so I fell asleep in my physiology textbook instead.

My alarm erupted at half past six. Much to my surprise, Maggie's joined the fracas. She must have snuck in during the wee hours of that chilly morning. After silencing her claxon, I expected my sister to drag her groggy body out of bed, but instead, she rolled back into her comforter.

"I'm skipping breakfast," she muttered. "I'll see you in class."

I pulled a heavy sweater over my unruly curls. "No, you're not. We have an exam, and you need calories to fuel that overpowered brain of yours."

"Are you sure you can't just grab me a muffin?"

Her dawdling annoyed me. After promising to "get me through this," I thought she understood how much help I would need.

"No," I replied. "I need you to explain the estrogen-progesterone cycle to me again. If I want a decent technician, I need to ace this test."

Thirty minutes of badgering later, I stripped the blankets from my listless sister and bullied her down to the cafeteria. I couldn't be entirely heartless, however—I still needed her mercy. So after my tutor slouched into one of the communal tables, I scurried about to bring her a cup of coffee, a bowl of oatmeal, and a pen. She'd just finished diagramming the structure of luteinizing hormone when Nolan slid his tray next to mine.

"Hi, ladies."

His usual cheer was laced with a sizable dose of caution.

"Good morning," Maggie grumbled.

They didn't speak beyond that. Nolan scraped some jam over a bagel.

I tried stimulating the missing conversation. "So . . . how was Serrano's?"

"Fine," they replied in unison.

The acrimony between them could've been cut with the spoon Maggie twiddled, so I pivoted. "Does anyone have plans for the weekend?"

"It's my first free Saturday in almost two months," Nolan complained. "My buddy Josh has been trying to get permission for some of the guys to head to Vegas for a quick outing, but I don't think there's any way Dr. Rubino approves it. Therefore, my bet's on video games and Texas Hold 'Em, as usual."

I looked over at my sister.

"I've got to drive to Barstow," she said. "Their clinic sequenced some eggs from a new recruit, and they think they've got a novel mutation. Dr. Carmichael wants me to bring back a sample so we can run more tests."

Nolan brightened. "Let me do it. I'll grab a car from the pool—it's what, an hour or two?"

Maggie looked up from her porridge with dismay.

"It's not a big deal," Nolan implored. "Collecting samples is technician scut. As a Mendel, you've got better things to do—fancy research and important reading and whatnot."

"No."

My sister's adamant reply was cut with affection. "I really shouldn't ask anything more of you," she finished.

"Maggie, I want to." Nolan's eyes locked onto hers as his eyebrows reached for reassurance. "I want to."

She grabbed his hand. "It could make the difference."

The bell rang, and whatever discussion Maggie and Nolan were having in the subtext got lost in the clamor of bussing trays and bustling students. After clearing the cafeteria's double doors, Maggie and I would go left for our physiology class, and Nolan would go right for his fertilization lab.

Maybe then she'd tell me what was going on.

But it was at that juncture that Nolan swept my sister into a desperate embrace, digging his hands into her shoulders just as he did in his driveway so many years before. After my sister kissed his forehead, he shuffled off without another word. When Maggie and I turned toward our own destination, she changed the subject back to our exam.

The details she provided only addressed female hormone production.

Though fleeting, that tender moment between Maggie and Nolan was enough to send the entire convent atwitter. Not only with rumors about their courtship, but with gossip about partnering preferences more generally.

May would soon be upon us, and it was time to develop our lists.

For me, selection was agony. While there were plenty of lovely, smart, engaging men at the convent, I couldn't imagine myself in rural Idaho or backwater Louisiana with any of them. It wasn't that they were especially unappealing, but in an effort to impress, many of the technicians focused on showcasing their commitment. Technician after technician pitched me on their passion for our mission, their perseverance through training, and their penchant for hard work. Like Maggie, they'd become the disciples that the Mendelia so deeply desired—and that frightened me.

Given her outstanding performance, the faculty pulled my sister away at all hours of the day for additional training. Maggie went eagerly, but Nolan was left a bit of an orphan. He preferred waiting for her in our room and spent most of his lonely nights lying on her bed and bouncing a tennis ball off the opposite wall. Most of the time, I could ignore his inadvertent metronome and attend to my reading, but on one unassuming Tuesday, Nolan wanted more than my ambient company.

"So who's at the top of your list?" he asked.

The question startled me out of a paragraph on persuasive psychology. "Maggie." I sighed. "It was supposed to be Maggie."

"You still haven't moved on? My, my, my, you've got some serious catching up to do," Nolan teased. "Why don't you go ahead and put my name down?"

If only. But instead of indulging in that fantasy, I rolled my eyes. "Maggie's going to pick you and you know it."

"That's true." He bounced the ball again. "But what if I don't pick her?"

The suggestion kindled a hope I long thought extinguished, and I almost fell out of my chair. "Are you insane?"

As much as I hated to admit it, I found myself wishing he was. I might be too for thinking I could compete with my sister. Because once—just once—I wanted him to pick me.

He returned a rakish smile. "I am not—so yes, I will pick her." A deep breath followed. "But I almost didn't. I almost didn't come to Tehachapi at all. When Val chose the convent in Manhattan, I almost went with her."

Aloof to the fact he'd inadvertently stoked—then smothered—my feelings, Nolan kept his eyes on the painted cinder block and resumed his individual game of catch.

I balked. Not just to tend my wounded heart, but to seize on the other detail he'd mentioned.

"Wait—you got to pick?"

I'd long been under the impression that Maggie and my selection of Tehachapi had been a fortuitous twist of fate.

Nolan chuckled and held the ball. "Not exactly. The Mendel who recruited us pulled some strings."

His eerily familiar story betrayed the serendipity I'd originally believed in, but no sooner had my brow furrowed than Nolan's thumps resumed. Organizational conspiracy, it seemed, would have to wait. The heart of his confession demanded further exploration.

"So why didn't you?" I asked, satisfying my perfunctory duties as a friend.

"My mother. She's the one who pointed out Val didn't need me."

My head filled with flashbacks of my own mother warning against clingy love interests. "Isn't that a good thing?"

"Val's beautiful, articulate, kind. But she's all of those things without me. We could've stayed together and stayed happy, but I wouldn't have made a difference in any perceptible way. Not in her life, not in the world, not even in our hometown." Nolan sat up and racked the ball in an empty flower vase on Maggie's desk. "And isn't that what we all want? To make a difference?"

Gallant *and* reflective? My sister really was too lucky.

I turned back to my book to hide my envy. "Honestly, I just want to get by."

Nolan seemed to take the hint. "Right, and at this point, that requires a list. Let's get to it." He stood up and peered out our shoebox-size window. Sometimes he could spot Maggie transiting the quad on her way back. "How about Derek Chatterjee? Nipping at my heels in terms of DNA extraction."

I winced. "Too much for me. Anyone who can compete with you probably is."

Nolan flipped around Maggie's desk chair and folded his arms across its back. "Not so much for A-listers?"

"I'm not an A-lister," I reminded him. Grades would factor into our final assignments, and while I wasn't failing, I wasn't first rate either.

"That's what I've always wondered . . . what brought you to the Mendelia, anyway?"

"What do you mean?" I asked. While I completely understood his question, I needed time to formulate a more acceptable answer.

He pulled at his chin. "I don't want to say you don't care, but it's not like you're in love with the work. Not the way most people here are."

His accusation landed much more like an exoneration, and I almost felt relieved to be found out. Especially by him. Now, I could at least tell *someone* that I'd never turn out to be the reproductive evangelist my employer hoped I would become.

"I've tried, Nolan, I really have. I know this is some of the most important work anyone can be doing right now. But I can't have people counting on me to make their babies or break the Limit. I'm not a hero. Not like everyone else here is trying to be."

"But you show up to class. You do all your assignments. You're making decent marks. You're obviously trying."

I threw my head back and groaned. "That's because I don't want to fail. I don't want to go back to Hawley, and I don't want to disappoint Maggie. I know I can't have it both ways, so I try not to complain, but, ugh."

"Looks like you've gotten yourself into quite a bind," Nolan chuckled. He stood up to pack up his things while I stared at the ceiling.

"I know," I said. "I just want a steady job in a normal place where I can have a regular life. The Mendelia offered me that. I just need to get through."

I sat up. "For what it's worth, I do feel badly about my motivation."

Nolan snickered. "Nobility wasn't an admissions requirement," he said. "You just need to find another con artist."

I cocked my head. "And where would I find that?"

A sprite dazzled through his eyes. "Not in the places you're currently looking."

I gestured for him to continue, but Nolan checked his watch instead.

"Looks like she'll be later than usual tonight. Give her my best, will you? I'll see you both at breakfast." He took two steps down the hallway before hollering back. "And have a list by then!"

CHAPTER 15

Nolan was right. I wouldn't find a good partner in any of the "right" places—the top of the class and the convent's partner-matching events were filled with too many eager beavers. The wrong places—the superintendent's office and the remedial classes—were no good either. I didn't want someone who might actually depend on me. No superstars, no slackers. I needed someone average. Someone unremarkable.

Someone like me.

I dined alone for the next few days. Not only did I need to purge the growing affection I felt for my sister's boyfriend, but the cafeteria made for an excellent perch from which to observe the student body. Each meal, I tried hard to scan for technicians who hadn't caught my eye before, those who didn't stand out in any particular way. Like zebras in a herd, however, it was difficult to distinguish individuals inside the morass of mediocrity. Luckily, Nolan enjoyed picking them out—and though Maggie may have been able to make more tailored selections, he was available and she was not.

Theo Park. That was the name at the top of Nolan's list. Nolan had to remind me that I'd partnered with him for several experiments during Introductory Microbiology in the previous term. I couldn't remember much about our interactions, other than stumbling over him during lab as we repetitively offered each other first choice of pipette or first turn with the centrifuge. The near-constant deference led to a pileup of experimental errors as we both missed timers, miscounted droplets, and mismanaged temperatures—our polymerase chain reactions were all but completely spoiled. That being said, Theo seemed far more interested in being respectful than being revered. Nolan's opinion of him confirmed my nondescript diagnosis: Theo was pleasant, if not a bit plain.

I probably had the same reputation.

The search for sameness didn't surprise me—having spent most of my life with a twin, I was most comfortable in the company of someone much like myself. While Nolan worried Theo and I may grow bored of each other when stranded together in Podunk, Nowhere, I knew he was a safe choice. Theo wouldn't push me, and I wouldn't make demands of him. We wouldn't challenge or better each other the way Maggie and Nolan would, but we wouldn't disgrace each other either. Our partnership would be comfortable. Ordinary. Predictable.

Everything I wanted my future to be.

"So we're done, then, right?" Nolan reclined on my sister's bed again and resumed bouncing his tennis ball.

I sat cross-legged on mine with a sheet of scrap paper. "Nolan, I only have one name."

"That's all you need." His tone was annoyingly nonchalant.

"You must be kidding."

"I am not. We've spent three whole evenings going through all 199 names besides mine. There's no one else here *you* feel good about. There's no one else here that *I* feel good about. Don't set yourself up."

He picked up his ball and bounced it again. "Last week you told me you hated failing, right? Well, if you submit Theo's name and it gets picked, you win. If they assign you to someone else and it doesn't work out, it won't be because you picked wrong. You can blame the Mendelia instead of yourself."

I strode across the room and snatched his ball midair.

"Don't be mad! I've absolved you of responsibility!" Smiling victoriously, Nolan sat up to see himself out.

I folded my arms. "It's a huge gamble, Nolan."

"It is." He winked. "But you can't lose."

How he could remain so chipper confounded me. "How do you do it?"

"Do what?" Nolan's gangly fingers gripped the top of the doorframe. His biceps were lean but neatly sculpted, and he pulled off three easy pull-ups before dropping back to the ground. Then, for the first time that I'd ever witnessed, Nolan closed the door.

We were alone. Together. And his shamrock eyes held mine.

He was waiting for an answer, I knew, but my mind could barely reach the memory of what he'd asked.

A beat passed before I located it.

"Act like everything's okay," I squeaked.

More questions careened through my heart. If I confessed, what would he think of my timid affections? What would he tell my sister? What would *I* tell my sister?

As Nolan sauntered toward my bed, the top of my throat cinched tight around what was left of my voice. I found myself yearning for him to touch me—not in any sexual way—but to reach for my hand or rub my back. I wanted him to do what I could not, in hopes that it might answer the one question that refused to abate.

Do you feel it too?

Unfortunately, after taking a seat at a respectful distance, Nolan answered only what I'd asked aloud.

"Might as well," he said. "Either the Limit's solvable or it's not. We don't know, and I suppose we can't until a hundred years from now. Either way, I know what I'm doing here is important."

I swallowed, then nodded along. Clearly, this wasn't the moment I'd hoped for, but it was important all the same. The Grand Canyon hadn't been so grand to start; it took years—eons—for the river to do its work. For people to realize just how majestic it had become. In time, maybe Nolan, too, would appreciate what I had to offer. He might even understand that I could love him just as much as Maggie—though maybe not as forcefully.

And maybe that could be just as good.

Guilt, I reminded myself. What I was supposed to feel was guilt. I was pining for my sister's boyfriend—no good could come from that. Not if I wanted to preserve our relationship.

Oblivious to my longing, Nolan continued his monologue. "I come from a really small town, you know. Nothing I could do there felt like it would ever really matter. But here, I might make a Limit-busting discovery. Tomorrow. Even if I don't, maybe I'll make the baby whose genius grandchild solves it. Sure, I'll probably die before it's all worked out, but when I do, I'll know that I at least planted some seeds of hope." He shook his head in embarrassment. "I'm sorry, I told myself I'd leave the kitschy farm jokes back in Minnesota."

Nolan moved back to Maggie's bed. "But in all seriousness, at this point, I think supporting your sister might be the best way to make a difference. She's so brilliant, the Mendelia seem to think she may be our best bet at finding a breakthrough. Maybe loving her is all I have to do to make a difference."

Love her?

Any thoughts of undervalued gorges crumbled in that instant, and the debris sank my heart down into the abyss.

I couldn't say anything now. I was too late.

To disguise my despair, I forced a snicker. "Are you really suggesting that love can break the Limit?"

Nolan gagged. "When you put it like that, I can barely stomach it. Thanks, Charlie. Now I need to go rethink my entire inspiration."

It took a whole month for me to reinter my feelings for Nolan. They resisted burial, especially when every sight of the boy revived them.

Unfortunately for me, such sightings would only increase in the coming months. Our second academic year would begin on July 1 with the Mendelia announcing partner assignments. And even though they hadn't officially announced their romantic coupling, Maggie and Nolan would be anointed a professional item on that date—much to my chagrin.

Before all this emotional activity, the convent broke for a week—a summer holiday for both the staff and students. The season brought recruiting weather to Tehachapi, and the valley became easy to love. Warm breezes rustled through waxy oak leaves, and the perennial grass had finally dried out into a gorgeous golden carpet. I guilted Maggie into spending one resplendent afternoon hiking around the windmill farm we'd passed through on arrival.

The sun had just begun to set when we reached the ridgeline, and fan blades swooped overhead. At the apex, Maggie regained cellular service and her phone began to buzz.

Three voicemails. All Nolan.

My sister called him back without retrieving them. With the phone pressed to her ear, she turned to face the desert, where great currents of air tussled at her obsidian tresses. I wasn't sure which was putting tears in her eyes—the wind or the conversation.

From what I could hear, Nolan had been in a bicycle accident back home. His hip had been involved, and Maggie asked about X-rays. Over the howl of the desert gales, I could hear him shouting that while the doctors would need multiple images to confirm, there didn't appear to be any permanent damage to his femur or pelvis.

"Thank you," she murmured.

It would be years before I understood why she closed that call with gratitude.

CHAPTER 16

I was in residency in Saipan when the Limit took its first country.

I'd just closed the clinic after a lackluster consultation with a 2* couple. They'd been reluctant from the outset—suspicious of the strings that must be attached to free government money—and I'd bumbled the pitch. When they walked out the door, I'd let go an audible groan.

Three more failed consultations and I'd be put on probation.

To nurse my disappointment, I took myself to one of the hotel bars. I'd only been in the South Pacific three weeks, and beachside sundowners hadn't yet lost their appeal. But I'd left the clinic in such a rush that I hadn't noticed it was only 4:00 p.m. I didn't need to risk developing a reputation as a lush—even if I was only ordering Shirley Temples.

To kill time, I considered calling my parents. A dose of mother's gentle reassurance would go a long way in improving my mood; my father would lend further assistance with a good joke or two. But those therapies would have to wait: considering the time difference, my call would startle the two from the depths of their predawn sleep. They'd certainly think someone had died, or had at least been grievously injured, and that just didn't seem fair. Not when the wound was only to my pride.

In the end, misery outmatched my modesty, and I ignored the hour to take a seat at the resort's thatched-roof bar. While I wasn't quite a regular, the bartender knew I always took my drinks virgin. When he wasn't slinging drinks, Patrick worked on one of the military barges that anchored semipermanently off the leeward coast. Despite being great symbols of military prowess, the loitering boats signaled a relative peace. The ships only moved off-island when there was trouble—either with the weather or North Korea. The crew got paid to loiter, too, but the salary wasn't much, and many of them took part-time side hustles to fund their vices. Drinking problems and divorce settlements didn't pay for themselves, Patrick noted.

Though the skies were clear on that unassuming Thursday, a thick Chamorro man took my order—not Patrick.

"I'll have a Dark 'n Stormy, please."

The man scanned me top to bottom. My South Pacific visage helped me at times like these; I looked more like a local than the rest of the patrons, and he recognized that.

"You want a rum floater?"

Patrick knew I was underage and wouldn't have offered, but in my current state, I wasn't going to refuse. "Sure." I sighed. "Patrick take the night off?"

"Not exactly. The ship recalled him early this morning."

My eyes darted to the horizon, which was all I saw.

"The whole fleet left around lunch." The bartender poured more rum over the ginger ale and passed me my drink. "That Supreme Leader must be up to something again."

A sun-dried tomato of a man three seats over took the bartender's assertion as a challenge. "I'd put money on another long-range missile launch."

After sweeping up a flush of abandoned napkins and ornamental toothpicks, the bartender agreed to take the bet. From the far side of the cabana, another churlish barnacle chimed in. "You can put me down for 'underground nuclear test.'"

"I'll take your money too." The bartender chuckled.

The tomato raised his empty pint glass. "Then what are you thinking, Francisco?"

The bartender poured himself a swallow of beer and downed it. "American prisoner execution."

The truth would arrive in the next day's headlines. And when it did, no man at that bar could collect any winnings, because "overnight capitulation of a ruthless dictator" was a wager no one had made. Word had gotten out that the Supreme Leader's firstborn son was a naught, and the subsequent coup brought down the country in less than a day.

※

When Theo and I had submitted our preference list for residencies, the Northern Mariana Islands hadn't been on it. I hadn't spent much time on that list at all, really; Theo just told me to pick the first three sunshine states I could think of. At the time, I was sure I'd run out my luck pulling Theo as a partner—there was no way my winning streak could continue. But someone at Headquarters correctly interpreted my haphazard selection of "California, Florida, Puerto Rico" as a general desire for sand and surf and then booked us on a twenty-four-hour flight to the other side of the world. The face value of the tickets—$2,000—was more money than I'd ever seen in my bank account.

For all intents and purposes, residency in Saipan constituted a humanitarian mission. While the airport could have fronted a 1950s postcard with its art deco terminal and cinematic scenery, the rest of the island looked unfortunately familiar. Neglected storefronts and overgrown vegetation fringed deteriorating roads. Blue-tarp roofs topped storm-damaged homes, and feral dogs strayed through empty parking lots. An insidious rust pervaded any surface it could find.

Saipan was more like Hawley than I was ready to admit.

After collecting my bags, I waited on Theo, who'd arrived a few days before to manage logistics. He'd picked up the keys for our apartments, fueled the rental Jeep, and stocked our pantries—all in a day's work for a good technician, and Theo was the best. The only son of Korean immigrants, Theo had enlisted in the Mendelia to spite his parents, who wanted him to become a doctor, a lawyer—some kind of upstanding professional with a braggadocious career. But Theo was far too relaxed for such a future. Much like the rest of us, Theo's definition of success had been completely reconfigured by the Limit, and he found himself far more concerned with good times and good people than good money and good prospects.

Theo had been on-island just long enough to give me a basic tour, the purpose of which was more about keeping me awake than providing helpful information. If I had any hope of acclimating to the eleven-hour time change, I needed to stay up—we were slated to start practice in just two days.

The first place he drove me was the clinic. Like most Mendelic facilities, it was nestled into the old post office—and unfortunately so. Calling the decrepit facility "shabby" would've been generous—the building was so run down, I couldn't imagine impregnating a woman there in good faith. Someone else must have felt the same, because tacked to the door was a handwritten note:

Mendel Services relocated to 3108 Sugar King Road.

Bleary eyed, it took me a minute to form a coherent question. "Is that even allowed?"

"If it isn't, who's going to stop us?" Theo chuckled. "Believe me, I don't think anyone here is going to mind."

We then made our way to the address listed on the door, where broad-leafed breadfruit trees engulfed a pink stucco cottage with a Spanish-tile roof. I couldn't imagine the government approving of such a whimsical abode, and I rubbed my eyes in disbelief. "Does the attending live here?"

"Dr. Fontanez? No. This is the clinic. Dr. Fontanez rents it on her own dime, though, since the post office is such a dump."

I tried to blink away my confusion, but Theo could tell I was in no condition for more complicated conversations.

"Let's get you to bed, Charlie."

After what felt like a week's worth of sleep, Theo and I began employing the skills we'd spent the last two years acquiring. We'd be supervised from afar by an attending Mendel who worked primarily on Guam, the busiest clinic in the region. Hot-tempered and hard-boiled, Dr. Fontanez knew exactly what she wanted as well as how to get it. She had good reason for such a ferocious approach. As the only fully licensed practitioner in the region, she served all three Pacific territories as well as some of the freely associated states, no doubt spending more time on airplanes than in consultations. We'd been detailed there as her reinforcements.

Dr. Fontanez flew in to orient us to the clinic. An hour after her flight landed, she called us into the Mendel's office and sat us in front of the consultation desk. The space had been converted from a teenager's bedroom and still burned hot with the scent of disinfectant. The Mendelia preached asepsis—it permeated all aspects of the institutional culture. But the approach fell flat in high-contact Saipan, where people hugged and kissed, shared food and beds and clothing, and communed with the earth and the sea just as frequently as they did with each other. Whether it was their faith in God or their enjoyment of the present, no one here seemed concerned about the next century, the next generation, or even the next month. Many simply ignored the crisis, Dr. Fontanez told us, which is why so few people had been reproductively screened. Even fewer sought Mendel services.

It was our job to change that.

"Rural assignments can be risky for new Mendels," Dr. Fontanez added. "We're on an island with a very culturally connected people. As mainlanders, you'll be physically and socially isolated. It can make fresh Mendels peevish." Her eyes slanted in our direction. "It happened to my technician during our residency in the Navajo Nation. Clients didn't trust him, he couldn't make friends, and when he finally got a date with a young woman in town, the tribal leaders almost ran him off. His restlessness matured into complete rage by the end."

Theo's face contorted. "So what happened?"

"After a bevy of client complaints, he was recalled to Headquarters and unceremoniously terminated. I'm still looking to repartner."

Dr. Fontanez turned to face the rear window, which glimpsed the backyard. A gentle breeze ruffled through the pearlescent blossoms of the overgrown plumeria tree. "As you can tell, we don't have a lot to work with here," she continued more sedately. "You're going to have to treat the clients in front of you with the tools at hand. I never want to hear you say 'if only' in front of the clients."

I couldn't tell if I was being intimidated or consoled. Either way, Theo and I seemed to have our work cut out for us.

Paradise, it seemed, was only a mirage.

⚭

Per Maggie's plan, my sister and Nolan deployed to the Marshall Islands, another facility under Dr. Fontanez's jurisdiction. And while the Northern Mariana Islands felt distant from the continent, the Marshall Islands may as well have been disconnected. In Saipan, if you ordered anything by mail, delivery took weeks—but it did eventually arrive. The same couldn't be said for Majuro.

I called Maggie on my way to work. "Did you get Mom's care package yet?"

My sister and I had been at our posts for almost two months, but I still found myself needing to call her every day. Even though she'd put an ocean between us, she'd always be my security blanket.

"I give it 50:50 odds for making it through customs," Maggie laughed. "Then 60:40 for falling off the delivery truck and maybe another 75:25 for the mailman helping himself to a snack."

I tried pulling my apartment door shut, but the lock wouldn't engage. The ambient humidity had warped the doorframe again, and there was nothing I could do but leave it slightly ajar. When I looked down the walkway, half the other apartments looked the same.

"Well, you're not missing much. Unless you enjoy pine-scented hockey pucks."

Maggie scoffed. "Is Aunt Frankie shilling bath products again?"

I shuffled down the concrete stairwell into the parking lot. The afternoon trade winds hadn't kicked up yet, and the muggy air stifled any zest I had for work.

"Not exactly." I sighed. "In her note, Mom says she knows we don't have much time to cook or clean, so she sent a few things to make it smell like home."

"Chocolate chip cookies?"

"With a little bit of sea salt. But the poor things didn't stand a chance against delivery delays and pine-scented dryer sheets."

Conifer-smelling laundry products weren't the only things that needed import. Planks of pine, cedar, and fir—while plentiful in places like Pennsylvania—all arrived by boat from the continent. And often too. Typhoons and tropical storms did quite a bit of regular damage, and the two-by-fours needed for reconstruction had to come from the mainland. And while Saipan treasured its connection to America—they loved their military boats and war history just as much as their chain restaurants and outlet malls—the Marshall Islands resented it, an artifact of the nuclear testing conducted there. Their animosity toward American science and government left Maggie wondering whether the Marshallese wanted a Mendel at all.

"It's a good thing I look like the people here," she said. "Or else I'd be just as sunk as the Bikini Atoll."

During those first few weeks in the South Pacific, Maggie entertained my need for small talk. But as time wore on, ambition replaced her hospitality, and work became all she could talk about. Her passion toed the line of obsession—but it was hard to argue with her results. She'd already convinced a couple in their fifties to procreate; the payout would pay off their mortgage. Maggie also persuaded a much younger woman into having a second child, but with a partner other than her husband.

These were serious victories for someone only in their second month, and Maggie was already earning back eggs.

I, on the other hand, failed to thrive. Just like in training, I found it difficult to insert myself so intimately into other people's lives. While I worked with several couples who seemed quite happy to let me make their reproductive decisions for them, I found myself unprepared for that kind of trust. Who was I to choose how children were produced? Why was I the right person?

At the end of our third month, I picked up a voicemail from Maggie announcing that she and Nolan would be coming to Saipan the next day. I bristled at the impromptu visit, unsure how she could afford such a luxury when our salaries barely covered the brow-raising costs of Pacific Island living. But as much as I tried to find fault with my sister's impractical purchase, in the end, delight overpowered my disapproval.

I'd get to see her.

At curbside, I flung myself into my sister's embrace. As she rocked me and stroked my hair, I felt a comfort I hadn't in weeks. Months. Ages, it felt like. I could have luxuriated in her grasp for hours, but people—including Nolan—were starting to stare.

I pulled back. After a minute's worth of compression, I could barely exhale my question.

"Maggie! What are you doing here?" I asked. "Ugh, that flight must have cost—"

"Stop," she interrupted. "I missed you. And Dr. Fontanez asked me to come teach you a thing or two, so the Mendelia are picking up the tab."

The explanation took me aback. Sure, I was blundering through my work, but calling in my own sister to provide remedial training bordered on humiliation. If I didn't miss her so much, I would've taken offense.

We piled into the Jeep and I turned the ignition. "What do you guys want to eat?"

"Burgers. Cheap, greasy, oversalted burgers," Maggie said, forcing the buckle on her seat belt. "God, I never thought I'd miss fast food."

I caught Nolan's eye through the rearview mirror. "You good with that?"

He flicked down his sunglasses. "As long as you've got some antacids at your place. I'm going to eat way too much way too quickly and not mind regretting it later."

The nearest drive-thru was ten minutes down the highway. Two bags, ten burgers, and three milkshakes later, we made for a scenic overlook to overindulge in peace. I took us halfway up the island's central mountain for a view of the western shore, where the ledge was lined with seat-size boulders. We laid out the food across the Jeep's hood and settled in. Maggie and Nolan ate like they'd been starving, but I couldn't focus on the food until I knew more about their visit.

"So what does Dr. Fontanez want you to teach me?"

Maggie peeled the wrapper from her burger. "Nothing you don't already suspect," she said as she chewed. "Confidence. Bedside manner. Customer service."

My hands dropped to my lap. "Am I really struggling that badly?"

She was just opening her half-full mouth when Nolan broke in. "No," he said. "Well, probably not. It makes for a good excuse, though."

"What do you mean by that?"

"I think Dr. F. wants to check up on Maggie." He took a long draw from his milkshake. "No one's ever seen such a new Mendel perform so well so early, right, babe?"

Maggie shuddered at the endearment. Her mouth was too full for reprimand, but her eyes made do.

"Sorry, *miss*," he mocked. "But I'm sure Dr. Fontanez thinks we're up to something we shouldn't be."

Maggie had gone back to the Jeep for more food. I called back to her over my shoulder. "As the attending, I think it's pretty reasonable for her to be curious."

She returned with three burgers and passed them around. "Except she's not curious. She's dubious."

"Try envious," Nolan scoffed, snatching at a napkin swept away by the wind. "Dr. Fontanez does not seem like the type who likes to be upstaged."

CHAPTER 17

Regardless of their reason, Maggie and Nolan took advantage of their visit to Saipan. They spent their first few days stocking up on things and experiences that were hard to find in Majuro: shopping, restaurants, entertainment. Maggie and I even woke up at 3:00 a.m. so that we could call our father together before his swing shift. By day four, Maggie even managed to talk about something besides work. There was no amount of time, however, that could remedy Nolan's new skin tone. The sheer volume of freckles he'd accumulated made me wonder if he ever wore sunscreen. But other than his appearance, neither he nor Maggie had changed much since graduation.

They still felt like home.

Over the course of the week, Dr. Fontanez had several meetings with my sister and Nolan, many of which were brief and none interesting. Unsatisfied with what little she'd gotten out of them together, Dr. Fontanez decided to divide and conquer and cornered Maggie for an individual "chat."

While the rest of us knew Maggie was being interrogated, none of us worried. Dr. Fontanez and Maggie were evenly matched in terms of audacity and endurance. Cut loose from responsibility, Theo, Nolan, and I piled into the Jeep to find a way to occupy ourselves.

Nolan took the back seat again. "Have you two explored any of the historical stuff on the island?"

Theo shook his head and shifted into reverse. "Sorry, man, not really my thing."

"Dude, I've been talking to some of the old heads on my island, and they said that some *real* crazy stuff happened here during the war. Know anyone who could show us around?"

"Maybe." Theo seemed bored by the prospect but was far too polite to show it. "Is there something specific you'd like to see?"

Nolan pitched the expedition like a seasoned tour guide. "On the north side of the island, there's an abandoned radar site, an old pillbox, and remnants of a jail. Not to mention a suicide cliff where the Japanese jumped to avoid capture by the Americans."

Theo cringed. "Yeah, I've heard some of the guys at the hospital talk about that. I'll ask around."

Within hours, Theo found an aged phlebotomist willing to take us around. I declined the invitation. With the boys otherwise occupied, I'd get some more time alone with my sister. And while I understood it was natural and appropriate for her to spend most of her time with someone besides me, I still wanted to recapture the intimacy of sisterhood—even just for an evening.

After dropping Theo and Nolan at the hospital to meet their guide, I returned to the clinic to collect my sister. Having successfully defeated her inquisition, Maggie requested sushi. As a minor destination for Japanese tourists, Saipan had a decent selection of restaurants to satisfy the homesick. But without a reservation, the hostess could only find room for us at a sidewalk table. Even though we'd broil in the late-afternoon heat, we took it—counting on each bite of cold fish to offer a mouthful of relief.

Despite the reprieve, my sister grew increasingly uneasy over the course of the meal. I could tell there was something she didn't want to tell me, and we danced our conversation around whatever she didn't want to share. It felt like that night in Tehachapi when she tried to avoid telling me she was about to put thousands of miles between us. In the absence of tequila, I could only hope that a bellyful of fatty tuna would lower her guard.

It did.

Maggie exhaled deeply while swirling some wasabi into her soy sauce. "I need to talk to you about Nolan," she began.

Between bites of marbled salmon, I mumbled, "Sure, go ahead." There was nothing she could say that was going to surprise me. She and Nolan had obviously coupled, and in a much deeper way than Mendelic partnership. The real mystery was why she had to hide that from me.

Maggie laid down her chopsticks and heaved out what was bothering her. "I need you to know that we're together. More than professionally."

Unimpressed, I continued chewing.

"I think you know he's loved me for a long time," she continued. "And, well, I'm starting to reciprocate."

A twinge of jealousy twisted my nerves. But Nolan loved my sister, I reminded myself. And he deserved love too.

That's what a friend would say.

"Mags, that must feel great," I answered. I popped a California roll in my mouth to avoid having to elaborate.

"It does," she said, but her fingers fanned up over the edge of her plate. "But I don't want it to distract from my work."

I almost felt badly that my sister's first instinct was to guard against judgment in the name of the Mendelia. "Well, I'm going to hope that it does."

Her mouth hung open like a dying carp.

"I'm not completely heartless, you know. You both could use a little 'extracurricular activity.'"

Maggie blanched at the suggestion.

I winked. "Just a little. It'll be good for you."

We returned to my apartment to find Nolan and Theo feasting on noodles and a few cold beers.

Nolan drummed on the patio's wicker table with alcohol-fueled gusto. "Ladies, ladies, ladies! I've got to tell you what I've learned!"

"Don't tell me you found a genetic unicorn in the recesses of some Chamorro war relic," Maggie taunted.

"I didn't! I found something far more irrelevant and delightfully inconsequential." Nolan made room on the wicker couch for Maggie and gestured for her to take a seat.

He used his index finger to drill into the cushion. "It was right here, on this very island, that one of the war's most exciting new devices was manufactured. An innovation! An invention! A feather in the cap of the United States Marine Corps!"

Nolan grabbed a pen to scribble something on the back of his takeout menu. The doodle was barely discernible as some kind of windmill. He pushed the drawing in my direction. "I present to you," he projected, "the *Saipanese Windwasher*."

He looked around at our smug, expectant smiles and continued.

"If necessity is the mother of invention, then creativity must be its father! Never mind the atomic weapons that passed through these islands—no, American ingenuity is truly exemplified by this novel combination of barrel, crankshaft, and propeller."

Maggie and I looked at each other and then back at him.

"I don't get it," we said simultaneously.

"Ladies, it's a rudimentary washing machine!" He gestured toward the jungle. "Can you imagine beating back enemy combatants through this oppressive thicket of vines, fighting through unrelenting sun and salt and rain, only to have to think about washing your clothes?"

He stood up and turned his patio chair into a lectern.

"On one hand, uniforms are important. They create a sense of belonging, of pride, of control—they make soldiers feel like they are part of something. Something larger than themselves! On the other, what's the point of clean socks when you've got disease and sharks and kamikaze Japanese to worry about . . ."

His gaze drifted into an individual void as he trailed off.

Maggie gathered up the boys' empty cans from the table. "Nothing like a good repetitive task to take your mind off certain death."

It was a truth that sucked all the oxygen from the room until Nolan snapped back to recapture the more jovial mood.

"And that's just one thing I learned on the tour! More inane facts and useless trivia available on request."

We filled the rest of that night with more beers and more stories. The neighbors let us borrow an old boom box and a few cassette tapes, so the Beatles' greatest hits sputtered in the background while we played cards and slung jokes. It wasn't until the stars had begun to fade that Maggie and Nolan retired to my bedroom. Theo looked ready to excuse himself as well, but as he reached for the door, he hesitated.

"Can I see you outside for a minute?" Theo spied the bedroom door. "It's about work."

I followed him out onto the concrete walkway. The advent of dawn was silent but for the chorus of native insects. Theo said nothing while he waited for the door to close, then looked to the windows to confirm they were shut.

"Okay, it's not about work. It's about Nolan. But I didn't want to say it in front of them."

Theo's eyes darted about. "At the end of our tour, Nolan asked Mateo, my phlebotomist friend, to take us to the sweatshops."

"Excuse me?" I coughed, certain I'd heard something wrong.

"I know," he continued. "Mateo's too nice a guy to say anything, so we went, but it got really weird."

"What did he want to see?"

"Everything. Nolan asked about the place's history, how many different garments they produce, where they get their materials. I think the guy in charge thought he was some sort of advance man for Nike or something." Theo folded his arms and took a deep breath. "Nolan spent the most time in the dye rooms, though. That was too much for me—those chemicals really freak me out."

I shook my head in disbelief. "I don't understand."

"Me neither." Theo shrugged. "But I thought you should know."

Like the windwasher, textile factories were a relic of Saipan's past. As a territory, Saipan wasn't required to abide by domestic minimum wage standards, and the island thrived on making clothing that could be stamped as "Made in the USA" but sold at the price of "Made in China." When labor reform became trendy, the industry collapsed. What few factories remained were completely dilapidated; their laborers, undocumented Vietnamese migrants.

Why Nolan wanted to bear witness to this, I did not know. After Theo retreated to his quarters, I began clearing the napkins and bottles and take-out containers and tried not to think about what he'd shared. Instead, I focused on savoring the last few moments of a night that had otherwise been a gem—the first and only evening we hadn't talked about the Limit.

Friendship, for once, had eclipsed the crisis.

It was a glimpse into what our lives could have been.

CHAPTER 18

Maggie and Nolan rose early the next morning. The angry light of daybreak streaked through the blinds while my two miscreant guests opened and shut the cabinets in search of breakfast. It wasn't long before Maggie popped her head over the back of the couch.

"Charlie," she whispered, awaiting a sign of wakefulness. I slipped my hand out from under the blanket and waved.

"I'm taking Nolan to the hospital."

I bolted upright. "Is he all right?"

"Nothing urgent," she assured. "Just his back. He's too tall for the laboratory equipment in Majuro, so his posture's been terrible. We're going to get him checked out since Saipan has more specialists."

Grateful not to have to address an emergency, I withdrew into my cocoon. A trip to the hospital would take Maggie and Nolan at least half the day—and I was glad of it. While I loved their company, I'd had more fun in the previous five days than I'd had in the previous five months. They didn't need me as much as I needed sleep.

I figured I could doze until lunchtime, at which point Maggie and Nolan would startle me awake with the slam of the door, the call of my name, and the rustling of bags of hot food. But that wasn't what woke me.

It was my cell phone, which trilled obnoxiously just two hours later.

Maggie cut in before I could even manage a greeting. "Charlie, you've got to come to the hospital right away."

"But I thought you said it wasn't an emergency?"

"Just get in the car," she begged. "I'll meet you at the front gate."

I pulled on some leggings and a cardigan. Long sleeves weren't usually necessary in the local climate, but they were in the hospital, which was kept inordinately cold. If I was going to be there awhile—and by Maggie's tone, that seemed possible—I wouldn't regret the coverage. I tied my unwashed hair into a sloppy bun and stuffed my stockinged feet into my favorite clogs.

The hospital was twenty minutes from our building, near the most urbane parts of the island. Built into the foothills of the dormant volcano, then painted white, the sprawling terraced three-story complex gave the impression of bleached coral. When I pulled through the main gate, I found Maggie standing beneath a flame tree, its slender branches thrusting crimson petals high into the cloudless sky. She'd tucked one of the blossoms behind her ear, which made me think whatever she had called about was less of an emergency than she'd intimated.

She leaned in through the passenger-side window. "Thanks for coming. I had one of the maintenance guys save you a parking spot." I followed her finger to a heavyset man with a half sleeve of tribal tattoos climbing into an old-model pickup. When he noticed us, the janitor gave Maggie an encouraging thumbs-up; she hollered effusive thanks in his direction even though his windows were closed.

That's when she hopped into the Jeep. Somehow, Maggie managed to slam the door so energetically I thought she might tip us over. I glared at her, then puttered over to take the parking spot. No sooner had I shifted into park than my sister bounded out of the vehicle with the same enthusiasm as when she'd entered. Flustered and perturbed, I moved slower and needed more than a few moments to gather my purse and lock the doors.

"Maggie, what is going on?" I pressed, still shoving the keys into my bag.

She brought her fists to her chest, where they shook with delight. "We're getting married, Charlie!"

"What? Here?"

She grabbed me by the elbow and led me inside.

"I got bored in the waiting room, so I started wandering around. Eventually I found the chapel and spoke with the minister. After I explained everything, he agreed to do the ceremony!"

"Everything?"

I needed to hear this justification myself.

"That Nolan and I have been in love for years." She swooned, dodging visitors as we walked. "And since we're based in Majuro and you're our closest family that this would be the perfect occasion!"

I winced. Just the night before, Maggie had been reluctant to talk much about her relationship with Nolan. Now she was ready to marry him? Memories of my mother's didactic tirades about Aunt Frankie's compulsive indiscretions flooded back into my mind. How my sister escaped such inundation eluded me.

Instead, glee teemed in Maggie's big brown eyes as she looked to me for approval.

As much as I disliked the situation, she wasn't doing anything wrong. My sister hadn't done anything to deserve my ire, and I chided myself for the cynicism. While it was easy for me to cast Maggie's decision as rash, perhaps I just needed to see it as uninhibited. Passionate. Daring. The same things that made her successful as a Mendel might also support her relationship.

Maybe I had something to learn.

"I'm sure the minister was happy to hear you weren't pregnant," I hedged, still not quite believing what I was talking myself into.

We both snorted. By that time, she and I had covered half a mile of hallway and still hadn't arrived. I stopped her in the middle of the corridor and took her hands.

"And you're sure you want to do this?"

"I am," she said. "I've taken a real shine to him, Charlie. He's doing so much for me. As a technician, but also as"—she dropped my hands and returned to walking—"a partner."

What should have been an easy sentence to finish seemed somehow painful. We rounded a corner to find an unlabeled metal door. She held it open for me.

"Okay, this is it."

"It" was a classroom with old linoleum tile and fluorescent yellow lighting. A few mismatched pews sat before a shoddy podium, and a simple crucifix hung against the farthest wall.

I suppressed my objections. "Nolan's excited too?"

"Oh yes. This was his idea," she said, snapping back to her original vigor. "He's got to be close to being done by now. We should go find him."

Maggie and I retraced our steps back to radiology. After taking seats in the waiting area, we chatted about the details of the shotgun-style ceremony until Nolan emerged from the treatment area. Still tucking in his shirt, he scanned the room for a familiar face and lit up when he found Maggie's.

"Can they do it?"

She threw her arms around him. "They will!"

Maggie turned back to me, a smile threatening to burst her rosy cheeks. "I'm so glad you're here."

"Me too," I offered, looking past Maggie to Nolan. "How's the back?"

The energy in his smile matched my sister's, but somehow it intensified as he answered my question. "Needs more tests."

The optimism unsettled me. I'm sure it must have shown on my face, but Nolan never noticed—his eyes remained locked on my sister's.

"Let's do this."

And they did. Completely and totally saturated with reckless romance, Nolan and my sister made their way to the chapel. On the way, Maggie snatched some flowers from one of the nursing stations while her beau checked his reflection in the mirror over a handwashing sink.

Twenty minutes later, they were married.

I was the only witness.

When the three of us returned to the Jeep, Maggie and Nolan took the back seat together so they could hold hands. Nolan placed the marital paperwork under the passenger seat, out of his new bride's way. I keyed the ignition.

"Sir, madam—may I escort you back to the honeymoon suite?"

After a hearty laugh, quiet bliss pervaded the car. My sister tucked into Nolan's shoulder—she was still coming down from the impassioned high of a spontaneous island elopement. Nolan kissed the top of her head and gazed out the window, halfway spellbound himself.

"Ladies, as excited as I am about what just happened, I think we should keep it between us for the time being. I'm glad you got to be part of it, Charlie, but getting anyone else involved right now is just going to be a headache."

"I agree," Maggie added, as if on cue. "You know what they say—if Headquarters wanted you to have a spouse, they would have issued you one."

I pulled onto the main road. "But at the convent, they told us the Mendelia allow marriage."

"They do." Maggie nodded. "The Mendelia profess their disdain for relationships between scientists, but it's got real benefits for them."

Nolan swooped in. "Yeah. I mean, what do they expect, sending a couple of twentysomethings off to the far-flung corners of the earth? Better we cavort with each other than the locals."

Maggie reclined into Nolan's lap so she could pop her feet out the window. "Or worse, the clients," she groaned. "I hear it happens more often than you'd think."

Nolan stroked her curls. "Marriage is convenient—until, of course, it isn't," he added. "Remember Hugo and Clarice from the convent? They just got divorced last month."

I hit the blinker to turn onto the beachfront highway. "How do you know?"

"You do know I have friends besides you two, right?"

"So the Mendelia just sent them away from each other?" Separating scientists seemed like an incredible waste of training.

"Clarice got to stay at the clinic. As the Mendel, she has rank. Hugo was relocated three hundred miles away before the court even finalized the paperwork."

Maggie blew out an exasperated sigh. "Can we not talk about divorce when we've only been married ten minutes?"

"Sorry, love. I just think getting the Mendelia involved is a bad idea."

Nolan was right. If Maggie's work was already under scrutiny, marrying her technician wouldn't help.

"Plus, it'll be more fun to have a big celebration when we get back to the States," Nolan continued. "Residency will be over, we'll finally be making some money—we can throw a great party."

A mile up the highway, we stopped at a roadside shack for celebratory smoothies. While I thought it a shame we couldn't honor the occasion more festively, the newlyweds were too enamored with each other to miss champagne and caviar. Nothing but the ring of Nolan's phone could interrupt their joy.

He put the call on speaker and laid the phone on the table.

"Mr. Kincade? It's Dr. Matuna from the hospital."

"Yes, sir."

"I have good news and bad news," the doctor clucked. "I don't see anything obvious on the images of your spine we took this morning. This is the good news—no major problems with your disks or vertebrae. But considering your persistent pain, I'd like to refer you for a CT."

Much to my surprise, Nolan pumped his fist in excitement, which he quickly contained. "And the bad news?"

"The bad news is that we don't have that machine here on the island—I'm going to have to send you to Guam."

They exchanged a few administrative details before Nolan ended the call.

Maggie grinned from ear to ear. "This is great news."

"Yes, and I'm due to provide the Mendelia a new sample next month, so the timing's excellent," Nolan continued. The two toasted their Styrofoam cups with a squeal.

"I don't get it," I finally interjected.

The paramours startled, then dropped their eyes to the floor.

"Well, uh, if I've got to go to Guam for this scan, I can just swing by the clinic and make my deposit while I'm there," Nolan said, swiveling his empty cup on the table. "It'll save shipping from Majuro, which is a disaster most of the time."

Maggie bit her lip. "So, Charlie, in terms of the reception, do you think we should have it in Hawley or . . ."

Not wanting to spoil our last night together, I let my sister continue with her redirection. Whatever she and Nolan were up to, they didn't want me to know, and I didn't have time to find out. Not with them leaving the next day. So instead of prosecuting the truth, I let Maggie expound upon dresses, the guest list, and menu options. The conversation carried us back to my apartment, and as we pulled in, Nolan spotted Theo emerging from his unit.

Nolan stood up to shout from over the roll bar. "Theo! Maggie and I got married!"

My technician barely realized that he was being addressed and searched for the source of the voice. I spun around toward the back seat.

"I thought you said we weren't supposed to tell anyone!"

Nolan smirked. "Don't tell anyone!" he hollered again.

In a more reasonable tone, he addressed me directly. "We have to tell him. It wouldn't be fair to leave you with no one to gossip with."

Theo hustled down the stairs. "Well," he started, without a single note of surprise, "I suppose a celebration is in order."

Nolan leaned out the window. "Can you find us some beers?"

"You leave tomorrow, right? The people here love any excuse for a party. A wedding and a farewell should be more than enough."

Ninety minutes later, Theo's island connections dropped off an oversize cooler. Nolan and Theo heaved it into the Jeep along with some picnic blankets, and we made for the overlook one more time. No one knew it would be our last night together.

Except maybe Maggie.

CHAPTER 19

I drove the lovebirds back to the airport shortly before dawn. Their slackened mouths breathed heavily in unison as I turned onto the highway and clicked on the radio ever so slightly. The clearest station carried a story about the government diverting funds away from cancer research to better support Limit-breaking initiatives. Tragic that the people of today had to suffer for the babes of tomorrow—but necessary.

I turned it off. Without the lull of the host's hypnotic voice, Maggie surfaced into consciousness.

"Hey," she said, her eyelids still ringed by last night's eyeliner. "Thanks for the shuttle service."

"No problem," I replied. "Thank *you* for coming all this way. Any last tips for me before you go?"

When I glanced at my sister through the rearview mirror, I could see she was fighting back comment. Recollections of prom dresses, unfortunate shopping incidents, and critiques of my timidity flashed through my brain.

"Never mind," I interjected. "You don't need to say it."

Maggie reached past the headrest to squeeze my shoulder. "I won't say anything except . . . you might consider acting like me just a little bit more."

"Brazen, reckless, irreverent?"

"Yes, all of the things you don't like. But please note that I didn't say you had to *be* like me. You just have to *act* like it. And just a little. You'll be amazed at what it can do."

For once, her response felt like consolation rather than castigation. I gripped her fingers. "I'll try," I said. "I promise."

When I pulled up to the terminal, Maggie and Nolan poured themselves out of the car. After slinging their bags onto their backs and bringing me in for a few goodbye embraces, they tucked into each other and plodded through the airport's automatic doors. Doors that slid shut a little faster than I expected and cut short the last time I'd ever see them together.

The warm island morning was just cracking over the horizon as I trundled back home. The intensity of the daylight washed the sky white while the sun's golden yolk spilled out over the sea, foiling the crests of the low-slung waves. Beautiful, no doubt; but for me, common. The only thing I concerned myself with was getting back to bed. My shift at the clinic started at noon and would be full with every consultation I'd put off during my sister's visit.

While I went to bed knowing it wouldn't be an easy day, I completely underestimated exactly how punishing it would be.

The drive from my apartment to the clinic wasn't long. I could've walked, as Theo often did, but I needed the Jeep to run house calls later in the afternoon. The vehicle's body had accumulated some unfortunate rashes since we'd first picked it up—sunshine and sea spray had peeled away the topcoat on the hood, and the wheel wells had pimpled with rust. But parked alongside the humble cottage clinic, the homely Jeep looked appropriate—even comfortable. It, and I, might finally be fitting in.

In many ways, the clinic was still unmistakably a home. Its two bedrooms had been renovated into offices—one for the Mendel and counseling services, the other for the technician and labs—but the floors still bore scuffs from twin-size beds. Theo and I had filled the kitchenette with various creature comforts: a coffee machine, a toaster oven, a radio. The living room served as reception, and the vestiges of its previous life worked well to welcome our guests: a colorful braided rug spanned most of the floor, while dated wooden bookshelves framed the back window with charm. Theo had added a few potted plants for some liveliness; I couldn't be bothered to take care of one more living thing.

That afternoon, lethargy fogged my mind as I stared down at the desk. Concurrent needs overwhelmed me: I needed to peruse the appointment book, review the day's charts, and brew a new pot of coffee—and I couldn't decide which to do first. The ring of the clinic phone decided for me.

"Saipan Mendelia Clinic," I spluttered, still half-asleep.

"Dr. Tannehill? It's Dr. Fontanez."

Her voice was assertive and well caffeinated. After completing her investigation of my sister, Dr. Fontanez had deployed to Rota, another island in the Marianas archipelago. The people there only got Mendel services once a quarter, so her days would be busy and full. She couldn't afford to be on the phone for long, and probably wouldn't enjoy it.

"Good morning . . . uh, afternoon, Doctor. I'm . . . I'm reviewing the schedule—"

Dr. Fontanez interrupted before I even needed to bluff.

"Dr. Tannehill, a longtime patient of mine is bringing you a new baby today. They're flying in from Tinian. All you need to do is complete the registration forms and take some blood for screening. Make sure Theo is careful with the sample, though—we can't have this one contaminated."

Theo had dropped a swab during his first week, and Dr. Fontanez still hadn't forgotten.

"You can review the chart for background . . ." Dr. Fontanez faltered, distracted by the distant call of a client demanding her attention. "But you're going to have questions. I promise I'll get to them."

She hung up.

My stiffened brain tried vainly to interpret her directions. What she described seemed so routine that there should be no need to brief me, but yet she had called. I returned the phone to its cradle and my attention to the appointment book. "Dibrova" was scrawled in red ink across the 4:00 p.m. slot. Inside the desk, I found a matching chart five times larger than any I'd ever seen.

I restrained my interest. Two other appointments preceded the Dibrovas', and I still needed to prepare. My career was on the line. First, I had a 2:00 p.m. with a new couple, the Aguons. Preliminary intakes were always the simplest, and I felt confident that I could land this one. But my 3:00 p.m. would be more involved: Ms. Sablan was needy—she'd eat up most of our time with small talk, and then want more. With her on my docket, I wouldn't have any time to preview the massive stack of intrigue contained within the Dibrova file.

Unless I skipped coffee and dove right in.

Satisfying my curiosity would free up my mind and improve my focus on the other clients. Theo would agree, enabler that he was.

It was all the justification I needed.

I peeked inside the file. Inches of yellowed carbon copies splintered the folder's spine. More paper generally meant more pregnancies; by that measure, there had to be at least a dozen different children between these folds. But for as many pages as there were, the file was conspicuously devoid of particulars. Most of the forms were blank.

What little detail I could locate about the family was found in the cover sheet, which summarized the couple's background. Petro and Lesya Dibrova, 5* and 3* respectively. Ukrainian born. In 1970. A picture of them was clipped inside the folder—they looked handsome, happy, in love. Nothing shocked me until I scanned the list of pregnancies and needed to count on my fingers.

Twenty pregnancies. Fourteen live births. Ten children surviving past two years of age. The woman described by this file had spent the vast majority of her life pregnant. Thirteen of the children had been screened, and they'd all scored 2*—expected, given their mother's status. No further genetic assessments or sequencing had been conducted.

I pried my eyes from the specifics, which seemed troublesome, if not abusive. Six miscarriages was plenty but not excessive, considering the sheer number of pregnancies. Four children dying before age two was much more concerning. As I considered all of this, an unfamiliar car pulled into our front lot. The Aguons.

I closed the Dibrovas' folder and returned it to the desk. There was no way Theo hadn't noticed its peculiarities. I knew he'd been in early—Theo preferred to work both the lonesome hour of sunrise and the bustling minutes of sunset. The schedule afforded him the indulgence of luxuriously long lunch breaks—which was where he probably was at the moment.

But it was time for me to switch gears.

After a chorus of sunny greetings, I shuttled Bendison and Ina Aguon back into my personal office and began the consultation. They provided all their basic details eagerly, with him laughing often and her following with giggles. We spent more than a few minutes discussing their recent wedding: no sooner had the bride been kissed than her family began pestering them about starting a family.

"My uncle said we should come and talk to you," Bendison said. Though his voice was round with poise, he pressed his fingers together nervously. "That you might be able to get us some money or something?"

I donned a practiced, professional tone. "Don't be embarrassed. A lot of clients come to us for the very same reason. Have either of you been screened?"

Bendison perked up. "Yes, ma'am. Just like everyone else in the fifth grade. I'm a 1* and my wife's a 5*."

I cringed. Any children Bendison fathered would be naughts. According to policy, I was supposed to advise against this. It would be one thing if Ina was also a 1*, or even a 2*, but as a 5*, she'd be forfeiting valuable—if not critical—generations.

"That's helpful," I started. Unsure about how to deliver bad news, I reverted to the best option I thought possible. "Have you thought about using a donor?"

Bendison bristled. "Why? I'm not a naught."

I hadn't meant for the suggestion to be taken as an insult, and I stuttered as I tried to get back on message.

"I-I understand. But if Ina's eggs were fertilized by a higher-scoring sperm . . ."

He blew an angry breath out through his nose. "Look, ma'am, I don't know what you're suggesting, but we want to have children with *each other*, not some random guy."

"I know," I said, feeling my control over the conversation slip. "It's just that . . ."

Ina yanked it completely away by picking up her handbag. "I don't think we want to do this anymore," she said.

Bendison dogpiled on her refusal. "Yeah, we'll just take care of it ourselves."

My stomach lurched as the screen door slapped closed behind them.

As Bendison and Ina pulled out of our driveway, I realized I should've just supported their original plan to have a child together. If I'd just gotten them into our system, if I'd just focused on winning their trust, perhaps for their second or third child I could have suggested a donor. But the first was always emotional. With the first there was no reasoning.

I should have known.

Any probation the Mendelia would put me on would be brief. There was no reason to keep me in Saipan if I kept fumbling basic consultations. Two more strikes—all of which were possible with the number of cases I had that day—and I'd be back in Hawley.

I hadn't finished berating myself when Theo pushed through the door.

He set down a few carryout bags. "Did you see the file?"

"Yes," I said, and blinked back into the present.

As I struggled to switch subjects, an herbaceous perfume of hot pepper and mint hit my nose. Motsiyas. Theo produced the neatly packaged take-out box of savory chicken sausages from his bag and dropped it on my desk. He'd correctly predicted that I'd need something to soak up the previous night's follies.

Theo dug into a bowl of Spam-studded rice. "I know they told us we'd run into these kinds of things, but I never thought I'd see *twenty* pregnancies."

The taut casing of the sausage snapped as I bit through it. "Yeah. It's amazing she can even carry one anymore—her cervix should be incompetent. It's a wonder the babies don't just fall out."

"Maybe she's on constant bed rest," he snorted. "But with nine other kids? There's no way she can just put her feet up."

I packed my cheeks with more of the ground chicken and leafy greens. "So they're bringing in their youngest?"

Theo had taken a seat at the registration desk and was sifting through the file. "Yeah, for screening. There's no clinic on Tinian, so they have to come here—and this was the earliest he could get away. At least that's what Dr. Fontanez's note implies."

I couldn't shake the feeling that this was some kind of test. No one could actually *want* that many children.

"They've got to be pulling down at least ten thousand a month in benefits, right?"

Theo paused for some quick estimation. "I'd be surprised if it wasn't closer to twelve. This one will bring them close to fifteen."

I felt my eyes bulge. "You don't think they're extortionists, do you?"

"If they were, they wouldn't be living on Tinian. That place is a shithole. Most people there are just trying to make enough money to leave."

Theo was right. It was hard to make a life on Tinian, where the economy relied almost entirely on a casino. But the money that passed through the gambling house rarely touched the hands of anyone who actually lived there. Wealth came and went with midlevel Chinese executives who seemed to enjoy having their fortunes slowly eaten away by video poker machines. Since winnings were wired back directly to bank accounts in Shanghai, the casino hardly needed chips.

The crunch of gravel drew Theo to the front window, where afternoon sunlight still poured through the gauzy drapes.

"Looks like Ms. Sablan is rolling up. She just needs consultation, right?"

Before I could answer, Theo had gathered up the Dibrova paperwork and was retreating to his lab. "I'm going to dig into this file a bit more while you handle her."

He winked cheekily as he closed the door. "Good luck."

With the click of the latch, I recognized the real reason Theo had brought me lunch: prepayment of the apology he'd need for abandoning me to Ms. Dora Sablan. In my short tenure on Saipan, I'd already met with Dora at least a dozen times. She frequented the clinic every week and felt so comfortable in our space that she no longer knocked. Nor did she feel the need to manage her noise and scraped her handbag against the wall as she clopped into the living room. Dora also dressed just as loudly as she carried herself—that day, a canopy of hammered silver accessories spilled out over her tropically magenta dress; she'd even donned her bedazzled slippers.

As she showed herself in, Dora dropped an obscenely large sunbrella in the corner and hollered. "Ms. Charlie! I made fresh titiyas for you this morning! And I've got questions about a man!"

Even under the best of circumstances, Dora was a difficult client. She was never unfriendly, but her expectations were just as impractical as her outfits.

I emerged from my office quietly, hoping to recalibrate Dora's volume. "Good afternoon, Ms. Sablan," I whispered.

"Ms. Charlie, what do you think about me partnering with an albino midget from Tunisia?"

"The Mendelia"—I paused, unable to determine whether she was kidding—"would encourage it."

"Well, I regret to inform you that I haven't met that man yet." Dora winked, satisfied with her ruse. "But I did have a date with that new golf course manager. He has a full head of hair and a rare blood disorder."

What people now advertised as their most attractive qualities still astonished me.

"But he expected me to pay for dinner, seeing that *I* was the one who asked. And then didn't even walk me to my car!"

I sat down opposite her and settled in for a long conversation. "I'm sorry to hear that."

"I know most men my age have already had their fill of women, or at least relationships with 'em." She tapped her belly. "But I need a *real* father for these eggs of mine. Not just a good time."

Dora and I had spent many hours talking about her predicament. She was one of the few women on Saipan who'd chosen to defer childbearing: the financial incentive was especially attractive considering her 7* status. But Dora was also exceedingly picky when it came to men—inconvenient when pickings were already slim. Chamorro men and women tended to couple early and breed immediately. Her personal choices deviated too far from these norms and alienated her from most potential partners.

But a 7*? At forty-five? Her windfall would contain more figures than her zip code if she could only pick someone. But even that kind of money wouldn't be able to buy Dora the one thing she wanted most.

Love.

Dora continued to twitter along merrily, stringing together tidbits of local gossip into one continuous monologue. While there was no hurrying Ms. Sablan, my patience was draining through a hole the size of the Dibrova file, and I found myself checking my watch. Ms. Sablan noticed my distraction and let fly the question that had truly brought her in that day.

"Ms. Charlie, how much longer should I wait?"

She'd caught me unprepared, and for once, honesty slipped past my guardrails. "If you want a good man, Dora, forever. But if you want a child, not much longer."

Loneliness pooled in her eyes.

"We can always use a donor," I reminded her.

"Ms. Charlie, I do beg your pardon, but I'm starting to think I need a matchmaker more than a Mendel."

She was, of course, exactly right. I couldn't manage a reply—only a regretful smile as Dora showed herself out. Theo heard the front door close and opened his simultaneously.

"Doesn't sound like we'll be seeing her again."

While Theo bore no affection for Dora, he delivered his prognosis mournfully. He knew how important it was to keep clients like Ms. Sablan, both for the Mendelia and for me. I'd lost five clients in as many weeks, and my career now hung in the balance.

Dora's departure redoubled my concern with the Dibrova case. I needed a win—or to at least prevent another loss. My job—my whole future—depended on it. Theo looked like he could see the anxiety percolating through me. He pulled over the chair. "We have ten minutes before Petro arrives. Here's what I've learned.

"Lesya miscarried her first six pregnancies long before she and her husband even arrived on Guam. When they did, they sought Mendel care. They managed four live births after that, but all of those children died before reaching two years of age. I found notes about a criminal investigation, but no conclusive results. The Dibrovas didn't have a viable child until their relocation to Tinian in 1999. Lesya has delivered a healthy child every year since."

Theo capped his diatribe with the detail he found most peculiar of all.

"They've seen Dr. Fontanez exclusively."

CHAPTER 20

The scrape of a battered yellow taxi van's arrival interrupted Theo's briefing. A useful alarm, really. Theo and I crouched before the front window to glimpse our incoming clients. While I wanted to witness what condition Lesya was in after weathering twenty pregnancies, the only thing I could really see were hands inside the vehicle passing the driver cash.

After yanking open the sliding door, a lanky, disheveled man stepped out. Cradling an infant in his arms, Petro looked underslept but not unkempt—not at all unlike the many new parents we often saw. While the driver unloaded a single backpack from the trunk, Petro reached back into the vehicle to coax out another passenger. The woman he brought forward, however, was not the woman I expected. Not a woman at all. As the driver closed the rear hatch, Petro offered his arm to a school-age girl as she cautiously stepped down from the minivan.

Once she'd steadied herself, Petro slung the backpack over his free shoulder. He made an attempt to thank the driver, but his hands were too full to offer a proper gratitude.

As the taxi pulled away, Theo and I startled into activity.

"That can't be Lesya, right?"

"Has to be a daughter," Theo replied before opening the front door. He smiled and waved as the group tottered across the lawn. While Petro's chestnut hair complemented his impressive tan, the girl looked far more wan. Though just as lean as her father, she was angular in all the wrong places and remarkably pale. Long blond hair hung limp around her inexpressive face, but her lips were fat and full. As they crossed our front lawn, Petro tried to engage her in conversation, but the girl returned little more than a sneer. He waved back at Theo and waited patiently for his daughter to shuffle forward.

Theo held open the storm door. "Good afternoon, Mr. Dibrova! How was the flight?"

"It would be better if you didn't ask! I've never gotten used to the small planes." Petro's accent was pleasant, if not completely subdued. He pushed his bundled infant in Theo's direction. "Could I please ask you to hold her? My back is sore from the journey."

Petro rolled his head from shoulder to shoulder in search of relief. With no car seat or stroller, he must have carried the infant in his arms for at least six hours. My own neck ached in sympathy.

Theo reached for the bundle and smiled. "It's the least we can do."

Having unloaded his precious cargo, Petro returned to the front steps to help the older girl navigate this final obstacle. Theo followed behind them, babe in hand. I noticed an unusual lift in one of his eyebrows as I poured cups of water for our travel-weary guests.

After confirming he'd not forgotten anything in the car, on the lawn, or anywhere in between, Petro took a seat at the registration desk and gestured for Theo to return the baby, which he did—but not without shooting me a contemptuous glance.

Damn it. Something was already wrong. And right when I didn't need it to be. I waited for him to say something, but no words came.

Whatever his objections, Theo decided to keep them to himself.

Unsure of how to proceed, I started with a standard greeting.

"Welcome, Mr. Dibrova. Thank you so much for coming all this way."

Petro's nervous eyes scanned the room. "Thank you so much for having us. I'm so sorry it took us so long to bring the baby in. I know you like to see them sooner, but with all the others, I just couldn't get away."

His gaze swept through the room again. "Is Dr. Fontanez not in today?"

The moment felt fragile, and I tried to remember what my sister had advised. To act like her. Maggie wouldn't fear a little discomfort, so I tried projecting her confidence. "I'm sorry, Dr. Fontanez is away in Rota for the week. Given your delay, she didn't want to cancel, so Theo and I will conduct the screening instead."

"Ah, very well," Petro replied. "You are her students?"

"Residents, actually. We completed our training earlier this year and have been practicing with Dr. Fontanez for three months now."

As the words spilled from my mouth, I realized how young and inexperienced they made us sound.

Petro gracefully ignored the misstep. "And you're liking Saipan?"

"It's . . ."

I'd yet to develop a good answer to this question, even though I received it regularly. Saipan, as far as I was concerned, was fine. I could tell most of the ex-pats hoped to hear some kind of romantic yarn about how I'd found my home in paradise—or at least a humorous rebuttal about why island life wasn't suiting me. The locals, on the other hand, expected me to feel drawn back to the States. Though I missed my parents, I wasn't yearning for Pennsylvania, and this befuddled them. Home was such an important concept to them that my agnostic feelings about geography brought pity. Even though I had a roof over my head, I was homeless in their eyes.

". . . not the States," I finished.

Petro laughed. "I understand exactly what you mean. I would miss modern health care and decent restaurants, too, if I hadn't already gotten used to their lack in Ukraine. There, we blamed the Russians. Here, it's the distance. Both are tyrants."

There weren't many similarities between a failed communist bloc and a far-flung tropical island, but Petro had found them. I smiled in amusement.

"The sunshine and the people, however, are both great improvements," he quipped.

Petro then went on to introduce Vesna, whose eyes darted to mine at the sound of her name. They were soft, but empty, and quickly flitted away.

She was ten, Petro said, and just starting fourth grade. She liked cats and always took care to feed scraps to the strays that lived around their house. Throughout this biography, Vesna never spoke a word of her own. Her mouth twisted into something between a smile and a scowl, and she dabbed it often with a kerchief. Her fingers curled tightly into the fabric, her knuckles white with strain.

As curious as I found Vesna's behavior, I couldn't afford the distraction. I needed to focus on the one thing that would make this consultation successful: the baby's screening.

I transitioned the conversation to business. "All right, Mr. Dibrova, I'm sure you remember our process. We begin with a brief assessment of baby . . ."

"Zlata," he offered.

"Baby Zlata. Then we'll gather details about her birth."

Petro nodded in agreement. For once, I might make it through a consultation unscathed.

"After we're done, Theo will take some blood. Then we'll get you on your way."

Petro's face toughened. "I'm sure Dr. Fontanez told you, but we only do the screening for our children. Not the more extensive sequencing."

"I understand," I lied. At that point, I would've said anything to make sure he didn't bolt. I nodded to provide further affirmation, though it was suspicion I really felt.

"Vesna, would you mind staying here with me while Dr. Tannehill speaks with your father?" Theo was already reaching into the bookshelves for a board game.

Vesna agreed. She separated easily from her father, and Petro settled into my office with the baby.

"So," I started, trying to recapture our rapport, "tell me about your little one."

"Ah. Born eleven weeks ago and did not give her mother too hard a time."

"She looks well."

From what little I could see, the baby was good-sized and active. She gurgled and cooed and made all the other noises infants normally did.

"And your wife, how is she?"

Petro tickled the baby's feet, and a flurry of kicks followed. "Tired. I know she should be here, but she dislikes the airplane even more than I do. Someone needs to stay home with the older children, anyway."

"And Vesna? She likes to travel?"

"Not especially." He looked over his shoulder to check on her. Theo was setting up the game, and Vesna looked completely enthralled. "But she's been acting out at school lately. When she had a seizure last week, we thought we should keep her home for a while."

"A seizure? That sounds serious."

"She fell and hit her head on the playground. The nurse said not to worry, but I can't help myself. That's why I have her here with me—to keep a better eye on her for a while."

In the ten minutes we'd spoken, Petro seemed like an earnest, competent father. I started feeling guilty for having judged him by his file.

"So your wife—she gave birth at home?" The practice was common on Tinian, where medical services were even more scant than Majuro.

"Yes. Her labor was only three hours. Zlata came out crying and fed immediately. Now, she eats well, she poops well, and she's starting to smile. All seems fine."

"It certainly sounds like it," I said. Maybe this would be an easy consultation after all.

The baby then started fussing more purposefully. Her tiny arms stretched out from the swaddling clothes, reaching upward like signal flags to request some kind of relief.

Petro rose from his chair. "I need to fix a bottle. Can you hold her?" When he passed the bundle over the desk, I finally laid eyes on the child's face.

Stolen. It was the first word that crossed my mind. The child was Asian, and obviously so, with a hearty shock of ink-black hair and heavily lidded eyes. She was beautiful and healthy, but most definitely not Slavic. I raised my brow and blinked, trying to clear my mind of the malicious explanations. Trying to remember my training, which was supposed to have prepared me for such disturbing possibilities.

Zlata writhed and struggled, her increasing volume intensifying Petro's haste; I heard him fumbling with the hot tap and scoops of powdered milk. Bouncing Zlata gently, I let instinct care for the child while the rest of my brain tried to untangle the truth.

No wonder Theo had scowled at me.

Petro returned with the bottle and passed it to me. Zlata took it and sucked aggressively, her trembling lips struggling to draw down the warm milk. When she finally settled into the rhythm of the feed, Petro opened his arms. I felt tempted to withhold her, perhaps use her as leverage for more information. But I couldn't risk losing these clients.

Out of my depth and completely adrift in a sea I did not know, I transferred the baby back to Petro, who basked in Zlata's tranquility.

The screening, I reminded myself. The only thing that really mattered was the screening.

"Shall we go to the laboratory?"

Petro bounced his way across the clinic into Theo's room without direction. I shouldn't have been surprised—after all, the man had been to the clinic at least a dozen times for all his other children.

Other children.

Eight of them. Where had they come from? Were they stolen too? The chorus of questions was interrupted when Petro turned back with one of his own.

"Would you call us another taxi? I know this won't take long, and it's best we get going right away."

Should I let them go? Make them stay? Why didn't Dr. Fontanez prepare me for this? Theo must have seen the wild in my eyes, because he decided to assert some control.

"Of course we will, Mr. Dibrova."

Theo rose from the seat and then pushed me into it. "Charlie," he said. "Take over this game for me. I'm getting whooped."

His expression assured me that he knew what was up.

Vesna giggled. It was the most emotive I'd seen her since she'd arrived.

I tried to compose myself. Just as soon as the Dibrovas left, Theo and I would sort everything out. Certainly there had to be some kind of reasonable explanation.

Explanation.

Dr. Fontanez said she'd provide one. She'd promised. We just needed to get her on the phone. Whatever she told us, it couldn't be worse than what I was imagining.

I took a cleansing breath and turned to Vesna.

"Are you winning?" I leaned over the desk to assess the status of the game.

"Not yet. Theo was helping me." Her elbow jerked erratically as she finished the sentence.

"Where did you leave off?"

Vesna tucked a wisp of flaxen hair behind her ear. "It's my turn. You're ahead by three, though."

I fondled a sterling game piece. "Don't worry, I'll change that. We'll get back to the game just as soon as I call a cab, okay?"

Vesna attempted to nod, but her chin jerked slightly to the left. Something wasn't right, but I wasn't sure it was wrong either. I ignored it. I needed to get these clients out of my clinic. I needed to call Dr. Fontanez. So instead of pursuing further questions, I shuffled through a stack of business cards and placed the order for the cab. The call took longer than it should have, and I found myself tidying the desk to keep my hands busy. Appointment book, closed. Case files, drawered. Vesna's now-empty paper cup, trashed. The girl watched my every move with a vacant gaze, knurled fists buried in her bountiful skirts.

When the operator confirmed our address, I turned back to the game, but Vesna's hands never moved to her pieces.

A full minute passed.

"Shall I spin for you?" I offered.

"Yes, please," she said. "It's my turn. You're ahead by three."

The plastic arrow swiveled around a rainbow dial and landed on four. I moved her piece accordingly.

"Thank you," she said. "It's your turn. Then it's my turn. You're ahead by three."

She repeated the score another time, as if I hadn't heard. When I opened my mouth to ask why, Zlata's cry pierced the wall behind me.

The unmistakable sound of a successful blood draw. The Dibrovas were one bandage away from completing their visit. Theo opened the door and Petro shuffled out of the room, soothing his infant. Vesna must have sensed the imminence of their departure and rose from her chair. Though she had balance, Vesna seemed to lack coordination, and the transition from sitting to standing sent her limbs akimbo. Petro moved to assist, his free hand wrapping around the older girl's shoulders to contain her flailing arms. Despite his intervention, Vesna upset my abandoned coffee mug and sent it splashing across their paperwork.

I pulled the file off the desk and shook it dry. Theo tried to comfort Vesna and locate napkins simultaneously, which meant he did neither well. Petro apologized profusely until the taxi arrived and honked, at which point he collected Vesna and made for the door before either of his daughters could incite further chaos.

Their departure was capped by a final question at the door.

"The money will start next month, yes?"

CHAPTER 21

Theo and I stood in silence long after the van disappeared.

"I don't know where to start," I said.

"I do," Theo scoffed. "By calling the police."

"On what grounds?" While there were many, Theo would know which were most egregious.

He released a sharp breath. "Abduction. Abuse. Trafficking. Definitely fraud."

All these crimes had increased since the Limit. Lots of people wanted high-screening infants, and many would go to great lengths to get them. Initially, the public had been shocked to hear that babies were stolen and sold, but now only the most outrageous cases made the news.

This, I had to admit, could be one of them.

I moved back to the registration desk to pick up the phone. "Shouldn't we call Dr. Fontanez?"

"What if she's in on it?" Theo retorted. "Dr. Fontanez has been involved with the Dibrovas since they came to the islands. There's no way she doesn't know."

"But she told me we'd have questions—and she was willing to answer them."

"I'm just saying that before we talk to her, we need to have a plan." Theo put his mug of lukewarm coffee in the microwave. "Something's not right."

"Can't we call Maggie first?"

Theo looked frustrated that I was reaching for reassurance. "Have they even landed yet?"

I checked my watch. "About an hour ago. They'll be home by now."

Theo hovered while I dialed. We both stared at the phone as if concentrating hard enough might compel her to answer.

Thankfully, she did.

I put her on speakerphone. "Maggie? Theo's here with me, and we need to talk with you about a client."

Theo briefed her on everything he'd gleaned from the file. When he was done, I described my phone call with Dr. Fontanez, and then together, we recounted the consultation: Petro's behavior, Zlata's appearance, Vesna's presence.

Theo then began ranting about how Petro was probably running a black-market baby farm. "Why does he need the government money? Shouldn't the bounties be enough?"

"I don't think we have enough information to make any assumptions," Maggie replied. "But let's run through the indicators. Any signs of excessive spending?"

"No," I asserted. "Petro's lifestyle looked pretty average by island standards. They didn't seem to have much, and nothing they wore was brand name. Petro didn't describe any nonessential travel or extravagant purchases. It looked like they were just getting by."

"Any signs of detachment from the infant?"

"No," I replied. "He seemed rather adoring, actually. Of both of them."

"He obviously got attached to the one he couldn't sell," Theo snipped.

"But that's another strike against the baby farm hypothesis," Maggie said. "Perhaps Zlata's got a distant Korean relative." She paused. "I think you should call Dr. Fontanez."

Theo ran his hands through his hair in frustration. "But she could be enabling it. She might not tell us everything."

"Whatever she doesn't share will be equally informative," Maggie chided. "Actually—you already have a sample for Zlata, right? Any chance you were able to get one from Vesna? If you can compare their sequences, you should be able to tell if they share parentage. That'll give you some insight into whether there's something to be concerned about."

Theo sighed. "There wasn't a reason to take a sample from Vesna. We don't just stick everyone who walks through the door, you know."

"What about hair, saliva, nail clippings, anything?"

I scanned the room for things Vesna would have sat on, brushed against, or made incidental contact with, but she hadn't moved much while she was here. I combed the chair where she'd sat for any errant hairs—her dishwater blond would have stood out against the craggy sateen. But then I remembered.

There'd been a cup.

I peered under the desk and found it in the trash bin.

Theo rolled his eyes. "I'm not a crime scene investigator, but I will try."

I handed him the cup, which he was careful to handle by the bottom. He placed the vessel on his lab bench and drifted over to the sink to wash his hands. "For Zlata, though, I only have enough blood to run the screening or the sequencing—not both."

I braced for the impending debate, which Maggie unabashedly began. "I vote for sequencing. It's the fastest way to get answers."

"But if we stick with the screening, as Petro *requested*," I implored, "then he'll trust us. Maybe then he'll just tell us the truth."

Maggie scoffed. "That's a big maybe, Charlie. You don't exactly have a track record for getting what you want out of clients."

Even Theo winced. It took a moment for the air to clear, but as sisters, we'd had plenty of fights that got cruel before they got productive.

I gritted my teeth. "I'm trying to act like you. Like you said once—grow a backbone?"

"Ugh, this is not what I had in mind. Don't you want to know if these girls are related? If they are, you don't really have a problem."

I was in no mood to break the rules. I needed to keep these clients happy. I needed to keep Dr. Fontanez happy. I needed to keep my job.

"But Petro only wanted us to run the screening. We don't have authorization for any additional tests."

"But the sequencing will tell us what we need to know," Maggie rebutted. "If you won't sign for it, I will. Just fax me the paperwork."

The argument stalled. Maggie wasn't interested in my caution. She knew my reluctance; she'd seen it her whole life. And I couldn't admit to her that I was scared. Not now, not ever. She didn't even know what that term meant.

We continued to quarrel. I was searching for a referee when I noticed Theo in the kitchen rifling through Petro's backpack. He'd forgotten it in his rush out the door. Theo stopped his excavation when he encountered a few slips of paper.

"Good news," he interrupted, his eyes on a pair of airline tickets. "They don't leave until tomorrow."

The squabble between Maggie and me arrested.

"Why is that good?" I retorted.

Theo had already started repacking the formula canisters, diapers, and burp cloths into the bag. "Maybe we can find them. Ask more questions. Get another sample from Zlata."

"I agree," Maggie chirped.

The suggestion made me queasy. Asking questions could only lead to trouble. Not to mention that we didn't know where they were or how to find them.

"Petro has to come back there, right?" Maggie continued. "Since you have their tickets?"

Theo shook the formula can. "While those can wait until tomorrow, Zlata's going to be hungry a lot sooner than that."

He was right. It was just past 5:00 p.m., and most grocery stores on the island had closed. Formula would be impossible to find at this hour.

"Do we even know where they're staying?" I asked.

"Not exactly," Theo answered. "But Petro deals cards at the casino on Tinian. He's staying with another croupier here. We chatted about it during the blood draw."

I rubbed my temples. "Is that really enough to go on?"

"Yes, actually. There's only one gambling house on Tinian, and the same company operates another here on Saipan. Everyone who works in that industry knows each other." He zippered the bag closed in preparation for delivery. "If I go and talk to some of them, we'll be able to figure out where they're staying tonight."

"How do you know all this?"

Theo dropped Petro's backpack on the reception desk. "What do you think I do on all those long lunch breaks?"

I was taken aback, mostly by the idea that Theo had a vice. Laughter erupted from below us as Maggie lost her composure.

I stood up to pace the room. "I have appointments the rest of the evening. I can't afford to go gallivanting around through the underbelly of Saipan."

"You don't have to. Today's remaining appointments are just intakes, no labs. I'll take care of the legwork . . ." He took two steps toward his laboratory. "Right after I get Zlata and Vesna's samples sequencing."

Maggie piped up from the phone. "He's right, Charlie. Once you have the sequences, you'll know what you need to ask Petro. Maybe nothing. But if there's anything ugly, you'll at least have some evidence."

Two against one. While I'd lost the battle, I could still negotiate the terms of surrender. I turned to Theo. "Promise you won't speak to him. Figure out where he's staying, but don't go there without me."

"Go ahead and fax me that authorization form too," Maggie added.

I directed my next petition to the phone. "Please let me call Dr. Fontanez before you do anything. She might sign it if I tell her what's happened. It would be better to have an attending take the risk."

I was certain we were all about to lose our jobs, but Maggie seemed nonplussed. Even if the Dibrovas made a complaint, it may not go beyond Dr. Fontanez, and she wasn't going to fire us, because we were the only help she had.

If only my sister's sense of security had been contagious rather than congenital.

"Fine," Maggie said. "But if you don't get what you want out of her, send it to me."

Theo picked up the cup. "By the way, Mags, is Nolan around? I need to ask him a technical question about preparing this saliva sample."

Her end of the line went quiet, and for much longer than was needed for what should've been a simple answer. Her voice returned with a quiver. "He's still sleeping off last night, unfortunately."

In the background, we could hear the unmistakable sounds of clanking porcelain and uncontrolled retching.

Theo and I exchanged quiet grimaces.

"No worries," he replied.

"I'll go ahead and try reaching Dr. Fontanez," I said.

We exchanged some perfunctory goodbyes as I clicked off the speakerphone.

Theo lifted and replaced the receiver just in case. "That was weird."

I stared at the phone in confusion. "He didn't seem ill when they left."

"Maybe the beers caught up with him."

"But we didn't have that many."

We left it there. The other mysteries were far more pressing.

While I disliked Maggie's approach, I was grateful she had one. I couldn't handle being in charge. While Theo headed into his lab to prepare the samples, I sat at the registration desk trying to summon the courage to call Dr. Fontanez. The clinking glass and humming machines abated what could have been a deafening silence.

It took me fifteen minutes to consider my options. Should I call her now, before dinner, or later that evening, just before bed? How should I start the conversation? I tried rehearsing a few scripts. None sounded as poised or conclusive as I wanted them. But in the brief period I spent making these preparations, Theo finished his tasks, grabbed his hoodie, and put one foot out the door.

"I'll meet you back here at eight o'clock," he said, then squeezed my shoulder. "We're doing the right thing."

This was the first time Theo had ever touched me in an intentional way. We'd bumped into each other at the desk and grazed hands in the kitchen, but neither of us was the type of person to need much physical contact. While he may have been desperate to assuage my doubts, he was gone a moment later.

Now, but for the constant ticking of the old office wall clock, I was alone. Theo had set off for the gambling district without a second thought. He didn't have a master plan about where he was going or who he was going to talk to. Nor was he concerned with the risk. Neither was Maggie. Both of them just made things up as they went along. And it worked.

That, I decided, was exactly what I needed to do too. To execute, and not overthink.

I faxed the sequencing authorization form to Maggie and dialed Dr. Fontanez.

On the first ring, she answered.

"How'd the appointment go?" she asked. Her words clicked along so quickly I was sure she was more eager than I was to have this conversation.

"Fine," I replied. "We collected a sample from the child. A healthy girl, by the looks of it."

"And Petro?"

I fidgeted with the phone cord. "He was, well, disappointed. Mostly that we weren't you."

"To be expected, for how long they've been under my care."

I mustered my nerve. "Dr. Fontanez, can you say a bit more about these clients? It's a large file, and Theo and I didn't quite understand some of the details."

"That's a polite way to introduce the elephant in the room, Charlie." Her shamelessness stunned me into submission.

"Petro is functionally sterile," she continued. "Probably due to radiation from the Chernobyl accident in Ukraine. He was living in Pripyat when it happened and spent too much time trying to get too close to the plant before the evacuation. Teenagers," she scoffed.

"Petro didn't know about his infertility until Lesya miscarried all of his children. Turns out it wasn't her fault—after some extensive testing, we determined his DNA was too damaged for their offspring to be viable. It's a miracle he's alive at all, really. They've been using alternate fathers ever since."

I noticed she hadn't said "donors." While it wasn't a prevailing practice, using men for live sperm donation wasn't uncommon in places with unreliable mail service and inadequate freezer space. But the husbands often took issue, and jealousy overpowered practicality more often than not. Petro would've set an agency record by agreeing to it ten times.

"As deeply religious people, Petro and Lesya are slightly ashamed of what they've chosen and don't like it documented. They're worried that some kind of Orthodox police will be sent to condemn them for their 'nontraditional' practices. I'm not sure how a Ukrainian priest could ever find his way to Tinian, but that's their concern."

She laughed at the absurdity.

I pressed out a breath between pursed lips. "Sounds easier to explain than running a baby farm."

"I'm sorry, what's that?"

"When we saw that the baby was Asian . . . well, we jumped to a few conclusions."

Dr. Fontanez took the confession in stride. "It's fair to be suspicious—I didn't give you much to go on. As a family, they're quite the rainbow. But they all seem to end up with Lesya's mouth. Small, but with beautiful lips.

To your point, though, Petro *has* selected some unusual fathers. I wouldn't be surprised if some of those traits start to become more pronounced now that the children are older. Height, weight, hair color, eye color, heart problems—you know the drill. Theo's running the screening?"

"Yes," I replied, feeling guilty for not reciprocating Dr. Fontanez's truth. But there was still a chance I could mop up this mess as long as we could get another vial of Zlata's blood. I silently thanked Theo for ignoring my mulishness.

"Excellent," Dr. Fontanez replied. "Though it might be better if I deliver the results to Petro myself. Call me in the morning?"

I swallowed hard.

We had just a few hours to find them.

"Will do."

CHAPTER 22

I returned the phone to its cradle.

Everything we had encountered that day supported Dr. Fontanez's account. The Dibrova case was disturbing, though not particularly scandalous. At the convent, we'd heard stories of clients and circumstances that were far, far more ghastly. *Actual* baby farms and the like. The longer I thought about it, the more Petro's condition seemed pitiful, but not any more despondent than Dora's. At least he and Lesya had found one another.

I tried calling Maggie to recall the form but couldn't reach her. It didn't matter—once Theo's machines had finished their work, we could destroy the sequencing results as well as the paperwork. We'd then return the diaper bag, at which point I'd tell Petro that we'd accidentally contaminated Zlata's sample and take a second to run the screening.

We were one white lie away from redemption.

With my mind finally at ease, I could continue with my last consultation—a house call. The couple lived on a remote part of the island and didn't have a vehicle, so I met them in their apartment to confirm their desire to volume breed. For once, the conversation went smoothly, if not a bit longer than expected. By the time I finished, the sun had relinquished the sky to a thumbnail moon, but the full veil of darkness had not quite unfurled.

I drove back to the clinic in meditation. I'd finally notched a success in my belt, and in just a few hours I'd be able to salvage another. After pulling into the drive, I noticed the lights in the living room already on. Theo was back.

Victory, it seemed, was already home.

I found my technician in his laboratory, his machines emitting their usual melody of whirs and beeps. I leaned against his doorframe.

"Now it's me with good news."

Theo kept his eyes on his work. "About Rodeo Pete?"

His caustic tone disoriented me. "I'm sorry, what?"

"Rodeo Pete. That's what they call him on Tinian, apparently."

My face asked the question my words could not.

"He rents out his wife to other men, and apparently she bucks like a bronco."

A gut punch of disgust dissolved my triumph. Of all the obscure things I'd presumed that day, I'd never suspected prostitution. Pimping, rather. I felt myself grasping for some kind of reason that could explain away such horrendous accusations as rumor or slander. Anything but the truth. But stories like this didn't grow from nothing, I knew. And as grotesque as it was, the allegation corroborated what Dr. Fontanez had told me about the alternate fathers.

Perhaps both tales were true.

I briefed Theo about my call with Dr. Fontanez, but her explanation didn't quite placate his suspicions. He said that the men in the casino talked about their use of Lesya in ways that sounded nonconsensual. Sometimes violent. And while we both knew men to embellish such things, the stories about their encounters had been far too consistent.

The sequencing machine dinged. Theo rolled back his computer.

"I'm sending these to Maggie."

I was in no place to contest. Since my sister had been the one to sign for them, she was the only one who could access the results. With four clicks and one dramatic keystroke, Theo sent the file.

"The croupier Petro's staying with lives on the north side of the island, near the softball field. The pit boss said he's not hard to find."

The last thing I wanted was for this to escalate further. "Shouldn't we just report him? Let the Mendelia sort it out?"

"Probably," Theo replied. "But that baby deserves to eat. It's been almost five hours since her last bottle. Let's take care of her first; then we can deal with the abuse."

There wasn't much I needed to grab since I'd just walked in the door. With my purse slung over my shoulder and the Jeep keys still in hand, I grabbed Petro's backpack and waited on Theo to shut down the lab. The drive would give us time to plan our confrontation.

We wouldn't need to. When we opened the front door, there stood Petro, shrieking infant in his arms.

"Oh good, you're still here," he called, just barely exceeding Zlata's emphatic howls. "I left my bag. Can I make a bottle before you close up?"

Theo led him into the kitchen. I held Zlata while Petro mixed. While I knew Theo wanted to interrogate him, neither of us could manage it over Zlata's caterwauling. Once the milk was ready, she took it eagerly, each suck more peaceful than the last.

Petro cut in at the first possible moment. "Thank you both so much. I should be going. Vesna will be anxious for our return."

Theo blocked his exit. "Not so fast there, *pardner*."

The sarcasm that dripped from his voice could've pooled on the floor. The color in Petro's face went with it.

"Petro, we need to talk to you about Lesya," I started.

He fumbled for his wallet in a panic. "She told us this day would come. Let me get the letter."

I joined Theo in the doorway. "Who is 'she,' Petro? Lesya?"

"No," he sputtered. "Dr. Fontanez."

Petro handed me a wad of paper. The men stood quietly while I unfolded the tattered typewritten sheet.

> *I, Lesya Olena Dibrova, hereby understand my deteriorating condition and consent to continued breeding as long as possible over the course of my shortening life. I have asked my husband, Petro Oleksander Dibrova, to select reproductive partners on behalf and for Dr. Linda*

Jimenez Fontanez to make medical decisions concerning my pregnancies. For all intents and purposes, this document constitutes durable power of attorney.

Lesya's curvaceous signature swept across the bottom of the page. The red-ink stamp of a notary provided official certification, as well as the date: September 7, 1999.

I drew in a deep breath. Petro sensed that I had finished reading and layered another document into my hands. A ragged sheet of notebook paper, flimsy in comparison to the heavier legal form. The handwriting was feminine, but not Dr. Fontanez's. Delicate Slavic characters loped along fading blue lines.

"I know you can't read this one," he said. "But it explains why."

I passed both papers over to Theo. His eyes darted down the page, then jumped to the next. "Petro, what's wrong with your wife?"

The kitchen had become a courtroom, and Petro knew he was on the stand.

"She does not leave the bed anymore," he said, his voice soft and vulnerable. "She cannot walk; her muscles are too tight. She spasms badly, and often. She stopped speaking last year. Dr. Fontanez said this is to be expected."

Theo's face creased. "Why would she expect this?"

Choking on the last few sucks from her bottle, Zlata swallowed quite a bit of air. Petro moved her to his shoulder and began to drum lightly on her back.

"The radiation. We're from Pripyat, you know. Near Chernobyl. We were teenagers when the reactor exploded. My wife went to watch the fire with some friends from her building. They say that everyone out that night received significant doses of radiation. Many of her friends died of strange cancers and other ugly diseases. For Lesya, this is her end. Contraction and contortion."

I shook my head in disbelief. "So why does she want so many babies?"

"Lesya loves children," he said. "Our children, and all children. But the radiation—it altered her DNA. She has mutations now. We think she can beat the Limit.

"I know it sounds crazy, but our first baby screened very high. Higher than he should have, 8* I believe. But Georgiy was a sickly child who rarely cried; we weren't sure what was wrong. We brought him in for screening at two months, and he died a few days later. Dr. Fontanez told us we must keep trying. That Lesya might save our species. My wife found new purpose after that. All the tragedy of Pripyat finally felt justified."

Zlata let go a satisfying belch, and Petro began to bounce at the knees. For the babe, sleep was not far behind and her father knew it.

"Lesya signed those papers ten years ago, when she was still of sound mind. For her, it was not a difficult decision; I was the one who needed persuasion. But in the end, I did not feel I could deny my wife this satisfaction after all she had suffered. Losing Georgiy almost broke her, and this seemed like the least I could do."

Theo turned back to the living room to pace. I resigned myself to a seat at the registration desk and blew my bangs out of my face.

Sensing that his hearing was complete, Petro's tone switched from defense to explanation.

"Lesya always wanted a big family—she comes from one herself—so we try as often as she can. Zlata is our tenth. I'm sterile, from the accident, so I select her partners. It's much cheaper to have them come in person. The casino on Tinian provides good selection, especially with tourists passing through."

Theo grimaced.

"I know of my nickname," Petro acknowledged. "And I do charge them for the privilege. All of it goes directly to Lesya's care. The government money supports the children, but I need more for her physical therapy, her medical supplies, and all the equipment to keep her comfortable.

"I'm careful with whom I choose. Dr. Fontanez taught me what to look for. Apart from a clean bill of health, she told me to look for men with uncommon features or conditions. Not hair dye or piercings, but wide-set eyes or shortened limbs. Men with small ears or misshapen teeth. Men who might also have unusual DNA."

I could not help but think of a blackjack table surrounded by genetic defects with Petro poised suavely at the head, dealing cards and evaluating his options.

Quite the perversion of James Bond.

"They know what I'm doing," he continued. "Many believe me to be a desperate man, unable to accept my wife's condition, or an immoral one, profiting from it. Some are curious as to why I haven't been stopped, but the men I work with are not generally men of principle. They do not object to the opportunity."

He kissed Zlata's hair. "And now we have ten beautiful children—though none have ever screened as high as Georgiy. Depending on Zlata's results, I think perhaps we will try one more. Lesya's light is fading, but the children will still have each other."

Zlata stirred a bit in search of a more comfortable position. Theo and I rearranged ourselves a bit, too, seeking the same.

Petro looked to me. "May we go now? Vesna will worry since we've been gone so long."

Their taxi was still idling outside. I couldn't see any reason to keep him, but Theo probably did. I glanced at him.

He nodded his permission. "But before you do, I need another sample from Zlata. I spoiled the last one."

The men shuttled back to the lab once more. Aggrieved by the heel stick, Zlata yelped but quickly settled back down in the comfort of her father's arms. While Theo activated the screening machine, I gathered the feeding supplies from the sink and helped Petro into his backpack. A cordial wave concluded the visit as he ducked into the taxicab.

After the van pulled away, Theo resigned himself to the floor and lay spread eagle on the multicolored rug. He sighed. "What a day it has been."

I took a seat against the wall. A solemn "yeah" was the best I could muster. Several minutes passed before I prodded him with my foot. "Why'd you pull the second sample? I thought Petro's story checked out."

Theo kept his eyes on the ceiling. "Petro may be off the hook, but we're not. Dr. Fontanez is still going to want screening results."

A twinge of panic crackled through me. "Oh God, I almost forgot."

"That's what I'm here for."

After that, the room was quiet but for the din of Theo's machines. While they worked, he and I tried to release the tension that had accumulated in our bodies: his fingers and toes reached for the corners of the room, while I massaged the hardened muscles in my neck.

The reprieve was brief. When the clinic phone rang, we looked at each other, both too wary to answer. Theo finally heaved himself onto the chair to pick it up.

"Maggie, Maggie, Maggie, please slow down," he pleaded. "Let me put you on speaker."

When he hit the button, my sister's voice thundered out with all the force of a runaway train.

"Charlie, can you hear me? There's something really, really wrong."

I dropped my head into my hands. How could today get any more complicated?

"Yes, Maggie, go ahead."

"The sequencing results you sent. These girls do share a mother but not a father. But they've also got Huntington's. It's bad. Over one hundred sequence repeats."

Theo flinched. "Wait—isn't that one of those disorders that's . . ."

"Incompatible with life? Yes," Maggie answered. "It causes the neurons deep in your brain to break down. It explains Vesna's tics. Based on her age, she's got a juvenile presentation, which is usually associated with paternal transmission. Did Petro exhibit any symptoms?"

"No."

I swallowed, knowing full well who'd given Vesna the condition. But I wasn't sure how to catch Maggie up. Theo glared at me, knowing it needed to be done.

Maggie rattled on. "That means it's coming from Lesya. With so many repeats, her condition is probably fairly advanced—I'd be surprised if she's not bedridden. There's no way she's been able to consent to these pregnancies. Most would have been medically inadvisable."

"Maggie, a lot has happened since this afternoon," I said.

Everything I knew spilled out of me.

"Well," Maggie scoffed. "Lesya's condition definitely isn't related to radiation, I can tell you that."

Theo reclined in the chair. "I don't understand why Dr. Fontanez never sequenced these kids. If she thought there was something special in their DNA, she would have run the test."

"That's because she knows about the Huntington's," Maggie raved. "She probably discovered it when she analyzed Georgiy's samples. If he screened at 8*, Dr. Fontanez would have sequenced him, but his DNA probably showed the breakthrough as well as the disorder."

"Then why didn't she report it to Headquarters?" I asked. "Wouldn't she want to collect her reward?"

"You can only collect if the breakthrough is *viable*," Maggie chided. "Georgiy died. I'm sure she wanted Lesya to try again in hopes the next child would survive."

Theo and I exchanged knowing glances while Maggie continued to unfold her argument. "She's been lying to Petro and Lesya so they feel safe continuing. If they do, she might be able to repeat Georgiy's success. But there's a serious risk to the children, as you've seen."

"Statistically, half their kids will have inherited the disorder—so, *probably* five, but *possibly* more. Each gets a 50:50 chance, though I don't think many will reach adulthood with this many sequence repetitions. It's completely unethical to have Lesya procreating."

"Unless her husband lets Dr. Fontanez have a say in it," huffed Theo.

Maggie ignored the jab. "How long until we get Zlata's screening?"

It was as if she spoke the result into existence. The hulking machine released a digital croon just as the inquiry left her lips.

Theo toggled into the computer. "She's coming in as a 5*."

While we all knew what that meant, it was Theo who said it aloud. "Damn."

Maggie was the first to find more words. "Who knows what her father is, but that's definitely higher than her mother's. She should be, at most, a 2*."

The computer made a few clicks and whirs. Because Zlata was already three months of age, her screening results were automatically sent to the central database at Headquarters. Her sequencing results went with it.

We'd just notified the Mendelia about a child who'd broken the Limit.

I think we all expected the phone to ring. For someone from Baltimore to recognize the discovery—then congratulate us, maybe send some champagne. To at least ask some questions. But instead, a resounding silence filled the room, and disappointment rained down like confetti.

"Headquarters will call in the morning," Maggie started. "It's the middle of the night over there, so no one's seen the results. But I'm sure they've been flagged by the system. You guys should go home and get some rest."

I took a seat on the desk and slouched. "What about Dr. Fontanez?"

Maggie had no patience for politics. "You should report her. Then confront her."

"Tomorrow?"

"Yes," she asserted. "And only because you're too tired now. You and Theo better get ready to run the whole clinic by yourselves, by the way, because they're going to bench Dr. Fontanez immediately."

Theo's throat bobbed. So did mine.

"And the Dibrovas?" I asked. Someone still needed to tell Petro.

"There's no reason you can't tell them everything," Maggie concluded. "Considering Zlata's results, you need to get more information about her father. See what Petro has on him. Headquarters will want to follow up."

"But what about the children?"

Five little children, physically and mentally decaying.

Five hospital beds.

Five coffins.

Possibly more.

"Honestly, Charlie, I don't know. But make sure to talk to Petro about Zlata's father first," Maggie said. "The other news may be . . . too catastrophic."

There was nothing left to say.

"Good night, guys, and good luck. Call me after. I'll be around."

There was a gentle click on the line as Maggie hung up.

Theo slapped his knees. "Well, I'm not going to be able to sleep. Might as well file that report."

I put my palms over my eyes and then dragged them down my face. "Where do we even start?"

"It's the government, Charlie. There's a hotline."

My naivete annoyed him at times.

"Have you ever heard of this happening before? Reporting a supervisor?"

Theo swiveled in the chair. "No. Headquarters spends a lot of time making Mendels, so they're not inclined to let anyone go. But this case is pretty egregious. It'll make the news—and not in a way that Headquarters will like. They'll do the right thing."

I hoisted myself up from the desk and grabbed my bag. "I can't take any more. I need some rest."

"You do," he affirmed. "You'll be talking to both Dr. Fontanez and Petro tomorrow, and that's not going to be easy."

"Take the Jeep," Theo continued. "I'll stay here and make the report. I'll also reschedule tomorrow's appointments. There's no way we can see other clients."

I squeezed his shoulder just like he'd done mine. "You're the best, Theo."

"We'll get through this, Charlie."

CHAPTER 23

I limped home and crumpled into bed. Petro's fate tormented me that night—what brief and fitful sleep I accomplished left me restless and regretful. While the recollection of our discovery should have buoyed my spirits, it only embittered my already sour mood. Tragedy had taken its rightful place on the throne of my emotions; any potential joy had been fully and completely subdued.

After I showered, I returned to the clinic and found a dozing Theo draped over his rolling chair. I eased the lab door closed, hoping to afford him a few more moments of sleep while I bustled about the kitchen. He deserved the rest after finishing a day I could not.

I considered our charge over a strong cup of coffee. Headquarters would probably call around 8:00 a.m., our publicly listed opening time. I needed to speak with Dr. Fontanez before then—no doubt the Mendelia brass would be trying to get her side of the story, too, and I didn't need them tipping her off. I thought about calling Dr. Fontanez right then, but prudence curtailed my impulse.

There'd be safety in having a witness.

Theo could serve, once he was awake. But I hated waking people—it felt so intrusive. And so I puttered about the kitchen and tried to steel myself for the approaching storm. Minutes ticked by, but Theo still snored. I busied myself tidying the living room. Loudly. When the clock struck seven, I planted a cup of coffee on my technician's desk in hopes the aroma would coax him back to consciousness. But after several more minutes of continued snoozing and boisterous chores, I was forced to be merciless.

A quick vacuum of the living room did the trick.

Theo emerged from his lab, stretching his eyelids. "You're just doing that to wake me up, aren't you?"

I clicked off the Hoover with an apologetic smile. "I didn't want to startle you."

"Couldn't have been any more startling than yesterday."

Yesterday. It was hard to believe it had all happened in one afternoon. Shame prickled the back of my neck. I shouldn't have been surprised that I'd cowered—after all, I could barely summon the courage to wake someone up. And while I'd spent most of the previous day punting away my responsibilities, Theo and Maggie had unflinchingly embraced them. Petro and Lesya's mettle was unmistakable, too—if not misplaced. Even Dr. Fontanez had enough confidence in her conspiratorial plot to lie to my face.

Surrounded by people so much more assured than myself, I could only feel inadequate. And I hated it. I wanted to feel something else. I wanted to be something else. I wanted to share in the privilege of conviction they all enjoyed.

And there was no reason I couldn't help myself into it.

I turned to the phone and called to Theo. "Are you ready?"

Dr. Fontanez picked up on the first ring.

"Good morning. I assume you have Zlata's results?"

I delivered the news in my most stoic tone. "The baby screened 5*."

Whatever happened on the other end of the line sounded equal parts excited and flustered. "I'm sure you know what this means, Dr. Tannehill. We must have her sequenced immediately. When Petro comes by this afternoon, make sure to draw another sample. Take two. If you can, convince him to stay on Saipan a little longer. I'll catch the next flight back."

"Dr. Fontanez, we already did," I said.

"Convince them to stay? Excellent."

"No," I said. "The sequencing."

Her voice hollowed. "Oh. Have you told Petro?"

Her arrogance incensed me. "About the screening? No. About the Huntington's? Also no."

Theo gawked at me as the line went dead. I tried calling back, but Dr. Fontanez didn't pick up.

Theo rolled his lips and took a sip of coffee. "Well," he said, "I think that tells us everything we need to know."

Since Dr. Fontanez was not going to self-incriminate, Theo and I prepared for the call with Headquarters. As Maggie predicted, they called exactly at eight. But instead of a chorus of eager and inquisitive administrators, the line connected us to just one disinterested lab supervisor who sounded decidedly unimpressed. Without asking a single question, he directed us to secure a second sample from the child and rerun the screening.

Theo deposited his mug in the sink while I spun aimlessly in his chair.

"They must get a lot of false positives," he said, pumping some soap into the sponge. "It's the only thing that explains their indifference. But we still have some time before Petro arrives. Can I get you some breakfast?"

I kept my eyes on the ceiling while I kicked in circles. "Theo, if anything, I'm the one who owes you."

"Don't worry about it," he said, an irreverent smile warming his cheeks. "I have plans."

Theo returned an hour later with a bottle of midgrade champagne and a box of fresh crepes. If we weren't going to receive any formal recognition from Headquarters, Theo thought we might as well mark the occasion privately. I uncorked the bottle while he plated the beautifully folded mango-filled flapjacks, and we took a seat in the backyard.

"Cheers," he said. "To us, and also to the Vietnamese, whose immigration to this island brought us delicious French cooking."

The bubbles stung against the back of my throat, and I stifled a cough. "Really, Theo, I don't know how you get your hands on so much alcohol."

Theo flourished his hand around his cheekbones. "Look, I'm Korean, and my mother taught me how to take care of my skin. Most people can't tell if I'm fifteen, twenty-five, or forty."

"So you just go up to the counter and buy it?"

Theo carved off a bite of crepe. "Yep. Generally, the cashier would rather make the sale than challenge me." He gestured back to the clinic. "As we've learned, profit is a pretty serious incentive."

"But let's get back to the reason we're celebrating," Theo continued. "You put on your big-girl pants today, and from where I was sitting, they looked pretty good."

I dropped my fork. "I thought we were supposed to be celebrating the discovery."

Theo helped himself to the whipped cream. "That too. But in some ways, this is just as monumental."

The observance offered a brief distraction from the drudgery ahead. I was not unfamiliar with delivering bad news to parents; crushing hopes and dreams was part of the job of managing the unborn. But never before had I needed to devastate a parent who'd already become so thoroughly attached to their child. Not a baby, not a pregnancy—but a living, breathing, laughing, loving *child*. A child with their own hopes and dreams. Petro had loved Vesna for ten years, and now I had to tell him that her life would end much sooner than he'd ever imagined. Not to mention the fact that the tragedy wouldn't stop there.

The same was in store for his other children, thanks to Dr. Fontanez's lies.

But first, as Maggie advised, I needed to deliver Zlata's results. Petro would be over the moon with pride in Lesya's courage and joy in their victory. Leading him to this high knowing that ruin would follow felt impossibly cruel.

But it was the only way to get details about the father.

The Dibrovas' taxi rolled into the driveway just before noon. Petro, Vesna, and Zlata emerged from the vehicle, their careful movements now completely explained. Vesna's dysfunctions seemed more obvious now—not because she was any more impaired, but because I could see beyond the shroud of the present. Huntington's was eroding her normal, healthy youth in the same way the termites riddled the bones of a home.

Collapse, although eventual, was assured.

Theo met Petro on the lawn to carry their bags. I provided beverage service once they sat down: a cup of coffee for Petro, water for Vesna, a bit more for Zlata's bottle. What little hospitality we could offer seemed a small act of mercy.

Petro eyed his cup in suspicion. I couldn't blame him for thinking we might want to poison him. After his revolting reveal, lesser Mendels may have tried.

He finally broke the silence. "Will Dr. Fontanez be calling in?"

"Unfortunately not," I started. "She's gotten caught up in some . . ."

I looked at Theo. Once again he had nothing to say.

". . . other business. But I have some far more interesting news."

Petro's eyes brightened.

"Zlata screened 5*."

The man's mouth fell open. "Oh my God."

I kept my face straight. "You can understand why we're going to need as much information about the father as you have."

"Of course," Petro stammered. "But I don't have much. He played cards at my table about one year ago, and all he could talk about was his heritage. He said he was from an island north of Japan. Part of Russia. He said he was one of the last of the Ainu people."

Theo and I exchanged confused looks. I'd never heard of such a place or its people. I scavenged a notepad and started scribbling notes.

"I asked what brought him to Tinian, and he said he'd made it big in the fishing industry. He gave me a business card in case our restaurant needed a supplier. The card's back at home, in my dresser."

I hadn't expected it to be this easy. I should've delighted in it, really. Maggie would have.

Petro's eyes scanned mine for satisfaction. "This is good, right? This is very good?"

I laid my pen aside. Nothing that would be said over the next few minutes needed to be documented.

"I have to tell you, Petro, we found something else in Zlata's results."

Betrayal petrified his expression. "I thought you weren't supposed to do any more tests."

Theo stood up and cocked his head toward the backyard. "Vesna, why don't you come outside with me. There are some flowers in the yard I'd like you to see."

Both Petro and I understood the intervention and held our tongues. Once his daughter was out of earshot, I continued.

"We had to, Petro, because of the screening results."

A white and convenient lie.

"And we found something troublesome."

An understatement of extreme proportion.

"Zlata has Huntington's."

Petro didn't speak for a minute. Zlata squealed and sputtered, and for the first time, I didn't see Petro engage. His eyes stayed with mine.

"What is 'Huntington's'?"

I couldn't continue looking at him. Instead, I rested my forehead on the heels of my hands and kept my eyes on the desk. "It's a genetic disease that causes the nerves in your brain to break down like overused electrical wires. The first symptoms include small spasms that worsen over time. Eventually, it's . . . incompatible with life."

I looked up just as his mouth tightened. The thought of having to deliver more devastating blows sickened me. But making him wait, making him suffer—that was even more torturous. Continuing was my only compassion.

"The way you describe Lesya's condition—the convulsions and contractions—well, it's consistent with the later stages of the disease."

One of Petro's knees bounced anxiously as his eyes brimmed with fear. "But Dr. Fontanez said it was from the radiation in Pripyat."

"She lied to you, Petro. I'm sorry."

He wiped away an escaping tear. "But why?"

I took a deep breath. "Dr. Fontanez wanted Lesya to continue reproducing. Georgiy's screening was very promising, but if she told you about the Huntington's, she knew you'd stop."

Petro stewed on this in silence.

"I also need to tell you that Vesna has it. The drooling, her stumbles, that seizure—these are all early indicators."

He looked away. "And how many of my other children?"

"We don't know exactly. We'd need to sequence them. Vesna is the only one old enough to show any symptoms. But since they all share Lesya as a mother, some"—I stumbled past a lump in my throat—"and possibly all may be affected."

Petro covered his mouth with his free hand and shook his head. "I don't know what to do with this."

Peeling away the bitter rind of clinical tone away from my voice, I addressed him with a tenderness that I've never been able to replicate.

"Me neither."

We struggled through the remainder of the conversation. Petro's mind was elsewhere, and understandably so. He complied with the rest of my requests: to draw blood from him, Zlata, and Vesna; to sequence samples from the rest of his children; to help us locate the man who fathered his infant. I named a few dates that Theo and I could visit Tinian to conduct the work, making clear our deference to his schedule. His responses were uncharacteristically tepid.

The only thing left to do for them was to call a cab. The taxi arrived while Theo was applying the family's bandages and I overpaid the driver on the promise he wouldn't bother Petro for a tip.

Petro ushered Vesna into the vehicle as I held their bags. "Would you like me to come with? I'm happy to help you get to the airplane."

I knew I should go all the way to Tinian with them, but I couldn't bear to watch any more of the train wreck I'd caused.

"No, thank you." Petro had hardened to granite; his tone smooth, cold, inert.

The driver bustled around the front of the car to close the door behind them. Despair overwhelmed me as the van retook the main road. I stood stock still on the fringe of our front yard thinking of all the tribulations that lay ahead. Dead mothers, dying children, survivors' guilt—it was all too much.

Theo interrupted my nightmare with a call from the front door. "Maggie's on the line."

I flopped in the nearby chair.

"How'd everything go?" she asked.

"With Headquarters? They didn't sound impressed. We got instructions to reconfirm the discovery."

"And how'd Petro take it?"

"Considering we just destroyed his entire family, the fact that he only seemed completely heartbroken might count as pretty splendid."

She blew past my hyperbole. "He's left, then?"

"Yes, they're on their way back to Tinian. Plane should be leaving in an hour or so."

"Why didn't you go with him?"

I took offense. "I offered. He refused. You said it yourself—I'm the only Mendel here now. I can't go traipsing all over the Pacific. I've got clients here who need me."

An administrative excuse to disguise the fact I couldn't face the terrible suffering I'd accidentally wrought. Contemptible, even for me.

"He did let us take more samples from the girls," I continued, in hopes that I might drag the conversation away from my deficiencies. "We learned a bit about Zlata's father too."

"And?"

"He's Ainu, apparently. I don't know what that means."

"I do," Theo chimed in. "According to some of the databases I've looked at, they're an understudied indigenous people from islands between Hokkaido, Japan, and Kamchatka, Russia."

"Any chance we can get a sample from him?" Maggie's tone was undeniably perky.

All I wanted was for the day to be over, and the fastest way to that particular end was to satisfy Maggie's questions.

"I have no idea," I said. "He left Petro a business card, so we might be able to get in touch. But who knows if he'll talk with us."

"You sound pretty defeated for someone who just saved the human race," she quipped.

I pushed my hands into my hair, where they tangled in my curls. "I know this should be exciting. I know I should be rejoicing. I know I should be having better feelings about all of this, but I don't."

Maggie didn't seem to know how to reply. For everyone's sake, I tried to lighten the mood. "Also, you're the one who signed the sequencing authorization, so you'll get the credit."

"I promise to share," she teased. "Especially with Theo."

My technician raised an eyebrow. "How many eggs do you think you'll earn?"

"Hmm, what's the exchange rate on miracles these days?" she mocked. But my question had snagged a substantial thread, which she pulled on more sedately. "To be honest, I don't know. It probably depends on how the Mendelia rate the discovery, how replicable it is, and whether humanity needs to suffer Huntington's to break the Limit."

Theo and I kept Maggie on the line for the rest of the hour speculating about Dr. Fontanez's punishment. We strategized about our visit to Tinian, discussed the best ways to prosecute justice for Petro. But the heroics we had planned were promptly snuffed out the next morning—along with the entire Dibrova family.

Every news channel and radio station covered the familicide. Ten children, drowned by their father, their bodies placed lovingly back in their beds. His invalid wife—smothered under a pillow. Prior to hanging himself from the ceiling fan, Petro Dibrova placed a note on the door that said: "Do not enter, call the police." But when his wife's nurse arrived the next morning for her shift, she did not yield that direction. After keying the door, she shrieked at such a volume that the neighbors called the police. They then gave interviews to anyone who would listen.

The subsequent hours, days, and weeks smeared together, and guilt rendered me entirely useless. Maggie, on the other hand, took command. She had the sense to call the Tinian police and have them hold the bodies so that we could collect samples before burial. The local officials wanted to get the Dibrovas in the ground as soon as possible to stem the flow of the grisly story, so we didn't have much time. Theo grabbed the next available flight after Maggie authorized it—generally, travel needed to be approved by an attending, but Maggie knew Dr. Fontanez wasn't going to give us anything. She then handled everything: the paperwork, the schedules, the interviews, the expenses. I couldn't tell whether she was driven by a sense of conquest or culpability, but she found time to call me every night before bed.

"How are you doing, Charliebear?" she asked.

Each night felt heavier with the clamminess and contentiousness of the day.

"Pretty terribly, thanks for asking," I answered. "Headquarters won't stop calling about the children's sequencing results. They think we're hiding something."

We certainly hadn't meant to. Theo just hadn't been able to process them. We'd run out of medical-grade saline and hadn't had time to reorder it. Not only had we been besieged by all of Dr. Fontanez's abandoned patients, but it was hard to prioritize the work that had just recently traumatized us. Whether Zlata's mutation broke the Limit wouldn't be changed by when we analyzed it.

"Speaking of, does HQ have anything to say about our favorite villain?"

Maggie, I knew, would be hunting for news about the forthcoming investigation. I was, too, to be frank. But from what little I could surmise from my near-daily conversations with Mendelia leadership, the program was neither particularly interested nor completely prepared to pursue the case. Their lack of enthusiasm chafed at me—if Headquarters didn't feel the need to make an example of such malpractice, perhaps we should've left well enough alone.

If we'd had, perhaps the Dibrovas could've remained blissfully ignorant—and very much alive.

At least for a little while.

I choked on regret. Every time I thought of Petro and his children, remorse reached up to strangle me.

How had this happened? How had something so innocuous conflagrated into such an abomination? Embers of suspicion had been whipped into an inferno of agony with nothing more than a few conversations. A few tests. Twelve people died. And horribly too. At my hand? Not exactly. But I hadn't used that hand to help. I hadn't reached out, hadn't helped them hold on. Hadn't hugged, hadn't held, hadn't wiped away tears. There were so many things I could have done differently to contain the catastrophe, but there was one that haunted me most.

If I'd only gone with them.

But cravenness had won the day despite my best attempts at confidence, and conviction, and all the other maxims my colleagues pitched so easily. I hated them at that moment, and almost as much as I hated myself. Had I been an angrier person, perhaps I could have used such hate to burn through my guilt, my sorrow, my sadness. But unable to sustain such a fiery heat of anguish, my rage cooled to misery in a few days' time. The ashes of my discontent flared only when my sister closed our nightly conversations with the same empty reassurance she'd used since we were small.

"I know this is hard on you, Charlie, but remember—we were just trying to help."

When things settled down a month later, Theo and I closed the clinic for a week. That was as long as we could go before Headquarters would nag us about seeing clients again. In the absence of Dr. Fontanez, we had to manage several islands' worth of patients, and they numbered in the thousands. Each needed my care when I had none left to give.

When we returned to the office, Theo and I found a week's worth of mail piled up under the slot. Among the government forms and credit card offers was a greeting card adorned with brilliant yellow sunflowers.

Inside was the business card of an Ainu fisherman.

Petro wanted us to continue. And that broke me.

CHAPTER 24

Relief came only when the friendly face of an old professor arrived on the island two months later to assume Dr. Fontanez's vacancy. Theo and I had been juggling hundreds of cases across Saipan, Rota, Tinian, and Guam—until Dr. Varghese placed us both on leave.

"To rest," she assured us. "It's not punishment."

By then, we had no will to disbelieve her.

For the next three weeks, I lay in bed as relentless tides of doubt washed away what little remained of my confidence. I cried more than I ate, fussed more than I slept. Though I still washed, combed, and dressed, I couldn't bring myself to engage in much more of life. If Petro couldn't engage in anything at all, why did I deserve more than him? Maggie's calls slowed down as well. She'd grown impatient with my melancholy and doubled down on her own casework instead.

My parents, however, still called often—but were relegated to voicemail most of the time. Despite their best efforts, my mother and father couldn't quite figure out the time change, and when they did, it didn't matter—depression had so fully dismantled my sleep schedule that I couldn't guarantee I'd be awake at any given time. When I missed their connections, I was glad of it. Shame had convinced me I didn't deserve sympathy.

Like Maggie, Theo eventually found himself recovered enough to return to work. Though he spent most of his time at the clinic, he made time to visit me often, and even tried coaxing me back to the world outside my apartment.

"Hirao and Taitasi Olapai are ready to go. If you can pick the gametes, I'll take care of the rest."

He'd come over that morning to share a bowl of fresh coconut pudding from one of the street vendors down the road. Theo had mentioned this couple a few times before in hopes that some low-hanging fruit might inspire me to stand up and pull down a victory.

"I just don't think I'm ready," I said.

After slopping a heavy portion of custard into his bowl, Theo shoved his computer into my lap. "I've already pulled up the database."

"But what if I accidentally give them a child with Huntington's?"

"You won't," he said, his voice garbled by the spoon he held in his mouth. Theo's hands were busy keying in search commands. "All the samples in the main bank have already been screened for genetic disorders. Those kinds of hazards only exist in the restricted collection—and don't worry. Headquarters doesn't ship those this far."

I scrolled through the database while Theo washed my dishes and folded my laundry. As the sun reached high noon, he poked his head back into my bedroom with a trash bag in hand. "If it's really that hard, I can get you a dartboard while I'm out."

"I know, I know, I'm sorry. I'm just worried that whatever I pick might mutate."

"If it'll smooth your feathers, I can run a preimplantation screening," he said. "Before we bring in Taitasi, I'll pull a few cells off the embryos and sequence them to make sure nothing's wrong."

The insurance policy was enough. After reviewing the seemingly endless options, I selected a 4* egg from an Inuit girl with blue eyes and a 5* sperm from an autistic Irishman.

The dartboard could have done the same job.

Theo placed the order, and the samples arrived from Baltimore within the week. After combining them and letting the embryos divide for five days, he extracted a few cells, spun them down, and inserted the DNA into one of his machines. Such testing was a luxury—since the Mendelia only cared about *viable* sequences, they avoided investing precious resources in embryos that may not endure pregnancy.

And in this case, our investment did appear wasteful—there was nothing unusual about the embryos' sequences to report.

"Except good news," Theo ribbed. "They're all 3*. And normal all the way around."

I shrugged. "No help to the Limit, though."

"Nope. Not by her genes. But who knows what she might discover. And don't forget the Olapais. We're giving them three more generations and a chance to be grandparents. They'll be thrilled."

Except they weren't. While Theo and I deposited three healthy embryos inside Taitasi's womb, none implanted. Mad with frustration, I drove to the clinic to resign.

"You need to finish," Dr. Varghese protested.

"Why? My clients are unhappy, my placements are duds—don't try to tell me I'm not terrible at this!"

"I didn't say you need to practice."

Her assertion stopped me in my tracks. "Excuse me?"

Dr. Varghese put down the chart she'd been reviewing. "As long as you finish your training, you'll be licensed. Once you're licensed, you can teach. Or work at Headquarters. Recruit. But there's far fewer options out there for someone who's not quite a Mendel."

As dejected as I felt, I couldn't deny the logic. I'd also never conceived of Mendelic work outside clinic walls.

Perhaps my future wasn't entirely bankrupt.

"I'll make you a deal," Dr. Varghese continued. "Promise me you'll get through these next six months, and I'll do what I can to get you a job at the convent."

While I wasn't sure I wanted that job, there was one thing I did know: any job that didn't require making babies would be a major improvement.

I spent the next six months struggling through the minimum number of consultations needed to graduate. In return, Dr. Varghese kept her word and arranged an adjunct faculty position for me back in Tehachapi. I'd be assigned to teaching the classes on genealogy and familial investigation.

I'd never have to work with a client again.

※

Breaking the news to Theo was the hardest.

Three days before I was supposed to leave, I still hadn't told him, so I decided to tackle the conversation in the only way I knew how: by playing cards. But my apartment was already half packed, and it didn't look like I was in the process of finalizing such a dramatic change. In an effort to hide just how far I was along in the process of abandoning him, I halfheartedly shoved my swollen luggage into a nearby coat closet just before his knuckles rapped against my door.

Per our custom, Theo let himself in while I sat cross-legged on my bed and shuffled the deck. What game would best facilitate this conversation? My parents had chosen Five-Card Stud to inform us about the Mendelia. Cribbage seemed too complex considering the circumstances, Old Maid too silly. And as much as I would've liked to architect a more artful delivery, my confession slipped out before I could even make a suggestion.

"Theo, I don't know how to tell you this, but . . ."

He leaned against the doorframe as his widening eyes tracked around the half-empty room. "You're quitting. I know. The only thing that's really surprising me is how quickly you've packed."

Shocked to have been read so easily, my dismay must have showed on my face.

"Do me a favor," he said. "Never play poker."

The barb stung, but not as much as watching Theo add more textbooks to my duffel. I couldn't let him pack for me—not after everything he'd already done in service to my depression. Helplessness only intensified my hopelessness.

I knelt beside him and shoved in some notebooks. "It was you who kept me going, you know."

Theo laughed and shook his head. "Your fear of failure kept you going. The thought of Hawley—having to go back there."

"Well, to be honest, Tehachapi isn't all that different," I said. "Somehow I keep ending up in different versions of the same place. Regardless, I feel pretty awful about hanging you out to dry like this."

He zippered the duffel and dropped it by the door. "Well." He smiled. "You might as well call me a beach towel, because at least you've hung me in paradise."

"Will you repartner?"

"Maybe," he said, after opening the utensil drawer and dumping it into a take-out bag for me. "But I'm with you—I'm not sure I'm cut out for this."

I strode into the kitchen to let my chin drop.

Theo scorned my confusion. "You weren't the only one disturbed by the Dibrovas."

"But what will you do instead?"

Theo smirked while he rolled the silverware into a hand towel. "I don't play casino games for nothing, honey."

※

Compared with my miserable performance, Maggie finished her residency with flying colors. The Dibrova case hadn't damaged her half as badly as me—if anything, it emboldened my sister. Because while the Dibrovas' story was tragic, it also held promise: Zlata was the first known child to screen higher than her parents and survive past infancy.

Breaking the Limit seemed more possible than ever before.

Maggie spent the remainder of her time in Majuro racking up increasingly radical consultations and proportionately successful results. The Dibrova case amplified her notoriety, and my sister developed a reputation for doing things that other government officials could not: getting her clients more and more money for their growing families.

There was also the rumor that she might save the species.

"That's the legacy the Marshall Islands really deserves," Maggie said. "Not as a cradle for nuclear war."

Despite—or perhaps because of—her intrepid attitude, Maggie's patients continued to trust her. Take risks with her. She celebrated with them, too, treating all of her expectant mothers to a laudatory brunch of Tannehill French toast whenever she successfully implanted an embryo. Dr. Carmichael, too, sent his congratulations by way of a state-of-the-art PCR machine. The equipment would only accelerate her achievements.

In contrast, my retreat to Tehachapi went completely unrecognized. Between the altitude sickness and the jet lag, I couldn't leave my room while my soft island body acclimated. The cloudless summer skies of bone-dry Tehachapi leached away moisture, and I spent the first few weeks battling cracking cuticles and chapped lips with vat upon vat of Vaseline. But if this was my punishment for all that had happened, I supposed I was getting off light.

My withdrawal from Saipan became a popular topic of gossip on campus. While the students couldn't fathom my reason for trading a tropical paradise for a craggy mountain dustpan, the more seasoned faculty didn't even have to ask. They'd seen dozens of Mendels succumb to island fever and presumed the same had happened to me.

Except for Dr. Carmichael, who spotted me in the cafeteria the week before class. "Maggie! Whatever are you doing here?"

I made room on the counter for his tray. "Hi, Dr. Carmichael. I'm Charlie, actually."

He pulled a plate for the salad bar. "Oh, I do beg your pardon, dear, I forgot you were twins. Tell me, what brings you back to the convent?"

"I'm teaching, sir. Introductory Genealogy."

He dotted his greens with a few croutons and a spray of shredded cheddar. "Ah, the art of ancestry. Using the past to predict the future! So important, so important. Have you done any teaching before?"

"No, sir, I haven't. Do you have any tips?"

"Not many, dear, but you won't need them. Stepping away from practice is like stepping back from a campfire. You can still draw warmth and light from the work, but you aren't so painfully close. Teaching is a much easier job."

Those were the words I needed to hear.

※

Over the next few months, I found both my professional and personal footing in Tehachapi. As Dr. Carmichael predicted, I found instruction to be much more comfortable than insemination. My students' questions seemed more answerable than my clients', and I enjoyed flexing my expertise in addressing them. I also made friends at the convent in a way I never had before and took meals with colleagues from all over campus. My calls to Maggie grew fewer and further between.

The dry spell between us snapped with some unfortunate news.

"Nolan left," she said, her voice cracking through the long-distance connection.

The words almost dizzied me. "Your apartment?"

That seemed like the only reasonable answer.

"Yes, our apartment. Our apartment, the island, the Mendelia, me. He went back home."

I wasn't sure which I felt more: shock, sympathy, or a sense of opportunity. Guilt snuffed out the latter, and I grasped for a more sympathetic response. The best I could offer was an indignant, "Why?"

"We've been working on an experiment," she said. I could almost hear my sister tonguing her teeth. Words weren't coming to her easily, and that meant there was misdirection afoot. "Unfortunately, it hasn't gone the way we expected, and we had a spat about it."

Finally, her voice swelled with resignation. "I don't know what to do."

Although my mind swirled with questions, it stuck on the words I'd never before heard her say. Maggie was always the one to scheme, strategize, plot, and overcome—surely she must be working on some way to mend their relationship. But the despondency in her voice disturbed me. The whole situation did. And as much as I wanted to, I couldn't pain my sister with more questions.

If she wanted to share more, she would. She always had before.

Her entire affect changed after that. Our next few calls grew graver and graver as reality pulled my high-flying sister back to earth. She yearned for Nolan and longed to reconcile, but with 6,800 miles between them, plenty of things got in the way. Clients, namely, and their baggage—the byproduct of Maggie's aggressive approach.

"Latasi Kaipat came back today," she started.

On the eve of the convent's holiday break, I sat at my desk grading term papers. The name didn't ring any bells. "I'm sorry, who?"

"One of my first clients. She was already married with one child but wanted another because they needed the money. I told her that while a second child would double their income, using a different father would triple it. So she did."

"So . . . what's the problem?"

"Her husband couldn't get over it; her parents think she's a whore. Latasi can't even step foot inside her church anymore. And she wants me to help."

I put down my red pen. "Can you?"

Maggie stifled a scoff. "We make babies, not families. Latasi got the children and money she asked for. I'm not sure what else she thinks I can do."

Latasi wasn't the only client coming back either. Maggie had advised many of the women in Majuro to pursue the same course. Alienated from their social circles in their greatest time of need, these young mothers returned to Maggie for guidance. Her naughts did too. The embryos my sister had concocted were risky, borne from eggs and sperm containing highly volatile DNA. Many of the women miscarried; others birthed babies with terrible malformations. While Maggie had promised these mothers bundles of joy, they'd received swaddling blankets of tubes and wires instead.

Heartbreak in Majuro was now just as common as it had been after the nuclear testing.

※

The last time I spoke with my sister was New Year's Eve. Well, it was still New Year's in California's cold and dreary mountaintops. In Majuro, 2009 had already begun with another perfect sun-drenched day.

Despite the exceptional conditions, a listless fog still hung over my sister. "Do you ever think about our mom and dad?"

I checked my watch. I was due to go out with some of the other faculty for margaritas and still needed to get ready.

"Jim and Sherry? A lot. Our biological parents? Probably not as much as I should."

"Being Marshallese has really helped me here, Charlie. My clients trust me so much." Maggie paused. "And maybe I've abused it, just like that godforsaken adoption broker."

I tried to interrupt her but couldn't get traction.

"The Marshallese are a really beautiful people," she continued, her confession accelerating. "It's not something that struck me when I first got here, but now I wonder how I ever missed it. They have an incredible attitude about community. Everything is given and shared and borrowed and returned. No wonder our parents thought our adoption was temporary. Talking to everyone here, they're proud to be *part* of something rather than *apart* from something. I've spent my whole life trying to be special, but now I'm wondering if I've gotten it all wrong. *This* is how humanity should continue."

"It will, Maggie," I cut in. "But it's going to take people like you to save it."

"I'm not sure what I'm trying to save anymore."

Before I could refute her, Maggie volleyed a question I'd long hoped to avoid. "Charlie, do you remember the Dibrovas?"

As if forgetting such a thing could ever be possible—but I held my tongue.

"Headquarters reached out to me earlier today. They found a critical sequence in the Ainu DNA that was activated by the Huntington's. It won't save the species, but it's advancing some other research. They're awarding me four eggs."

She didn't sound half as excited as I thought she'd be.

"That's great to hear," I said in a vain attempt to buoy the mood. "At least some good came of it."

"A pittance for those children."

A silence hung between us. My moral wounds were still too fresh; I wasn't ready to revisit my guilt, nor did I need to burden my fragile sister with my intractable grief.

I desperately needed a change in subject.

"Did you ever find out what happened to Dr. Fontanez?"

An honest question, despite my more evasive motives.

"She's in Miami now," Maggie answered. "The Mendelia moved her to an urban clinic so they can keep better tabs on her. Because the program's still struggling with recruitment, they can't afford to fire anyone."

Unfortunately, Maggie didn't lose track of what I was trying to ignore.

"I wish they could go to you," she said.

The suggestion did nothing to alleviate my discomfort. I wanted a night out with friends, not the additional responsibility of my sister's progeny. Or her dejection. I'd been there, I'd wallowed in mine, but if I could pull through, she certainly would. She just needed time. And to think about something else.

"What about Nolan?" I suggested.

He was still her husband—at least in theory. If the two of them had actually gone through with the paperwork, the eggs would've been his joint property. Maybe the sound of his name could pull her off topic.

"They'd be wasted on him," she replied.

She said it with sorrow instead of contempt.

CHAPTER 25

Somehow, once again, my life changed irreparably another month later. So dramatically, in fact, it made surrendering my ovaries for bait-and-switch employment on a distant island in the South Pacific seem quaint.

A whistleblower.

At the end of January, an unnamed complainant came forward to cry foul against the Mendelia. Their objection was not one of malpractice but of misdirection: the Mendelia was not the scientific safety net that leadership proclaimed but a two-bit carnival sideshow. The practitioners, the clinics, the financial incentives—all part of a sophisticated farce to sedate a nervous public.

The Mendelia, they claimed, was a sham.

When the news first broke, the convent fulminated with whispers, hearsay, and scuttlebutt. At first, most suspected the whistleblower to be some kind of aggrieved Mendel with misplaced revenge, but with every passing day more students found reason to convert to the theory of grand governmental conspiracy. Conveniently, it explained our program's slow rollout. The dilapidated facilities. Its persistent understaffing.

After all I saw in Saipan, I wasn't sure what to believe. When I tried calling my sister, she didn't pick up.

On Tuesday, February 3, Dr. Rubino rolled a microwave-size television into the convent's cafeteria and called on all the staff and students to take a seat. The auditorium would've provided a much better venue, but there was no way the leadership would risk using the convent's crown jewel to showcase its downfall. As part of the faculty, I was afforded a choice seat at one of the front tables, but could still see very little. The tiny screen featured a distant congressional hearing room, and from what I could tell, an expert scientist, the Mendelia's director, and a vacant chair all sat before a glossy wooden conference table. The twelve senators on the dais were impossible to make out, but it wasn't hard to tell the gallery was full.

Everyone was watching Congress hold the Mendelia to account.

The chairman of the committee, Senator Brian Mulroney, introduced the scientist first. An international expert on the Limit, Dr. Irfan Ahmad testified that he'd comprehensively audited the scholastic underpinnings of the Mendelia. His findings should be interpreted as reassurance: the science behind Mendelic practice—the physiology, the psychology, the sociology, all of it—was valid.

The remarks softened my unease very slightly.

At least we hadn't been completely deceived.

Content with this explanation, the chairman moved on to the director. I recognized the large woman by her flaccid cheeks and protuberant eyes—while she'd never visited our convent, Director Winifred Byrne's portrait had hung in the auditorium ever since I'd first arrived. Brassy hair and a tweed jacket did nothing to abet her aged appearance. Despite her considerable size, she somehow looked mousy.

With little preamble, the director spoke her truth hard and fast.

"As a program, the Mendelia was never truly intended to break the Limit. While the fundamentals of our practice are sound, we've never been funded at a level to achieve that objective. At current investment, the Mendelia amounts to a sophisticated form of palliative care: our work provides a significant amount of psychological comfort to the masses as our species' inevitable fate draws near."

The audience gasped, then turned to each other to exchange furtive questions. An unflappable Director Byrne folded her hands over her notes and waited for the hubbub to subside. While she did, a few junior staffers furnished some dramatic-looking charts at the front of the room.

"Every person in this country deserves a purpose," she remarked. "And for many, that means making a contribution. Our program provides that illusion, and our clients partake of it willingly. We provide mercy in despondent times."

The director then gestured to the colorful posters her minions had put on display.

"In this respect, the Mendelia is succeeding. Suicide rates in the country have dropped; average lifespan is slowly increasing. In comparison to other nations, the United States is attriting generations far more slowly than its peers. These population-level changes cannot be attributed to the microscopic experiments of science-led programs.

"And despite its financial handicap, our work has recently returned some unexpected results. Just last year, an attentive practitioner in the South Pacific territories located a unique DNA sequence that advanced our broader understanding of the Limit. We're proud to have shared that discovery with researchers around the world."

Several of the senators tugged at their jowls. For me, hearing the Dibrova case touted as victory turned my stomach. But that upset paled in comparison to the total upheaval that came next.

After thanking the director for her comments, the chairman turned his attention to the vacant seat and explained that it had been held for the final witness: the whistleblower. As he finished this introduction, the mahogany doors at the rear of the room swung open so that a tiny Hispanic woman could swagger through.

I almost fell out of my chair.

An alabaster clinic coat draped over her blood-red dress, Dr. Fontanez looked ready for battle.

She took a seat at the table of witnesses, and I felt my insides clot with fear.

"Chairman Mulroney, thank you for inviting me to this hearing today," she began. "My name is Dr. Linda Fontanez, and I'm a practicing scientist at the Mendelia's clinic in Miami. As you know, I've expressed concern about the program's ethics, and today I will be expounding on those complaints.

"As I've detailed in my written testimony, I have reason to believe that the Mendelia are acting in bad faith—both with Congress and the American people. The program leads their clients to believe that their personal reproductive choices are nationally important. That their individual decisions might save the species. But from what I've witnessed both in training and in practice, this is, quite simply, blatant propaganda."

Chairman Mulroney interrupted. "Isn't that what your director explained just a few minutes ago?"

The question pushed Dr. Fontanez onto her back foot. "I'm not sure. I was . . ."

"In another room," Senator Mulroney finished for her. "That's why we cloister you with a television, Dr. Fontanez. Ought to pay better attention to it next time—it seems you've been upstaged."

Such a political assassination couldn't have been coincidence. I wasn't sure whose side the senator was on, but it certainly wasn't Dr. Fontanez's.

"Then . . . then I need to inform you about something even more disturbing," Dr. Fontanez said.

Senator Mulroney's eyebrows lifted.

Dr. Fontanez leaned into her microphone while she fumbled for her narrative. "There are at least a handful of practitioners taking our protocols to irresponsible lengths. The children they're making are little more than mutants."

My jaw clenched. Based on what my sister had told me, Dr. Fontanez's accusation might have merit—but that could be sorted out another day. Right now, on national television, I could only pray that our former supervisor wouldn't torpedo my sister in a last-ditch effort to save herself.

"I have firsthand knowledge of the extent of this abuse," Dr. Fontanez continued. "Because in one case in particular, the practitioner was a resident of mine."

Oh God. It was happening. Please no. Please no, no, no.

Dr. Fontanez's tongue swiped across her bottom lip, seemingly enjoying the taste of the kill.

"Dr. Maggie Tannehill."

Shit.

The whole cafeteria whipped around to look at me. The scrutiny might have disturbed me if my mind hadn't already engaged in imaginations of how Maggie might be pilloried. Hostile courtrooms, belittling interviews, shadowy jails cells. Could there be worse? Maybe there should be if my sister in fact committed such heinous crimes. But I shouldn't think like that. Not at a time when she needed me.

I kept my eyes on the television as notions of an ugly future raced behind them.

For his part, Chairman Mulroney looked not at all fazed by Dr. Fontanez's revelation. Instead, he reclined in his seat and swiveled his pen between his knuckles.

"Sounds more like a criminal matter than a congressional one. And as her supervisor, shouldn't you have been keeping a closer eye on her?"

"If only you'd allow me to explain . . ." Dr. Fontanez stuttered.

"No 'if onlys,' Dr. Fontanez. Considering that we've gone almost twenty years without a breakthrough, perhaps more extreme applications of Mendelic practice might be necessary."

Dr. Fontanez withered in her chair.

Chairman Mulroney's mouth twisted into a serpentine grin. "To that end, it sounds like the Mendelia is executing its mission exactly in line with congressional intent. We do write the checks, you know. And based on what I've heard today, they might need a plus-up."

The hearing concluded without further spectacle. Director Byrne and the expert were thanked for their time and dismissed; Dr. Fontanez was largely ignored. The camera zoomed out to show an audience of suits and skirts drifting away from their chairs to exchange handshakes and business cards.

While the bombs our director had dropped were enormous, the dust had already begun to settle.

Only time would tell whether my sister would survive the fallout.

CHAPTER 26

Gunshots are insidious wounds. Looking at one, you might wonder how a person could even die of such an unassuming injury: entrance wounds are trim, symmetrical, almost tidy. Some are no larger than your pinkie finger. But as a bullet passes through the body, tissue and bone absorb the round's enormous force as it slows. Without the stabilization of speed, it starts to tumble and yaw, ripping open a new cavity all its own. Unsatisfied with this destruction, the projectile punches out the back of its new home at several times its original size. In like a pencil, out like a pancake. That wound peels back muscle, bleeds profusely, and drains the body of life.

Exit wounds are messy.

Exit wounds kill.

For the Mendelia, the shot had been fired in Washington, but the exit wounds were felt at the convents, in the bodies of its practitioners. Some students were so emotionally injured that they began packing their bags before Dr. Rubino could even turn off the television. A few others had pulled out their cell phones to book airline tickets home. The air of the mess hall thickened with disgusted questions: Is this real? Should we stay? What do we do?

Call Maggie, I thought.

My sister was already in a fragile state. Surrounded by the broken hearts of her desperate clients and fully consumed by her own, the news of the Mendelia's fraud would gut her. And this didn't even account for the fact that she'd been denigrated on national television. By name, no less.

I needed to talk to her.

I retreated to my room to call, but no one picked up. Just as I finished leaving a message, a familiar trench coat passed by my door.

"Dr. Carmichael," I called.

When he turned, I saw that the thin man's hands were full of luggage.

"I didn't think you'd—"

"Have morals? I'm a scientist, Charlie, not a sociopath. The fact that some students have taken our practice to unapologetic extremes appalls me."

I blinked through my disbelief. He had to know he was talking about Maggie. He was the one who'd trained her.

I sputtered through my rebuttal. "But I thought Dr. Ahmad said the science was real?"

"And who do you think wrote his testimony?" Dr. Carmichael said, adjusting his cap. "Dr. Ahmad is an old friend of mine. The work is still worthy, Charlie. It's just that I can't lend my talents to corruption, no matter how convenient they make it. I'll find work elsewhere."

"Is that what I should tell the students?"

"Only if they need to hear it," he replied. "Figure out what they want to do, then help them get there. Just like we do with clients."

I spent most of the next few days trying to reach my sister. Though I called her after every meal, each one rang through, and I was relegated to leaving increasingly frantic voicemails. When I wasn't on the phone, students crowded into my office for counsel about whether to quit. But while they came to me on the pretense of advice, I knew what they truly sought was validation.

I gave it to them without a second thought.

"Am I throwing my future away?"
"I don't think so."
"Is this the right thing to do?"
"Of course."
"What will my parents think?"
"That you made the right choice."

By the end of the week, the population of the convent reduced to a fifth of its prehearing numbers. Housekeepers and janitors now outnumbered anyone teaching or learning. It wasn't long before we got word that Mendels and technicians all over the country were abandoning their posts. Dr. Rubino put me in charge of organizing a roll call of all the clinics west of the Mississippi.

"Isn't this a job for Headquarters?" I asked, completely uninterested in phone calls that didn't involve my sister.

She heaved an enormous directory onto my desk. "As you can imagine, they're a bit busy."

"What about the Kansas convent?"

Annoyance dripped from the administrator's words. "Kansas is covering the South. No one can reach Ponce de Leon."

"The whole convent walked away?"

Dr. Rubino turned without answering my question.

The next day, I put what was left of the demoralized student body to work on the phones taking inventory of which clinics could still operate. Thousands of clinics in twenty-four states meant we had at least a week's worth of work. But only one call mattered to me.

I still hadn't reached Maggie.

I could only hope that she'd retreated into herself to lick her wounds. That wouldn't have been unlike her—the few times she'd flubbed tests in high school, she'd banished herself from contact with me until she'd fully recovered her ego. But given all that had happened over the past months, I couldn't shake the feeling that such an outcome wasn't in the cards. Normally, I would have checked on her, but with the entire Pacific between us, there was nothing I could do but call.

Petro was right—the ocean really was a tyrant.

The roll call project absorbed most of my time. I was grateful for the daytime distraction; with the time change, I wasn't going to reach my sister during California's waking hours. I tried staying up into the wee hours of the morning to catch her before work, on her lunch break, between clients—but still, nothing.

Nothing but intensifying dread.

In the mornings, I worked through my call list.

- La Grange, Texas: Could not be reached. Presumed inoperable.
- Ladora, Iowa: Mendel, AWOL; technician, present. Clinic inoperable.
- Lafayette, Oregon: Mendel, present; technician, present. Clinic operable.
- Laguna, New Mexico: Mendel, undecided; technician, AWOL. Clinic TBD.

I had one more call before my lunch break.

"Lake Crystal Mendelia Clinic," a female voice answered.

"Good afternoon," I started. "My name is Charlie Tannehill. I'm calling on behalf of Headquarters to assess your clinic's operating status. Is your Mendel still on duty?"

"I am," she replied.

"And you plan on staying?"

"I do."

"Your technician?"

"The same."

"So you're able to operate normally?"

"Yes."

"Thank you for your time," I concluded.

"Wait—is this Tehachapi?"

The question bobbled me from my script. "It is."

"I thought your name sounded familiar," she said. "Charlie, Nolan's not well."

"Excuse me?" I sputtered.

"This is Val Proctor. Nolan came home from Majuro a mess. He looks awful and feels worse. And he hasn't been able to reach your sister in weeks. Can you help?"

Val. The name strummed a memory that I couldn't quite put a finger on. Though she'd asked me for help, my shaking hands hung up on her as my breath quickened. If my sister wasn't even taking Nolan's calls, something far more sinister must be afoot.

My numbing fingers could barely punch in the numbers to reach Saipan.

My voice cracked when she answered. "Hi, Dr. Varghese, it's Charlie Tannehill. I'm sorry it's so late there."

The warmth of Dr. Varghese's voice made for an immediate salve. "No trouble about the time, dear. You know I'm a night owl. Tell me—how's the convent taking the news? How are you?"

"I'm worried about Maggie. I haven't been able to reach her all week."

"Come to think of it, I haven't either. She's so independent—I don't usually need to check up on her. Do you know if she saw the hearing?"

"I don't. She hasn't returned my calls, and it's not like her to ignore me."

Dr. Varghese's voice dropped. "You're right to be concerned," she said. "Let's see . . . she hasn't gotten a new technician yet, so we can't send them to check on her . . . but . . ." Her voice stretched as she reached for something. "I know some of the hospital staff in Majuro. Mary is a charge nurse, and I have her number right here. She won't mind making a house call."

"Thank you, Dr. Varghese," I whispered. Any remaining hope faded with every word.

"It's Brinda now. I'll call you back as soon as I hear."

The next morning, housekeeping slipped a summons under my door. A mandatory meeting. For the entire convent. At 3:00 p.m. that afternoon. This time, in the auditorium.

The new superintendent would be discussing the future of our practice.

As we made our way over, the hallway filled with rumors about the termination of the Mendelia writ large and details of our severance packages. I wasn't interested in the speculation—whatever the Mendelia offered, it wouldn't cover the loss of our jobs, our homes, and our future. It wouldn't make Maggie call me. It was useless.

With Dr. Carmichael's departure, Dr. Rubino had taken the helm. When she took the stage, she brought no slides, no posters, no notes. She looked appropriately disheveled for a week's worth of chaos: long sleeves rolled up, suit jacket forgotten, reading glasses tucked into a wrinkled breast pocket. Whatever news she was about to deliver would be unadulterated, unpackaged, and raw. She spoke like a Gatling gun—short sentences, fired off quickly, each word cutting off the last.

The Saipan discovery had been convincing.

Resources were being increased—the scientific mission shored up.

The work was important.

We were important.

More important, perhaps, than ever before.

Temptation tickled my interest. Dr. Rubino had just promised that we'd be able to continue our work, now with more funding and support. She offered a future that so many desperately wanted—needed—and if we could just ignore the slippery pangs of doubt, we could even enjoy it. But it was hard to quiet the murmurs that reminded me that this might be another iteration of what the Mendelia had already admitted to: misdirection, delusion, deceit.

At the end, there was no applause. After Dr. Rubino excused herself in silence, I shuttled back to my dormitory, nagged by thoughts of my sister. Even if they were false, these messages were exactly what Maggie needed to hear. That her work mattered. Not only had it advanced scientific research, but it secured the future of the entire program. If that didn't inspire her back into practice, it might at least constitute grounds for her and Nolan to reconcile. Their failed experiment could be set aside—or perhaps run anew, given the fresh investments in the program. The warmth of the fantasy sustained me as biting winter winds hounded me across the quad.

I'd just arrived at my room when my phone rang, and a flush of optimism coursed through me as I picked up.

"Mary visited the clinic this morning," Dr. Varghese began. "The manager of the post office hasn't seen it open in weeks. I gave her your sister's home address and she visited the apartment. No one answered, and she couldn't locate Maggie's vehicle. I've already called the police."

The inside of my chest began to burn as I realized I'd been holding my breath.

Deep down, I knew there were only two possibilities. Maggie was either dead or she wasn't, and the Majuro police would soon find out which. Until then, my sister was neither—uncomfortably strung between two opposing fates.

The fairy-tale ending, the one where Maggie was overworked and out of touch, had already vanished.

The next best case, the one where Maggie was depressed and reclusive—but still very much alive—was evaporating.

The worst possible outcome seemed more probable by the minute.

As illogical as it was, I held on to hope. The Mendelia had conditioned me to seek the unlikely, and so my mind reached for it, unwilling to concede to the overwhelming evidence. Harrowing thoughts of razor blades, pills, and suicide cliffs pried at the corners of my mind. I did anything I could to stay busy. I reorganized my desk and swept away pencil shavings. Then I turned to my laundry and put away my shirts and pants. Finally, I dusted and mopped and performed all the other chores housekeeping usually took care of.

I might as well have been building a windwasher.

When my desk was clear and my clothes were stowed and my floors were spotless, the phone rang once more.

The Marshall Islands Police Department. They'd found Maggie's car—at a beach near the airport—but not her body. Not anywhere on the island. No persons of interest, no signs of a struggle. Her wallet was still in the cupholder. A small bag of things in the trunk. Perhaps an accidental drowning, the officer suggested.

"It happens more often than people realize," he said. "Could she swim?"

I don't remember answering, only hanging up.

CHAPTER 27

How long could I go without eating? Two days.

Without showering? Three.

Without stepping outside? Five.

More now, since Theo couldn't come calling.

How did I know? The Dibrova case. Some might have thought that such a recent tragedy would've left me hardy, or fit, or somehow otherwise equipped to handle my sister's sudden death.

But this hell was different.

This hell was deep.

While the Dibrova case had pained me, Maggie's death left me gasping for air. Sure, I'd ached for Petro and his family, but thinking about Maggie left me gouged. Gutted. Grief must have spooned out my insides, because after a week, I felt like little more than a husk. Dry and listless, I might have died in my room had it not been for the housekeeping staff. Of dehydration? That would've gone on the record. But heartache would be more accurate. And loneliness, closest of all.

My parents must have sensed my torment, because they called every hour, on the hour. Their voicemails begged me to pick up. The panic in my mother's words reminded me of my new responsibility: their one and only daughter.

That's what brought back the sobs.

A week later, we had a service for Maggie. It was just my parents and me.

Mercifully, the funeral was one of just a small handful of administrative items I had to take care of. In the Mendelia's records, Maggie had listed me as her next of kin, but she didn't have much of an estate. No pets, no investments—nothing but a credit card bill I could settle once I'd signed for her final paycheck. In terms of personal effects, Dr. Varghese put what few personal items my sister owned into the mail so that the Mendelia could dispose of her apartment. As her employer, the Mendelia took care of notifying her technician too.

While there was no way I could have made that call myself, I was desperate to know how Nolan had taken the news. We hadn't spoken since he left Saipan, but Maggie never faulted him for their separation. If anything, she'd blamed herself. And while I wasn't sure he would share the details of their dispute, I wanted him to. My sister had transformed into someone entirely different after he'd left, and I was starting to suspect only he knew the reason.

When I called to invite him to the funeral, Nolan picked up the line without answering.

I queried the dead air. "Nolan?"

"Speaking," he answered.

I could tell he held his hand on the hilt of sharper words.

"We're going to have a service for Maggie in California," I continued. "I wanted to know if . . ."

"No, thank you," he said, and hung up.

There wasn't time for further pursuit; my parents were due to arrive the next day, and we hadn't decided where to honor my sister. As her twin, my parents left the decision to me.

Springdale meant nothing to her, and Hawley would be an insult. Majuro, too expensive to ever visit.

That left California. The place where she'd grown to be her best self.

I'd decided to take my parents to the end of the Santa Monica Pier. Cliché, but neither my parents nor I had the wherewithal to find a better option. When we arrived, however, I almost wished we'd had—the adjoining sidewalks and beaches were thronged with people interested in anything but solemn remembrance. The boardwalk itself was saddled with a noisy arcade. As we passed, my father tried to lift our spirits by challenging me to a round of Skee-Ball, which I unceremoniously lost. In an effort to help me save face, the carnival barker awarded me a consolation pinwheel.

Its pink metallic fan turned splendidly in the brisk ocean breeze.

The pier continued more placidly beyond the carnival: the weathered planks now belonged to quiet fishermen and the serenity of a near featureless ocean. Bare but grand, the view commanded reverence with its relative simplicity: an infinity of sun, sky, and water; instinctively and relentlessly captivating.

My family took a seat on one of the communal benches to wait for some railing space. In the crook of her elbow, my mother cradled a bouquet of sweet pea flowers we'd spent all morning procuring. It took no less than three visits to insensitive florists across the city for us to locate such an unusual arrangement, and each inquired as to why we wanted such pedestrian blooms for such an important occasion.

My mother's glare sufficed for an answer.

It wasn't long before one of the anglers grew tired of the ocean's emptiness and abandoned his post. What remained of my family then sauntered up to the railing and stood, taciturn, but for the pinwheel, which thrummed in the near-constant wind.

We were all waiting for someone to say a few words. In any other circumstance, it would have been Maggie.

Gusts tugged at the sweet pea blossoms and plucked away their bubblegum petals to scatter them into the sea. My mother knew not what to do but to watch the flowers deteriorate. She hadn't received such a privilege with her daughter, whose death had all but ambushed her. My father must have recognized this sadness, and it bit him in anger. With a grizzled beard and cheeks as ripe as cherries, he snatched the decrepit bouquet from my mother's unsuspecting hands and hurled the entire thing into the Pacific.

"I know all good things come to an end," he blubbered, unable to stop his tears. "The spectacular ones just go a bit faster."

Try as we might, my family could not avoid speculating about Maggie's death. While the Majuro police seemed confident of its inadvertent nature, no one in our family could shake the feeling of premeditation.

To answer the officer's question, of course she'd known how to swim. She'd been a lifeguard, the star of the swim team. But would she have heeded a riptide warning? I couldn't be sure. Whatever she'd learned at the convent left her so plucky, she laughed in the face of risk. Risk, it seemed, had finally laughed back.

But there wasn't enough evidence to confirm a suicide either. No note, no witnesses. Intent? Perhaps. The dishonor of her practice in Majuro had finally caught up with her, and unlike Petro, Maggie's clients were still alive enough to complain. But she must have been keeping such shame from my parents, because they never brought it up. Instead, my father and mother seemed convinced that the Mendelia scandal must have crushed her when Nolan's desertion had already weakened her resolve. Maggie was prone to impulsion, they reminded me, and haste could've gotten the better of her. With every passing minute, they seemed certain of it. She was their daughter, after all, and no one could know her better.

Except me, I thought. And there was so much more to it.

I withheld that reality even when my father caught me in the parking lot.

"You don't think . . . she was actually making mutant babies, do you?"

My eyes dodged his as I slid inside the sedan. "No. Dr. Fontanez had no idea what she was talking about."

It should have been an easy question to dismiss, given Dr. Fontanez's fall from grace. But my father's inquiry hinted at his doubt. Deep down, he, too, knew what Maggie was capable of. He knew of her gumption. But graciously, he took my word when I brushed him off and never brought the question up again.

Whether I was protecting my sister or my family, I didn't really know. As it stood, my parents had an understanding about their daughter's death that they could live with. Insisting on the truth would only reopen their wounds—and perhaps bleed them dry.

Throughout their visit, my parents and I willfully ignored Nolan's absence. Over dinner, when we retold stories of Maggie's finest moments, his name was omitted, his presence glossed over—until, at last, it wasn't. My father stumbled into mentioning her beau when recounting one of Maggie's finer moments.

"Do you remember graduation?" He volleyed the question over an appetizer at an oceanside restaurant not far from our hotel.

"At the convent? Of course," I said, and discarded the variegated tail of a coconut shrimp into a nearby bowl.

As valedictorian, Maggie had made a school-wide address during the ceremony and used her platform to whip the entire class into believing that we, the seventh graduating class of the Tehachapi convent, would finally break the Limit.

"She sure looked like a real champion, hoisted up on Nolan's shoulders like that," my father chortled. "I thought we were going to end up waiting on them 'til midnight with all the hands she had to shake."

My mother's face soured as my father recalled that victory lap. Even though Nolan hadn't amounted to more than a step stool, she resented the recognition.

Speaking his name seemed to summon him. Moments later, my phone rang. When I spied Nolan's number under the table, I excused myself to the sidewalk to take the call.

"Nolan," I answered, a bit more harshly than I intended.

"Yes, it's me, Charlie. How long are you going to be in California?"

I looked out at the sunset, where a half-moon had slipped into the cotton candy sky. "We leave tomorrow. My parents have a morning flight from LAX, then I'm headed back to the convent."

"Great. I'll be landing right about then. Can you give me a ride downtown? I'll throw in lunch for your trouble."

While his audacity appalled me, I censored my revulsion.

Amnesty would be a fair price for details about my sister.

"Sure," I said. "But why? Our service for Maggie was two days ago."

"You'll see," he clucked.

That night, grief visited again. I was grateful, then, to be sharing a room with my parents—not only for the company but for my father's snores, which drowned out my pitiful blubbering. I wanted so badly for this to be over. For it to be a dream. For it just not to *be*. Because no matter how Maggie had died, at her own hand or not, she was still gone. There was nothing I could do, say, think, or pinkie promise to change that. Ever.

Exhausted by helplessness, or perhaps the sleeplessness, I downed three cups of coffee before dropping my parents at the terminal the next day. After I did, I kicked myself for taking on the burden of whatever Nolan needed. I just wanted to go home and cry. And cry again. And maybe cry forever. But the combination of caffeine and obligation got the better of me, and I darted in and out of airport traffic in search of the man I'd last seen in Saipan. And I would have missed him but for his tousled shock of ginger hair, because the vibrant man I once knew had winnowed into frailty. Withered flesh hung from his anemic frame, and a prominent brow cast ominous shadows over sunken cheeks.

While I'd expected my sister's death to have been hard on him, I hadn't expected for it to take fifty pounds.

His twiggy fingers pulled open the car door. "Fancy meeting you here," he said.

"Where . . . where can I take you?"

The words were innocent enough, but a poor substitute for my real questions: Why did he look like a corpse? What was going on? Nolan was obviously unwell with something far more destructive than resentment.

"The university hospital," he replied.

"I thought you said you wanted lunch?"

"I said I'd buy it, not eat it," he parried. "Clearly, I don't have much of an appetite these days."

CHAPTER 28

We didn't measure distance by miles in California—minutes were far more accurate. For example, while the university hospital was situated an unimpressive twelve miles away, Los Angeles traffic would quintuple that into a full hour's drive. Long, for sure, and longer still because of the company. Not only was Nolan generally crotchety, but we couldn't quite agree on what to talk about. Gentle chitchat lasted only a few moments, and I didn't feel it was my place to pry about his condition. Maggie was the only thing we had left in common, and even she was gone. Strained and uncomfortable, we kept an armistice of calculated silence until the hospital appeared on the horizon, at which point I began searching for a place to park.

Nolan noticed the shift of my attention. "There's a cookie place two streets over. They've got a few spots on the curb."

After locating a meter, I clumsily groped the inside of my bag for spare change. Nolan, however, stretched out of the car like a man stepping into his own kingdom.

"It's free for the first two hours," he said, reaching toward the sky. "And I don't think we'll be here that long."

The bakery itself looked neat. Candy-striped awnings trimmed massive front windows featuring crisp gold-leaf signage. Inside, industrial mixers, massive refrigerators, and giant racks of baking sheets dominated the space. Half a dozen men bustled between the oversize appliances, measuring, mixing, and rolling out cookies—hundreds of which were on display in at least a dozen varieties. The line of customers wrapped around the block, and no one looked to be leaving with less than a box.

We queued behind a gaggle of students, and Nolan leaned over with instructions. "Cookies are three for a dollar. My treat, considering the fortune your sister left me."

I ignored the jab. While his joke may have been misplaced, his bitterness was not.

The fact that I didn't rebuke him must have meant something, because a meek smile broke through his churlish frown.

"You should get the chocolate chip," Nolan said. "They sprinkle a little sea salt on top."

The instruction irked me. I craved details about our current circumstance, not about the cookies. In the absence of more direct answers, I searched Nolan himself for clues. Every word, every glance, and every gesture could be a tea leaf. Surely I could divine something from them if I stared long enough.

After five quiet minutes, he grew tired of my fixation. "Charlie, I have cancer."

I'd been waiting for him to say it. There weren't many other reasons for him to look so gaunt.

Nolan kept his eyes on the display case. "It's aggressive and unusually so. I'm getting experimental treatment."

"Is that why you didn't come to her funeral?"

It was an ambush he'd prepared for. "No. Maggie drove me out after the diagnosis. It was too much for her; she said she couldn't live with it."

His callous choice in language twisted the knife still lodged in my heart.

Realizing his unintended cruelty, Nolan winced. "Honestly, Charlie, if I thought she'd meant that literally, I would have stayed."

Devotion imbued his voice in a way I hadn't heard since our last night in the islands.

"But as soon as the diagnosis was confirmed, I made one last deposit with the Mendelia like we'd planned . . ."

His mossy eyes finally met mine. ". . . and then she told me to leave."

Ahead of us, the coeds were settling up with the cashier, and we'd be called for orders next. I snuck in one more question.

"What do you mean, 'like you had planned'?"

It was his turn to recoil. "She didn't tell you?"

I said nothing, but my face must have twitched with a twinge of betrayal, because Nolan chuckled.

"Well," he said, "before we get started on that, you're going to need one of those cookies."

After the teenagers made their way out, Nolan stepped up to the counter. Through the shop window, I watched as he made some friendly banter with the cashier. One by one, each of the men behind the counter greeted him with high fives and handshakes. Nolan was obviously a regular, if not favorite, customer. When he attempted to pay, the cashier firmly refused him—but Nolan shoved all the bills from his wallet into the tip jar, anyway.

He rejoined me with two hefty boxes.

"You'll want to take these back with you to the convent," he said, bobbling the six dozen cookies. "You'll be a hero in the break room."

Having spent most of the day cooped up in transportation, Nolan insisted on walking the rest of the way to his appointment. Despite his weakened condition, I was in no position to deny him small pleasures. I did, however, carry the bakery boxes.

We both knew our next destination. The four main towers of the hospital enclosed a manicured courtyard where doctors and patients alike took more than a few minutes to catch some fresh air. During our training, the convent had sent us to this hospital to observe complicated implantation procedures, and we'd always found it easier to make the harder decisions under the open sky.

On this day, like homing pigeons, we returned.

Nolan heaved irregular breaths as we took a seat on a polished redwood bench. The short walk had winded him, and it took more than ten minutes for his two-word sentences to ease into three, and then five. There was no way for me to help him but to wait, and this seemed to pain both of us.

Finally, he swallowed one last gasp. "From the beginning, Maggie had a plan," he gurgled. "Even in Tehachapi, she was ready to conduct radical experiments based on the theories she'd developed with Dr. Carmichael."

Whatever had happened had started at school? She seemed so happy then—so confident, so comfortable. Besides succeeding, I couldn't recall much of what Maggie had been up to at the convent—I'd been too preoccupied with my own survival.

Maybe that's why I'd missed the signs.

Nolan pushed the cookies in my direction. "I'm not going to continue until you have some. They're delicious."

Obediently, I nibbled at one.

"That advanced coursework she took? The after-hours labs? Dr. Carmichael had her convinced that the South Pacific was full of genetic anomalies. Between the nuclear testing and the presence of ancient DNA, Maggie was sure she'd strike genealogical gold."

He paused and nodded again toward the cookie.

I took another mouthful.

"The Marshall Islands were the furthest we could go within the confines of US border agreements," he continued. "Initially, Headquarters didn't even want to send us there—too remote. But given her budding reputation as the program's prodigy, Maggie had pull. Majuro had a US post office, she argued, and she wanted to go."

With that, Nolan unwrapped a cookie of his own. There was something relieving about watching him eat.

"And Maggie wasn't alone in her excitement. I was pretty pumped about the research potential too." He wiped a few errant crumbs from his chin. "But the people alone weren't enough.

"As much as she wanted to work with the Marshallese, Maggie thought the most gains could be made by formulating interesting embryos. Given our distance from the continent—and regular supervision—she thought she'd be able to get away with more. But unfortunately for her, Headquarters wouldn't ship her restricted samples since so many of them spoil on the transpacific flight. So after weeks of talking it over, she and I determined that if we wanted to work with more volatile DNA, we'd have to bring it with us. In the end, I agreed."

Valentine's Day. Echoes of that awkward breakfast conversation rang in my mind. I could feel my eyes widening.

"What do you mean you 'agreed'?"

He picked up another cookie. "To start acquiring mutations. Mostly through radiation—it's why I was in the hospital so often. The bike accident, the back pain—I got pretty good at convincing doctors to order X-rays. You can get yourself a lot of them if you visit different clinics and know how to complain."

I didn't fully register the horror I felt, though I saw Nolan looking for it. I could feel his eyes scanning mine—any trifle of outrage might compel him to stop. With an oversize swallow, I let disgust flow past me.

If Nolan needed to feel safe to continue, I could feign understanding a bit longer.

Content with my abiding tolerance, he continued. "After that, I started exposing myself to mutagenic chemicals, which is why I asked to visit that garment factory. The dyes they use can get pretty nasty. But when I threw up the next day, I knew I had to back off. Too much, too fast, too sick. Nonetheless, I kept updating my samples with the Mendelia so Maggie could use them in her work."

He stopped to inspect me again. Unsure of what to say, I took another bite of cookie.

Nolan's eyes lifted skyward. "I knew it was risky. I knew what I was getting into. But Maggie believed in it. And I believed in her."

Blind allegiance. From him to her, and her to the Mendelia.

Unfathomably imprudent.

No, that was too generous.

Unfathomably stupid.

All of it was so goddamn *stupid*.

Despite all the anguish I'd felt in the preceding days, I couldn't help but feel my anger provoked. Maggie was dead, Nolan was dying, and none of this would've happened if she hadn't always pushed so hard. Hadn't asked for the inconceivable. If my sister could've just settled for . . . for . . . normality, maybe they'd both still be alive.

Unaware that my temper was flaring, Nolan balled up his cookie wrapper and lobbed it into the trash. "We agreed to stop once the first tumors appeared. Treatment wasn't available in Majuro so I had to fly to Guam—and only at night, to avoid additional radiation." He raised a spindly middle finger toward the sky. "Sunlight's a bitch."

"Unfortunately, I didn't respond to the therapy. And I didn't have the heart to tell your sister"——at last, his voice faltered—"until I had to. Last September, I was hospitalized for a couple of weeks so they could take a part of my lung and a couple of feet of intestine. After that, I got a lot sicker a lot faster. That's when they told me I had six months to live."

A dewy coating formed over Nolan's eyes. "When I told Maggie what the doctors said, she was angry. She told me to get out. She'd never said things like that to me before, even when we'd argued." He rolled his chapping lips and wiped away a tear. "I stayed at first, thinking she just needed time to process, but whenever she saw me, she winced. Like I'd failed her or something. We had the same fight every night for two months. After Thanksgiving, she couldn't take it anymore and threw me out."

It was all he could do not to break down. I might have, too, but for my burgeoning ire.

How could she have done this to him? She was supposed to love him, not harm him. *Him.* The one I could've loved. A peptic surge of jealousy scalded my insides, which had already been rendered raw from two weeks of grief.

"I never heard from her again." Nolan's sigh was thready and weak. "I tried calling her at Christmas and New Year's, but she never picked up. I knew she was busy with cases, but I thought she'd at least want to *try* patching things up. But she didn't. She loved her work, and in the end, she chose it over me."

I didn't know what to say. What Maggie had done to Nolan almost seemed more grievous than all those unfortunate children she'd heedlessly made.

"I don't understand," I said flatly, filling the dead air.

"Me neither. But you don't need to. What's done is done, and understanding won't change anything. I've tried."

I couldn't bear to talk any more about my sister. I couldn't stomach the image of her, haughty and self-possessed, berating the man who'd sacrificed himself for her ambitions. I tried convincing myself that he must be exaggerating, that he'd become irrationally embittered by some transgression far smaller than what he described.

But I found I didn't want to think so little of the man I once loved.

An intrusive, unwelcome thought, I tried dismissing it from my mind with a change of subject. But there was only one left to switch to, and it wasn't more positive.

"So how's treatment?"

Nolan shrugged. "Like most things in my life, a waste. But since your sister already convinced me to donate my body to science, I might as well continue. The doctors are studying my tumors to see if they can learn anything. I'm near the end now—they're counting down in weeks.

"But," he said, resigned, "at least there's cookies."

Nolan checked his watch. "Time for me to head up."

My eyes flicked to his. "Can I join you?"

"I can't imagine why you'd want to."

He was right. I didn't want to. It was almost too painful to look upon my sister's ugliest indiscretion. To see Nolan tortured. I hated her for what she'd done, and for leaving me with the consequences. But now I had to stay. Abandoning him now seemed impossibly cruel.

I felt Nolan watching the weights and balances tilt behind my eyes.

"It's what Maggie would've done," I murmured.

"*Should* have done," he snipped.

I didn't disagree.

Nolan and I collected our things and made our way toward the western tower. Having spent my entire career in neglected, faraway places, I'd forgotten what it was like to be in such a modern facility. Here, the needy brought with them all kinds of afflictions, and like the prophets of old, the doctors had become renowned for managing them. Curing them, even. If Nolan had any hope, it would've been within these four walls—but the high priesthood of healthiness had already told him there wasn't.

The oncology suite felt emptier than it actually was. Sterile at best and hostile at worst, the spartan room would've been the crown jewel at any convent or clinic. But Nolan didn't comport to the chamber's severity. Instead, his conduct at the front desk was just as friendly as it had been at the bakery. I found myself coveting the congeniality he could extend to others but not to me. And while I understood why he was fickle, I missed that part of him—dearly so.

When Nolan was brought back to the treatment area, my phone vibrated with an incoming call.

A convent number.

I stepped away into the hallway.

"Dr. Tannehill? It's Venita Rubino. How are you today?"

I put a finger in my ear to block out the surrounding commotion. "Good afternoon, ma'am. What can I do for you?"

"I was so sorry to hear about your sister," she said, her voice dripping with artificial sympathy. "We're finalizing some things on our end, and I was wondering if you could forward me a copy of her death certificate."

"But we've already received her final paycheck."

"There's a lot that Headquarters can do on the administrative front without formalities, but disposing of Maggie's eggs is a legal matter. We need documentation to begin the process."

I stopped. My mind replayed her words to make sure that I'd heard them correctly. "Already?"

"We're recruiting, Charlie, and we need room in our freezers. After the hearing, Congress cut us a huge check, and they want us staffed up as quickly as possible. Maggie's eggs are, well, a liability. Not to mention that her genetic material is already overrepresented in our library because of yours. As a Mendel, I'm sure you understand."

I didn't. I didn't understand her reasoning, I didn't understand my feelings, I didn't understand why she was calling me now.

I did understand, however, that I was being dismissed.

"I made the request to Majuro last week," I said. "But mail travels slowly across the Pacific."

Half truth, half prayer. I'd been away from the convent for almost a week, and it was entirely possible that the document was already sitting in my inbox.

"Once you have it, be a dear and send a copy along."

It was almost too much.

Maggie dead, Nolan dying, and now the Mendelia, flushing away the last parts of my sister without her consent. How much more could go wrong? How much more could I endure?

I darted back into the waiting room to hide my demolished mind behind a vacant stare. By that point, I wasn't sure I could survive in this terrible reality unless something changed. But Maggie's death was incontrovertible, and Nolan's seemed not far behind. Just thinking about how irreversible everything was revived the helplessness that had tortured me all night. I *hated* feeling so impotent. So inept.

I needed to do something.

Unfortunately, there was nothing I could do for Maggie or for Nolan. The most malleable part of my atrocious existence was the Mendelia—an organization alive enough to desecrate the remains of my sister.

Maybe that was something I could change.

Nolan broke my trance by taking the seat next to mine.

"Hi," he asserted.

For him, not much had changed since the beginning of the appointment—except for his forearms, which were now bandaged from the volley of blood draws.

"Hi," I whispered, distance in my gaze as well as my voice.

He noticed my detachment. "Well, you seem involved."

"I am," I admitted. "I'm working on . . . a plan."

He slapped his knees with his bruising hands, and we both took our feet. "You Tannehill girls and your plans. Let's get back to the airport. Los Angeles traffic will give you plenty of time."

Our ride back was just as muted as the first. Nolan leaned against the window to rest his eyes while my mind worked to process everything I'd heard in the past two hours. When I finally pulled to the curb at the terminal, I looked over at the boy I once hoped would be mine and wondered if this would be the last time I'd ever see him.

"You'll call me when it's time?" I asked.

Nolan was checking his pockets to make sure he hadn't forgotten his wallet or phone. "Only if you tell me about this plan of yours. I'm not agreeing to any more Tannehill girl plans without the details up front."

A fair request.

"I will," I promised, and peeked out over my sunglasses so that he could see the honesty in my eyes.

"And . . . ?" He gestured saucily for more detail.

"I don't have them yet. I need to think everything through."

Nolan cracked the car door. "Quite unlike your sister."

CHAPTER 29

As I drove back to Tehachapi, my mind turned faster than my wheels. Though the trip took a solid three hours, I found that I still needed more time to register my sister's crimes. To consider her eggs.

To figure out what to do next.

And it all had to be done before that death certificate arrived.

When I got back to my dorm, I checked my mailbox. Empty, thankfully. I reminded myself it would be an incredible feat for a notarized legal document to find its way across thousands of miles of water in just a few days. But the improbable was delivered by a custodian just after dinner. Not the officially stamped envelope I was expecting, but an unassuming shoebox. Wrapped in butcher paper, it bore an address in Dr. Varghese's elegant script and a postmark from Majuro.

Her things.

Though my family had already honored Maggie's passing, this package somehow made my sister's death all the more real. Sorrow weakened my knees while the weight of the shoebox threatened to drop me to the floor. Instead, I crumpled into bed and cradled it like the child my sister would never have.

Though it pained me to open, I slipped a finger under the flap.

Tearing through the paper revealed a picture of sweet pea blossoms—the framed art Nolan had gifted her that first Christmas here at the convent. Under that, a few selfies of her and Nolan at the beach. In all of them, my sister sparkled with the same exuberance I'd seen in the hospital the day of their wedding. After everything Nolan had shared, I felt relieved to see that she might have actually, really, loved him. Even if he couldn't see it, I could. The photographs revived my hope that Maggie wasn't the monster Nolan described.

Perhaps he'd just misunderstood.

A few assorted notebooks and papers filled the remainder of the box. Handwritten details about certain patients, a few extravagant Punnett squares and pedigrees. A copy of her collection contract—nothing that didn't look like work. As I leafed through her chart papers, I savored my sister's penmanship. Strong, sharp, eagerly scratched—a lasting and appropriate approximation of what could have been her legacy.

Nothing would be written in the same hand again.

At the bottom, I found a few loose-leaf computer printouts. One that caught my attention featured a travel advertisement: white sandy beaches shaded by dancing coconut palms. The scene I'd always hoped would satisfy me. Below was an itinerary. And a receipt.

Both had been struck through with an angry red X.

The flight plan beneath it read: MAJ->HNL->ORD->MSP: $1652.63

Majuro to Minneapolis.

She'd planned to see Nolan.

I would have called him immediately if envy hadn't overpowered me. If he was going to get some satisfaction, some explanation, I certainly deserved some too.

She was *my* sister. My twin.

I flipped over the sheet. There had to be more than just four airports and an oversize strike mark. There had to. Pages must be missing. Pages with a better justification for what she'd done and why she'd done it. And why she'd given up.

Why she'd left me.

I knew it was unfair of me to think like this. But I was the one who had to live through this hellscape of grief, not her. And I needed to know.

Desperate for something more, I returned to the shoebox for clues. I tore through Maggie's artifacts again and again but found no more revelation. In the absence of hard evidence, I started constructing hypotheticals: Her car had been found at a beach near the airport, hadn't it? From the police report, it sounded as if she'd even packed a bag. Had she stopped for one last farewell cleanse in Majuro's clearest waters before heading to the plane? Or had she been washing away her shame after canceling the tickets?

I couldn't tell. And I'd never be able to. As much as I yearned for it, only Maggie knew the truth—and she'd taken it with her, by intention or not.

The rest of us were left to write our own stories.

I was about to close the box when the printout caught my eye again. While the package carried the date Dr. Varghese had mailed it, the receipt differed. January 25, 2009. Maggie had bought the tickets a full three weeks earlier, and well before the hearing too. If that was the day she died, my sister would've missed the Mendelia's confession. My parents' understanding of her motivations couldn't suffice: Maggie would have been spared the disgrace of her inspiration. Never suffered that humiliation.

But then I realized how little that mattered.

She'd disgraced and humiliated herself just as badly destroying Nolan.

A silent scream escaped as I mouthed the only words I could imagine her saying.

"I was just trying to help."

My future, my career, my pride, my sister—all of them had been taken from me. All ruined by forces beyond my control. I'd accepted that, as best as I could, but this package spoiled the one thing I'd been holding on to: my sister's memory. This itinerary removed any doubt that my sister had been ignorant of what she'd done. And she'd done it to the man I'd loved the most. Now, any recollections I had of her as an indomitable spirit—vivacious and persistent, courageous and kind— were corrupted by a terrible reality. Was I really supposed to spend the rest of my days remembering her as an overambitious psychopath?

I wouldn't. After everything that had happened to me, I deserved one happy thing. I would bury the ugly truth. No one else had seen her note, and Nolan—the only other witness to her heinous mistake—would pass in just a few weeks' time.

As the last survivor of her terrible indiscretion, I could protect my sister from shame.

I fell asleep convincing myself of it.

※

The eggs. That's all that mattered now. Theirs was the only fate I could hope to change.

I could only hope it would change mine.

Maggie wasn't the first Mendel to die before appropriation. Car crashes, heart attacks, other untimely deaths—they all took their fair share. According to the contract, any eggs a Mendel left behind were forfeit in the absence of a certified legal directive. But even when the Mendelia had one on record, spouses and siblings struggled to secure what was rightfully theirs. In the name of freeing up freezer space, the Mendelia rarely waited a week before flushing them.

I shuddered at the thought. But given what I'd heard in the hearing, I shouldn't have been surprised. The Mendelia had wooed my sister into practice on false pretenses, then manipulated her passion for their own benefit. Disposing of her hard-won prizes would be easy work by comparison. As angry as I was with my sister, I couldn't let this abominable agency desecrate the last parts of her.

I couldn't let them win.

But what would I do with fifteen eggs?

Maggie had earned back four from the Dibrova case, three from other minor genetic mutations, and eight from superlative consultations—an unprecedented take for someone so young. Given that Mendels used three eggs in every implantation, fifteen eggs amounted to five placements. Five placements meant at least five opportunities for discovery—at least that's what Dr. Carmichael still believed. But even if they didn't break the Limit, these eggs could still create life.

Five placements meant five children.

Five mothers.

Five families.

But did any of it really matter? After all, in five generations they'd all be naughts.

I could have revolved through that confusion for the rest of my life. But with my sister's eggs on the edge of the Mendelia's toilet, I was going to have to act. And not because I knew what to do. But because doing nothing meant failure, and I was done doing that.

⚇

Spite was incredible fuel.

After steeling myself over breakfast, I marched down to the superintendent's office and pushed past a protesting secretary.

I offered a handshake across the desk. "Dr. Rubino."

The superintendent raised a finely plucked eyebrow at her apologetic assistant, who did nothing but hold up her hands in surrender.

"Hello, Dr. Tannehill," she purred. "Any word on your sister's paperwork yet?"

"No, ma'am. But I did want to talk to you about Maggie's eggs."

"And what of them?"

I'd practiced the line all morning. "I'd like to take custody."

Unimpressed, Dr. Rubino reclined into her leather office chair. "For what purpose?"

"To continue her research," I lied.

The superintendent swiveled to face the window behind her. "Unfortunately, Dr. Tannehill, by law and by policy, that cannot be done. We'd be in violation of the collection contract and ultimately, Maggie's human rights."

Not knowing what to do with my hands, I crossed them over my chest. "But as you mentioned before, Dr. Rubino, Maggie and I are twins, so, uh, her genes are my genes and therefore . . ."

"Clever," she interjected, still gazing out over the meadow. "But not the first time I've heard such an argument from twins under similar circumstances. Those eggs did not come from your body, Dr. Tannehill; we have witnesses who can attest to that. And therefore, you have no right to them." She spun back to glare at me. "The Mendelia take bodily autonomy very, very seriously."

With blood in the water, Dr. Rubino stood up to circle her prey, high heels clicking on the concrete floor.

The superintendent liked to play with her food.

"Even in the face of the Limit, we cannot force people to delay reproduction. We cannot impregnate them either. We cannot compel an unwilling body to do anything against its resolve, even if it might save the species. We can only incentivize. We can only reward.

"Think of medicine," she continued. "Thousands of people die every year waiting for blood, bone marrow, organ transplants. All of these tissues could be forcibly collected if doctors were only allowed. But they aren't. Not without consent. If I would let you have these eggs, Maggie would have fewer rights than a corpse, whose organs I could not harvest even if it would save the life of the next Nobel Prize–winning scientist."

If Maggie had heard such a thing, she would have spit. Whoever could break the Limit could have whatever organs they needed, Nobel or not—that's what she'd believed. The species needed a future more than it needed morality.

"Restraint is one of the pillars of the Mendelia, Charlie. You know that accusations of eugenics and government-controlled reproduction run rampant. Much of the public think that the Mendelia conduct their business with irreverence for the law and disdain for humanity. Indulging your request—using Maggie's body in a way she did not intend—would only confirm the public's suspicions."

"What about my eggs? Will you dispose of them too?"

A churlish question, but the only one I could summon.

"If and when you leave the Mendelia, we are, by contract, obligated to do so."

She finally went in for the kill.

"To protect our reputation—and our mission—the Mendelia must honor their word. My refusal of your request is part of that."

My patience curdled.

She made it sound so legitimate. So sensible. So fair.

And it would have been, but for what I'd seen just a few weeks before.

Nothing the Mendelia said could be trusted, even if it sounded true.

"I don't believe you," I snapped, and left without another word.

༄

I would've called my sister if I still had a sister to call. Exasperated, I stalked the still-clean floors of my dormitory like a caged animal. Maggie would've known what to do, how to retaliate. I yet again needed her to stand in for me, like she so often had. But without my sister to take my place, I had no choice but to take hers.

She'd told me as much at the airport.

I flopped into a nearby chair to stare at the ceiling. To defeat the Mendelia, I needed to think like Maggie. Act like her. Figure out what she would've done, and then do it.

But what was that? What would right my capsizing ship?

I returned to the shoebox for inspiration and found it in the collection contract.

༄

My sister would've known that the only recourse was legal. Two days later, I returned to Dr. Rubino's office prepared to counterpunch. This time I made an appointment. On Friday afternoon, her assistant showed me in at exactly one o'clock.

"Good afternoon, Charlie. I suppose this means you have news from Majuro?"

"I do not. I am here, again, to *formally* request custody of my sister's eggs."

Dr. Rubino didn't take her eyes off the forms she was reviewing. "Dr. Tannehill, I already explained."

"In that case, I would like to exercise my sister's right to arbitration."

She put down her pen. "Excuse me?"

I crossed my arms with confidence. "To arbitration. It's in the collection contract."

Dr. Rubino was not a woman easily unnerved. Though she stared at me for a few moments, the twitch at the corner of her eye suggested she knew that I'd cornered her. Given the Mendelia's delicate political standing and recent public embarrassment, it would be prudent for her to deflect any additional attention by redressing my complaint quietly.

And that's what she offered.

"We have a man in Bakersfield who handles these things," she announced. "I'll make our counsel available."

I didn't let my guard down until she latched the door behind me, but once it had, I whooped my way down the hall. Silently, of course—but with enough of my sister's enthusiasm to draw a few eyeballs.

However sweet, the victory fleeted away later that afternoon. Reaching the arbitrator Dr. Rubino had mentioned turned into a wild-goose chase through the Bakersfield phone book: it took fourteen calls and three hours with the Kern County Bar Association, the public defender's office, and several other lawyers to locate the esteemed Kenneth W. Kolb. It took far less time for him to tell me that he was the only qualified attorney in at least a hundred miles and that his availability was limited to next Tuesday.

I had only three days to prepare.

There was no use scrambling for legitimate legal aid—there weren't any attorneys in Tehachapi that didn't belong to my adversary. I considered calling Theo or Dr. Varghese for help but decided against that, too—they didn't need their professional reputations tarnished by my vengeance. I was going to have to represent myself entirely by myself.

What little remained of my sister depended on it.

※

Tuesday came quickly. The drive out of the mountains would take at least an hour, so I planned to get an early start to give myself two. But on that morning, impulses to stay and go fought each other while minutes ticked by. I abhorred conflict, and fighting the Mendelia would be nothing but. I took a centering breath and reminded myself that Maggie's eggs could not be won at the convent.

I had to go to Bakersfield. And I had to go now—before doubt changed my own mind.

Anxiety slunk between my thoughts, stalking my composure and heightening my senses. I found myself noticing the clock, the temperature, my clothes, my breath. Misfortune was on my tail, I could feel it. It was only a matter of time before something terrible happened. I'd spill my coffee, crash my car, lose my way—something would penalize my progress. Something always had.

But on the drive, to my earnest surprise, nothing did. For once, I felt like I'd escaped fate's wicked clutch. The drone of the road soothed my frazzled nerves as craggy mountainsides slumped into rolling hills and finally open oak savanna.

It, and I, felt gloriously empty.

I found Mr. Kolb's office near the more industrial part of town. The squat concrete building had been hard to locate, and I felt grateful for the extra minutes I'd built into my schedule. The blocky exterior stairs brought me to a shabby second-floor door, where I knocked politely. After one long minute, a man I could only assume to be Mr. Kolb ushered me inside.

"Exactly on time," he said, and gestured toward a plastic folding chair beside his unstaffed reception desk. "Please, take a seat. The conference room is nicer, but I wouldn't want anyone to think I'm showing you any kind of favoritism. You know how it is."

"Thank you, sir. I understand, sir."

He looked like a man who valued honorifics.

"Would you like some water?" Mr. Kolb toed into what looked like an empty box under the desk.

"No, sir," I said, offering a timid smile. "Thank you, sir."

"Good, because I don't have any. I'm sure they'll be here shortly anyhow."

I had my doubts. The Mendelia weren't half as nervous as I was and had no reason to have left early.

Over the next few minutes, I took care not to project any signs of impatience. I resisted eyeing my watch, though Mr. Kolb checked his often. I watched him review and recycle the front pages of the newspaper and then start visiting the conference room window to scan the parking lot. When ten minutes tripled into thirty, so did his irritation.

"I know you drove a long way. How long are you willing to wait?"

His aggravation was a gift only the Mendelia could give. I called back to him without a single note of annoyance.

"As long as you are, sir."

Mr. Kolb helped himself to another cup of coffee. He was about to sprinkle in the powdered creamer when the overdue knock finally arrived.

Though drabber and more disheveled, the attorney at the door looked just as young as I was. Even prior to the hearing, the convent struggled to recruit talented counsel—the banal work of contract and administrative law didn't draw many intellectual heavyweights. What few lawyers the Mendelia could retain were unimpressive, inexperienced, and always watching the door.

Ms. Noda looked to be one of them.

Mr. Kolb scolded the mousy woman for the delay and gestured for me to stand up.

"Ms. Noda, Dr. Tannehill, let me show you to the conference room."

CHAPTER 30

When Mr. Kolb announced our Tuesday meeting, I briefly considered spending the weekend trying to become a lawyer. When I realized I didn't even know where to find books on contract law, I gave up on that particular quest. The only tool I had any hope of wielding was one the Mendelia had given me.

I'd use genealogy against them.

During my time on faculty, I'd taught my students the art of climbing through family trees. I'd shown them how to pull back branches to find siblings with intellectual differences, grandparents with physical deformities, distant cousins with unusual conditions. We'd gone over how to pick through the tree's fallen leaves and use deceased relatives to surmise a family's pattern of death. Moreover, I'd taught them the value of this information and how it could reveal important secrets.

It was the only hope I had of subverting Mr. Kolb.

There was no magic to genealogical research. No pipettes or vials or fancy machines. Only records. And at his age, Mr. Kolb had plenty. I spent that Saturday at the Bakersfield library sifting through public documents: marriage licenses, birth certificates, property titles—when properly assembled, they painted a pretty detailed picture of Mr. Kenneth W. Kolb. The eldest of five siblings, Mr. Kolb had lived in California's Central Valley for all his life and spent most of it married to his high school sweetheart, Donna Pavlovitch. Though they never had children of their own, Mr. Kolb's four sisters had plenty. They'd all taken their husband's names, however, which made my job four times harder.

It took a full day's work to account for all twelve Kolb nieces and nephews: ten living; two dead. While I found a news article describing the toddler's tragic swimming pool accident, the death certificate for twenty-seven-year-old Jennifer listed no cause.

Could any of this be exploited? Possibly. According to the birth date listed on his marriage license, Andrew Corden, one of the nephews, was thirty. At that age, he and his wife could be trying for children. Since the Kolb family showed no signs of independent wealth, the couple may be seeking financial benefits through the Mendelia.

If so, I'd find their records in our database.

Given my position at the convent, I was allowed access to individual genetic records without restriction. Most practitioners weren't afforded such a privilege—privacy, like autonomy, was a protected right, and Mendels could only analyze the genetic data of clients under their direct care. That's why, when I took a seat in the convent's library and opened up Andrew's sequencing report, I halfway expected someone to sound an alarm.

Had the Mendelia known how I planned to use Mr. Corden's data, they would have.

Andrew had screened as a naught. Perhaps more interestingly, though, he'd been tagged as a carrier for cystic fibrosis. Another well-studied genetic disorder, CF drowned its hosts in their own sputum—but it took two copies of the gene for the condition to express. As a carrier, Andrew only had one and would show no symptoms. But given CF's heritability, the defect would splinter back up through the Kolb family tree and offer reasonable cause for Jennifer's unexplained death.

That was something I could use.

After we'd settled into our seats in the conference room, Mr. Kolb convened the session. He was not a man for grand introductions, and after reviewing some of the basic administrative details about the proceedings, he turned to me.

"You'll both get time to make your arguments, but Dr. Tannehill, why don't you get started."

I thought about Maggie. Her moxie. Her nerve.

I took a breath.

"Mr. Kolb, do you know what it's like to lose a sister?"

The old man balked. While I knew I was supposed to start with some kind of opening statement, nothing I had to say was as important as what Mr. Kolb had to realize. For that, questions would do a better job.

"All right, m'dear, not the most traditional of starts, but since you're a guest in this profession, I'll go with it. My answer is no, though I did have a niece who died young."

My inexperience made for helpful disguise.

"And what did you do with her body?"

"We buried her. Underneath an oak in my sister's backyard. Took more time and permits than I thought it should, but that's what she wanted."

He seemed proud to have executed his niece's wishes. Another useful tell.

"Did she have a will at such a young age?"

Mr. Kolb glowered. Whatever delight he'd taken in my amateur interrogation was starting to wear thin. "She did. But that's because she had a terminal disease."

"And did she die at home?"

"No. She died in the hospital. It all happened a lot faster than we thought it would."

Embarrassment flashed over him, and he closed his mouth to stem the flow of more personal detail.

I took the spillage as a sign that I was breaking through Mr. Kolb's stony defenses but kept my celebration to myself. If the taciturn man sensed my trap, the jig would be up—so I let his utterance slip by unacknowledged.

"So what happened after?"

"Her death?" Frustration simmered behind his stale blue eyes. "Her body was taken to a funeral home. We picked a casket and put her in the ground. Pray tell, Dr. Tannehill, where are you going with this?"

I parried his outburst placidly. "No. Before that."

Placing his elbows on the table, Mr. Kolb steepled his sinewy fingers against his face. He then shut his eyes, making his reaction harder to read. When they opened, cold calculation had replaced the heat of indignity.

"They took her to the morgue. There was a medical examination. She wanted her tissues donated to science."

A carefully calibrated reply. Mr. Kolb was not going to make the same mistake twice, but that left plenty of room for me to stumble.

"So they removed her lungs?"

His voice ripened with suspicion. "And why would they do that, Ms. Tannehill?"

I'd sprung my own trap. Of all the personal details Mr. Kolb had let by, he hadn't mentioned the CF. I'd just revealed how far I'd trespassed into his privacy.

When his beady eyes searched mine for malice, I made sure he found none.

He would surely punish my hubris. The misstep should have been enough for Mr. Kolb to call my bluff, embarrass me in front of my enemy, and then let Ms. Noda run me through with technicalities and legalese.

But none of that happened.

"I believe they did," Mr. Kolb conceded.

Confusion swirled into my panic. Why wasn't he berating me? Mr. Kolb's relentless stare instead telegraphed an understanding. Some kind of unspoken compact that Maggie probably would've understood.

Desperate for the stay of execution, I entered into it not knowing the terms.

"And then what happened to them?"

Mr. Kolb rolled his cheap pen over the expensive desk. "Dr. Tannehill, could you make your point plain now?"

My point. I had spent most of Monday crafting it and most of that morning rehearsing it in the car. I had practiced all sorts of inflections and intonations to deliver it in the most exacting way. And now it was time.

"Shouldn't *all* parts of your niece be handled in accordance with her wishes?"

The conference room held silent. Even Ms. Noda seemed stunned.

Mr. Kolb replied with a crisp, indubitable, "Yes."

Agreement. Simple, powerful agreement. From the mediator. The only advocate I really needed.

"Mr. Kolb, much like your medical examiner, the Mendelia are custodians of tissue," I continued, confidence surging through me. "While they may hold my sister's eggs in escrow, they do not have the right to act upon them."

Ms. Noda interjected. "Our contract says otherwise."

I ignored the remark. It needn't convince her—only Mr. Kolb. And I almost had.

"Like your niece's lungs, my sister's eggs were separated from her body. Like your niece, my sister wanted her tissues used in a particular way. Do you think Jennifer would be happy to hear that the examiner just tossed her lungs in the trash? No. She wanted to advance the research into cystic fibrosis, just like my sister wanted to advance research into the Limit. Maggie signaled her intent when she signed the Mendelia's contract, just the same way your niece did when she signed her will. And while the Mendelia may have authority to flush away the remainder of her ovaries, fifteen of those eggs were earned back. They deserve to be handled according to my sister's wishes. And that's what I intend to do."

I stood for a moment and allowed the power of my performance to resonate. I wasn't sure at which point I'd taken my feet—I hadn't intended to. But the lines, the gestures, the exchanges with Mr. Kolb—all of it had carried me away.

"But the collection contract," Ms. Noda stammered, "is still a contract. The Mendelia's authorities are clearly stated in that document, and your sister assented."

Mr. Kolb's gaze hadn't shifted from mine even though Ms. Noda was trying to catch his attention.

"The Mendelia offered the contract in bad faith," I replied, speaking more to Mr. Kolb than to her. "Their fraudulent intentions were established in the congressional hearing earlier this month."

Ms. Noda sagged back into her chair. Even she knew that this case would be won or lost on the merits of my argument, not hers.

Mr. Kolb, it seemed, had heard enough.

"Thank you, ladies, for your time. I'll be rendering my decision in the next few days. You'll receive it by certified mail."

After collecting our things, Ms. Noda and I departed just as unceremoniously as we'd arrived. As I made my way to the car, I felt my enthusiasm giving way to exhaustion. I wouldn't be able to maintain the air of Maggie's confidence much longer; I needed to get somewhere that I could finally shed my disguise. I was keying the door to my rental when Ms. Noda caught up with me.

"If you weren't already a Mendel, I'd say you'd make a great lawyer."

I fumbled through the key ring. "Thanks."

"For what it's worth, I agree with you. I have to argue otherwise because I need to get paid, but I think you're right. And more importantly, *he* thinks you're right. I hope you get what you need."

Whether she meant the eggs or revenge, I never found out.

CHAPTER 31

When I returned to work the next day, the Mendelia had devolved the convent into a hostile landscape of inconvenience. While they couldn't legally drive me out, the Mendelia weren't prohibited from expressing their displeasure by declining my meal card or revoking my access. After the custodian stopped delivering my mail, I knew it would only be a matter of time until I'd find my laundry service suspended and the lock to my dormitory changed.

It didn't help that word of my insurrection was already making the rounds. Most of my colleagues and all of my friends found it prudent to keep a safe distance from me. I couldn't blame them—the Mendelia had revealed themselves to be a sly and vindictive adversary. Though I'd known that winning back Maggie's eggs would not come without cost, the rejection still stung. I reminded myself that my sacrifices paled in comparison to those of Nolan or the Dibrovas.

Mr. Kolb's decision arrived within the week. After digging through the mailroom myself, I ripped open the goldenrod mailer: cross as he was, the arbiter had awarded me full custody of Maggie's earned-back eggs, as well as the rights to place however I pleased.

Mr. Kolb did, however, limit my placement authority to thirty days. He'd bought one part of the Mendelia's argument, but perhaps the smallest: their need for freezer space.

I'd won. I couldn't believe it. I started flapping the paperwork around like I had when Maggie and I had received our admissions letters, but this time there was no one to embrace. No one to celebrate with. Any delight I felt in slaying Goliath further dissolved when I considered the logistics of placing fifteen eggs in thirty days. A tall order, even for a practicing Mendel with eager clients and complete support from her clinic. And I had none of those things. While Mr. Kolb had ordered the Mendelia not to obstruct or impede my work, the program would offer me little grace and no assistance. I'd be lucky if they didn't actively subvert my efforts.

I needed to get started. But eggs were nothing to a Mendel alone—I wasn't trained to perform implantations. I didn't have the equipment.

I needed Theo.

We hadn't spoken since I'd left the island, but Dr. Varghese kept me appraised of his prospects. After Saipan, Theo had gone home to Seattle to try his hand as a substitute teacher while he worked through the repartnering process. I was glad to hear that he was teaching—it was one of the few professions that wasn't in major decline. The world still needed high-quality education, at least for a few more decades. Unfortunately, according to Dr. Varghese, it wasn't going well. Neither was his hunt for a new Mendel. While I knew I should've been racked with guilt, I had only enough empathy for one tragedy at a time.

"I need your help placing eggs," I said, after Theo picked up my call.

My technician pushed through his stupefaction. "Charlie? I thought you were back at the convent."

"They're Maggie's eggs, Theo. I won them in court."

It crossed my mind that he might not have heard about my sister's death, and I winced at having to explain. But whether he was already informed or too polite to ask, Theo replied with what could only be described as perverse delight.

"Oh my God—congratulations! I'm sure the Mendelia put up a fight."

"Not a very good one," I replied. "But I only have thirty days."

"That's impossible. Aren't there a dozen or something?"

"Fifteen." I sighed. "Can you come? I need a technician."

His reply was unqualified and full throated: "Sure."

"I don't know how to thank you, Theo. God knows the Mendelia won't help." But as the relief passed, unrelenting doubt reared its ugly head. "I don't understand why you are doing this."

"Me neither," he said. "I can only tell you that this sounds better than spending another day with horny, hormonal teenagers."

It was the first time I'd laughed since I heard about Maggie.

"Look," Theo continued. "Four of those eggs came from the Dibrova case, right? That family still needs avenging. Where do we start?"

"I haven't figured that part out yet."

Theo smacked his lips. "Well, you have one whole evening to work up a strategy—I'm packing a bag and meeting you at LAX in the morning." The distant sound of a zipper confirmed his intent.

"I'll meet you at the airport, but I don't think there's any use coming back to the convent. I've been excommunicated here. Let's just plan on grabbing a flight," I said.

I could almost hear Theo smile. "And you said you didn't have a plan."

"It's not a plan. It's a step."

In the right direction, hopefully.

We hung up. By morning, I needed to know what to do. Or at least where to go.

Thirty days had already contracted into twenty-nine.

That night, sleep ignored my restless mind as it galloped through my anxieties with all the uncontained frenzy of a spooked horse. How was I supposed to place these eggs? When paired, would they produce the horrible mutations that Maggie intended? Would I accidentally create another Lesya? Another Petro? My conscience gnawed at these worries until they splintered to bone.

As the unrelenting sun warmed the winter sky, I tried to focus. With Mr. Kolb, I'd argued that Maggie's eggs had been specifically and purposefully earned and should therefore be used according to her wishes. But what were those wishes? Had my sister died the brilliant researcher that I first knew, I would've known exactly how to put her eggs to work. But she perished as someone entirely different—and I had no idea what that person would've wanted.

An unhelpful conclusion, and one wrought with complication. But while I could no longer know how Maggie truly felt about her work, there was one thing that I felt certain about: her feelings. I had a shoebox. I could hold her final emotions in my own two hands. And what its contents told me was that Maggie felt shame. Complete, insufferable, shame.

Had she not been immediately responsible for Nolan's death— had the cancer developed spontaneously and unfortunately—my sister would've seen him through to the end. She'd have taken him to every appointment, shaved her head in solidarity, and rubbed his back while he puked up his guts. And she would've done whatever it took to make sure his life had meaning, because that's all he ever talked about wanting.

And while Maggie wasn't around to deliver this kindness, I was. Her eggs were. And if I put them to work with Nolan's sperm, then maybe, just *maybe*, something might come of his sacrifice.

My sister's redemption might still be in the cards.

I still didn't know where to begin—but Maggie always did.

In Majuro.

Maggie had very deliberately chosen to practice in the Marshall Islands. While she'd always professed its research potential, I knew there was more to it. Majuro offered a chance for her to go stand in our biological parents' footprints. Feel the faintest connection. Pretend that they could be found.

Her curiosity about our parentage piqued in our teenage years, when Jim and Sherry helped us explore our origins as part of an eighth-grade history assignment. Paperwork from the adoption fraud revealed that our biological father had emigrated from Namdrik Atoll after his friend found work on an industrial poultry farm in Springdale, Arkansas, and sent word back. My father—and many men like him—followed. They brought along their brothers, fathers, uncles, and friends, and when they'd finally saved enough money, they sent for their women. And so, an entire Marshallese city grew up in the homely foothills of the Ozarks. A little piece of the South Pacific half a world away.

Just like Saipan, the Marshall Islands saw its fair share of missionaries, and many of the people brought their faith with them to Springdale. As immigrants poured into the region, a crop of Marshallese churches sprung up. Baptist, usually, but a few others as well. Maggie and I contacted one of the larger congregations just after our fifteenth birthday. Pastor Black knew his flock well, he said. He knew their number, their stories, their lineage. But most importantly, he said he knew our father, and that he'd be happy to talk.

We'd placed the phone on the kitchen counter and hovered over it.

"Ah, Vaitea, yes," Pastor Black started. "Always sat in the third pew. Came over in 1986, maybe."

Maggie looked at me, and I nodded. The year matched the date from the papers.

"The church was smaller then, so he and I talked a lot after the sermon. He had a job at the poultry plant, of course, in the hatchery. A delicate touch, that one. After he'd gotten a few paychecks under his belt, Vaitea sent for your mother, and it wasn't long before she was pregnant. They wanted to book the baptism as soon as they felt you kick."

I looked up from the phone to smile at Maggie. She was dabbing away a tear.

This was the first time we'd ever heard how wanted we'd been.

"The blessing of twins surprised your folks, as it did most people at the time. But your parents were ready to give you girls everything they had. Including those Dixie names of yours—they'd picked those before you were even out of your mother's womb."

Charlotte Mae and Magnolia Bea. But success in the American South required assimilation, and our parents had given us a great foundation. Little did they know that we'd end up in Pennsylvania. After near-constant Yankee torment by the Heathers and Emilys and Paiges, we'd stopped using our proper names.

I hadn't realized what a gift they had been.

"When you finally arrived, oh my, was your father in tears. He told me that his own mother had miscarried several times after the nuclear testing. Celebration was in order whenever a baby made it through delivery. And this time, that joy doubled."

The shine in his voice began to dim as he finished that sentence. While Maggie and I already knew what he'd be saying next, it was always painful to hear.

"But so did expenses. Double diapers, double formula, double cribs. Your parents turned to the church for help. I must confess, I was the one who pointed them to that deceitful adoption broker. She'd been a member of our choir ever since I arrived, but after an ugly divorce, she was trying to strike out on her own. I can't believe I didn't see the signs. For this, I will be judged by the Lord."

Any additional reprimand from us would be negligible by comparison.

"Shortly after signing the papers, your mother found a job at the local school, in the cafeteria. Your father took extra shifts. They worked as hard as they could to earn enough money to support you, and when they did, they came back to me. They didn't realize that . . . I didn't realize that . . ."

"That you'd all been duped," Maggie finished.

"I could barely explain it to them. They didn't show up to church for weeks. There was no recourse then—not until the lawsuit. But ten years had passed, and your parents had gone back to Majuro to take care of their parents. I didn't know how to find them.

"I don't doubt that they're still hoping for your return."

I didn't wake the next morning, only because I'd never fallen asleep. By the frosty dawn, poise had replaced my panic, and I strutted out into the morning mist with a moxie I'd only ever known one woman to have. Though I didn't have a plan, I finally had a purpose.

The rest would surely follow.

I arrived to find LAX swarmed with travelers. Most looked shabby and comfortable—lots of sweatpants and oversize cardigans. But not Theo. He never left the house without a starched collar and slim-fit jeans. I spotted him cuffing his sleeves from across the concourse and waved.

"I'd almost forgotten what a hellhole this airport is," he said. "But you're ready to get us out of here?"

I reached into my purse for the tickets. "Yes. I want the first egg to go to a Marshallese couple."

"Charlie, the trip to Majuro takes at least three days, not to mention that there may not be any clients left to work with considering how Maggie left things. Sperm samples usually arrive damaged because shipping is so unreliable, which means that . . ."

"Theo," I said. "I bought us tickets to Arkansas."

CHAPTER 32

Placing a baby with a Marshallese woman would balance Maggie's karmic checkbook. Not for the loss of my biological parents, but for all the families she'd left broken back in the islands. Was it idealistic? Definitely. Rational? Not exactly. But it was just as good of a reason as any, and it gave me a place to start.

My best chances were in Arkansas, in the same town in which I was born. Springdale still hosted the largest Marshallese population on the continent, which clocked in at nearly ten thousand. Of that, roughly half would be female, and 20 percent of that would be naughts. From there, I subtracted the preadolescent and the postmenopausal populations; I needed someone with the right hormones to carry a pregnancy. On top of everything, they'd need to be interested. According to the back of my napkin, the needle I was looking for was located in a two-hundred-person haystack.

While it wasn't a long flight—our measure for that had been completely redefined by transpacific travel—it was a long day. Theo and I had gotten a very early start but didn't arrive in Springdale until almost midnight. We took the first cheap motel we could find.

After breakfast, we got started by establishing a clinical beachhead. Theo made contact with the Springdale clinic, and while the staff seemed friendly at first, a chill settled into the room after they scanned his badge. As he told it, they knew exactly who he was and who he was with. There'd been no need to discuss whatever I'd done.

My job was to find Pastor Black. From what I remembered, he sounded just as capable as the Mendelia at helping us locate eager naught couples. Getting back in touch with him proved the most significant challenge—I didn't remember the name of his church, and the listing for "Black" in the phone book was two pages long. It would've taken me days to comb through all of them, though I can't say I wasn't tempted. The alternative was far more painful.

I needed to call my mother.

After the lawsuit, my mother had grown increasingly cagey about talking about our adoption. She never fully recovered from the accusation and took any mention of Springdale, Pastor Black, and the Marshallese as a threat. My request would involve all three.

I picked up my phone and dialed home. As it rang, I pulled open the drawer of the bedside table and flipped through a few pages of the Gideons Bible in hopes that God had some advice on how to broach such a sensitive subject with my mother.

He didn't, at least not before she picked up.

"Charlie? It's so good to hear from you!" my mother chirped. "Have you made any placements?"

I sighed. "I'm hoping you can help me with that, Mom."

"And how's that, darling?"

While she sounded eager, I knew her enthusiasm wouldn't last.

I took a deep breath. "I need to get in touch with that pastor in Springdale who helped Maggie and me learn about our biological parents. You don't happen to still have his phone number, do you?"

"But why?"

Behind the innocent question, I could hear my mother sharpening her claws.

"The placements, Mom."

"Well, I hope you aren't using Maggie's eggs to try and correct for some kind of . . . cosmic injustice," she spat. "Giving some Marshallese woman a baby won't fix the fact that you and your sister were stolen."

Though I'd expected her bitterness, it was no less hard to swallow. And as much as I wanted to, I couldn't tell my mother that she was incorrect. Not without explaining my sister's crimes.

Oblivious to my predicament, my mother barreled on. "There are plenty of other deserving women in the world who want babies, too, you know."

The barb shredded what little was left of my patience. "Like who, Mom?"

"Your aunt, for one."

I dropped to the bed. I hadn't thought much about Aunt Frankie since the funeral. When she hadn't been able to afford the flight, I'd just moved on. I certainly hadn't considered her for a placement. No wonder my mother was so upset.

"Mom, it's not like that at all, I promise. I'm placing some of the eggs here because Maggie thought the Marshallese people carried ancient DNA. There's no time for me to fly to Majuro, so my best chances are here. I'm just continuing her research."

A partial truth, but one we could both believe.

"The same research that drove her damn near insane? What if the same thing happens to you? I can't lose both of you, Charlie, I just can't."

"You won't, Mom, I promise. It's different for me."

The little reassurance I could offer was at least honest. Good, bad, or otherwise, I wasn't my sister. I didn't have her instinct. I didn't have her conviction. At least not yet.

"I'm coming back to Pennsylvania," I finished. "I'll tell you more then."

Surprise lingered in the air.

"When?" she asked.

"Give me a couple of weeks."

In exchange for the promised visit, my mother surrendered the name of Pastor Black's church. His secretary made an appointment for the next day and assured me he wouldn't be hard to find.

On Day 27, Pastor Black received us on his front lawn with a full embrace.

"Good morning, my friends!" he cried, thumping Theo hard on the back. "Welcome to the First Baptist Church of Springdale."

The old man ushered us into the main sanctuary. The church was a dinky little thing without many places to sit but for the pews. Theo and I chose a spot two rows back from the altar. The midmorning sun cast flamboyant shadows through the stained-glass windows; the heavy perfume of spring stifled the air.

Pastor Black sat immediately in front of us and leaned over the backrest. "Please, tell me how I can be of service to you today."

I swallowed. "You may not remember, but a few years ago, you received a phone call from two Marshallese girls in Pennsylvania . . ."

Pastor Black slapped his hand on polished wood. "Who were looking for information about their biological parents! We got a lot of calls that year from other children looking for the same, but no other twins."

"Well, sir, my sister died last month . . ."

He reached for my hand before I could finish. "I'm so, so sorry for your loss. Never easy, and especially tragic for someone your age."

"Thank you," I said, eager to move on. "She was a Mendel, and I'm here to place some of her eggs."

"In Springdale?"

I nodded. "I think it's something she'd want."

Pastor Black stood up and raised his hands toward the wall-size cross. "Well, Ms. Charlie, I can tell you that the people here will be thrilled to learn of the return of their children. I am certain we can find good families for them." He winked. "There are many here."

After taking the night to think, Pastor Black called us in the morning. We met him on the front steps of the church, and he handed us an offering envelope with five Marshallese names scrawled on the back.

"All good people. *Worthy* people. I won't make the same mistake twice."

Theo and I thanked him and bounded down the stairs.

"Sounds like we've got a family for each batch of embryos," he said. "We'll be wrapping this up in no time."

I ground to a halt under one of the giant hickory trees near the sidewalk. "We still have to talk to them, Theo. I'm not giving my nieces and nephews to just anyone."

Theo picked a few of the nuts out of the grass and pitched them into the adjacent wood. "Fair. But where are we going to hold the interviews? I don't think there's any way the Mendelia will allow us to use their clinic."

"We'll have to be careful. The Marshallese here are suspicious of anything involving the government. We can't have them bolt."

Theo turned back to the clapboard building behind us. "It's going to have to be the church, isn't it."

"It's who they trust." I took several paces toward the car while Theo surveyed our new office. "And Theo," I called. "You'll probably have to perform the procedures there too."

He hustled to catch up with me. "Not quite a manger in Bethlehem, but I'll make it work."

※

Theo and I spent Days 26 and 25 in fruitless conversation with four of Pastor Black's couples. Whatever he'd seen in them, I did not: one just wanted the money, another thought it would impress the congregation, and the third hoped to appease their nagging parents. The fourth didn't even show up. It became very clear to me how he'd misjudged Ms. Fabiola Lang: Pastor Black was remarkably and unfortunately generous.

The final couple wasn't available until Day 23, and having already disqualified the others, I wasn't optimistic. When this interview failed, I'd need to make a decision: continue to sift through the haystack of Springdale or try my luck elsewhere. Both sounded like Sisyphean tasks. If making just one placement was so hard, there'd be no way to make four more in three weeks.

I reminded myself that this was not how Maggie would think. Not how Maggie would act. I'd found a way to emulate my sister for the major acts of my performance, but even between scenes, I needed to find a way to tap into her endurance, her poise. Pretending to be someone I wasn't sapped my energy, but exhaustion would be a small price for success.

I was just trying to conjure Maggie's energy when a tiny knock broke my reverie.

Arno and Bujen Ajik peered through the front door.

According to Pastor Black's notes, Bujen and Arno were both naughts. Like most Springdale men, he worked at the poultry factory while she ministered to the elderly. Despite their busy schedules, both wanted children.

This was their first interview with a Mendel.

I began by reciting the same Mendelic script I'd used for every other interview. "Thank you so much for taking the time to meet with me today. I'm very excited to evaluate your application for placement. While I've already reviewed your file, I'd like to hear a bit more about the family you're trying to build."

The Ajiks exchanged nervous smiles and then grasped hands.

"Pastor Black says you've been attending his church for almost a decade now?"

It was Bujen who spoke first. "Oh yes, Ms. Charlie," she started. "We come every Sunday to hear Pastor Black. During the week I come spend time with the old folks too. Lots of old folks here in Springdale, and they need someone to talk to them and make sure they're getting enough to eat."

"Not many people seem all that concerned with their elders these days," I affirmed.

Bujen sat up to the edge of the pew. "Ms. Charlie, that's exactly what's wrong in the world right now. So many people are concerned about what's going to happen that no one is worrying about what's already passed."

Her response splashed over me like a bucket of cold water and left me equal parts startled and refreshed. Arno noticed my surprise and shot his wife a disconcerted look.

Bujen blushed. "I'm sorry, Ms. Charlie. I can get a little excited about all of this."

"It's fine," I said, delighted by her enthusiasm. "Please, continue."

"It's just that today, people are making babies just to beat the Limit. All that seems to matter is that these kids are born and what they screen at. But if we don't show people they matter beyond that, what are they besides failed experiments?"

A contagious spirit flowed freely from Bujen's lips, and it was hard not to catch an eddy of inspiration.

"That's why I work with the old folks. No one else seems to care, but I do. Maybe that's how I can make a difference."

I wanted to pour her a margarita.

Bujen and I moved quickly through the remaining interview questions. She softened, as did I, and the entire sanctuary seemed to fill with light. It was then that I felt like I could truly see Bujen—beyond her broad nose, full lips, and sturdy figure, I found an endless source of warmth. Of community. Of beauty. All the things Maggie described.

I dismissed her and Arno in full confidence that they'd fulfill my sister's vision.

CHAPTER 33

Theo took blood from Bujen the next day. Based on her hormone levels, she'd be prime for implantation on Day 8—a little more than two weeks away.

Back at the motel, Theo opened his laptop to place the order for Maggie's eggs.

"So what do you want in terms of sperm? Marshallese, I suppose."

"Actually . . ." I said, not quite knowing what to say. While Theo didn't know how damaged Nolan's sperm might be, he still might not like that I planned to use it.

I needed to tell him. Theo was putting his career on the line for my vendetta and didn't even know the reason. He was trusting me in the same way Nolan trusted Maggie—and I was abusing it. Just like she did.

"Actually what?" he replied, his tone much more stilted than before.

I looked out the window at the restaurant across the street. "Actually, can we get a drink?"

He looked at me over his horn-rimmed glasses. "You don't want to use Nolan's, do you?"

"If we go now, we can still catch a few minutes of happy hour."

He rolled his eyes. "Give me twenty minutes. I need to clean up."

Given its neon lights, earsplitting music, and tacky decor, I expected the chain restaurant across the street to be far fuller than I found it. But its bar sat vacant in the middle of the floor, with a heavily tattooed brunette racking the glassware instead of pouring drinks.

It was a Monday, after all.

Not wanting to disturb what little peace this bartender probably ever got to enjoy, I pulled up to a lonely high top and ordered a bottle of light beer. I picked at its soggy label. Somehow, I needed to explain to Theo that I wanted to combine Maggie's eggs with Nolan's sperm—ethically complicated for a number of reasons—without revealing what had happened between them.

A feat only my sister would've had the gall to pull off.

As promised, Theo strode through the door at exactly half past four, his hand busy polishing his glasses in the hem of a crisply pressed polo. His signature style looked out of place in such a working-class town, and his drink order only emphasized the difference.

"Gin martini, dirty, with blue-cheese-stuffed olives," he said. "Please."

He took the barstool next to mine while I nursed the end of my drink. I didn't know what to say or how to say it, so I opened and closed my mouth a few times trying to start the conversation. When none of them were particularly successful, Theo took over.

"It's okay, Charlie, you don't have to tell me. I figured it out in the shower."

The bartender huffed as she delivered Theo's persnickety cocktail. The transaction gave me a moment to consider my reply. I wasn't half as good as my sister at keeping secrets—if Theo had already figured everything out, I'd probably blown my own cover somewhere along the line. Any hopes of preserving my sister's memory had washed down the motel's drain.

But as Theo himself had once said, there was no harm in asking.

"And what's that?"

My technician took a sip from the lip of his angular glass. "Well, we're out here placing Maggie's eggs because she was a risk-taker, and probably one with a lot of unfinished business. Your sister was itching to beat the Limit, and you're carrying on her work by making babies with her ex-husband's sperm. I assume this to be some kind of restorative justice or emotional fantasy." Theo's second sip lengthened into a long draw that finished with a pop. "To be clear, I just want to say that I think it's well deserved."

I didn't refute any of Theo's theories. It was helpful he'd come up with his own story. And as far as I could tell, his truth could coexist with mine.

I cocked my head in his direction. "Do you know about Nolan?"

Theo tossed back the end of his drink and flagged the bartender for another. "They never should've sent someone so pale to somewhere so bright. Melanoma's a shitty way to go."

"So you guys talk?"

He shook his head. "Not a lot, but he's helping me repartner. Nolan's always had a good read on people."

My cheeks lifted. "He's the one who suggested I put you at the top of my list."

"Same. Anyhow, his sperm's as good as any, I suppose. If the cancer was genetic, the Mendelia would have flagged it."

At that point, I suspended my campaign for honesty. Because as polite as he was, Theo was a gossip. If he'd known about Maggie's experiment, he couldn't have resisted mentioning it—not with a glass of gin in his system. Which meant Nolan must not have mentioned it.

With that omission, I knew everything I needed to about how Nolan felt about my sister—or at least how he wanted her remembered.

Excused. Exonerated.

Undeservedly so.

※

The intervening days passed fretfully as I struggled to approve another couple. I interviewed a half dozen more as Pastor Black paraded them through the sanctuary. By the morning of Day 12, I settled on other plans entirely—and bought Theo and me tickets to Scranton.

"Are you senseless?" Theo was busy turning the motel room dresser into a laboratory bench to prepare for Bujen's implantation. "With Pastor Black's Rolodex, we could place all of the remaining eggs over the next few days and just be done with it. We're almost out of time."

I took a seat on the bed, well out of his way. "Theo, besides Bujen, no one here has worked out."

"Well," he tutted. "Maybe if you'd just . . ."

"Lower my standards? That's not what Maggie would've done. And I've got to go to Scranton. For my mother. I'm sure you understand."

Theo snapped his gloves into the trash. "No, I do not understand. My mother is twice the handful yours is, and I don't feel the need to run back to her. Also, if you count the five days it takes the embryos to mature, we barely have a week left. You might as well call the convent and just have them flush the rest."

I traced the quilt's paisley embroidery with my finger. "We'll be able to do at least one more. I've already picked the mother."

"And where is she?"

"Pennsylvania."

Theo glared at me over the bridge of his nose. "Don't tell me it's your aunt."

"And why not?"

"You've only ever talked about what a terrible candidate she is!"

He was right. In Saipan, I'd derided Aunt Frankie's potential as a parent. Although her personal circumstances were much more stable now, she was still riddled with flaws. For one, the drug addictions had left her looking incapable of enduring even the most temporary challenges of pregnancy. Beyond that, regular unemployment, unstable relationships, the inability to self-manage—there were so many reasons why not.

But Maggie had seen promise. She'd said as much at our lockers just three years prior. Based on Aunt Frankie's recovery, Maggie was certain she'd be able to rise to the challenge. And even if she couldn't, Maggie knew that our foolhardy aunt would be working with a safety net. Because for the past twenty years, Aunt Frankie had dumped each and every one of her personal problems on my mother. A baby would be no different. This challenge, for once, would be welcome: that baby would be her grandchild.

"The child's not for her," I tried to explain.

Theo dropped his pipette onto an aluminum tray with disgust. "Wait, so now it's you who's running a baby farm?"

I lay back on the bed to escape his condescending glare. "Please just start cooking the embryos."

"Do you even know if she's fertile?"

A practical and important question—and a sign he was entertaining the possibility.

"My mom was just complaining about the cost of tampons last month. At her age, I can tell you she's not buying them for herself."

With the plug for the portable incubator in his free hand, Theo knelt beside the dresser and groped for the electrical outlet.

"But that doesn't tell us anything about Frankie's timing."

I stood up to help him pull back the furniture. "Biologically, we get three good days a month, right?"

"In the best-case scenario," Theo said. He fumbled the plug into the socket, and the machine began to hum.

"That's one in ten," I said. "Don't tell me you've never taken those odds."

He adjusted the incubator's dials and checked the settings before turning back to face me. "But we need *her* three days to hit at the end of *our* ten-day window." His brow raised. "Don't try to out-gamble me, Charlie Tannehill. I know what I'm doing with probability."

Of course he was right. The situation wasn't ideal, and it pained me to think about how unlikely it was for things to work out. But this was the hand I was dealt, and I was doing my best to play it.

Of one thing I was certain: while I may not win, I wasn't going to fold.

I picked up my purse and slung it over my shoulder. "Theo, I need you to trust me on this."

"You're starting to sound like your sister."

"If only," I scoffed. "See you in a few."

In the shower, grief caught up with me again, as it so often did when I was quiet and alone.

I'd only gotten to mourn my sister a week before Nolan's rapidly deteriorating condition completely displaced my despair. And although it was cancer that was killing him, Nolan and I both knew it was Maggie who was truly at fault. I wasn't sure who to be angrier with: him, for adding to my sorrows, or her, for leaving me to manage his death.

A miserable inheritance, really. And I needed to make it a good one too. Because if Nolan's life got the conclusion it deserved, maybe Maggie's would be redeemed.

Pitiful inspiration, no doubt, but more purpose than I'd ever felt before.

Maybe that was what my sister had really meant to leave me.

Drawing back the shower curtain, I saw what could've been my sister. It was when we were sopping wet that we looked most alike—water seemed to dilute the few small differences between us. Damp, dark curls sagged over supple, toasted skin. Long lashes kissed heavy eyebrows set over deep mahogany eyes. But Maggie's had always been brighter than mine, which was why, in the end, I knew it was my own reflection and not that of my beloved twin.

After toweling off, I slipped into some flimsy panties and a well-worn T-shirt. After three years in the Mendelia, I didn't own much that wasn't branded with the agency insignia, but this one was a favorite: the convent's seal, silk-screened in delicate pink over forest green cotton. These colors paid homage to the notorious sweet peas that first revealed the secrets of genetics—the science that now threatened to both destroy and save us. I'd purchased the shirt when Maggie and I first arrived in Tehachapi.

The memory disintegrated when knuckles rapped against my door.

It was time for me to decide. I could yet ignore his knocking—Theo would forgive my change of heart and never mention the inconvenience. But as I approached the door, I realized what the Mendelia had always known: choice was, and always had been, an illusion.

I pulled open the door. "Come on in."

CHAPTER 34

Heavy clouds crowded the sky on the morning we performed Bujen's placement. The sparse morning light was best in the church's southern transept, so Theo and I pulled the altar table near one of the larger arched windows.

Bujen looked horror-struck. "Are you sure it's appropriate . . ."

Pastor Black gestured for her to lie down. "Don't worry, my dear," he whispered. "Our Lord in heaven approves . . . and more importantly, the congregation won't know."

I smiled throughout the procedure and tried to focus on how much good would come of it—not only for Bujen, but for Nolan. But as much as I wanted to consider the procedure a victory, I couldn't quite escape the thought that I might be creating a monstrosity. Even though the Mendelia's system hadn't flagged Nolan's DNA as seriously corrupt, I knew what he'd done. Even minor damage could precipitate major consequences.

If the worst happened, I might render myself no different than my sister.

Risk was necessary, however. Maggie had known that, and now I needed to act like I did too. So, despite my reservations, Theo and I moved through the procedure. Our timing, our scripts, our steps were all perfectly synchronized. Implantations were supposed to run like well-staged theater: every step blocked, every line hit. This, I figured, must have been how Maggie and Nolan had worked—hand in glove.

Twenty minutes after removing the final syringe, Theo and I headed to the airport. Without a clinic to monitor Bujen's hormone levels, it would be a full three weeks before we'd know whether the embryos had implanted, and we couldn't wait—half of Day 8 had already transpired, and we needed to get to Pennsylvania.

I left Bujen with a handful of pregnancy tests and my phone number. She promised to follow up.

Theo and I arrived just in time to check in for our flight. I passed through security with ease, but Theo got pulled for additional screening. Between the chemical solutions he handled and his electronics, it happened a lot. I knew they'd be a while, so I took a seat near a window overlooking the runway.

And then my phone rang.

Had something happened to Bujen? Had we forgotten something? Whatever confidence I'd mustered at the church shattered with that ringtone.

I answered the call gingerly, as if my tone could somehow ward off bad news. "Hello?"

"Dr. Tannehill, it's your old friend Kenneth Kolb."

The breath went out of me. Mr. Kenneth W. Kolb had no reason to be calling. Whatever he had to say could not be good news.

"Mr. Kolb, sir, how are you?"

"My nephew Andrew Corden met with a Mendel yesterday," he said, his voice thickening. "I don't suppose you've heard that name before."

The jig was up. I covered my eyes and prepared for the worst to finally arrive. "I have, sir."

"Something curious happened at his appointment."

I knew where this conversation was headed: into a trap, just like the one I'd laid for him.

Unfortunately, this was a punishment I deeply deserved, so I honored my virtue by falling—no, jumping—into it.

"And what was that, sir?" I gulped.

"He said that the Mendel 'apologized.' For someone 'inappropriately accessing' his genetic records."

I gazed out the window, in search of how Maggie might respond. My sister, I decided, would've been bold enough to tell the truth.

"That was me, sir," I admitted. "When I was researching your family for the case."

"You were trying to manipulate me," he growled.

"I was, sir. It was the only advantage I could get over the Mendelia."

He blew past my explanation. "Andrew also said that he and his wife were granted a placement. That they'll be receiving a 4* embryo. Was that your doing?"

"It was not," I answered, although I sincerely wished that it had been.

"Well, to be honest, Dr. Tannehill, you've had three chances to lie to me just now and you didn't take one. Maybe your invasion of my privacy was just a momentary lapse in judgment."

The tension in my body released as I slumped back into my chair. "That's gracious of you, sir."

"You remind me of my Jennifer. Too clever by half but three times as wholesome. Girls like you deserve the benefit of the doubt."

"Does any of this change your mind about the eggs?" I asked, eager to move on from the purity test.

I could hear him rustling through papers. "No. No matter how you made your point, it was still the right one—and now your profound honesty has bought you another month."

I couldn't believe what I was hearing, so I thanked him before he could change his mind. "I appreciate it, sir. You didn't have to do that."

"You're damned right I didn't have to. I wanted to. And you can stop calling me 'sir.' There's nothing left I can do for you, so you can stop kissing my ass. I'll send out a revision to my decision shortly. Where should I mail your copy?"

I snatched a glance back at security. The bomb dog seemed to have determined that our incubator wasn't a threat, so Theo was getting a final pat down.

"Pennsylvania," I stuttered, giving him my parents' address. "I can't tell you how helpful this is."

"And I don't need to know. Go forth and do good work, Charlotte Tannehill."

※

With a stroke of his pen, Mr. Kolb reset my clock to thirty-eight days. A blessing, by most accounts, but one way, a curse. When we'd left the motel, I'd all but accepted that Frankie would be my last placement. Now, with more time, I had no excuse but to try and place the rest of Maggie's eggs.

But I was out of ideas.

Theo talked some sense into me on the flight. At the rate I was moving—one placement every three weeks—Mr. Kolb's bonus time wasn't enough to make all the placements possible. It was, however, enough to make our one remaining placement a lot more probable. For Aunt Frankie, we could align the in vitro fertilization with her natural cycle, improving our odds of success.

While Maggie wouldn't have settled for anything less than five full placements, for me, these few would set a record.

Maybe that could be enough.

※

Landing in Scranton marked the first time I'd returned to Pennsylvania in almost four years. As far as I could tell, the city hadn't changed much. The March roads were sloppy with snowmelt, and the trees looked miserable—both would benefit from more sunshine and drier weather. Both were still two months off.

When my parents picked us up, they took us out for sushi—a small celebration for my victory over the Mendelia. The restaurant had been a childhood favorite of mine, and I found unexpected refuge in being in such a familiar place with such familiar people. The strain of the past three weeks dissolved as I put in an order for miso soup and matcha tea.

My father flinched. "No fish?"

"Not after that flight," I muttered. "I need something to soothe my nerves."

Another half-truth, but the trip *had* been turbulent.

After the waiter collected our menus, Theo and I made small talk about our adventure in Arkansas. My parents greatly enjoyed Theo's dramatic retelling of Bujen's less-than-immaculate conception and took no shame in filling the restaurant with hearty guffaws. When the waitstaff delivered our dishes and stepped back so that we could enjoy the meal, my father segued to the more important parts of our conversation.

"So what's bringing you back to Pennsylvania?"

While I'd promised my mother the visit, I hadn't signaled my intent. At the time, I hadn't had any. But I'd just spent the past three weeks in Arkansas convincing myself that placing an egg with Aunt Frankie was prudent, safe, and consistent with my sister's intentions.

If my parents agreed, I was ready to take the next step.

I eased my teacup back onto the tray. "I need to talk to you about Aunt Frankie," I said. "I might have a placement for her."

"Is . . . that allowed?" my mother asked carefully, very well knowing that it wasn't.

"I don't think that matters anymore. But I need to talk with both of you before I speak to her."

My parents put down their chopsticks and nodded.

I smoothed my napkin across my lap. "Are you ready to be parents again?"

My father opened his mouth to reply, but my mother broke in first. Sadness trembled in her aging face. "I know you can't know this Charlie, but just because your kids are grown doesn't mean you've stopped being a parent."

"You're right," I said. "I'm sorry. But I think we all know that if I give Aunt Frankie a baby, most of the responsibility will fall to you."

Doubt wrinkled my father's face. "Aunt Frankie's still young enough to carry a pregnancy?"

"She should be, assuming you haven't heard her complain about hot flashes yet."

"And because of her advanced age," my mother continued, tiptoeing around the potential slight, "we wouldn't have to worry about the expense of it, right?"

I took a slurp of soup. "She's forty?"

My mother nodded. "Will be next month."

"I feel safe in saying that this baby will pay for itself."

My mother plopped her napkin onto the table affirmatively. "Then I don't see why not."

"Your mother and I still need to discuss it, Charlie."

While I suspected my father was in agreement, I understood why he didn't want to make such an important decision in a restaurant. But there wasn't more to say, at least not there.

Theo decided to stay down in Scranton that night. While my parents made sure he knew he was welcome in their home, Theo suggested that they take some well-deserved alone time with me. Jim and Sherry clucked in appreciation, but I knew my friend had ulterior motives. The local Indian casinos were just up the road—not that I could blame him.

After dropping Theo at his hotel, my father drove the rest of us back to Hawley. I was eager for the comforts of home; I hadn't considered staying anywhere else. But I also hadn't properly braced myself to set foot inside my childhood bedroom. *Our* childhood bedroom. Maggie's books and blankets and postcards still lined every shelf and wall and windowsill. Every token of hers made for a bramble of grief, and stepping into that room was like stumbling into the briar patch: there wasn't a place to sit or look or stand or cry that didn't tear open my heart.

Before the night was over, I felt like I'd bled out.

I went to bed that night wondering if such episodes would ever stop. Then I wondered if I even wanted that, because it meant I would finally have to accept my sister's death. Acceptance might lead to forgetting. And forgetting meant moving on.

I wasn't ready for that. I wasn't ready to be alone. I wasn't done needing my sister.

I might never be.

CHAPTER 35

I slept that night, though I don't remember falling into it. The quiet reprieve must have taken me only after I'd cried myself to exhaustion. And I would have stayed in that dreamless haven had the overpowering scents of baking spice and citrus not revived me.

I waddled downstairs in one of Maggie's old terry cloth robes, my eyes still puffy from the previous night's tears. My father stood over the griddle with a spatula.

"We're glad you slept. You had a big day."

Slices of French toast sizzled in the pan.

"We also know you're in a hurry to place Maggie's eggs, so your mother and I spoke this morning."

My mother handed me a cup of coffee just the way I liked it—a splash of cream and two sugars already stirred in. "We know it's Maggie's egg, but you haven't told us about your plans for the father."

I set the mug aside. "I haven't gotten that far yet," I fibbed. "Does it matter?"

"No, not really," she answered. "As long as it's not Nolan."

"He left her there on that island," my father huffed. "And we all know what happened next. It's hard to say we'd be excited about him fathering her child."

A reasonable position for two parents of a dead daughter, but they didn't know enough about what had happened to determine the real victim. To do that, they'd need to know about the experiment, the cancer, and the fact my sister had thrown Nolan out when he needed her most.

And I didn't want them to.

"Let me see what I can work out with Aunt Frankie," I said. "It will be *her* baby."

Lying got a bit easier with every distortion of truth.

"Of course, Charlie, of course," my father muttered.

"And how has she been these days?"

"The same. On her second job of the year already. The video-rental place went under after Christmas, so she's stocking shelves at the liquor store again."

"No less happy for it, though. You know how she is," my mother added on her transit toward the laundry room. "Can't keep a job, hangs out with the wrong people, spends her paycheck on things that don't matter. One week it's crystals, the next it's essential oils. When she got roped into a pyramid scheme selling leggings last year, I had to buy three dozen pairs just to bail her out."

This, I realized, was what life looked like in Hawley—no matter who you were. With my collapsing career as a Mendel, such a future wasn't yet out of the question.

"You know I might end up back here in a couple of weeks, right? There's no way the Mendelia will keep me around after all the trouble I've caused them."

My father took a sip of coffee. "I thought you couldn't get fired from the government."

"It gets easier when you misbehave."

My father cocked an eyebrow. "You? Misbehave?"

If only he knew.

"Well, you know how Frankie is," he continued. "There'll probably be a vacancy in the liquor store in about two months. I'll have Mr. Weinberg hold it for you."

The joke drew a chuckle from me, and my father grinned at the sight. He rapped his knuckles on the table in satisfaction. "You know what they say, Charlie—you can never go home."

The knock seemed to summon my mother, who fussed her way back into the kitchen, restocking the paper towels and dish soap as she went. When I deposited my dishes into the sink and started washing them, she batted me away.

"I've taken care of your father for thirty years," she chirped. "The least I can do is take care of you for a week."

Care. It was exactly what I needed. Arbitration, Arkansas, Aunt Frankie—the sheer number of choices I'd made in the preceding weeks had worn me threadbare. Even the smallest decisions felt overwhelming—what to eat, what to wear, when to sleep. But that was work mothers did well.

For the first time that I could remember, I wasn't afraid to be home.

After clearing away my plate, I had nothing left to do but plan. It was Day 37 now, and I needed to figure out my next steps.

The shower offered the best peace and contemplation.

First, I needed to talk to Aunt Frankie. While I was certain she'd want Maggie's egg, I wasn't sure how she'd feel about Nolan, given his role—or lack thereof—in her death. Sure, I could've told her that the embryo was already set, but I knew I'd risk losing her. Like an insolent child, Frankie generally refused outside guidance and direction. I needed to let her choose—or at least let her think that she was choosing.

The latter, I determined, seemed most reasonable.

Once she'd concurred, Theo could go ahead and procure the samples. Then we'd have to cook the embryo for at least four days. Five would be better, but we were already pressed for time. I didn't even know where Aunt Frankie was on her cycle. She'd probably need hormones, which meant needles would be involved, but based on her past, Aunt Frankie probably wasn't afraid of them. That being said . . .

The cart of my mind ran too far afield of reality's horse. Nothing else could happen until I spoke with Aunt Frankie, so I needed to focus on brokering that deal. And while I was finding it easier and easier to ignore the slippage of minutes, the loss of hours and days still loomed.

These eggs, and my authority to place them, weren't getting any younger.

After toweling off, I returned to my bedroom to call my aunt before better judgment could suppress the impulse.

My mother must have heard me leaving a voicemail, because she cracked the door and poked her head in. "Darling, Aunt Frankie works the swing shift. I don't think you'll be able to reach her tonight, but if you try her in the morning, you two might be able to grab lunch before she goes in."

"Thanks, Mom."

She knelt to sop up my footprints. "Don't worry about the short notice—not really fond of planning, that one."

I dropped down to assist. "Mom, how did Aunt Frankie take Maggie's death?"

She clutched at the bath towel. "Not well," she said. "But she didn't relapse, and that's the best we could've hoped for, I suppose.

"When we told her what happened, Frankie ran out of the house howling with grief. You know your aunt—she's a runner. Then, we didn't hear from her for a week. But she showed up the next Sunday for supper, right on schedule. Right now, everyone does their best not to bring it up."

"That helps, Mom. Thank you."

She gathered up my towels in a hamper and then made her way back down to the hallway.

"I really want this for you," I called. "And for Frankie. But mostly for you."

My mother cast her eyes to the ceiling to stymie her tears.

"Charlie, I want you to know that any way this turns out will be fine by me. Your sister would be proud of you for just trying to help. And so am I."

Per my mother's advice, I called Aunt Frankie the next morning. She was giddy, if not manic, to hear I was making time to see her. Little did she know it was Day 36 and time for me to get down to business.

Nolan's death depended on it.

Shortly before noon, I drove my father's truck back toward the highway. The nearby on-ramp hosted a smattering of underused conveniences, including a run-down gas station and a family-owned sandwich shop. Their "lunch rush" constituted three other vehicles, whose out-of-state plates may as well have read "just passing through."

Just like me, hopefully.

Aunt Frankie pulled her rusty hatchback into the parking lot at ten minutes past one o'clock—remarkably timely by her watch. My mother had told me that Frankie would need to leave for her shift by two, so I had just under an hour to figure out whether she could handle a baby.

Maggie's baby.

After slinging her car haphazardly into a parking spot, my aunt exploded out of the driver's seat. Screaming my name, she ambushed me with an embrace at least five separate times, none of which I could return with equal gusto.

Frankie either didn't notice or didn't care.

After the overzealous greeting, we made our orders at the counter—a tuna sandwich for her and a salad for me. She chided me for not getting something heartier, but I'd had my fill of Spam and other cured meats during my time in Saipan. The bill took me by surprise when it came to only $13.27. I'd forgotten how cheap food was outside of paradise.

We withdrew to a table near the front window. As she dug into her meal, I laid my napkin and my hands in my lap.

"Aunt Frankie, I need you to consider something for me."

She popped open her bag of chips. "What's that?"

"When Maggie died, she left behind some of her eggs. I get to decide how they're placed, and after thinking it over, I'd like one of them to go to you."

Aunt Frankie pulled a handful of napkins from the steel dispenser and dabbed at her eyes.

"This is not how I wanted it, Charlie," she replied. "I'd trade just about anything—including this baby—to have your sister back."

Me too, I thought. If only I could control death the same way I controlled life.

Frankie balled up the wasted paper on the table. "And I'm not sure I should accept something from the people that accused her of such nastiness. I feel like I'm being bought off."

Frankie was right to distrust the Mendelia. I did too. But my aunt's misplaced hesitation was jeopardizing the future that she and my mother most definitely deserved. That's when I recognized it—her uncertainty.

Aunt Frankie needed purpose just as much as I did.

That I could give.

"This isn't blood money, Aunt Frankie. The Mendelia would've flushed these eggs if I'd let them. And there's a reason there's so many. Maggie was incredible at what she did." The look on my aunt's face suggested she was enjoying the melodrama. I lowered my voice and leaned across the table. "And I believe she was onto something. Maggie's eggs might just hold the discovery she was seeking."

Frankie's eyes widened. "Is that why you're here?"

"Yes. I'm just trying to finish her good work. And I need your help."

Aunt Frankie fidgeted with the sobriety pendant that hung around her neck. "You . . . think I can do it?"

"Have a baby?" I leaned back in my chair. "There's no reason why not. I've seen women much older than you have completely successful pregnancies."

"But no other Mendel has agreed."

I reached for her hand. "That's because they don't know you like I do."

Aunt Frankie tucked some errant strands of tawny hair behind her ears. The flecks of gold in her hazel eyes dazzled in the afternoon sunlight. For a brief moment, I could have sworn she was my mother.

"Isn't this something you said you'd get in trouble for?"

"Yes. But my time as a Mendel is over," I said, returning my fork to the bowl. "They'll be kicking me out after I place these eggs no matter what I do."

"And what did you do to deserve that?"

Three construction workers stomped through the door, hard hats tucked under their sausage-like arms. Their racket made for a useful distraction from the question I didn't have time to answer. I leaned back into the conversation.

"What I need to know, Aunt Frankie, is whether this is something you still want."

"I do," she said. "I always have, Charlie. And I promise I'll turn things around for the baby. I'll probably need Sherry to help with homework and piano lessons and all the smarty-pants things that you and your sister did. But for my part, I'll do my darndest to be the best possible mom. You know I'm good for it."

"I know you are."

Deep down, I didn't. But Maggie had, and I'd decided to trust her. While I didn't enjoy manipulating all these people, if I wanted to secure the future my family deserved—and that my sister had hoped for—it had to be done.

I could bend my morals. Even theirs, perhaps.

Aunt Frankie finally took a bite of her sandwich. "So who's the father?"

"That"—I smiled—"is something you get to decide."

"You're going to let someone like me do the choosing? That doesn't seem very wise."

"The fact that you recognize that, Aunt Frankie, means you are. So I brought you some options . . ."

Though I'd convinced Frankie to take the placement, I was still nervous she'd balk over Nolan. On the plane, I'd spent hours reviewing my psychology texts, devising the best ways to suggest and entice. While I'd prepared a whole strategy to persuade her, my aunt rendered the whole thing moot with a single line.

"Can it be Nolan?"

I almost choked on my half-chewed greens.

"I know Jim and Sherry won't like it," she continued. "They still blame him for what happened to Maggie. But Charlie, the hours I spent on the phone with her, she always went on and on about him. The way she spoke, Charlie, I can't really explain."

Finally, I knew with whom my sister had shared her love-drunk diatribes. Not with me—but with someone who understood intoxication.

Aunt Frankie grabbed another napkin. "I don't know exactly what happened on that island, but I do know Maggie and Nolan loved each other. And this baby should be born of that love, even if it didn't last."

I was more than happy to agree. Now, I just had to hope she wouldn't run.

CHAPTER 36

With Frankie on board, Theo and I could proceed with making the embryo. As much as I wanted my parents' approval, Aunt Frankie's consent was all that we needed. And in the end, I knew my parents wouldn't refuse a grandchild.

My mother had wanted one for far too long.

After seeing my aunt off, I collected Theo from Scranton and brought him back to the house for dinner. On the way back, I briefed him on my conversation with Aunt Frankie.

"Sounds like we can go ahead and get the fun part started," he said as he stared down Pennsylvania's granite canyon walls. The serpentine road coursed along a swollen stream choppy with the previous days' rain. "Where do you think I should have the samples sent?"

"The Scranton clinic? I know they won't do much for us, but they'd just have to sign for a delivery. We're not asking to use their space or clientele or anything."

We cornered around a rocky outcropping, and I honked to alert any oncoming traffic. The scenic route gave us time to work out our plan's details, and it was a beautiful, if dangerous, drive. Theo turned off the radio to respond to my suggestion.

"You're asking *me* to have *your* dead sister's eggs sent to the clinic nearest your hometown. Where you still have family. Fertile, *female* family."

"Frankie and I don't share a last name—or any genetic material, for that matter," I said. "By the time the Mendelia figure it out, you and I will have finished."

Theo's expression deadpanned. "You're not the first person to try something like this, you know."

I knew it wasn't a great idea. The Mendelia patrolled for nepotism, and far too often it was far too easy to spot. And even though Mr. Kolb had given me license to place Maggie's eggs however I pleased, he hadn't given me permission to break the Mendelia's rules. Having my sister's eggs sent to my aunt would set off all sorts of alarms.

I put up a hand to defend against his incoming rant. "Theo—"

"If you pick up an ethical violation, Headquarters will have grounds for an injunction against your work. Then they'll tie us up in administrative knots until the clock runs out . . ."

"Theo—"

He checked his wristwatch. "Which occurs, I'll remind you, in just thirty-six days."

"You're right, Theo."

The concession jerked him out of his tirade just as we emerged from the river gorge.

"I'm sorry." He sighed. "I'm just not used to you taking risks."

I thumbed the steering wheel as we rejoined the highway. "Neither am I. Is there anywhere else we can have it sent?"

"Your parents' house is no better. Neither is my motel. To be honest, anything in this zip code is going to raise flags."

"What about my dad's police department?" I suggested.

"Do you think he could sign for it?"

Perhaps, I thought, but shook off the idea like a wet dog. I couldn't endanger my father's career by making him an accessory to our crime. He'd lose his pension. His pride. But the catalog of reliable people in my life had thinned considerably in the past two months.

I blew out a frustrated breath just as we passed the old post office—and a better idea leaped into my mind.

"What about a convent?" I said, barely able to contain my excitement.

Theo squinted. "In what world does that make sense?"

"Not Tehachapi. Baltimore."

"You mean Headquarters?"

"It's only a few hours from here," I started. "You could just drive down and pick the samples up."

Theo paused. "Are you sure you're feeling all right?"

The question confused me. I didn't expect to feel badly for a few more weeks. "What do you mean?"

"It's just that you're not usually the one figuring out solutions."

※

The next day, Aunt Frankie left me a voicemail.

"Hey, Charliebear, it's *your* Aunt Frankie. *My* Aunt Flo just arrived, so I'll be down for the count this weekend—but I thought you should know."

Great news. The start of her cycle meant Frankie would be ready to impregnate in just two weeks' time. That, and she hadn't shifted her opinion on the whole "having her niece's love child" thing. Day 21 would be here before we knew it.

While I dropped off tampons at Aunt Frankie's, Theo placed the order for Maggie's and Nolan's samples. He decided to fetch them on Day 26—combining them then would give the embryo a full five days of development and the best chance of implantation. Waiting for that day to arrive pained us, however—there were only so many hands of slapjack we could play. But when it did, the day brought far more disappointment than delight.

Maggie's eggs were ready for pickup, but Nolan's sperm hadn't been moved.

I pulled Theo into my room after dinner to avoid causing a scene. "Do you think they figured us out?"

Theo shrugged and leaned into a bookshelf. "If they did, would they tell us?"

"Sample retrieval doesn't usually take this long, does it?"

"They might have to ship it in from Guam. Most samples are brought back to Headquarters for analysis, but the Mendelia may have left some back in the islands if Maggie was using a lot of it. No sense in shipping that stuff both ways."

I massaged my forehead. "But don't you have to start the cook?"

"Ideally, yes." Theo sighed. "Five days of development is better than four. But we can take our chances all the way down to two."

"And after that?"

He bit his lip. "We'll have to find another mother. Frankie will be past her prime."

I collapsed into my unmade bed with a groan.

Theo sat down. "Charlie, you know if you choose a different sperm, we *could* get started tomorrow."

But they had to be Nolan's babies. I was doing this for him. My dying friend would take no joy in hearing that I'd combined his wife's eggs with someone else's seed. Hell, Nolan might consider it tantamount to cheating.

I refused Theo with another pillow-muffled grunt.

"Stubborn," Theo scoffed. "Just like your sister. Well, there's nothing else we can do at this point but wait. You should get some sleep—we still have a few more days."

I found it impossible to rest when there was nothing to do. Any chirp from Theo's phone drew my attention, and I found myself begging it to ring. It did, finally, on Day 25, but not with a call from Headquarters. Just Theo's mother, checking in again. She did the same on Day 24 and Day 23, until Theo finally asked her to stop. We did our best to protect Aunt Frankie from our emotional roller coaster, but by Day 22, I needed to start thinking about how I'd break the news. If she wasn't impregnated by the end of Day 21, Aunt Frankie couldn't receive an embryo—and my custody of Maggie's eggs would run out before she'd cycle again.

I didn't know what I was going to tell her. Our plan had completely fallen apart. Whether it was with denial or despair, Theo and I spent the morning of Day 21 milling about my parents' kitchen without words.

Luckily, neither of us had to say anything. Just before my father came down to fix breakfast, Theo's phone twittered once more. Suspecting it was yet again his mother, Theo removed himself to the office—but not a minute elapsed before he came bounding back into the room.

"It's here," he said, and plopped onto the bench in the front entryway to grab his boots.

I covered my face with my hands at the tragedy. "It's late."

"Very. But that's no reason not to try."

I peeked through my fingers to shoot him an impudent glare.

"I'm serious, Charlie. I'm bringing the portable incubator with me. You said it's not far? The batteries should last long enough. I'll fertilize the eggs in the truck and bring them back with me tonight."

"I thought you said we wouldn't have enough time?"

Theo pulled a knit cap down over his head. "You were right about me taking those one-in-ten odds. Hormonally speaking, today is the best day to impregnate your aunt. With every hour that passes, she's less fertile, and those embryos need at least twenty-four. But if we can prop Frankie up on hormones for just one more night, there's an outside chance we might be able to pull this off. There's no reason not to try."

While I wanted to share in his excitement, I couldn't find it in me. Instead, I flashed back to my dorm room, where I'd clung to that irrational belief that Maggie might still be alive. Hope had been a terrible tease, and I wasn't sure I'd survive its temptation again.

Theo's confidence, however, remained unperturbed. He grabbed my father's keys. "You get everything—and everyone—ready. I'll take care of the rest."

Once Theo was on the road, I rallied my nerve and my mother to complete the preparations. She called a neighbor to borrow their car, and we sped down to the liquor store and ambushed Aunt Frankie with a syringe full of hormones. Mr. Weinberg didn't love what he saw but said it wasn't the first time he'd stumbled upon someone shooting up in his storage closet.

He sent her home early.

When we got back, I tasked my mother with decluttering my bedroom and sanitizing the bedsheets. I fashioned a basic set of stirrups from broom handles and belts—rural practice had long ago sharpened my ability to improvise. As my mother flapped a freshly boiled sheet over the mattress, we spoke about how best to corral Aunt Frankie.

A change of her mind was the only ending we could not abide.

CHAPTER 37

Theo returned from Baltimore twelve hours later with his portable incubator riding shotgun.

Despite his victory, Theo returned testy and irascible: the combination of mid-Atlantic traffic and convent bureaucracy had aggravated his temper. While he was tight lipped in front of my parents, I knew he'd do better spending the night alone at his hotel—and I insisted on driving him there, even if that meant having to wake in the wee hours the next morning to retrieve him.

"Before we go, can I grab a shower?" he said. "I'll be a better person if I can wash off this exasperation."

I looked at him and then at my watch. The later we left, the less sleep I would get.

"I promise I'll be ready in less time than it takes to navigate a Maryland toll plaza," he said, and turned to the stairs.

As soon as he turned on the spigot, Theo spewed forth the fountain of expletives he'd been holding in for the past half hour. He'd spared my parents his vulgarity, and for that I was thankful. I wasn't sure what I'd done to deserve such a good friend.

But I still needed to tell him.

Theo reappeared five minutes later, toweling off his hair.

"Feel better?" I asked.

He pitched his towel into the washing machine. "Not entirely," he said. "But at least I got to see parts of the country I hadn't before, and that was nice. Who knew Pennsylvania had so much roadkill?"

I snorted in amusement.

"Look, I'm trying to be positive!" he said. "Sensationally irate was not a good look. Also, the facility in Baltimore was incredible. State-of-the-art equipment, massive classrooms—their dorms even had full-size windows. I'm telling you, we drew the short straw with Tehachapi."

When he finished, I gathered my resolve and looked over from the couch. "Theo, I need to apologize."

"For what? Getting us into trouble that'll get us thrown out?"

While he didn't entirely understand my motivation, I took comfort in the fact that Theo understood precisely how all of this would end. That, I figured, would suffice.

"You can tell them I lied to you," I said, still grasping for some kind of deliverance for him. "That I tricked you into impregnating my aunt."

He took the seat beside me to rub my knee. "I won't need to do that, Charlie. By the time they figure it out, I'll have quit too. I made that decision when we made the first placement."

By the time I returned home from the hotel, my parents had already gone to bed. I was relieved to find Aunt Frankie tucked into the old leather couch and covered with one of Maggie's quilts. She'd at least decided to wait until morning to bolt.

Morning came early, at least for me. With all the running around, I was only able to get a few hours' sleep, and it was still frosty and blue when I went out to warm up the truck. When I pulled up to Theo's hotel, the driveway was empty but for one traveling family getting a sunrise start. I flashed my headlights to rouse Theo, who'd glazed over on one of the couches in the lobby. He climbed into the cab and shoved his hands against the heaters.

"The zygotes seem to be enjoying their stay at Château de Incubator," he said, nodding at the machine between his feet. "One's already on the verge of dividing."

Too early for more banter, the rest of the drive passed silently. The roads thickened with traffic as sunlight breached the horizon and we wove our way back to Hawley. When we stepped through the front door, the crackle of fresh eggs and bacon heralded our return. My father was busy managing the griddle, but my mother looked fully engaged in conversation with my aunt at the kitchen table. I was about to feel ashamed for my premonitions about Aunt Frankie's possible flight until I saw my mother's pleading eyes, and I made my way over to their coterie.

"I'm sure there's nothing to be worried about," my mother crooned, "and no, I don't think you need to go into work to tell them that you'll be calling off this afternoon. I'll go ahead and call them for you, and if Mr. Weinberg really needs someone to cover your shift, I can step in."

The poor woman looked as if she'd been treading water for an hour. "Charlie, be a dear, and come reassure your aunt that everything's going to be all right."

I took my cue as well as my seat. "How are you doing, Aunt Frankie?"

Her eyes dropped to her lap. "Oh, I don't know," she said. "This is just such a big decision, and I'm just not sure if it's the right time, or the right way, or . . ." She pulled at her necklace as she spoke. "I'm just not sure it's right."

As I put my hand on her knee, the wild in her eyes began to dim. "Is there anything I can do to make it feel more 'right'?"

"I don't think so. It's just . . . I guess I'm not sure if I'm ready to be this responsible."

Despite all her flaws, Aunt Frankie was at least aware of them.

"No one ever is," I said, stroking the top of her thigh. "We'll get you through this, Aunt Frankie."

Theo appeared at my side with a loaded plate. "You need to eat," he insisted. "And your mother agrees with me." He nodded to his accomplice, who was loading the dishwasher.

"Frankie, can I get you anything?" His offer to her was laced with a much more generous tone.

"Sherry says I should start cutting back on the coffee. For the baby. Can I have some orange juice?" She looked to me for permission.

"As much as you want. Great choice."

As I picked through my scrambled eggs, I explained to my aunt the details of the upcoming procedure. Theo had already combined the egg and sperm, and in a few hours, we'd move upstairs to implant the embryo. Her job was easy—she'd just need to lie on Maggie's bed the same way she did for any routine gynecology visit. Most of the tools we'd use would be the same: gloves, speculums, stirrups. The only new addition would be a small tube that we'd insert into her uterus to pump in the embryos.

Thank goodness Frankie had only had juice, because my explanation turned her an unfortunate shade of green. It was time to move on to other things.

"Dad, how about a game of cards?" I suggested, eager to turn the babysitting over to someone else. Dutifully, my father got Aunt Frankie started on a game of crazy eights while I ducked into the laundry room to marshal my regiment.

"She seems calmer now, but I think it's best if we let Aunt Frankie come down a little more. Too much, though, and she might fall victim to more flighty ideas. Can we be ready to go in an hour?"

I looked at Theo, who had the most preparation to do.

"You built the stirrups, right? And the bedding's ready?"

My mother and I nodded.

"Then I just need thirty minutes."

"Then I'll go tell Jim to start losing that game," my mother replied.

I dismissed the huddle and made my way upstairs, flanked by Theo. When we got to my room, he heaved his overladen suitcase onto my unmade bed while I placed the incubator atop my unvarnished dresser. Over the next few minutes, he and I barely spoke. He set up the microscope while I completed the paperwork; I sanitized the space while he prepared the trays. The scripts and the stage directions were instinct, the actions and reactions rote. With it, mastery had brought along an extreme sense of composure.

When everything was in place, I called down to my mother to bring Aunt Frankie up.

I handed her an unfortunate paper gown. "You'll need to take everything off—shirt, pants, underwear, all of it."

Aunt Frankie's arms tightened as a shiver passed through her. "Can I at least keep my socks?"

A contamination risk, according to policy. "We can make that work," I said.

My father, who'd followed his ladies up the stairs at a respectful distance, turned toward us.

"Is there anything you need me to do besides stay out of the way?"

"Why don't you guard the stairs?" By that point, I doubted Aunt Frankie planned to make a run for it, but he'd feel useful with an assignment. "Oh, and throw some more towels in the dryer."

He made a beeline back toward the laundry room. "You got it, Doc."

After settling Aunt Frankie into the master bedroom to change, my mother stepped into the hallway to give her some privacy but didn't entirely close the door. We could hear the bumbles of Frankie's undressing but no other suspicious noises. None that suggested that she was crawling out the bedroom window, at least.

Content with Frankie's commitment, my parents watched as Theo and I moved through our final tasks, checking and rechecking the equipment and supplies. They'd never seen us work before, and by their gawking, I could tell that our harmony impressed them. Not to mention it was the first time they could see me as an established professional and not a directionless child.

Just as Theo and I were about to finish, a brisk draft slapped open my parents' bedroom door, and I spotted a paper doll standing at the threshold. Knock-kneed from the cold, Frankie toddled toward us, the boxy exam gown crinkling with her every move. Her socks were patterned with windmills—Maggie must have sent them from Tehachapi.

"Aunt Frankie, you look ready," I called. "Now it's time for us to uphold our end of the deal."

She shuffled over the creaky wooden floors into our ragtag clinic. I asked my father for the dryer-warmed towels and placed them over Frankie's chest.

"Oh, that's much better. Thank you." There was a formality in her tone that made it feel like she was addressing me like a doctor, not a niece.

Theo and I returned the courtesy by treating Aunt Frankie no differently than any other patient. We narrated the maneuvers as we performed them: Theo spread her legs as I handed him the speculum; he inserted the beak as I passed him the syringe. My mother stood at the head of the bed and held Aunt Frankie's hand. This scene, I noted, might look a lot like the birth.

The procedure went smoothly, aside from its conclusion. As Theo withdrew the syringe, I was suddenly overcome—not by joy or relief, but by a sudden pang of nausea.

I ran to the bathroom to empty my stomach.

My mother was the first to holler, "Charlie, are you all right?" but neither she nor Theo could do very much, as they were still tied up between Aunt Frankie's legs.

"Yeah, Mom, I'm fine," I lied, and heaved again into the toilet.

My father pulled back the pocket door. "Well, this doesn't seem like it's part of the act."

"First time for everything, I suppose." I stood up and spat some bile into the sink, only to find my sister gazing back at me through the mirror. My father must have seen her, too, as a puckish smirk crept across his wrinkled mouth.

After I was done retching, my parents helped Aunt Frankie off the bed and back into their room. While she dressed, I tried convincing everyone that my sudden upheaval was just related to nerves. Theo and I had already started repacking the equipment when I noticed a voicemail on my phone.

Nolan.

His message was barely intelligible; his voice sounded painfully coarse. Sharp and stilted breaths interrupted his deranged and disoriented sentences. Though I couldn't make out what he was trying to tell me, I knew exactly what he meant.

It was time.

CHAPTER 38

Theo was making some tea when I dropped my luggage at the front door.

"I need to go to Minnesota."

He pulled the whistling kettle off the stove. "I'll go grab my bag."

I winced. There were still conversations I needed to have with Nolan that Theo needn't hear. "I need to go alone. At least for now."

Theo would've pressed for justification had my mother not crossed the room and her presence handicapped his ability to pry. He shot me a wounded look instead.

"Is there anything you need me to do?"

Guiltily, I broke away from his gaze. "Can you stay a few days and help my folks keep an eye on Aunt Frankie?"

He poured some of the boiling water into a gilded porcelain cup with a sigh. *"No problemo."*

"I promise, I'll have a better idea when I need you once I get there," I said, trying to salvage what little remained of his goodwill.

He wouldn't meet my promising eyes.

"Charlie, do you even know where 'there' is?"

The question cracked my confidence. While I knew Nolan had retreated to his family's home in the southern plains of Minnesota, I'd never actually been there. Or sent a letter. Or even asked. Since he hadn't been returning my calls, I might not make it much farther than the airport.

"I do."

My mother piped up from the laundry room, where she'd been eavesdropping. After making her way to the junk drawer, she presented her trophy: a long-forgotten thank-you note from Mrs. Kincade, sent to my parents after they hosted dinner for our convent graduation. The envelope carried a return address from Lake Crystal, a small town two hours outside the Twin Cities.

I kissed her forehead and booked a flight.

After an uneventful flight the next morning, I continued Day 19 with a long drive south through an ocean of corn. Outside the metropolis, the roads straightened and navigation simplified with every mile; Nolan's house was easy to find, just one turn and two stop signs off the main highway. Strangulating ivy crept up the old brick Victorian as its ancient shutters pulled at their hinges. The rest of his yard was immaculate, though, and filled with all sorts of well-groomed shrubs and flower beds. Had the greenery not looked so tidy, I would've thought the home was abandoned.

I left my rental at the curb and followed a footpath to a side door on the attached sunroom. I'd just finished knocking when I noticed Nolan's carcass splayed out over a cushioned wicker couch. For a moment, I thought I'd arrived too late—but he stirred at my rapping.

Nolan hobbled slowly across the sun-bleached rug, his crepe-paper skin peeling at every crease. His knees didn't straighten, and what remained of his shriveling muscles hung limply from his bony frame. It pained me to watch him unlock the door.

"Nolan," I whispered. More suddenly than I expected, I felt myself sinking into emotional quicksand. Pity, anger, sorrow, fear—they all would've swallowed me whole had I not been so distracted by the features of his failing body. Hands, hair, lips, joints—they all seemed to exist in a state somewhere between revolt and decay.

The man I could have loved was almost dead.

I could've cursed my sister right then. Not just for what she convinced him to do, but for loving him. Because I could have done that, too—and without this tragic end.

"You didn't have to come all this way, Charlie," Nolan said.

I shook off my jealousy with a curt nod. "Of course I did."

The cadaver motioned for me to step inside. "No, no, not 'of course,'" he said. "You have big, fancy faculty things to be doing."

"Well, uh, not as much as you would think."

Nolan didn't look like he could stand for long, so I helped him with a graceful collapse into his sofa.

"I'm sorry about that phone call," he said. "The tumors are pumping all sorts of toxic metabolic byproducts into my bloodstream—they can really make me loopy."

The sound of conversation summoned Mrs. Kincade. As she poked her head in from the kitchen, she blanched at the sight of me. I knew the feeling—it was the same one I'd felt just the day before, when I saw my sister standing opposite me in the mirror.

I offered a handshake and some clarification.

"Hi, Mrs. Kincade. It's Charlie."

She put a hand to her chest and shuddered—from embarrassment or relief, I couldn't tell.

"Of course it is." She sighed. "Would you like something to eat?"

It took us a full five minutes, but we successfully moved Nolan from the couch to the kitchen, where he eased into an overstuffed armchair that his mother dragged in from her office. I took a barstool at the center island while Mrs. Kincade sliced up some fresh fruit. We then made a valiant attempt at small talk, but there wasn't much to be had. All paths of conversation led back to my sister, his condition, or their experiment—nothing Nolan and I wanted to talk about, at least in front of his mother.

And I still needed to tell him about the eggs.

"How are you feeling?" I asked.

Nolan smirked. "Not that much worse than before, but I look it. They're not treating me anymore, and I can't travel to Los Angeles for study. I'm in hospice now, I guess. Just a week or two more, so says my doc."

Mrs. Kincade stopped scrubbing the dishes. Her head hung low as her ruddy hands gripped the farmhouse sink. Even though she'd heard those words before, their very mention seemed to further dismantle what little courage she had left.

Either unaware or unconcerned with his mother's anguish, Nolan barreled on. "At my last appointment, my oncologist told me I didn't need to come back. He said he'd be happy to sign my death certificate, though. That was fun—nothing like having to worry about paperwork even after you die."

It was too much. After a brief sob, Mrs. Kincade darted out the back door.

"There," Nolan said. "I thought that'd be enough to drive her out."

I swallowed. "Do . . . do you mind if I stay?"

"For the night? Or for my death?"

"The latter, I suppose," I said with a punctuating sigh. "It's what my sister should have done."

Nolan didn't appreciate the irony. "If Maggie wanted to be there for me, she could've waited to kill herself until after I was gone," he said. His body boiled with anger. "But no. When she heard that her beloved Mendelia wasn't all it was cracked up to be—when she finally got called out—she gave up. Like everything we believed in, everything we worked on, *me*—didn't even matter."

"You can't know that," I countered.

"Know what? That she didn't love me? Like hell I do."

"That she died by suicide."

I realized then that her actual manner of death didn't matter. He'd chosen to believe in a version of her death that vindicated his emotions. Such strong emotions, too—I had no hope of refuting them.

I could only introduce doubt.

"Nolan, there's something else."

He was the only one I could ever tell. Nolan was the only other person who'd fully understand the words on that page. And not only did he deserve to know what she'd written, he wouldn't live long enough to tell.

The tease was enough to stunt his accelerating rage.

"I found a receipt in the box of her things Dr. Varghese mailed me," I continued. "For airfare. She purchased tickets from Majuro to Minnesota a week before the hearing. Maggie never knew about the fraud. She was going to come see you."

"Then why didn't she?"

I offered him the theory I'd chosen to believe. "She couldn't accept that she'd destroyed something she loved."

Had he been strong enough, I'm sure Nolan would have stormed out of the room. But prisoner to his own weakness, he could only produce a sneer. "I'm not sure she ever loved me."

I dropped my fork onto my plate. "I can tell you that she did. Because she changed. After you left, Maggie started seeing her clients as humans instead of experiments. People instead of results. She recognized she'd ruined a lot of lives—not the least of which was yours."

Nolan scoffed. "Not exactly the difference I was hoping to make."

"So now it's my job to make sure that your death—and hers—are not in vain. It's the only way I can live with what you've done. And I'm the only one who has to do that, just so we're clear. I can only hope you enjoy your just deserts."

He cocked his head at me. "So that's what you've been planning?"

"Yes."

"Doesn't exactly sound like I'll be getting a box of cookies."

"No, nothing as delicious as that. But maybe something more satisfying."

"And when do I get to know?"

I brought my dishes to the sink. Out the window, I spied Mrs. Kincade pulling weeds around the mailbox. "Soon."

"You promised, Charlie." A note of anger had returned to Nolan's voice. "That was your end of the bargain."

"And I won't let you down. Not like my sister."

I cursed under my breath. I needed to put these last eggs to work. If Nolan had a few weeks left, then so did I.

It wasn't time to give up.

From what I had seen, Lake Crystal was an especially small town, which probably meant there weren't many suitable naughts. I'd gotten lucky with Pastor Black and with Aunt Frankie: finding, screening, and preparing a mother usually took a full month. Nolan only had two weeks. If I had any hope of making another placement, I needed referrals.

I needed a Mendel.

I slotted my plate in the drying rack. "Nolan, Theo's still thinking about repartnering, and he found a Mendel in Saint Paul," I said. "Considering the abundance of Scandinavian DNA around here, along with the Somali immigrants, he thinks it could be some pretty interesting work. Have you heard about anything?"

"Val's at the post office if you want to talk about that." Nolan yawned. "She's still the Mendel here, and I'm sure she'd love to bend your ear. But"—he slapped his knees—"I need a nap."

Val. The girl Nolan had broken up with for Maggie. The one I'd hung up on. I cringed at the irony. My mission now depended on the one person who probably took the least interest in seeing it succeed.

At least I had nothing to lose.

After helping Nolan up into bed, I let myself out. I found his mother still toiling in the front beds.

"Mrs. Kincade, can you tell me how to get to the post office?"

She peered out from under her broad-brimmed hat. "Certainly, dear. Just head back to the highway and then two blocks west. If you hit the railroad tracks, you've gone too far."

"Thanks. I've told Nolan I'll be back tomorrow."

"Of course," she said. "And Charlie—you should know that Val's started coming around since Nolan's been back. She never really got over him, even though he was head over heels for your sister."

She turned back to her tulips. "He still is when he's not angry with her."

While Nolan had never mentioned any residual feelings of his own, Mrs. Kincade had just confirmed that Val's were complicated. That, I'd learned, offered points of leverage. I just needed to pick one.

The post office was a thickset brick building set in the middle of a large asphalt parking lot. After pressing through the front doors, I asked the manager for the Mendel. She pointed me toward the back offices, where the clinic door was tucked behind the post office boxes. I waved my badge over the sensor.

Even though it beeped, the door didn't unlock, so I tried again. As a Mendel, I should have had access to any clinic I needed. But again, nothing. I'd been locked out.

I felt the fibers of my heart stiffen.

They knew.

Val must have heard me struggling, because she opened the door looking understandably confused. There were no other Mendels for the next fifty miles—and certainly none that needed to access her clinic.

"Excuse me—can I help you?"

"Val, it's Charlie," I said.

She, too, saw my face with recognition. "You . . ."

"Look exactly like Maggie," I finished. "I get that a lot."

Val led me back. Her space was even smaller than the cottage in Saipan—a single room with an exam table, lab bench, and administrative desk. I had no place to sit but the exam table, so I eased myself up.

"But what are you doing here?"

There was an edginess to her tone that put me on guard.

"Something for Nolan," I said. "I need a mother."

"For Maggie's eggs?"

"How did you know?"

"Everyone in the Mendelia knows," Val hissed. "Headquarters put out an advisory this morning. We've been warned not to aid or abet you. Something about an ethical violation."

I cringed. Just as Theo predicted.

I steeled my gaze. "Val, I know you have no reason to help me. But I thought you might want to help Nolan."

"Help him what? Die?"

I took the accusatory questions as a good sign. They corroborated what Mrs. Kincade had mentioned: that Val might still love Nolan. And if I could make her feel something, I could make her do something—one of the greatest lessons of the Mendelia.

I made my sincerest appeal.

"Die happy."

Val let go a long breath as she considered my petition. I was all but sure she would refuse when she finally let go a reluctant "okay."

Val then pulled open a file drawer to retrieve a manila folder: Kirsten and Roger Jacobsen. Naughts, and newlywed, they'd just come in a few weeks ago to seek a placement. Kirsten taught at the local elementary school, and Roger worked as a tractor mechanic—though they were young, Val felt they could provide a normal, stable household. She'd planned on giving them an embryo next week.

"It'll be an easy substitution," she said. "I'll keep the eggs I ordered on ice."

I kicked my feet against the exam table. "I can't thank you enough, Val."

"You can use the clinic for the procedure. Kirsten is already scheduled for next Thursday." She used a red pen to make a note in the appointment book.

"Really." I smiled. "I wouldn't be able to do this without you."

"I'm sure Nolan will be happy to know that Maggie's eggs are being put to good use. I suppose the last thing to talk about is sperm?"

My feet slowed gently to a stop.

"My technician's on his way into town." At least he would be, as soon as I could get Theo on the phone. "I'll have him place the order."

Val shook her head. "Not with the Mendelia's embargo on your names," she said. "I'll get Kofi to do it. What are you thinking?"

My answer would test her nobility, but I saw no way around it but the truth.

"Nolan's," I said.

Val's face shriveled almost imperceptibly, but enough to betray her true feelings. Inside, I knew righteous morality battled her petty instinct over creating her rival's progeny. And while it took several moments, virtue won the day.

"I understand," she said, though I wasn't sure that was true.

I heaved a great sigh of relief. "And I'd like to talk to them, if you don't mind."

"The Jacobsens?"

I nodded and hopped down from the table. "I want them to know."

"About Maggie?"

"About everything."

I paced circles on the floor while Val placed the call. Her exchange with the Jacobsens was choppy and uneven; neither Val nor Kirsten knew exactly what to say—neither Mendels nor clients enjoyed such disruptive surprises. Val closed the conversation with assurances that the placement was still on track and that I'd be calling them soon to explain.

For a moment, I almost felt bad for ruining what should've been perfectly routine.

I gathered my things to head back to the car when Val caught me by the hand. "Before you go—how is Nolan?"

She seemed uncomfortable asking. There was no way she didn't know about his condition, but she seemed ignorant of his more recent decline. I felt tempted to gloss over it—driving their reconnection still felt vaguely traitorous to my sister. But memories don't have feelings, I reminded myself. The dying still do. And with his end just over the horizon, Nolan deserved some joy. Val seemed most capable of delivering that.

"You should see him. Soon."

CHAPTER 39

The only privacy I could find was in my rental car. I'd been in Minnesota for most of the day but still hadn't found a hotel. Therefore, the unassuming four-door sedan was forced to serve as my breakfast table, my locker, my changing room, and now, my phone booth.

Kirsten answered my call with apprehension. I asked if she had time to meet me at the post office later that evening, and though Kirsten said she'd be happy to, she wanted her husband to join—and he wouldn't be able to get off work in time. Instead, she suggested coffee at one of the two restaurants in town. The diner was quieter than the bar, she said, and while I agreed, I couldn't help but feel like a drink might help take the edge off my news.

Ending the call provided the first chance to catch my emotional breath. I found it hard to believe that I'd started the day in my childhood bedroom. So much had transpired, yet there was so much left to be done. I crawled into the back seat to close my eyes and rest my heart.

A knock on the car window interrupted my meditation.

Val.

I sat up and cracked the door.

"My technician just got off the phone with the sperm bank," she said, helping herself in. I scooted over to make room. "Nolan's remaining samples have been restricted.

"From what Kofi told me, it seems that Nolan's last donations differed from his others," she continued. "They've been marked unstable. Do you know why?"

I almost told her. It would have made things so much easier. But Nolan had been very clear about the story he wanted to leave behind, and I didn't want to spoil his legacy. I bit down on the inside of my cheek to stop the truth from spilling out.

"I do," I said.

Val's eyes sharpened. I leaned into the back of the passenger seat to hide my face.

"And . . . you still want to continue?"

"I do."

These mutations were exactly what Maggie was hoping for. What Nolan was dying for. I couldn't say no. Not when I'd come so far.

Val could tell I was obfuscating the truth, but her midwestern sensibilities impaired her ability to snoop. She pushed her bangs out of her face and sighed.

"Well, no matter your reason, acquisition is going to take extra steps."

The headrest muffled my reply. "I suppose I need to get involved."

"Yes," Val answered. "Kofi couldn't explain why we needed this *particular* sample, and the administrator denied him. If you're going to hold your cards close to your chest, *you're* going to have to make the appeal."

In theory, Headquarters had no reason to deny a request for Nolan's sperm. While restricted samples were held back from general circulation, they weren't entirely unavailable—provided a Mendel could offer appropriate justification. After all, risk was a necessary part of the program. The Mendelia, however, wouldn't deny my request based on risk. This case was personal.

I thought of Nolan. Then Maggie. And all that I'd given to this callous, spiteful organization. For nothing in return.

Contempt steeled my resolve, and I punched the number for Headquarters into my phone. While it rang, I stepped out of my vehicle for some fresh air. The afternoon was tapering, and a nearby elm now cast its shade across the full length of the post office parking lot. It would be even later in Baltimore—I could only hope I'd catch someone before the end of their day.

Fortunately or unfortunately, I did.

"Good afternoon, Baltimore Gamete Bank. This is Dr. Linda Fontanez."

I almost hung up.

Of course Dr. Fontanez hadn't been fired after the hearing; the retribution would have been too obvious. But they hadn't allowed her to return to practice in Miami. Instead, the Mendelia buried her at Headquarters, where the powers that be could monitor her work—with a close eye on any infractions that might merit termination.

My voice cracked as I tried to mask my intimidation. "Good afternoon, Dr. Fontanez," I said. "I need authorization to use a restricted sample in a placement I'll be making next week."

"With whom am I speaking?"

Too exhausted to pull off another caper, I gave in to the truth.

"Dr. Fontanez, this is Charlie Tannehill."

The smack of her lips crackled over the line. "Well, well, well. Why in God's name do *you* need a restricted sample, Dr. Tannehill?"

"My sister died two months ago. I'm placing the eggs she earned back."

"So I've heard. It's the gossip across the agency, as I'm sure you know."

I stacked my feet on one of the painted parking space lines like a balance beam. The steps I took were as careful as my words.

"I'm just asking to use the sperm sample provided by her husband."

"Freud would probably have something to say about that," she taunted. "What's his name again?"

It took every ounce of my patience to say his name with neutrality. Dr. Fontanez's fingernails clicked away on the keyboard while the shadows of the elm danced across my imaginary tightrope.

"Let's see . . . ," she said. "Nolan Kincade made fourteen deposits in the past three years. Nine of them were put into use in Majuro by Dr. Magnolia Tannehill. Another three were recently ordered out by Mr. Theo Park—your technician, if I recall."

"Yes," I said, and kept my eyes on my feet.

"Two remain, and both were found to be seriously unstable with many genetic flaws. But for some reason you still want to use it. Smacks of hypocrisy to me, Dr. Tannehill."

I reached the end of the white line as well as my patience. "There's a difference between a calculated risk and a genetic certainty, Dr. Fontanez."

"You torpedoed my career, Charlie Tannehill. And for what? The sanctity of Mendelian ethics? You're lucky you don't have to answer to Petro Dibrova."

I recognized the provocation and muzzled my disdain. Dr. Fontanez had no legitimate reason to deny me Nolan's sample—at least not one that would pass muster with Mr. Kolb.

That, I realized, was my advantage.

I turned to face the setting sun. "Dr. Fontanez, you don't have any real cause to refuse my request," I started. "When I won these eggs, the arbiter directed the Mendelia to avoid obstructing my work. If you choose to do so, I will file suit. Given your current standing within the organization, this could be strike three."

The line held silent as Dr. Fontanez considered her options. She was choosing: her career, her pension, and her future—or me.

In the end, her greed was reliable.

"Enjoy having your cake and eating it, too, Dr. Tannehill," she spat.

I put the phone down on the roof of my sedan and smiled. I'd just felled Goliath—and not just Dr. Fontanez. The entirety of the Mendelia. I'd started with nothing and gotten everything that I'd wanted, from Maggie's eggs to Bujen to Aunt Frankie to Kirsten. Each of my triumphs had begotten another, each had emboldened me to try harder. *This* was the same sense of achievement my sister had known, and now I understood how she'd gotten herself into so much trouble.

Success was addicting.

⚛

The diner where I was supposed to meet Kirsten and Roger wasn't far from the post office. Nothing could be far from anything in such a small place. Lake Crystal was a town you could wrap your arms—perhaps even your hands—around, so I decided to walk.

Just two blocks in front of me, I spotted the couple. Raised on milk and midwestern portions, both were large, especially compared to me. Kirsten's lipstick was as fresh as her outfit; Roger's trucker hat looked conspicuously new. I regretted they felt the need to impress me.

After exchanging pleasantries, Roger asked the hostess for the booth in the back. The waitress offered us menus, but we collectively declined. Roger and Kirsten were too nervous to eat; I still felt queasy from Aunt Frankie's procedure. We did make a beverage order, however—coffees for them, a ginger ale for me. Once the waitress brought back our drinks, I turned our conversation to business.

I donned my most professional tone. "Thank you for taking the time to meet with me today," I said. "Val spoke very highly of you."

My eyes flitted between Roger and Kirsten—both stared at me, correctly suspecting the compliment was prelude to darker news.

"It's important to me that you know the child you'll be receiving is the culmination of my sister's research. The eggs you'll be receiving are hers and contain Marshallese DNA, which she believed to be especially promising in breaking the Limit. The sperm you'll be receiving is her husband's. His DNA has been identified as uniquely unstable, which might lead to more significant—and potentially important—mutations."

"I'm sorry," Roger interrupted, shaking a finger at me. "Can you please explain to me why your sister and her husband aren't having this mutant baby themselves?"

I looked him straight in the eye. "They're dead."

After blinking away his shock, Roger resumed his counterargument. "I still don't understand why we can't have our original baby."

Kirsten turned to her husband. "The Mendel gets to decide, Rog," she murmured. Her hushed tones just barely breached the hubbub of the busy diner. "If we want a baby, we have to accept what they give us. It's in the contract."

Kirsten then turned to me with more authority. "Ma'am, we saw the hearing," she said. "We know that Mendelia babies are experiments. We also know that most won't save the species. But that's not what we're here for. Roger and I are just trying to enjoy what we can of our lives—and for us, that means a child."

I blinked twice before responding. "I understand."

For once, I actually did. Reproduction had been the shared purpose of all living things for so long that even extinction could not derail it. This was what I'd learned during my short stint in practice. Procreation allowed creatures to persist beyond their individual lives and infinitely elude an inevitable fate, and by giving my clients children, I restored their tomorrows. I allowed them to defy what was certain—for a moment at least, and a generation at best. But when death finally came for people like Kirsten and Roger—and it would—they could die at least satisfied, having cheated life's only certainty.

For the living, that was enough.

CHAPTER 40

Did I really believe that placing these eggs would save the human race? I'd convinced Aunt Frankie of it. Had I told others that the gratification of children was far more important? The Jacobsens seemed to think so, and I'd agreed. My opinions had been inconsistent—and that had been useful. It was like owning two houses; I could occupy the one that suited me best and then leave it when it no longer served. But by that point, the maintenance had grown expensive, and no one ever knew where to find me. Despite the convenience, neither ever really felt like home.

After my meeting with Kirsten and Roger, I headed back to the highway to find a place to sleep. Lake Crystal was too small to merit a hotel of its own, so I headed back toward the interstate, fifty miles east. As I drove, the inky black night all but absorbed my headlights; while I could see the road, I couldn't make out anything too far ahead. To keep myself awake, I called Val—now that the Jacobsens had assented, Kofi could place the order.

"But how did you convince them?" she asked.

"The Mendelia?" I stifled the smallest laugh. "By pretending to be my sister."

"Don't tell me you actually pulled that stunt."

"Of course not," I replied. "Though that did work once for a sixth-grade math test."

"Then how?"

Gall. Guts. Grit. All the weapons Maggie knew how to wield so well but I'd been too afraid to ever pick up.

"I bluffed." I sighed. "Threatened legal action."

"I can't believe that worked."

"Me neither."

I could almost hear Val smile. "Better to be lucky than good. When are you going to tell Nolan?"

Not until I'd accomplished all that I'd wanted to. And we were close. Realistically, I'd be able to impregnate Kirsten before Nolan passed, but not anyone else. That, I decided, would suffice. Once she was taken care of, I'd be able to deliver to Nolan the largest dose of closure I possibly could.

"Soon," I said.

I found my exit a few minutes later as well as a hotel. Once I'd arranged a room, I called Theo and asked him to catch a plane. The tentacles of sleep then pulled me under and kept me for longer than I'd intended. The next morning, I was late picking up Theo at the airport, a transgression for which I could never quite apologize enough.

Days 18 to 13 were docile. Nolan's sperm arrived exactly on schedule, and Val supervised Kirsten's preparations, all of which progressed without incident. When we weren't busy at the clinic, the three of us spent time chaperoning Nolan through the throes of decline. We brought treats, played cards with him, and told jokes that would make even the most precocious of kindergarteners groan. But while the spring days grew longer with every passing day, his wakeful hours shortened.

His end, no doubt, was near.

On Day 12, Theo and I arrived at Val's clinic with our portable incubator in tow. Val, I knew, was taking a great personal risk by allowing us to use her facility and her clients, and in exchange, I let her sign the paperwork. If the combination of Maggie and Nolan's germ produced anything useful, the credit, the eggs, and the glory would all go to her.

According to the notes, Theo and I initiated Kirsten's procedure at 1:17 p.m. and concluded it at 1:42. What wasn't captured by the record was how perfectly we executed our last dance. Even Val seemed entranced. But perhaps most importantly, Kirsten left the clinic babbling wistfully about her plans for the nursery.

After tidying up, Theo and I strolled through the postal lobby together.

"It's a shame you're hanging up your spurs," he said. "I never expected to see you practice like this."

I tucked a loose curl behind my ear. "Me neither."

"Are you sure you want to? I hear Canada's got openings. Maybe France?"

"I'm sorry, Theo, I have to. If I keep going like this . . ." I paused to watch an eager teenager open a post office box and discover a pink slip. "I'll end up like Maggie."

"You know what they call gamblers who quit while they're ahead?"

I didn't. My cocked eyebrow begged for the quip.

Theo clapped me on the back. "Winners."

That was the last time I set foot in a post office for anything but stamps.

※

Theo caught a ride with Kofi back to the airport. After almost a month on the road, he needed to tend to some business back in Seattle. His mother, he said, had a new skin-care routine for him. I, on the other hand, needed to see Nolan. With the placements complete, it was finally time for me to share the totality of my gift. I called Mrs. Kincade to see if I could swing by; she said I'd better hurry if I wanted to catch Nolan before he needed another nap.

Naps often preceded death. But I had just one more call to make.

Dr. Rubino sounded as if she'd been licking her lips when she answered my call. For once, her posturing didn't faze me. I blew past her insolence to deliver my final message.

"Ma'am, I am resigning my position as a Mendel. Please revoke my credentials and terminate my access. When you do, go ahead and flush my eggs along with the remainder of Maggie's. I believe that's contractually obligated. Goodbye."

I hung up without waiting for her reaction. I didn't owe her, or anyone else, an explanation.

The spring breeze picked up just after I cast my future to the wind. I found its warmth energizing, promising even. Playful gusts carried me in the direction of Nolan's house, however, and I could only hope that they weren't also carrying away his final breaths. Each visit to his house began with this same anxiety, and I tried to settle my nerves: either Nolan was dead or he wasn't, and my haste would not change it.

As I approached the Victorian, I found Val scurrying down the driveway, her face buried in her hands. She collided with me to force an embrace.

"I told him, Charlie. I told him."

"About the Jacobsens?" I asked.

"That I still love him," she wailed.

I didn't know what to offer besides empty reassurance. "That's good, Val."

"He told me he still loves your sister. She left him, and he's still dying for her." I felt a resonant sob shudder through her. "Why couldn't he love me like that?"

Val carried on for a few minutes. I knew I should try harder to comfort her, but my mind was with Nolan, just a few yards away.

She pulled back. "I'm not sure how much more I can take."

"It won't be much longer."

My eyes scanned the windows for signs of life. Val had just been inside, and Nolan had still been alive then—but every minute that passed was one where we could lose him.

Val dabbed her streaky mascara on the cuff of her sleeve. "Are you going to tell him now—about the eggs?"

"I am."

"Maybe it'll help him stay a bit longer."

I put my hand on the cap of her shoulder. "I want it to help him go."

We parted with a hug. I trudged up the remainder of the driveway to the sunroom, where Nolan had curled up again on the wicker couch. The bones in his back added unusual contours to his shirt, and his shorts draped awkwardly over his skeletal backside. I tapped gently on the storm door, hoping he hadn't found his final resting place.

"Charlie? Didn't expect to be seeing you so soon. Not dead yet, you know."

"For once I'm here with good news, Nolan." He grabbed my hand for help sitting up. I took a seat beside him, still holding his hand. His once-mossy eyes had dulled to a lichenous gray. I could only hope my news would bring some light back to them.

"I'm pregnant."

CHAPTER 41

"It's your baby. Yours and Maggie's."

Nolan's swollen eyes threatened to pop. "Excuse me?"

"The plan I've been working on? This is it. I went to court, I won her eggs, I've been placing them with your sperm. I'm carrying one of the embryos."

His expression soured.

Not the reaction I'd been hoping for.

"Nolan, the work you and Maggie were doing was important," I said.

"The work we were doing was stupid. Can't you see?" He gestured across the room, where medical pumps, IV tubing, and bloodied gauze crowded every flat surface. "I'm dying. Right now. Your sister's already dead." He sank back into the couch and plucked a tennis ball from a nearby emesis basin. With a flick of his emaciated wrist, he bounced it off the interior wall.

His rejection reduced me to tears. Maggie's redemption hung on how well I could deliver his death, and now my chances seemed slim. I struggled to defend my reasoning. "Dr. Carmichael said that while it wasn't probable, beating the Limit was still very, very possible."

Nolan didn't respond. As we sat, every metronomic thump of the tennis ball ticked away another moment of his waning existence. Even if I could convince Nolan of his worth, he wouldn't be able to enjoy it for very long. Every passing moment felt like another immeasurable loss.

After seventy-three throws, Nolan broke the silence. "So how'd you pull it off?"

I couldn't have been happier to hear him speak. It didn't matter what he'd said—if we could dialogue, I might yet work this out. I summoned a resolve only my sister could've matched.

"Theo. It was the first egg we placed. He ordered samples for a woman we were working with in Arkansas but then marked them as spoiled when they arrived. The Mendelia replaced the shipment straight away. The benefits of bureaucracy, I guess. He performed the procedure in the motel."

"But there were more, weren't there?"

"Yes. Maggie earned back fifteen. The next placement went to a Marshallese couple in Springdale."

"That's where you were born, right?"

I felt like I was defusing a bomb—every sentence clipped a tangled wire that I could only hope wouldn't set him off.

"Right. Where my biological parents lived."

Nolan raised an eyebrow. "A bit of restorative justice, I suppose."

His approval, however mild, seemed to move us in the right direction.

"Bujen—the mother—you would have loved her," I said, trying to further lighten the mood. "She was so much like Maggie."

He ignored the reference to my sister, and the tennis ball thumped away. "Who else?"

My chest tightened. "Another went to Aunt Frankie."

His voice was fresh with candor. "I'm sure she was over the moon."

"She got there." I sighed. "But it was more complicated than that. Aunt Frankie is more complicated than that."

"Maggie always said as much. I wish I'd gotten to meet her."

Less confident that Nolan would approve of the last placement, I turned to face him with my most imploring eyes. "The last placement went to a couple here in town—Kirsten and Roger Jacobsen. Val helped me. I thought your mother might like having a grandchild nearby."

Nolan wouldn't meet my gaze. "That was *your* mother's dream, not mine," he muttered.

Another long silence. But no more argument.

"That leaves one more, right?"

"Flushed," I said. "I ran out of time. The arbitrator only gave me two months."

I saw Nolan reviewing the calendar in his mind. "That means you still have two weeks."

"But you don't," I countered. "Look, we made four more attempts at beating the Limit. That counts for something."

"You still believe that?"

I clapped my hands together. "Honestly, Nolan, I don't know what I believe. It's either all a waste or it's all meaningful, and it's all too much for me to sort out. The only thing I'm really certain about is that the Limit will remain unbeatable until it's finally beaten. Someone once told me that its victory was assured only if we stop trying."

Nolan sank back into the cushions. "That was me, wasn't it."

"At the convent. In our first year. And you were right—fraud or no fraud, we still need to try. Her eggs, your sperm, and now, this child." My hand went to my belly. "Maybe it'll figure the whole thing out."

"Probably our best chance at this point," he said, a note of sarcasm in his tone.

I parried with acidity. "And we've got four of them."

My sass reignited his anger. "Quadruplets, aren't they? Sounds like the family that Maggie always wanted."

I stood up. "Look, if Maggie were alive, I'd feel good about pleasing her. But she's not. The dead don't have feelings. You do. I do. And if you don't feel good about what you did, then I never will."

It was more reprimand than condolence. Stunned, Nolan sat back and pawed his tennis ball.

"If the science is true, Maggie's experiment had value," I continued, doing my best to channel my sister's fire. "And she couldn't have done it without you. Not just your body, but your love. Your devotion.

And the odds of discovery are better than most, considering Maggie's Marshallese DNA and your mutations. Who knows what'll happen.

"But if it's all garbage, if the Mendelia really is just rearranging the existential deck chairs, then we've at least made four children for four mothers who now will have four happy families. If you really believe that we're all really doomed, you've at least given a few more people one last chance to enjoy one of the few things that makes us fundamentally human."

And fundamentally alive. That's what I'd told myself in that Arkansas motel room. Anything that didn't reproduce didn't stand a chance against the Limit. We'd be extinct much sooner than later if people like me just gave up. Sure, I'd been afraid about how hard it might be to love a child, but it couldn't have been any harder than trying to love my sister. She'd lost her own life and taken others down with her, and yet I still wanted to protect her. To love her.

This child might allow me to do that.

"And maybe, just maybe, this is all for me. Because I'm the one who has to live with the consequences of what you've done. I'm the one left to remember your disgrace. I couldn't let it amount to nothing, even if it was monumentally stupid. Really, I hate you both for leaving me. And I'll miss you more than you can ever know."

My rapid pulse reverberated inside my skull. I felt as if I was standing in Mr. Kolb's office again, preaching my beliefs to the only person I needed to convert. Pretending to be Maggie and succeeding at it. That's when I noticed the shadows darkening. The day was coming to an end, as was our conversation.

There was only one thing left for me to say.

"You know I've always loved you," I whispered. My voice splintered over the words. "Maggie did—maybe stronger and louder than I ever could. But I did too."

Nolan shook forth the beaded bracelet from under his sleeve. "So did I."

For the first time in months, I slept peacefully that night. I'd said—I'd sermonized—my peace, and with that load lifted, I could finally sink into rest. Visions of Maggie and Nolan saturated my dreams, and I would've stayed in the company of my two dearest loves had a call from Mrs. Kincade not startled me awake.

There was only one reason she'd be calling, I knew.

Nolan was gone.

I decided to stay in Lake Crystal for a few more days to help with the funeral arrangements. Mrs. Kincade didn't need a lot of help—Nolan had been dying for quite a while, and together they'd already picked the casket, the pastor, the burial plot. But I felt compelled to shoulder at least some of the remaining responsibility—whether it was for Maggie or for my child, I wasn't exactly sure. I also needed a chance to think about what should come next. I hadn't entirely thought through the decisions I'd made in the past two months. Like everyone else in my life, I'd decided to act and not to worry. And while I'd achieved what I'd wanted with the placements, I now needed to figure out what I was going to do with a baby.

Three days later, I found myself standing at the back of a two-acre cemetery. Nolan's grave overlooked a massive crop of soybeans—a plant with virtually no end in its genetic sight. His mother and her sister gathered along with a handful of cousins and friends. Val was conspicuously absent.

The pastor concluded Nolan's beautiful and foreshortened life with a gentle twenty-minute homily. Mrs. Kincade then hosted a small reception in the church basement to afford the mourners a chance to mingle. One of the church ladies positioned a flotilla of lemonade-filled Dixie cups alongside the three boxes of chocolate chip cookies my parents had sent. It wasn't long before the bereaved were happily chomping away and exchanging stories about Nolan. I spent most of my time explaining that I wasn't Maggie.

An hour passed before I spotted a willowy blonde peering down the staircase. Val was scanning the room, looking for someone. When her eyes met mine, I knew it was me.

She grabbed my elbow and escorted me to the yellow linoleum kitchen.

"I'm glad you're here. I thought you might've left for Pennsylvania already."

"You knew I'd stay for the funeral—where were you?"

"It's a small town, Charlie. Showing up to his burial wouldn't help my budding reputation as his jilted lover." She looked over her shoulder at the clutch of women who'd already noticed her arrival. "But there's something more important I have to tell you. Kirsten's pregnancy didn't take."

"Damn it." I sighed. At least it wasn't Frankie's. Or Bujen's. But our quads were down to triplets.

"There's something else."

Val fidgeted, barely able to contain what she was about to tell me. "Before you impregnated Kirsten, I pulled some cells off the embryo for preimplantation screening. I'm sorry, but when you told me you knew about Nolan's restricted samples, I couldn't help myself."

I should have known Val wasn't the type to be so easily cowed. She'd gotten the information she wanted, but not out of me.

"And?"

Her whole body stilled as she grabbed me by the shoulders. "Did you test any of the other embryos?"

"No. We weren't working in clinics. We didn't have the equipment."

"Charlie, the embryo screened 12*."

I couldn't comprehend the number at first; I'd never heard of a screening so high. Breathless, I could do nothing but stare. Val's fidgeting set in again—she was waiting for me to catch up. She needed someone to help process this miracle.

I finally managed a question. "Are you sure?"

"I'm not. I'm not a technician. But the machine ran fine."

"Charlie, and I'm sure you know this, but . . ." Val's cornflower eyes began to tremble as she fought back tears.

"You couldn't do the sequencing," I finished. "There was only enough genetic material for the screening."

She winced at the truth.

I covered my face with my palms. "And the rest has been flushed. Maggie's eggs, Nolan's sperm, even my eggs—they're all gone."

Desperation weakened her voice. "But there's still the two other embryos you made, right?"

"Three, actually."

"Three? Your aunt, the Marshallese woman—who's the third?"

"Me."

Val didn't ask why or how. She didn't need to. She looked relieved to hear that perhaps humanity's Holy Grail hadn't been flushed away.

It was my turn to grab on to Val. I took her by the wrist. "Have you told anyone?" I asked, with all hope that she hadn't.

"Not yet."

"Good. I'm not sure you should. The other embryos were all made from Maggie's eggs and Nolan's sperm, but not with samples that were restricted. They might not screen as highly."

Val nodded. "I guess we'll just have to wait 'til they get here."

"Thirty-three more weeks."

After a brief hug, she kept her promise to avoid a fuss and left out the back door.

I returned to the main room, where Nolan's family and friends were kissing cheeks and saying goodbyes. The basement had emptied during the short time I'd stepped away, and I joined Nolan's aunt in tidying up until she ran up to Mrs. Kincade to see the last of their family off.

Finally, I was alone. Alone with my thoughts. My consequences. My new reality.

It's going to be fine, I reminded myself. That's what my father would've said.

When Mrs. Kincade made her way downstairs, she must have seen me wiping down the last few folding tables.

"Oh, Charlie, you didn't have to do all this."

"I know, Mrs. Kincade, but I wanted to." I tipped the last table over to collapse the legs. Mrs. Kincade stood over me as I knelt on the floor and tried to work the joints.

"Did Nolan tell you?"

I slammed the heel of my hand into the rusty hinge, and the question came off more aggressive than I intended.

Mrs. Kincade must have been able to tell that I was expecting some kind of resentment. It would've been appropriate for the girls that destroyed her boy. But she withheld her response for so long that I was forced to look up—only to find a deeply maternal smile.

"He did. I didn't know if you wanted me knowing, so I haven't brought it up."

"That's kind of you, Mrs. Kincade," I said. "And I'm glad that you do. I hope that it means something to you."

"Most importantly, Charlie—it meant something to him. You gave his life meaning, even at the very end."

For once I felt like Maggie would've been proud of me. "I also wanted to ask if it would be too hard for you if I stayed here in town for a while. I like it here, and I'm not in a hurry to be anywhere else."

"Of course, dear. And you're welcome to stay with me until you get yourself sorted. I could use a few more footsteps around the house."

EPILOGUE

And so, my new life in Lake Crystal, Minnesota, began. I stayed with Nolan's mother for three weeks until I found my own place. Mrs. Kincade insisted I use Nolan's savings to make the purchase; he would've wanted it spent on the baby, she said. With his nest egg, I was able to buy a nest of my own: a small cottage near the lake, complete with baby-blue siding, crisp white trim, and sweet pea flowers that climbed a split-rail fence.

I shared all the news with my parents a month later, and to great jubilation. Val agreed to help care for my pregnancy, and after the birth I planned to find a job teaching. Finally, it seemed, I'd stumbled into the simple life I'd always wanted.

It just took a child to get me there.

※

Matilda Lou Tannehill was born a year to the day that I received my sister's package. Her fraternal twin, Andrea Magnolia Stewart, was born to Aunt Frankie just a few weeks prior. As expected, Frankie's body didn't carry the pregnancy easily, and she delivered the tot a bit prematurely—but with no other complications. Mattie and Andie both screened at 2*—expected, considering Nolan's status. Bujen's son, Sebastian, screened 2* as well. None of them showed any signs of the same genetic gift that we'd lost in that fourth batch, and I never reported what we found. Not because of my grievances against the Mendelia, no. But because successfully reproducing what I'd stumbled upon would be just as probable as finding it in another random combination. Lesya and her suitor, Nolan and Maggie—there wasn't just one pairing that could break the Limit. There were many.

And a whole agency was already dedicated to discovering them.

Finally, it was my turn to do what made me happy.

Prior to their extinction, periodical cicadas took seventeen years to prepare for just a few weeks of activity. The entire purpose of their lives came to pass in a single season. But some didn't mate. Some didn't deposit eggs in the ground. Some were swooped up by predators, crushed underfoot, or drowned in thunderstorms. Passion had nothing to do with the success of their species. Neither did talent or drive or heroics. It was a numbers game. They all made an effort, they all did their part—that's why they'd survived. Until suddenly—cataclysmically—they didn't.

Humanity, however, still might.

JINED ILO KOBO

There is a Marshallese phrase for the unbreakable bond between mother and child: Jined ilo Kobo. The Marshallese believe that this connection cannot be severed, no matter the distance between the pair, and no matter who raises the child. *The Beauty of the End* presents a deceitful adoption broker who exploits such Marshallese ideals—and unfortunately, it draws from recent history. In the past twenty years, in the states of Arkansas, Utah, and Arizona, at least seventy Marshallese children have been illegally trafficked to both unsuspecting and complicit families. At least one perpetrator has been convicted.

    I can only hope that this book continues to spotlight such abhorrent practices, and that all the victims—parents and children alike—can find comfort in Jined ilo Kobo.

ACKNOWLEDGMENTS

Science was, and always has been, my first love, and for that, I must thank my early educators—Jeannie Small, Paul Swenson, and Robin Groch. With that said, writing has made for quite the enchanting paramour, and for that I owe much gratitude to my agents, Sabrina Taitz and Margaret Riley King, as well as my editing team, Laura Van der Veer, Nicole Burns-Ascue, and Alicia Clancy.

Thank you *all* for inspiring, guiding, and believing in me.

As a scientifically trained policy wonk, writing fiction did not come easily to me, and I owe a great deal of appreciation to the instructors at the UCLA Extension Writers' Program for both their lessons and their patience. It was in these classes that I also gained my long-standing writing group, Aimee Clemens and Sonia Roman, without whom this story would not exist. Additional early reads and moral support came from the esteemed Alexa Danes, Jennifer Murphy, Erica Lee, Elizabeth Webster, Claire Corcoran, Joan Berna, and Gabbi Stienstra.

Lastly, I must thank my children, who mostly managed to stay asleep during my critical late-night writing hours, as well as my husband, Tom Beliveau, who loved me all the way through.

Thank you all for these magnificent gifts.

BOOK CLUB QUESTIONS

1. The Mendelia's reproductive incentives might help solve the Limit, but they also undermine many commonly held beliefs about family, romance, and childhood. Given these shifts, how do you think society within the novel would change in twenty years? In fifty?
2. This story explores certain topics related to reproductive ethics, including embryo creation and donation, selective genetics, and the commodification of women for reproductive services. Which Mendelian practice did you find most upsetting? Why?
3. In this book, global population collapse sparks nationwide concern about a woman's right to reproductive autonomy. In our own world, fears of global overpopulation, rampant in the 1970s, prompted similar discussions. If and when should society curtail women's rights for the greater good? What role should men play in that decision?
4. Charlie struggles to understand whether the Mendelia is actually an effective organization or whether its practices amount to an exercise in "rearranging the existential deck chairs." Which do you believe and why? In the end, does it matter if it brings people hope?
5. At the beginning of the book, Charlie is intent on

remaining childless. By the end, she chooses to have her sister's child. To what extent does Charlie's experiences with the Mendelia shape her attitude about motherhood? Was the decision to have children or not a major challenge for you?

6. Maggie's drive to break the Limit results in her demise. Is her ambition toxic or admirable? Is she a workaholic who got what she deserved, or a martyr for the cause?

7. The epilogue has a lot to say about the importance of individual effort and duty to society. What decisions have you made that might fit this model?

8. How much should ongoing crises and questions about the potential future sustainability of civilization affect a person's decision to bring children into the world today? Is it selfish to have children at the end of the world?

9. How do the girls change during their time with the convent? How do Mendelian values guide their choices throughout their lives?

10. What is the significance of gambling in the novel? How do odds, uncertainty, and wagers shape decisions in your own life?

11. Sometimes, the outcome of a catastrophe hinges on the actions of a single person. Aside from Charlie, are there other characters whose choices significantly affect the management of the Limit? Which are heroes, and which are villains?

12. Speculative fiction often offers insight into contemporary social issues. What parallels do you see between the conflicts presented in the novel and the crises of today (such as climate change)? What aspects of Charlie and Maggie's story can be universalized?

ABOUT THE AUTHOR

Photo © 2023 Melody Yazdani Studios

Lauren Stienstra's professional life in government has been instrumental in shaping her literary voice. From the front lines of the COVID-19 pandemic response to addressing the critical issue of climate change, Stienstra's lived experiences and deep-rooted commitment to public service have informed and inspired her prose. She holds degrees in physiology and crisis management, has studied creative writing at UCLA Extension, and is currently completing her doctorate in public health at Johns Hopkins University. These endeavors have not only broadened her understanding of the world's most pressing challenges but also fueled her passion for resonant stories that weave together the complexities of the world she knows so intimately. Based in Washington, DC, Stienstra is the mother of two children and two cats, both of which challenge her equally. For more information, visit www.laurenstienstra.com.